ROBIN SCHONE

BERKLEY SENSATION, NEW YORK

THE BERKLEY PUBLISHING GROUP
Published by the Penguin Group
Penguin Group (USA) Inc.
375 Hudson Street, New York, New York 10014, USA
Penguin Group (Canada), 90 Eglinton Avenue East, Suite 700, Toronto, Ontario M4P 2Y3, Canada
(a division of Pearson Penguin Canada Inc.)
Penguin Books Ltd., 80 Strand, London WC2R 0RL, England
Penguin Group Ireland, 25 St. Stephen's Green, Dublin 2, Ireland (a division of Penguin Books Ltd.)
Penguin Group (Australia), 250 Camberwell Road, Camberwell, Victoria 3124, Australia
(a division of Pearson Australia Group Pty. Ltd.)
Penguin Books India Pvt. Ltd., 11 Community Centre, Panchsheel Park, New Delhi—110 017, India
Penguin Group (NZ), 67 Apollo Drive, Rosedale, North Shore 0632, New Zealand
(a division of Pearson New Zealand Ltd.)
Penguin Books (South Africa) (Pty.) Ltd., 24 Sturdee Avenue, Rosebank, Johannesburg 2196,
South Africa

Penguin Books Ltd., Registered Offices: 80 Strand, London WC2R 0RL, England

This book is an original publication of The Berkley Publishing Group.

Cover art by Alan Ayers.
Cover design by Rita Frangie.
Interior text design by Kristin del Rosario.

PRINTING HISTORY
Berkley Sensation trade paperback edition / March 2009

Library of Congress Cataloging-in-Publication Data

Schone, Robin.
Cry for passion / Robin Schone.—Berkley Sensation trade pbk. ed.
p. cm.
ISBN 978-0-425-22593-6
1. Marriage—Fiction. 2. England—Fiction. I. Title.

PS3569.C52612C79 2009
813'.54—dc22

2008050461

PRINTED IN THE UNITED STATES OF AMERICA

10 9 8 7 6 5 4 3 2 1

Cry for Passion *is dedicated to justice,*
and the men and women who pursue it on our behalf.
Keep up the good fight, ladies and gentlemen!

Love is the flower of life,
and blossoms unexpectedly
and without law . . .

—D. H. Lawrence

Chapter 1

Men and women mobbed the Old Bailey Courthouse, voices joined in jubilation.

James Whitcox had won. Jack Lodoun had lost.

Again.

"Mr. Lodoun." The clattering footsteps that dogged Jack's heels picked up speed. "If I might have a moment of your time."

Chill, damp air licked his cheeks.

He turned up his collar: The soft wool blocked neither the cold nor the woman he had earlier examined, and who now followed him.

But the trial was over. And so was Jack.

He lengthened his stride.

"Mr. Lodoun." The hurried heel taps were losing distance. "Please."

He had only three more steps . . . two more steps . . . one more step to reach the curb and hail the approaching hansom.

Jack raised his umbrella.

"I am murdering my husband, Mr. Lodoun," froze his arm.

Before Jack, a sweat-streaked dun hurtled down the cobbled street, ears flattened, mouth working to expel a sawing bit.

"Please don't turn away." Behind Jack, the clear, cultured voice reverberated over the pounding of hooves and ringing celebration. "I need your help."

Need gripped his testicles. Simultaneously, the acrid stench of hot, damp horse slammed into Jack's face, freeing him from his paralysis but not the desire with which he daily lived.

"There are police patrolling the courthouse, Mrs. Clarring." Jack hoisted higher the furled umbrella. The sweat-streaked dun passed him by, spittle blowing from its mouth like cobwebs. The two-wheeled hansom cab rattled after the protesting horse. "If you need assistance in saving your husband, I suggest you inform them, rather than I, of your murderous intentions. If you need representation after you kill him, I suggest you solicit James Whitcox."

Each closing heel tap spiked his eardrums.

"You remember my name."

He had subpoenaed her. He had questioned her.

Now all he wanted to do was forget her.

Jack ignored the woman who would not be ignored.

Rose Clarring halted behind him, a throbbing reminder of the trial he had not won and the man to whom he had lost everything. "I don't want to murder my husband, Mr. Lodoun."

A four-wheeled cab edged closer to the curb.

Pain fused Jack's spine.

Seven months and three weeks earlier a woman had hailed a Clarence cab.

That day, also, had been a Wednesday.

She had died penned in muck underneath four wheels while Jack, cock satiated, drowsed between clean sheets damp with their sweat and their sex.

"I want to divorce him," jolted Jack out of the past.

Debilitating pain instantly gave way to castigating anger.

He could not board a four-wheeled cab, no matter that the cries of men and women who jeered his loss rode the crowded London street. He could not get on with his life, shackled by grief as the sweat-streaked dun was shackled to the two-wheeled hansom.

All he could do was lower his umbrella and face the woman whose testimony continued to knot his stomach. "Is your husband a bigamist?"

"No," she said, pale oval face rouged with cold. "Of course not."

There was only one certainty in Jack's life: parliamentary law.

"Has he deserted you?" he curtly probed, knowing the answer.

Small, black-leather-gloved fingers curled around the black gores of a slender umbrella. "No."

"Then I suggest you murder him, Mrs. Clarring, because no barrister can win you a divorce; whereas, should you rid yourself of your husband, I have no doubt Whitcox would win you an acquittal within a week of your arraignment."

She did not step back from his biting sarcasm. "I love my husband, Mr. Lodoun."

"So you said in the witness box."

Rose Clarring was thirty-three years old, a golden-haired, blue-eyed woman who stood ten inches shorter than his own five-foot, ten-inch frame. She looked like a pocket Venus in her stylish black bonnet and worsted wool cloak, a woman who would crumble at the slightest provocation.

Jack knew differently: In the witness box she had not once looked away while he deliberately baited and belittled her.

Rose Clarring stepped closer still until her femininity choked his cock and the churning mob at the end of the street shrank to the size of dark, bloated maggots. "You did a very great thing, sir."

A bark of laughter joined the cheers and jeers of those who thought otherwise; it came from Jack's mouth, but it contained no mirth. "I lost, ma'am."

"Because it was the right thing to do."

The bitter dregs of laughter dried up in his throat. "Are you accusing me of malfeasance, Mrs. Clarring?"

"If you intended to win the trial, Mr. Lodoun"—a sharp breeze rifled through the white egret feathers crowning her bonnet; it carried upward a faint waft of roses—"all you need have done was say that Mr. Whitcox and Mrs. Hart were lovers, and you would have done so."

And Frances Hart, a forty-nine-year-old widow who had joined the Men and Women's Club—an eclectic society of men and women who discussed sexology—instead of mourning the death of her husband with her family, would have been remanded into the care of her son, Jack's client, who would have committed her to an insane asylum. And James Whitcox, a man who never lost, would have learned what it was like to lose the woman he loved.

But Jack, sworn to uphold English law, had withheld key evidence. And he did not know *why*.

"Coventrys 'n chonkeys! A ha'penny, a ha'penny!" tumbled down the cracked pavement; it was chased by a masculine rumble. "Ginger beer, git it 'ere!"

The street vendors had found the mob.

"I can't help you," Jack said, breaking free of her gaze.

"If you were Mr. Whitcox, you could not," halted him mid pivot. Watery sun rays burst through scuttling gray clouds. The translucent gleam of a pearl earring riveted his gaze. Immediately the single gem was superimposed by a pearl necklace, a wife's recompense for bearing a daughter. "But you aren't Mr. Whitcox, Mr. Lodoun: You're a member of Parliament."

Rose Clarring's response was a sharp slap of reality.

Jack's gaze jerked upward.

Anemic light aureoled her black bonnet and danced on the tips of white feathers.

"And so you want me to petition Parliament for a private act," Jack harshly deduced.

"Yes."

There was no hesitation in either her gaze or her voice.

Only once, he remembered, had Rose Clarring hesitated in the witness box.

Is your husband here with you today? Jack had asked.

Her answer had been damning. The pain inside her eyes had kneed him in the groin.

"No," Jack said flatly.

Society did not approve of divorce. And neither did Parliament.

His position in the House of Commons was the only thing Jack had left.

Deliberately he turned his back on Rose Clarring and faced Newgate Street.

"Have you ever loved, Mr. Lodoun?"

A trill of laughter drifted on the grumbling passage of a carriage. Through the window he glimpsed the curve of a feminine cheek.

Silvery blond hair glinted in the shadows.

Jack's heartbeat accelerated, even as his mind jeered that he would never again hold the woman he loved.

Immediately the laughter and the carriage were gone, taking with them the spark of hope.

"Unlike you and the other members of your club, Mrs. Clarring," Jack bit out, fingers fisting around the wooden grip of his umbrella, "I am not compelled to share my private life with strangers."

The sudden blockage of the relentless breeze alerted Jack that Rose Clarring had stepped closer still.

"You do not approve of the Men and Women's Club," she said.

"I do not approve of women who deliberately jeopardize their husbands' good names."

"Would you rather a woman murder her husband?" prickled his shoulder blades.

Across the street, a man wearing silver-rimmed spectacles ducked inside Bailey's Book Shop.

Jack knew the man: He was a court usher. Jack knew what he sought: pornography.

One month, one week and four days earlier Frances Hart, James Whitcox and eight other members of the Men and Women's Club had sought the same sexual titillation at the Achilles Book Shoppe.

Rose Clarring had been among them.

But Jack had withheld that evidence, too.

"You said you wanted to divorce your husband"—he concentrated on the closing door of the book shop instead of on the woman who stood behind him—"not kill him."

"But I *am* killing him," glanced off his left arm.

Rose Clarring stepped around Jack.

"The love I bear him is killing him."

Rose Clarring stepped in front of Jack.

"The love he bears me is killing him."

Rose Clarring's pale, cold-rouged face turned up to his; the top of her head did not quite reach his chin. Her cloak, black as a widow's weeds, molded her body even as a blast of chill spring air battered his bowler.

"Every day he is dying, Mr. Lodoun, because I have not had the courage to stop it."

In the witness box—underneath the flickering gaslight—her eyes had been midnight blue. In the watery wash of sunlight, they were the pure, untarnished blue of cornflowers.

"Yet here you are, Mrs. Clarring"—Jack gazed over the white feathers blowing in the wind and searched the approaching stream of groaning, clattering conveyances for a hansom—"positively brimming with courage."

"Because of you," snapped his head downward. "And the way you looked at Mrs. Hart and Mr. Whitcox."

"I looked at them as what they were," Jack sharply rebutted, "a plaintiff and a colleague."

"You looked at them with envy." Her gaze did not waver from his; the feathers crowning her bonnet danced a macabre rite. "You know what they've found with one another."

Jack's lips curled cynically. "I can go out and buy what they have any night of the week."

"But you can't," she said quietly. Decisively. The scent of spring and roses teased his nostrils. "You can't buy passion. No matter how much one might wish to do so."

Her unshakable resolve exacerbated the loss that pulsed through his veins.

"And just how did they find this passion, Mrs. Clarring?" Jack's derision slashed through the stinging wind and the bump and grind of metal wheels skimming cobble. Amid the mob and over the street vendors' calls scattered voices sang, "*. . . Oh what a happy land is England!*" "By passing around French postcards? By sneaking into pornographic shops? Or did they discover it while reading so-called academic books that serve no other purpose than to detail sexual perversions?"

Rose Clarring did not glance away from him.

He realized with gut-clenching certainty that she saw within his eyes the secrets of the thirteen members of the Men and Women's Club; secrets he had been duty-bound to reveal, but which he had not.

The neatly written minutes detailing their weekly meetings were indelibly scrawled on his mind.

Provocative discussions. Damning disclosures.

Men and women questioning. Women and men revealing.

Loneliness. Desire.

"You're frightened," Rose Clarring surmised.

Jack was a barrister, but he was also a politician. Men whose lives depended upon popular opinion did not admit to fear. Grief.

Guilt.

"And what are you, Mrs. Clarring?" Jack riposted. "Your name will be in the papers tomorrow. You're a very pretty woman. Perhaps even your likeness will be printed. You will no longer be able to hide your clandestine meetings from your husband. He can put you away, just as my client attempted to put Mrs. Hart away. Only there will be no Whitcox to save you. I would be very afraid, were I you."

"Would you, Mr. Lodoun?"

"Yes," he said, fighting the sudden drumming of his heart and the soughing of his lungs.

She searched his gaze, as if she were the barrister and he an adverse witness. "What is more terrifying than living without love?"

Nothing, Jack thought. Nothing was more terrifying.

But he could not say that.

"You said your husband loves you," he shot back.

Pale sunlight infused her face. Shadow darkened her eyes.

"The first time I saw my husband," she unexpectedly confided, "I was watching my two youngest brothers. They were only nine and eleven. I took them to the park. They were quite a handful. When I warned them not to whip their hoop in the street, they laughed. They would have been run over by a cab had it not been for Jonathon."

The man to whom she had been married for twelve years, one month, three weeks and two days.

"This is not necessary," Jack brutally interrupted.

"But it is, Mr. Lodoun," Rose Clarring said, white feathers whipping the air; a guinea-gold curl lashed the slender curve of her neck. "He snatched them up, one under each arm, and whirled them around until their laughter filled the park."

Unwitting images flitted before Jack's eyes: pictures of a woman weighted down with packages instead of two children whipping a hoop; the figure of a forty-four-year-old man instead of the twenty-one-year-old boy Jonathon Clarring had then been.

But Jack, unlike Jonathon Clarring, had not been there to cheat a cab of death.

Forcefully he beat back the images. "The trial is over, Mrs. Clarring: Go home."

But Rose Clarring did not hear him, caught up in her own past.

"I laughed, too." The innocent happiness that flooded the cornflower blue eyes stabbed through him. "It was impossible not to be happy when I was with Jonathon."

But now she proposed to divorce him, a husband she loved.

"I don't want to hear this," Jack said harshly, suddenly choking on the scent of coal and manure, and the asphyxiating perfume of springtime roses.

"But I need to tell you," catapulted through the air. The brief glow of happiness drained from Rose Clarring's face. Inside her eyes he glimpsed the pain he had evoked in the witness box. "I need you . . . I need *someone* . . . to understand."

But Jack didn't want to understand this woman when the woman he loved lay dead in the ground.

A heavy omnibus lumbered past them, wood creaking, wheels groaning.

The barrister inside Jack noted that Rose Clarring's breasts heaved with the force of her breathing. He felt no triumph at finally shattering her composure. Not when the man inside him stared at those breasts and appraised their size.

Stoically Jack met her gaze.

Black vulnerability dilated her pupils; instantly it was swallowed by determination.

"I need to tell you," she repeated.

But no need went unpunished.

Jack couldn't say that, either.

"When Jonathon set the boys down, staggering and giggling," she continued, sunlight gilding the tips of her lashes, "he looked at me and said, 'I want you to give me a dozen just like these.'

"And I wanted to give him sons, Mr. Lodoun." The castigating wind drove home her earnestness. "I wanted to give him little boys with whom he could play. I wanted to give him little girls he could pamper. I wanted to make Jonathon as happy as he made me.

"You accused me of joining the Men and Women's Club in order to learn about prophylactics, but it wasn't preventive checks that robbed my husband of children: It was the mumps.

"I am a living reminder of every dream he ever dreamed. Every night when he is home alone with me, he drinks himself into a state of unconsciousness. As long as we are married, he will look at me and see only his inability to create life.

"Yes, my husband has the legal authority to do as you say." Jack watched dispassionately as Rose Clarring took a deep breath—small, round breasts rising . . . falling . . . egret feathers flogging the wind—and regained the inner resolve that had defied his earlier examination, and that had won the sympathy of twelve jurors, all men with wives and children. "But I have the moral obligation, surely, to end the pain that is crippling us both."

A distant bell pierced the whining, grumbling traffic and the muffled shouts interspersed with song. Three more strikes followed, Westminster Chimes announcing the quarter hour.

It was fifteen minutes after five: The trial had ended sixteen minutes earlier. In six hours and forty-five minutes, the first of June would end and the second day would dawn.

And where would he be? Jack wondered.

He had never fathered a child, but he had never wanted children. He had loved a woman, but he had not wanted marriage.

Jack stepped around Rose Clarring and raised his umbrella.

The flagellating breeze abruptly died.

"Who was the woman you loved?" catapulted through the stillness and stopped a hansom cab.

Jack stepped up onto an iron rung, spine straight; the cab tilted with his weight, instantly righted, his left foot anchoring the wooden platform. The gaze that followed him pierced the wool of his clothes, the flesh stretched taut across his body, the bones that held him rigid.

Swinging open the door, keenly aware of the cabby, who was a potential witness—every move he made, every word he uttered a matter of public record—Jack turned his head and caught Rose Clarring's gaze. Clearly, coldly, he enunciated: "Cynthia Herries Whitcox."

Daughter of the First Lord of the Treasury and wife of James Whitcox, Barrister, Queens Counsel.

Shock widened her eyes. Understanding slowly ate up her surprise.

He had represented one man for the sole purpose of destroying another. He had not cared that he would also destroy the members of the Men and Women's Club.

In that, at least, he had succeeded, Jack thought: Their lives would never be the same.

Jack had butchered their reputations in the witness box. The papers would serve them up piecemeal to a public hungry for scandal.

The condemnation Jack expected did not blossom inside the cornflower blue eyes. Instead Rose Clarring asked the question that every night robbed Jack of sleep: "Do you ever wonder, Mr. Lodoun, if she would be alive still had she divorced Mr. Whitcox?"

Chapter 2

A sharp snap of wood pierced the grating whine of wheels and a wafting chorus of ". . . God save the Queen! These times *are* times, seldom to be seen. . . ."

One second Rose stared up into eyes so blue they looked purple; the next moment the cab into which Jack Lodoun had disappeared merged into a stream of traffic.

Her gloved fingers clenched around silk, metal and wood.

She had needed him, and he had turned away. As if the stark yearning inside his eyes had been a figment of her imagination.

And perhaps it had.

Hot tears pricked her eyes.

What could she—a woman who inspired only pain in her husband—know about the needs of another man?

"Gi' ye a cab, missus?" permeated the disjointed cacophony of traffic and song.

Taking a deep breath, Rose turned.

Gentle, sympathetic eyes captured her gaze. They were on a level with her own.

The ageless, stooped man smiled a toothless smile. "'Ad a bit o' a lov'rs spat, 'ave ye?"

Memories of endless blue skies and smiling blue eyes slashed through Rose.

They had been lovers, she and Jonathon, when they married.

"Yes." Rose swallowed the loss that swelled inside her. "I would like a cab."

No sooner did she fish out of her reticule a copper coin than a hansom pulled up to the curb.

Rose pressed the penny into gnarled fingers. "Thank you."

Slowly—feeling as fragile as the old man who had procured the cab—she stepped up onto the eighteen-inch-high iron stair.

The cabby indifferently enquired: "Where t', missus?"

She could not go back to Jonathon's house that echoed with the lament of his unborn children. But neither could she keep the trial today a secret.

"Langham and Great Portland Street, please," Rose said.

The cab reeked of masculine cigars and feminine perfume. Blindly she closed the door on the celebration of another woman's victory and stared through water-spotted glass.

What should she tell her family? she wondered. The truth?

But what was the truth?

She *had* discussed provocative topics in the company of men. She *had* read books society deemed sexually perverse.

Above pointed horse ears, the black top hat and stiff back of a cabby materialized.

It had seemed so innocent two years earlier, congregating in the Museum of London, each meeting of the Men and Women's Club called to order with the rap of a gavel.

Rose braced herself as the cab she occupied lunged in between careening carriages.

The trial today had also been called to order with the rap of a gavel, she recalled. The impact had bored through the floor of the windowless room where she had waited, alone, to be called as a witness.

The left wheel of the cab dropped into a pothole. Immediately the seat shot up underneath Rose.

She grabbed a leather pull. The cab irrevocably jolted forward.

Through the streaked glass, storefronts gave way to brick townhomes. Each row a community. Each house a home. Every woman filling a niche: wife, mother, daughter.

The cab slowed, jerked, horse stepping backward . . . forward . . . halting.

Rose stared up at the gray clouds that striated a blue sky.

The wind had chased away the rain. But now the wind had died.

Rose *still* did not know what to tell her family.

The impatient jangle of a harness sliced through a creak of wood.

Reluctantly Rose pushed open the cab door.

A thin line of sunlight marked the four-storied brick town house that she had called home for twenty-one years, but that had ceased to be her home the day she married.

Her bedroom had overlooked the street. Blinds now shuttered the tall rectangular window.

Rose paid the cabby.

The white-enameled door swung open.

"Mrs. Clarring."

Giles, the black-haired, sixty-year-old butler who was no less stately than the town house, briefly bowed; simultaneously he held out an imperious, white-gloved hand.

"Hello, Giles," Rose said huskily, offering up her umbrella.

The folded black silk disappeared; instantly the white-gloved hand reappeared.

Rose gave up her black leather gloves . . . her cloak. . . .

Not quickly enough.

The butler tugged warm wool off her shoulders.

Rose transferred her reticule from one hand to the other, losing her cloak. Feeling unaccountably naked, she stepped forward.

A familiar clearing of a throat stopped her.

Tears stinging her eyes, Rose wiped her feet on the doormat. Head down . . . inspecting her handiwork . . . she asked, "Is Mother home?"

"Mr. and Mrs. Davis are in the drawing room."

She resolutely lifted her chin and squared her shoulders. "Thank you."

A comfortably plump man and woman—his graying hair thinning, her gold hair graying—were seated around the leather-tooled drum table that had for all of Rose's life been the center of the Davis family.

But it was neither tea, nor a puzzle, nor a game that occupied the man and woman.

Rose stopped short of the table, feet sinking into thick wool carpet, breath lodging inside her chest.

Judgment would not come on the morrow; it had come now, this evening.

Blue eyes—*her* eyes, masculine instead of feminine—glanced up and pierced her soul. "Do you think so little of us, Rose, that you let us learn about this in the paper?"

The hurt and betrayal inside her father's voice squeezed closed her throat.

Her mother had taught her how to pour tea at that drum table, Rose thought with a bittersweet pang. Her father had taught her how to play draughts.

Now *The Globe* spread across the tooled leather, black print summarily destroying thirty-three years of trust and respect.

Jack Lodoun had said she was a very pretty woman. Rose did not look very pretty in the evening newspaper.

Underneath the drawing capturing her likeness the caption

read: "Rose Clarring: A Woman in Search of Illumination or Fornication?"

"Do you think so little of me, Father," Rose managed, "that you think I would be unfaithful to Jonathon?"

"I didn't say you were unfaithful," the fifty-nine-year-old man harshly denied.

Rose held his gaze. "But it's what you think, isn't it?"

How ugly was the color of guilt.

He flushed. The gaze of the man whose eyes Rose had inherited slid away.

"Why didn't you tell us, Rose?"

Rose glanced down at the fifty-three-year-old woman who was taller than Rose, but who was golden-haired like Rose. "Tell you what, Mother?"

"Why didn't you tell us it was you who didn't want children? All these years we thought it was . . ."

The older woman's voice faded, unable to complete the thought: *All these years we thought it was* Jonathon *who did not give* you *children.*

The secrets Rose had kept from her family pushed up inside her throat.

Too late.

Their revelation would not now alter the future.

Rose drew in an unsteady breath. "Is that what the paper reports, that I joined the Men and Women's Club to learn about preventive checks?"

The face that all of Rose's life had shone like a beacon—pale with worry during childhood illnesses . . . flushed with pride at social recreations . . . wet with tears at her wedding—turned a dark, shameful red.

"Perhaps, Mother . . . Father"—Rose's corset squeezed her heart—"I didn't tell you about the Men and Women's Club because of your reactions now."

Or perhaps Rose had not told them because she had needed a

private place where she could be a woman instead of the mother others daily expected her to become.

"What of Jonathon?" Horror suddenly choked her father's voice. "Surely you didn't leave him to discover this through the papers, like you did with us?"

Rose felt the gaze of her mother and father more keenly than she had felt the stares of all the men and women inside the courtroom, judging her dress, her face, her voice, her marriage, her very worth as a human.

"I told Jonathon about the club," Rose said. A half-truth. Or a half lie. Jonathon had been unconscious from too much drink when she had told him about the club and the decision she must make.

"And the trial?" her father persisted.

"No." Rose met his gaze—his familiar face now blanched from shock—and braced herself. She had answered Jack Lodoun when he examined her; she would truthfully answer her father. "I did not tell him about the trial."

"Oh, Rose!" Her mother gasped in dismay.

Her father's face suddenly turned old and aged.

Because of *her.*

Darkness blotched Rose's vision.

"Mr. Davis, Mrs. Davis," cut through the tightening noose of emotion. "I prepared a tray. Mrs. Clarring no doubt missed teatime."

Rose gratefully turned to the impossibly black-haired butler who had in the past publicly frowned when she muddied his floors, but who had privately sneaked her cookies at bedtime. "Thank you, Giles."

Giles whisked away *The Globe* and deposited a silver tray on top of the leather drum table.

His hands were rock steady. Unlike Rose's hands.

Carefully she picked up a heavy, silver-plated teapot that radiated heat.

"You may go, Giles," her father shortly instructed.

Black tea leapt out of delicate, gold-rimmed china.

An ugly splotch spread over the silver tray like the blemish she now created on her husband's reputation. Growing with each breath . . . with each purchased newspaper . . .

Rose set down the teapot. Simultaneously the twin doors to the drawing room clicked shut.

"Why did you testify, Rose?" her mother asked pragmatically, more like the mother of Rose's past.

Rose stared at the still-growing stain. "I was subpoenaed."

By the barrister whom she had asked to win her a divorce.

A man who had accused her of joining the Men and Women's Club to learn about prophylactics, so that she need not be burdened by children. A man who—while guilty of loving another man's wife—had then accused her of joining the club in hopes of finding a lover who would give her the sexual titillation her husband did not.

What *had* she been thinking?

"You're a woman." Her mother summarily dismissed the legal laws of England. "You could have been excused."

"No." Stiffening, Rose met her mother's gaze. "I could not."

"Why not?" her father asked, cornflower blue eyes bright with hurt.

They're my friends stuck inside her throat.

In two years she had not made one friend of a club member, purposefully segregating her life from theirs.

"A man tried to commit a woman—a member of the club to which I belong—to an insane asylum, Father." Rose took a deep breath. "Simply because he did not approve of what we discussed."

"He's her son," her father objected.

"And he was wrong," Rose rebutted.

"It's not up to you to interfere in another woman's family," her mother adjured.

Rose snared her mother's gaze, a paler shade of blue. "If Father put you away, Mother, would you say that it's not my place to interfere?"

The color drained out of the older woman's face. "Your father would *never*!"

"But he could, Mother."

The danger to women had been made very evident inside the courtroom.

Rose captured blue eyes, *her* eyes. "*Couldn't* you, Father?"

Puzzlement shaded the hurt inside his gaze. "Do you think I don't love your mother, Rose?"

Rose remembered all the nights she had lain awake, crying from the pain caused by love.

"I think," she said steadily, "it's not always a matter of love."

Maternal concern enveloped Rose; Rose, the woman, derived no comfort from it. "Rose, you know your father and I love you."

And Rose loved Jonathon. And Jonathon loved Rose.

But he was not her father. And Rose was not her mother.

And love was no longer enough.

"I'm divorcing Jonathon."

The muted rattle of carriage wheels permeated the silence.

At night, lying in bed alone, the passage of a carriage was much louder.

Sometimes, Rose remembered, the loneliness of the passage had deafened her.

"I don't understand you, Rose."

A smile lifted Rose's lips; it contained no humor. "Then that makes two of us, Father."

"Are you doing this because of that club?" angrily demanded her mother.

"No," Rose said honestly.

But society would think so. Just as society now thought of her as an adulteress.

Impossibly, a small ember of hope sparked inside Rose.

"I love you"—she took a deep breath, slowly released it—"but the Men and Women's Club, the trial and my divorce have nothing to do with you. I hope you understand that."

Fleetingly Rose glanced at the bronze- and silver-framed photographs scattered throughout the drawing room.

Rose had five brothers, ages thirty-one, twenty-nine, twenty-eight, twenty-five and twenty-three. The framed pictures catalogued each and every one of their lives: their childhoods . . . their school days . . . their weddings.

Cameras had progressed even as the obligation to produce a family had not.

A baby boy—the son of her youngest brother—grinned into the lens of a Kodak that did not require a separate shutter. A tottering boy balanced on roller skates, the middle child of her oldest brother.

Bright marble eyes snared Rose's gaze.

A motionless rocking horse stood in a corner, horsehair mane tangled, gaily painted body chipped with age and use.

She and her brothers had rocked on that horse; now her brothers' children rocked on it.

In this room was everything her husband had ever wanted.

Squarely Rose met first her mother's gaze, and then that of her father.

"I hope you support my decision." She reached into her reticule and pulled out a card: The front—printed in elegant black font—bore Jonathon's address; the back of the card bore her own neat handwriting. "I've leased a row house. This is my new address. I hope, when I have my house in order, you'll visit me."

Their shock weighted down her shoulders.

"Enjoy your tea," Rose said, because there was nothing more to say.

The thick green carpet sucked at her feet. Outside the drawing room, the oak floor amplified each hollow heel tap.

"Your coat, Mrs. Clarring," elicited a sharp start of surprise.

Giles had always appeared out of nowhere, Rose remembered.

She held out her right arm . . . her left. "Thank you."

Mechanically she tugged on her gloves and grasped the proffered umbrella.

Giles thrust a column of paper into her left hand; it took Rose a long second to realize it was *The Globe*.

"It's not a very good likeness, Mrs. Clarring."

Tears blurred her vision. "You think not, Giles?"

But he did not answer, asking instead, "Did Mrs. Hart win her liberation?"

Rose had testified at two in the afternoon. The trial had ended four witnesses, two hours and fifty-nine minutes later. Too late for *The Globe* to print the verdict, but not too late to ruin Rose's reputation.

"Yes," Rose said. "She won."

There was no emotion inside the butler's eyes. "I sent the potboy to fetch a cab."

"Thank you," Rose repeated, blinking back the tears.

She had no choice but to walk the solitary course she had planned. The door to her childhood closed behind her.

Pale pink tinted the darkening sky.

A horse waited at the curb; it was as black as the hansom it pulled.

Rose slammed shut the cab door and sat down on cracked leather. Forcibly she concentrated on the descending dusk instead of her destination.

A lamp boy walked the pavement, lighting wrought iron streetlamps one by one. The teardrop-shaped flames did not disperse the gathering shadows.

All too soon the hansom jerked to a stop.

"Wait for me," Rose instructed the cabby.

Twilight was brick by brick swallowing the familiar town house, turning mellow gold into murky gray. Through a mullioned window she glimpsed Emily, the chambermaid, lighting a parlor lamp.

The shadow-dulled door did not magically open.

Rose slid a key into the lock. Simultaneously the door swung open.

Metal jerked free of metal.

"Mrs. Clarring!" the forty-year-old butler who came by his black hair naturally gasped, white-gloved hand clutching his chest.

"Justin," Rose returned, fighting to lower her fisted hand instead of clutching her own chest.

Between one blink and the next the butler's startled face transformed into an expressionless mask. Gloved hand dropping, he stepped backward in a half bow.

It was so obvious he had read about the trial.

Rose would *not* cry.

"Is Mr. Clarring home?" she asked instead, jagged key piercing her glove.

"No, madam."

Relief swept through Rose.

She would face Jonathon. But not tonight.

Please, God, she thought, *not tonight.*

"A cab is waiting outside," Rose calmly informed the stiff, disapproving butler. "Please have the trunk in my bedchamber brought down, and strapped onto it."

"Very well, madam."

The butler turned with a flap of black coattails.

Beyond the gleaming curve of a mahogany staircase, five closed doors barred her entrance.

She had betrayed her husband, the closed doors accused her. She no longer belonged in his house, they judged her.

Turning—swallowing back the nausea rising up inside her throat—Rose's gaze was captured by a gleam of silver.

Envelopes were neatly stacked on a tray. Folded beside the evening mail lay a newspaper that could only be *The Globe*.

Dropping the key into her reticule, she quickly, decisively strode to the cookie-cornered table. The first drawer contained calling cards . . . there a pen . . . a stack of notepaper. . . . The second drawer contained envelopes.

Rose blankly stared at a white sheet of vellum paper.

She saw the heavy silver ashtray—a wedding gift from her youngest brother—that set on Jonathon's desk. She saw the long-stemmed glass rose—a memento of her honeymoon—that lay upstairs on a nightstand.

There were so many memories inside these four walls.

The gold banding her ring finger throbbed, another memento.

Rose peeled off her black leather glove and twisted off her wedding band.

Gripping a thick metal pen, Rose stared down at the blank vellum paper that was weighted down by gold.

No words came to mind.

How did a woman tell a man whose body she had welcomed into her own . . . a man who had made her family his family . . . that she could no longer live on the emotion sustained by memorabilia?

Chapter 3

"Bloody shame you lost, Lodoun." Wood scraping hard oak flooring pierced the muted din of masculine rumbles. An acrid burst of smoke obliterated the oily black current that was the Thames. "Dreadful miscarriage of justice, if you ask me. Women joining secret sex clubs. It's all very well for the men, lucky dogs, but the very thought of our ladies . . . But there you have it. *Our* ladies wouldn't, would they? I pity Clarring, poor sod. Married to a bit of a slut, what?"

Slut infiltrated the muffle of alcohol.

Jack had told Rose Clarring she would be in the papers on the morrow.

He had lied: She had made the evening newspapers.

Laughter needled his skin.

The verdict of the trial had come too late to be printed, but there were no secrets between the courts and Parliament: Each and every MP knew he had lost.

Jack turned his head away from the bow window and dispassionately studied Blair Stromwell, a senior member of Parliament and the Chairman of Justice. "Do you know Jonathon Clarring?"

"What?" The senior man glanced up from *The Globe*. Gray smoke spiraled up from the brown stub of his cigar. "Don't you?"

Jack knew his reputation. Jack knew the desires of his wife.

She wanted a divorce. *A moral obligation,* she had claimed.

Jack lifted the crystal snifter—cupped between his fingers like a woman's breast—and drained body-warmed brandy.

The alcohol burned all the way down to his testicles.

He set the snifter down onto solid oak. The thud of crystal impacting wood—the sound of other glasses, of other MPs drinking and breathing politics—reverberated throughout St. Stephen's Club. Beside his empty snifter, amber winked in the bottom of a crystal decanter.

Every night when he is home alone with me, he drinks himself into a state of unconsciousness slammed through him.

"Why should I know Jonathon Clarring?" Slowly Jack raised his lashes and met the senior MP's waiting gaze. "I examined his wife, not him."

"Best damn stockbroker in London. The man's made me a bloody fortune." The Chairman of Justice punctuated his endorsement with a fresh billow of smoke. "See him. Tell him I sent you."

Jack had not before realized how thoroughly he disliked cigars.

Pushing back the heavy leather wing chair—wood skidding across wood—he stood. "I leave such things to my man of business."

"Lodoun." A frail hand weighted down his shoulder. "Pity you lost today. Mothers suing their sons. And winning! Dreadful, just dreadful. Take comfort in the knowledge you were in the right."

Bitter irony welled up inside Jack.

Slowly he turned, motion dislodging the hand that held him. "Was I, Father?"

Jack addressed the Father of the House.

The most senior member of Parliament—a man of seventy-five years who chaired the Select Committee of Privileges—was older than Jack's own father. Unlike his own father, the most senior member of Parliament knew the cost of ambition.

Empathy glinted in the senior MP's eyes. Or perhaps it was the flickering light that gave the illusion of empathy. "Did Stromwell here tell you that your name came up today in meeting?"

While Jack was in court, destroying an innocent woman.

The Chairman of Justice's gaze stabbed his back, sharp and appraising. His voice carried over the suffocating din of masculine conjectures: "I mentioned to Father what a splendid Lord of Appeal in Ordinary you'd make."

A Lord of Appeal in Ordinary sat in the House of Lords and adjudged the legal cases brought before it. Were Jack to be so appointed, he would for his lifetime be awarded the rank of Baron.

Such an appointment would be the pinnacle of his career. But no appointment came without a price.

Jack had learned that as attorney general. But he was attorney general no more.

"I didn't realize the appointment was available," Jack said neutrally.

"It isn't . . . yet." Reaching out a liver-spotted hand, Father squeezed Jack's forearm; there was strength yet in the aging fingers. "But it will be."

All it would cost was more silence, more compromises, more lonely nights.

A chorus of ". . . Shame you lost . . ." greeted Jack at each table he passed.

Each man suspected the truth, but no one dared voice it: *Shame you lost to a man you cuckolded.*

Jack collected his coat, hat and umbrella from the cloak clerk. A bowing, black-and-white uniformed man opened the door.

With distant irony Jack reflected that membership to St. Stephen's Club—a club that pandered to conservative Parliament members—cost more than the annual wages of the doorman whose liberty they were sworn to protect.

One second Jack stepped off the concrete stoop; the next second the bowed man who held open the door stood at the curb hailing a cab.

Jack was drunk. But the alcohol had not obliterated cornflower blue eyes.

The doorman waved away a four-wheeled Clarence cab and aggressively gestured to the driver of a two-wheeled hansom.

Anger sliced through Jack's pain.

Everyone knew. Nobody spoke.

Not Father. Not the Chairman of the Justice.

Jack had never spoken of it until this day.

Tossing the doorman a florin, he stepped up onto the cab.

"Where t'?" penetrated the wool scarf covering the cabby's mouth and nose.

A deafening chime vibrated the night, ended on a flat strike: It was forty-five minutes past eight.

Jack looked up at the black sky that was dominated by the Houses of Parliament, magnesian limestone shining like gold.

Where did Jack have to go?

He drank alone, surrounded by MPs thirsty for power. He lived alone, wedded to politics.

Jack gave the cabby an address.

Each turn of the wheel cried out: *I need* someone . . . *I need* someone . . . *I need* someone. . . .

Jack had gambled; his gamble paid off: The Achilles Book Shoppe was open.

A discordant jangle announced his entry.

Gaslit globes brightly illuminated the glass-plated store.

Respectable women in black bonnets with crowning white feathers and black cloaks leaned over tables piled high with books. Respectable men in dark coats with matching bowler hats roamed long aisles.

Rose Clarring could be one of those women. Jack Lodoun could be one of those men.

Jack shut the door on the night, closure eliciting another sharp jangle.

No one looked up. No one looked around.

Jack had no interest in the conservative men and women who comprised his constituency.

Sharp perusal stabbed through him.

But someone was interested in Jack.

He glanced to the back of the store.

A middle-aged clerk dressed in tweed caught his gaze.

He saw Jack's drunkenness. He recognized Jack's face.

He knew about the Men and Women's Club—a group of men and women who had congregated inside the shop on the evening of the twentieth of April—and he knew why Jack had come.

Jack strode to where the clerk stood. He said, only, "Show me."

Without question the clerk opened the white-enameled door bearing the insignia of "Latin and Greek Classics."

A wall of books with embossed titles in Latin and Greek—some of which Jack recognized, some of which he did not—confronted him. Two overstuffed armchairs were angled in a corner.

He had entered a reading room.

His fingers fisted around the grip of his umbrella.

There were no pornographic books to titillate the imagination. No artifacts to stimulate the body.

No hope for sexual satiation.

"Where is it?" ricocheted off gold and leather.

Jack's voice was harsh.

From drink, he told himself. He knew that he lied.

His testicles and his cock ached for that which he did not have.

"Behind here, sir." The man dressed in tweed pressed the middle panel of the bookshelves filled with gold-embossed books. The panel noiselessly swung inward. "In the basement."

Jack stared at the downward path of dark wool carpeting that Rose Clarring had descended forty-two days earlier.

There were no banisters to catch a woman tripping on a trailing skirt. But the stairs had not been designed with a woman in mind.

"When you're ready to leave," the middle-aged man neutrally instructed, "a clerk will show you the exit."

Jack followed Rose Clarring down into the dimly lit world of masculine pornography.

Behind him, the wall closed with a hissing click. Below him, wooden tables branched out into narrow aisles.

Too narrow, surely, for a wheelchair to maneuver, Jack remotely thought, yet a member of the Men and Women's Club was bound to a wheelchair, and he, too, had roamed these aisles in search of sexual satisfaction.

Jack stepped down off the bottom stair. The air was noticeably cooler than the air upstairs.

This wasn't the first time he had visited such a store, but it was the first time he'd visited this store. It looked and smelled much like every other pornographic shop.

The wooden tables bore the imprints of sweaty fingers. The flickering shadows reeked of male arousal.

Stepping in between a gap of oblivious men dressed in wool coats and felt bowler hats, Jack randomly selected a postcard.

A naked woman—lips curved in a knowing smile—with her left hand held apart another woman's naked buttocks to expose a darkly puckered anus impaled by a thin nozzle. A short hose connected the nozzle to a bloated rubber bag. With her right hand, the smiling woman who exposed the compromised anus squeezed the douche.

The dull throb inside Jack's groin sharpened.

He wondered what Rose Clarring would think of the picture. Perhaps, even, she had gazed at this postcard.

Had it excited her? Repelled her?

He wondered what the woman he loved would have thought of the act, commonplace in the world of male pornography.

She had liked it when he penetrated her between her buttocks.

Would she have been repelled if he had inserted there a syringe and directed warm liquid deep inside her? Or would it have excited her, as Jack was now suddenly excited by the thought?

Disgusted at the desire that had not died seven months and three weeks earlier, he flipped the card onto the table.

But he couldn't leave. He couldn't stop thinking.

Would she still be alive if she had asked for a divorce?

Jack moved away from the long table weighted down with boxes of postcards.

A glass showcase monopolized the end of the center aisle. Stoically Jack studied the contents.

"May I help you, sir?" enquired an impersonal male voice.

Jack knew Rose Clarring had visited the Achilles Book Shoppe. But he did not know what she had purchased. He did not know what excited her.

He did not know if the pain inside her eyes could be vanquished.

"Lay them out on top of the counter," Jack said shortly.

Consternation laced the clerk's voice. "Everything, sir?"

Gaze slowly rising, Jack penned the younger man with the authority invested in him by the Commonwealth of England. "Only those items made for a lady."

The clerk quickly, efficiently laid out the requested articles—pings of metal followed by a click of glass and the thud of leather—then discreetly stepped backward.

Hooking the grip of the umbrella over his forearm, Jack picked up a gold nipple bob and clipped it to the tip of his little finger: It pinched.

The image of a translucent pearl earring flashed through his mind's eye.

Rose Clarring had small, delicate earlobes, he remembered.

He wondered what size her nipples were. Were they smaller than the tip of his little finger? Larger?

Would her breasts fill his mouth as had those of the woman he would never again suckle?

The pain binding his finger spread to his chest; it did not restrict the flow of blood that thrummed through his testicles.

Jack pulled off the nipple bob. A dildo snared his gaze.

His fingers curled around hard leather.

Did Rose Clarring fuck herself at night, he wondered, and imagine a dildo was the flesh of a man other than her husband? Did she thrust it deep against the mouth of her cervix when she came, and pretend it ejaculated sperm that hadn't been robbed of its seed?

The memory of wet, hungry flesh gripped Jack.

Caressing his cock. Squeezing his cock.

Drawing from his aching testicles one spurt of ejaculate . . . two spurts . . . three spurts . . .

He dropped the dildo. He gripped the umbrella.

He turned from the showcase.

Everywhere Jack looked another memory surfaced.

The pump of fingers. The lick of a tongue.

The tangy scent of arousal. The slick taste of desire.

A moan of satisfaction.

Glass glinted; liquid glistened.

Compulsively he crossed to a round wooden table artfully arrayed with crystal-stoppered bottles.

Jack's throbbing glans recognized both the brand and the substance: Rose's Lubrifiant, a sexual lubricant he had purchased in the past, but not for a woman named Rose.

Chapter 4

Rose woke with a start.

The wooden banister she gripped dissolved into sweat-dampened sheets. The pounding of a gavel continued to pummel her eardrums.

I would be very afraid, were I you, squealed a coiled spring.

Rose's eyelids snapped open. Darkness dilated her pupils.

It was not a convicting judge's gavel that pounded the bench, she realized, but a metal knocker that pounded a door.

Rose's husband could put her away, the knocker hammered home. A possibility that had seemed dim in the light of day, but now she was surrounded by the dark of night.

For the first time in her life she was truly alone: No one would come to her aid if she called for help.

Reason galloped to Rose's rescue.

She had left a note informing Jonathon of her new address late in the afternoon, too late for him to file a lunacy order. Nor would a criminal so loudly announce his intentions.

Wrestling back the covers, Rose slid out of bed. Cold, hard wood curled her naked toes. Blindly she located a nightstand. Inside the top drawer, her scrabbling fingers stubbed a tin of safety matches.

Blue light sparked, shot up a plume of yellow fire.

Lifting an icy glass globe, she touched the burning match tip to a blackened wick. Light radiated outward, replacing darkness with bare, shadowed walls.

Blowing out the dying match—breath a silvery plume—Rose dropped the blackened stick into a small milk glass bowl and grabbed the candle she had earlier used to light her way up the stairs. Dancing yellow flame leapt from the wick of the oil lamp to the candle stub.

The urgent pounding spurred Rose forward.

Fluttering candlelight illuminated the dark length of the corridor . . . the steep descent of wooden stairs . . . a white-enameled door wreathed in shadow.

"Who is it?" Rose asked, heart tripping.

More pounding vibrated the door.

A warning. A promise.

It could only be Jonathon.

Now they would have the discussion they should have had twelve years earlier.

Rose unlocked the door and swung it open. "Jonathon—"

Eyes made black with shadow stared at her from underneath a rain-misted bowler. "I seem to always be the other man, Mrs. Clarring."

A wave of brandy fumes snapped back Rose's head. "You're inebriated."

"But not unconscious."

Unlike her husband, Jack Lodoun implied.

Raw betrayal slashed through Rose: It should be *Jonathon* who knocked on her door, not this man.

She gripped cold, damp wood. "It's late, Mr. Lodoun."

"A barrister and the law are much alike," Jack Lodoun returned, dark gaze holding hers. "You get one shot at justice. If you close this door, you forfeit your chance."

"I thank you for your consideration—"

"I assure you, I am not a considerate man."

"—but my actions outside the courthouse were impulsive," Rose determinedly finished. *And desperate,* the flickering candle flame underscored. "I don't need your services."

Light glinted off reddish-gold whiskers while shadow scarred the murky face underneath the mist-kissed bowler. "You no longer want a divorce?"

"It's no longer a matter of what I want." Unaccustomed bitterness tinged her voice. "I've seen *The Globe*. Because of *you*, sir, I have been labeled an adulteress."

"So like a child"—the harsh line of his mouth twisted—"you now want to hide behind your husband's coattail?"

The unexpected criticism stung.

"I have instructed my husband I will not contest a divorce," Rose said stiffly.

"But in order for him to win a divorce, he must first prove criminal conversation." The shadow-blackened eyes bored into hers. "Did you sexually converse with a man inside the Men and Women's Club?"

The injustice of his question tore through Rose. "You *know* I didn't."

"You forget, Mrs. Clarring, I am a man who made a woman an adulteress," lashed the flickering darkness. "What makes you think you are any more impervious to a man's need than she?"

Rose stared up at the shadowed eyes that showed no emotion, even as the illuminating candle flame dipped and spurted under the force of his emotions.

This man had loved another man's wife. He had paid dearly for his love.

As Rose continued to pay for hers.

"I don't," she said quietly.

Rose did not for one moment think she was more moral than another woman.

In the distance Big Ben struck: It was eleven o'clock.

"Prove it," Jack Lodoun abruptly commanded.

Rose's heart skipped a beat. "Prove what?"

"Prove that a woman's passion is worth a man's reputation."

Cold, wet air snaked underneath Rose's gown and crawled up her naked legs. "It is a woman who bears the stigma of divorce, Mr. Lodoun, not a man."

"As you reminded me earlier, Mrs. Clarring, I am a member of Parliament." The misty rain softened the harshness of night; there was no softness inside the dark eyes that stared down at her. "I assure you, every situation I accept affects my career."

Impossible hope was tempered by hopeless reality.

"And if I *should* prove to you that passion is as worthwhile as position?" Rose asked.

"I'll consider your situation."

But he would not *commit* to her situation.

"I'll consider your offer—"

"Now." There was no compromise in the dark eyes. "Or never."

"I'm not dressed."

"I know what a woman looks like."

Inexplicable anger arced through Rose.

"But you don't know what *I* look like," she retorted.

No man had ever seen her naked.

She and Jonathon had been equally virginal, equally clothed in their marriage bed, she shrouded in a gown, he in a nightshirt.

Shadow flickered inside the too-dark eyes. "Do you want me to?"

Did she want this man to see her nakedness?

"No."

"Then there's no need to worry, is there?"

Every fiber inside her body screamed that there was, indeed, a need to worry: He was an inebriated man who was not fully in control of his actions, and she was a vulnerable woman who was naked in her emotions if not completely in her dress.

Rose stepped backward. Jack Lodoun stepped forward.

He filled the foyer.

The door closed with an ominous click; she did not lock it. "How did you know where to find me?"

Rose had only given her address to her parents and her husband—

"A clerk gave me your change of address this morning," he said shortly.

—and to a clerk when she had registered at the courthouse, Rose belatedly remembered.

The candle flame flickered and fluttered, darkly revealing shadowed walls devoid of decoration.

Her progress was silent, naked feet softly impacting hard wood. Jack Lodoun's footsteps echoed behind her, hard wooden heels a jolting reminder of the damage he was capable of inflicting.

Rose stepped through yawning darkness.

Pain exploded inside her right foot, toes slamming into leather-covered wood.

Hot wax scalded her thumb and forefinger. Simultaneously the tilting candle slid free of her hand.

Rose straightened, fighting back tears. She suddenly felt as young as the child the barrister had accused her of acting like.

Gas hissed to life. Light aureoled a stooped figure, turning black into gray: a coat . . . a bowler hat.

Diamond-bright drops of water shimmered on gray felt.

The grip of an umbrella hooked a small, round table beside a heavy brass lamp base.

To the left of a masculine hip materialized a blue damask settee, a remnant of the former row house's occupants; to the right a sullen iron fireplace formed out of the darkness.

Jack Lodoun straightened. Turned. Underneath the brim of the rain-misted hat, purple-blue eyes snared her gaze. "Why is it that you answered the door, and not your butler?"

"I leased the house yesterday." The empty row house creaked a warning; innate honesty stiffened her spine. "I haven't had time to hire servants."

"Some would say, Mrs. Clarring"—his eyelids lowered, dark lashes shadowing his cheeks; blatantly his gaze fingered . . . cupped . . . weighed her breasts—"you've created an idyll trysting place."

"That may be, sir," Rose said with a calmness she did not feel, forcing her arms to stay at her sides instead of independently hugging her chest, "but since both my parents and my husband have this address, the trysts would be subject to untimely interruptions."

"Yet here I am." Slowly he lifted heavy lids; the blackness of his pupils swallowed the purple-blue of his irises. "And there's no one to interrupt us."

Rose did not glance away from the dark sexuality that glittered inside his eyes. Of one thing she was certain: "I am not the woman you desire, Mr. Lodoun."

The hiss of gas was deafening in the ensuing silence.

"If you want to end your marriage," he abruptly said, purple-blue irises shrinking the blackness of his pupils, "all you need do is prove that your husband is unable to give you children."

She forgot the dark excitement that had for one infinitesimal moment called to her. She forgot her swollen breasts that pulsed in time with her bruised toes.

Rose forgot everything but the husband she would not further betray.

"No," she said with conviction.

"Then you must not want a divorce," Jack Lodoun impersonally deduced.

But she did: just not at that price.

"My husband has been punished enough." Rose stepped around the heavy trunk that separated them, and advanced into the circle of light. "I will not publicly humiliate him."

"You don't think a divorce will humiliate him?"

He deliberately did not understand.

"A family is all my husband has ever wanted." Clearly she enunciated each word, forcing upon him the strength of her resolve. "I will not have men judging him because he cannot father children."

"Don't you?" Jack Lodoun returned.

Rose held his gaze. "No."

The truth.

Lashes flickering downward, he stared for long seconds at her left hand.

The white flesh circling her finger—the only physical evidence that remained of her twelve-year-long marriage—pulsed.

Abruptly his lashes lifted; purple-blue eyes snared her gaze. "How do you know he can't give you children?"

It was the barrister who now questioned her, and not the man who had appraised her breasts.

Rose took a deep breath, ignoring the rise of flesh that irrevocably proclaimed her femininity. "I told you Jonathon had the mumps."

Only six hours earlier, she had told him so. It seemed as if six years had lapsed since she had followed Jack Lodoun outside the courthouse.

"But mumps don't always make a man sterile." He pinned her with his frank appraisal. "Did you share his bed after he recovered?"

"We have separate chambers," Rose evaded.

But Jack Lodoun would not be evaded. "You denied him his conjugal rights?"

"My marital life is none of your business, Mr. Lodoun."

"It will be Parliament's business, Mrs. Clarring, should I petition them for a private act," he replied, gaze unwavering. "Do you or have you ever denied your husband his conjugal rights?"

Her throat tightened. "No."

"Do you or have you ever used preventive checks?"

"No."

No matter that *The Globe* printed otherwise.

"Does your husband?"

The cold lapping Rose's toes traveled up through her body. "My husband has never used a preventive check."

"Did mumps render him impotent?"

This private invasion was far worse than had been a public examination.

Rose forced herself to answer. "No."

"Was he able to sustain an erection?"

An empty ache spread through her lower abdomen. "Yes."

"Did he ejaculate inside you?" Jack Lodoun probed.

A rush of warmth spread deep inside her lower abdomen, the memory of the sperm her husband had spurted inside her.

Rose dryly swallowed. "Yes."

"And you have not once conceived?"

"No."

No matter that she had cried each night, praying to God that she do so.

"When is the last time he ejaculated inside you?"

Rose would *not* look away from those penetrating eyes. "The twenty-fourth of December, 1875."

Westminster Chimes distantly struck the quarter hour.

"Why now, Mrs. Clarring?" Jack Lodoun harshly asked.

For one dizzying second Rose felt as if she were once again standing in the witness box.

But then she had looked down into his eyes. Now she looked up into them.

"Why now . . . *what*, Mr. Lodoun?" Rose politely returned.

"Why, after being celibate for more than eleven years, do you suddenly want a divorce?"

"I told you."

"Tell me again."

"I saw the manner in which Mrs. Hart and Mr. Whitcox gazed at one other."

The explanation hollowly rang over the pop of a burning coal.

"Your nipples are hard."

Rose's breath caught inside her chest at the blunt, masculine observation.

Between one heartbeat and the next, Jack Lodoun shrugged out of his coat. Long, tapered fingers stretched out toward her. His wrist below a stiff white cuff was lightly covered by fine, reddish-gold hair that glinted in the gaslight. "Take it."

Over the all-too-familiar scents of brandy and damp wool wafted the unfamiliar fragrance of masculine spice.

"No." Rose clenched her fingers into fists. "Thank you."

"Take it, Mrs. Clarring." The long, tapered fingers were steady, the purple-blue eyes calculating. "Or I might imagine your nipples are hard from more than the cold."

Rose took his coat. It swallowed her.

His warmth. His scent.

Without warning, Jack Lodoun turned.

A darkly illuminated hand removed the gray bowler hat and dropped it onto walnut wood.

Gaslight danced on thick, wavy hair, turning brown into gold and gold into red.

Inside the courtroom, she remembered, he had worn a gray periwig.

No color had gleamed in the shadows.

Not on his head. Not on his face.

Not on the white-cuffed wrists that the black silk barrister's robe had revealed with each motion, each gesture.

He leaned over the flickering lamp.

Rose could not see what he did; she could only watch the stretch of his shoulders under a tailored black wool frock coat while her body prepared for his next question.

Jack Lodoun straightened . . . turned again in a semicircle, red-and-gold glinting sideburns bleeding into bristly whiskers. A small bump, evidence of a previous break, marred an otherwise straight nose.

Gripping the candle that had leaked hot wax upon her—charred wick flaming—he knelt in front of the fireplace.

Rose had lit a fire earlier, but now the coals were cold and covered with white ash.

Slowly, a deep red glow shone through the ashes.

A black sleeve slashed upward, white cuff flashing; metal clanged, the flue opening.

The deep red glow spread. The heat did not reach her.

Standing—yellow-and-blue candle flame flaring—Jack Lodoun confronted Rose. "You admit, then, that you want to divorce your husband so you can take a lover."

"I admit no such thing," Rose swiftly denied.

Eyelashes lowering, he brought the candle up to his mouth—his bottom lip was full, the top lip sharply delineated—and blew, his breath a short, definitive *whoosh*.

The flickering flame died.

Slowly his lashes—tips reddish-gold like the hair lining the sides of his face—swept upward; his eyes were uncompromising. "Do you really expect Parliament to believe you want to divorce your husband simply to spare him the pain of your presence?"

Jack Lodoun's cynicism burned hotter than wax.

"Yes," she riposted, breathing deeply to counteract the small pain he inflicted.

Parliament must grant her a divorce.

Jonathon needed, but so did Rose.

"If I am to be your barrister, Mrs. Clarring"—he paused, turned, placed the dead candle on the narrow wooden mantel, turned again before resuming, cold eyes riveting Rose—"I will accept nothing less than the truth."

"I have told you nothing less than the truth," she lied.

"You're not wearing your wedding ring."

Rose's thumb involuntarily sought the comfort of gold, found flesh instead. "Our marriage is over in all but name."

"But you don't want a lover," Jack Lodoun probed.

"No," Rose returned.

Silently he weighed her answer, as he had earlier weighed her breasts.

A burning briquet collapsed.

The slick slide of silk-lined wool rubbed her shoulders: chest expanding, breathing in . . . chest constricting, breathing out . . .

Abruptly the wait was over.

"I think you're lying," he concluded.

Rose stiffened. "You are at liberty to think whatever you wish, Mr. Lodoun."

"I think you do want a lover, Mrs. Clarring." The purple-blue eyes were inscrutable. "A man who will fuck you hard and often."

Fuck stabbed up between her thighs.

But words, like dreams, did not fill empty flesh.

"You, of all men," Rose reasoned, holding on to the truth that burned like bile, "should know a woman need not divorce one man in order to take another to her bed."

But Jack Lodoun was not interested in reason.

"I think, Mrs. Clarring," he purposefully continued, "you want a man to shove his prick up your cunt and spew his ejaculate inside you until you swim in it."

Thrumming blood and hissing gas filled her ears.

Coldly he waited for her reaction to words that no gentleman uttered in front of a lady. Words that continued to vibrate the air between them: *Prick. Cunt.*

. . . Spew his ejaculate . . . until you swim in it.

The ache inside Rose's pelvis spread to her chest. "If I took a lover, I would insist he wear a machine."

But again he did not acknowledge her response.

"I think you need a man to give you the children your husband can't," he deliberately charged, "so you can feel like a woman. And *that*, Mrs. Clarring, is why I think you want a divorce."

"Then you would be wrong." Rose hung on to her composure, all that was left after her day in court. "And I will thank you to have the courtesy to leave my house at once."

"Not until you admit the truth."

"I am not a whore, Mr. Lodoun, and you will be waiting here until purgatory freezes over before I say I am."

"Don't you want to feel your belly swell with a man's seed, Mrs. Clarring?"

A tiny flutter feathered her lower abdomen.

"No," Rose said, tears burning her eyes.

"Don't you need to feel that spark of life quickening inside your womb," he relentlessly parried, "so you can justify your desire for sexual satisfaction?"

"No," she said more strongly.

"Don't you get wet between your thighs, imagining a man filling you with his child?"

The wetness between Rose's thighs did not arise from a desire for children.

"No."

Her voice rang out over his.

"Are your nipples hard now, Mrs. Clarring, because you imagine a man tasting the milk you feed his suckling child?"

"No."

Rose's strident denial echoed over the hissing gas and crackling embers.

"Isn't it true, Mrs. Clarring," Jack Lodoun gently pressed; there was no gentleness inside his gaze, "that the only way you will ever have worth in a man's eyes, is if you bear him a child?"

Chapter 5

"I don't *want* Jonathon's child," silenced the hiss of gas and the pop of embers.

For one long second the cold, purple-blue eyes that judged Rose were wiped clean of expression.

Fleeting satisfaction surged inside her, admitting the truth she had in the past refused to acknowledge. "My breasts ache for a man, not a baby's suckling mouth."

Red and gold alternately appeared and disappeared inside Jack Lodoun's hair, the only movement inside the barren drawing room.

"Is that what you want to hear?" Rose asked, throat taut, nipples hard, sex wet with the desire she had for too long denied. Deliberately, she repeated, "I don't want Jonathon's children. I don't want any man's child. And *that*, Mr. Lodoun, is why I wish for a divorce."

She had loved Jonathon, but she had never shared his dreams.

"You said you wanted to give him children." Jack Lodoun impersonally watched her every inhalation . . . her every exhalation . . . breasts hidden underneath the mantle of his coat while she exposed emotions she had never before revealed. "'Little boys with whom he could play,'" he purposefully quoted. "'Little girls he could pamper.'"

Each barbed word dug into her skin.

"When we wed, I did want to give him children." Jonathon's gentle blue eyes superimposed the hard, purple-blue eyes of Jack Lodoun. "I wanted to make him happy. I wanted to be a mother to his sons and his daughters. But even more, Mr. Lodoun, I wanted him to love me . . . for *me*."

The hurt Rose had hidden for twelve years tore through her.

"But he didn't."

The dark, purple-blue eyes were free of the emotion that serrated Rose.

"Before the mumps, Jonathon teased and courted and wooed me." Rose spoke past the pain that squeezed her throat. "After the mumps, he did not once look into my eyes. But he stared at my abdomen that did not increase with his child."

An ember exploded, freed from the shock of her confession.

"I am a woman," Rose said, back stiff, chin high, breath ripping in and out of her lungs, "but I have a right to be wanted for myself. Because of *who* I am, and not because I have a womb."

Jack Lodoun's nostrils flared, as if scenting the veracity of her words.

Rose no longer cared if he thought she spoke the truth or not. She needed the liberation that came fully from disclosure.

"Yes, I want to be"—deliberately, she spoke with crude vulgarity—"fucked by a man. I want to feel a man's sex buried inside my sex, thrusting deeper . . . and harder . . . and *deeper* until he is a part of me, and all that matters to him is the pleasure we share together."

The man before her still showed no emotion, as if he were carved in stone. But stone did not glint with red-and-gold hair.

Stone did not smell of brandy and spice and rain-dampened wool.

"I'm not a whore, Mr. Lodoun, and neither you, nor a jury, nor every man in Parliament can make me feel otherwise. I deserve to be loved." Rose took a deep breath, painfully sensitive nipples stabbing her cotton nightgown; she exhaled, inflated lungs slowly collapsing. Calmly, resolutely, she concluded, "And I will not live for one more minute with a man who sees me as nothing more than an incubator for his seed. No matter how much I may love him, or him me. If you think that a woman's desire is shameful, then I will find another MP to represent me. But I don't think you believe that, Mr. Lodoun. No matter how much you may wish to do so."

His voice, when he spoke, was strangely removed. "Why would I wish to believe otherwise?"

Rose remembered the darkness that had shuttered his face, admitting the name of the woman he loved.

"Because," she said, "as long as you believe that career and reputation are more important than passion, you need not feel responsible for the death of Mrs. Whitcox."

The pain that blazed inside his eyes snatched away her breath.

Immediately the pain inside his gaze disappeared.

Labored breathing sounded over the hiss of gas and the pop of embers and the pounding of Rose's heart.

Jack Lodoun's pain. Jack Lodoun's breathing.

Jack Lodoun fought to control both.

"Not all men desire children, Mrs. Clarring," he bitingly offered.

Anger abruptly pumped through her breasts and her womb.

"Don't they?" Rose challenged.

"Some men want nothing more than to share the pleasure of a woman's body."

But there was no pleasure in his eyes, discussing the wants of a man.

The heat of his coat was burning her up. "Are you one of those men?"

"Yes." His pupils dilated until there was no color, just a yawning abyss of blackness. "I enjoy sex."

But Rose could not believe him. Not when for twelve years she had each night slept alone. *Because* a man could not impregnate her.

Impulsively she turned—the oppressive silk-lined wool that smelled of cold spring night and hot sexual man slithered off her shoulders—and flung open the lid of the trunk that carried everything she had taken from Jonathon's home. Feverishly she located the book of love sonnets with which her mother had gifted her upon completing finishing school, and the picture tucked inside it.

Turning—cotton gown swirling, swollen breasts bouncing—she thrust forward a French postcard. "Look at it, Mr. Lodoun."

Long, thick lashes shielded his gaze; dark shadow carved out his cheeks.

Rose studied Jack Lodoun while he studied the postcard.

A lone clip-clop of hooves rang out in the darkest hour before midnight.

"What do you see?" she demanded harshly, tensely waiting for his condemnation, he a man who had accused her of wanting a divorce for no other reason than to commit the adultery of which he himself was guilty.

Slowly his lashes—reddish-gold tips glinting in the flickering lamplight—lifted. "I see a man stroking his cock."

"Does not the sight disgust you?"

"Why should it?"

Why should it not?

Rose's heartbeat quickened, *too* fast, *too* hard, *too* dangerous. "Do you touch yourself, Mr. Lodoun?"

"Yes."

The admission was reluctant.

"But only when you do not have a woman in which to spend yourself," she challenged.

Shadow tautly delineated sharp cheekbones. "Not always."

"When?" Rose's voice rang out over the hiss of gas and the

popping crackle of burning coals. "When do you touch yourself? When you imagine a woman's sex overflowing with your ejaculate?"

"No."

Deliberately she reversed Jack Lodoun's earlier accusations.

"You don't get hard when you imagine a woman's belly swelling with your seed?"

"No."

"You don't get stiff and erect with desire when you imagine"—coldly, purposefully, Rose emphasized—"*fucking* a woman who is big with your child?"

"No."

"Are you hard now, imagining a woman suckling your son, warm milk dribbling down her swollen breasts?"

"No."

But the dark imagery she conjured lingered inside the purple-blue eyes.

"Isn't it true, Mr. Lodoun," Rose tautly charged, "that the only way you feel you will ever have worth as a man, is if you impregnate a woman?"

"No."

The harsh masculine denial was unequivocal.

Gaslight flared, light battling darkness.

"Touch yourself, Mr. Lodoun."

Touch yourself echoed in the shrinking confines of the naked, unadorned drawing room.

"Show me," Rose said, and wondered what would happen if he did not comply. Jack Lodoun had turned away from her outside the courthouse; she could not bear for him to turn away from her now, when she had alienated her family and her husband embraced his dreams rather than her. "Show me that a man can take pleasure in his flesh and not in his seed."

Chapter 6

The faint chime of a Westminster bell rang out, announcing the half hour . . . or the three-quarter hour. The world outside the four walls of the drawing room had ceased to exist.

Slowly—the black of his pupils eating up the purple-blue of his irises—Jack Lodoun reached for the front placket of his trousers.

"Everything," Rose said jerkily. "I want to see you naked."

Like the man in the postcard who unashamedly loved himself.

Dark color edging his cheeks, he shrugged off his black wool jacket.

A silk, gray-striped waistcoat hugged a starched white shirt and rode a band of black wool trousers.

The shape underneath the tailored clothing was undeniably masculine.

Rose had never before watched a man undress; she catalogued Jack Lodoun's each and every motion.

Long, tapered fingers freed the four pearl buttons fastening the gray-striped waistcoat. Wide shoulders bunched; at the same time, white-cotton-sleeved arms—there a shadow of flexing muscle—slid through silk. A dark gray silk tie—knotted like a noose—climbed a corded throat . . . blocked the flaring protrusion of a nostril . . . rifled red-and-gold glinting hair. Three gold studs winked in the gaslight; tapered fingers twisted and turned until stiff white cotton gaped in an ever-widening V and exposed flesh-colored wool. Black silk suspenders snaked over blindingly white sleeves.

There was no hesitation in Jack Lodoun's motions, no self-consciousness in his movements.

The white shirt escaped banding black trousers and inched up flesh-colored wool that molded jutting ribs . . . two button-hard nipples. . . .

White cotton fluttered to the floor.

Between one blink and another, the flesh-colored vest was jerked upward.

Red-gold hair winked in the flickering light: on his chest . . . underneath his arms. . . .

The vest cleared his head and fluttered to the floor.

Rose's breath hitched inside her throat.

Light and shadow danced on sharp collarbones, tautly defined muscular shoulders. Beaded brown nipples pierced the glinting bed of red-and-gold hair that arrowed down a tautly ridged stomach.

Jack Lodoun, Rose realized with a sharp pang, was a beautiful man.

A cinder exploded.

Rose abruptly became aware of the utter stillness inside the drawing room.

Her gaze shot upward.

His gaze waited for hers.

"Do you mind if I sit down to take off my shoes and socks?"

Jack Lodoun's voice was impersonal. Heat glowed inside his purple-blue eyes.

"No." Rose swallowed. "Please."

A sharp squeak of springs grated her skin, the blue damask settee protesting his weight.

Eyelashes shielding his gaze, he leaned over.

Thick curls shaped the nape of his neck, darker than the fine hair that covered his body. The muscles in his arms and shoulders alternately flexed and stretched, a living composition of light and darkness.

Velvet-covered wood impacted the backs of Rose's calves: She collapsed on the facing armchair.

Long, tapered fingers reached up underneath black wool trousers, exposed taut black silk. Unhurriedly, they peeled down socks and clinging braces.

A burning ache spread through Rose's chest, that she enjoyed this intimacy with a stranger she had known for less than twenty-four hours instead of her husband of over twelve years.

Squeaking springs overrode the pain of regret.

Jack Lodoun stood. Long, tapered fingers reached for the front of his trousers . . . liberated one button . . . two buttons . . . three buttons—pink shone in the widening gap of black wool—four buttons . . . *five* buttons . . .

Rose's breath rasped her throat.

In one smooth jerk, the black trousers and pink woolen small-clothes slid down over hips that were narrower than hers. Over thighs that were harder than hers. Over legs that were longer than hers.

Both his thighs and his calves glinted with red-gold fire.

Unerringly her gaze focused on the sex that jutted out of dark, wiry brown hair: It was both longer and thicker than the man in the postcard.

The blue veins striating Jack Lodoun's flesh pulsed. Unlike the bloodless flesh of the man in the postcard.

A pulse leapt to life deep inside Rose's breasts . . . her womb . . . her vagina . . . her clitoris . . . her eyes.

The plum-shaped head suddenly flushed a dark red: It jerked, reaching out to Rose.

Rose's breath hitched inside her lungs.

A drop of liquid pearled inside the tiny urethra—as if squeezed out by an invisible hand—and elongated to form a crystalline thread that shimmered, first in shadow, then in light.

Long seconds passed, he standing naked, she nakedly gazing at his sex.

Tentative, tapered fingers grasped the swollen shaft that was engorged with blue veins.

His sex was longer than his fingers. Thicker than his fingers combined.

He lifted the heavy flesh in his left hand. He kissed the tiny urethra with his right hand.

Rose's fingers clenched into fists.

Even as she watched, clear, shiny liquid crawled down the small cleft that cleaved the crown of his penis.

It was not seed that he cried, Rose realized—heartbeat accelerating, womb contracting—but desire.

His legs—long, muscular legs that were covered in fine, red-gold hair—shifted . . . parted. Gaslight poured between his thighs and cupped his testicles.

More confidently, the long, tapered fingers smeared glistening essence down and around the thickly swollen crown . . . ducked under a rim of foreskin . . . traced blue veins . . . circled pale flesh that graduated into dark red.

Rose felt the smooth skin. Rose felt the slick friction.

Rose felt the deepening desire.

Making a fist of his left hand, he gently pumped.

Up . . . down. Up . . . gathering more moisture . . . down.

Rose clenched her thighs, vagina weeping at the pleasure Jack Lodoun took in his touch.

With his fingertips he teased the small opening that cried crystalline tears, while with his left fist he steadily pumped. *Up* to the crown . . . *down* to the dangling testicles aureoled by gaslight.

Fingers caressing.

Fingers stroking.

Fingers pumping.

She wanted to speak of how utterly beautiful he was—touching himself—but she had no words to describe what she was witnessing.

Rose had seen naked men in the form of statues and paintings and photographs; neither marble, paint nor chemically treated paper compared to skin caressed by light and shadow. To flesh that cried for sexual expression. To human need that burned deep inside the body where moral and marital obligation did not penetrate.

The swollen glans jerked underneath a probing fingertip. Rose's clitoris jerked in sympathy.

Soughing breathing interspersed the hiss of gas and the crackle of embers and the slick rub of skin.

Something was happening . . . something that quickened her breathing and heated her skin.

His fisted fingers tightened. Rose tightened her two fists until her nails bit into the palms of her hands.

Abruptly the fingers that rhythmically rimmed the tiny opening to his urethra leapt downward and cupped the testicles that had drawn tight and close to his body.

A small, stifled groan snapped her gaze upward.

Jack Lodoun's head was thrown back, eyes squeezed closed in—her heart contracted in empathy, even as her vagina convulsively clenched—agony.

Rose saw on his face the joy he had experienced, loving another man's wife. She saw the loneliness he now escaped, living on the memories of the pleasure they had shared.

His penis pistoning deep into her vagina. Her vagina—crying

with need as his penis now cried—welcoming . . . embracing . . . treasuring the flesh that filled it.

One man. One woman. Two bodies. Two heartbeats.

Each straining to achieve that moment when they would cease to be two, and in their shared pleasure, would become one.

It was an intimacy Rose had dreamed about but had never before experienced until now, watching a stranger love another woman with his hand.

Without warning, the clenched eyelids snapped open. Purple-blue eyes pinned Rose.

First came the orgasm. Then came realization.

Rose was not the woman he loved. And the woman he loved was dead.

Silently she rose and left Jack Lodoun to his grief.

Chapter 7

"Hats off, strangers!"

The police inspector's traditional bawl ricocheted off white marble, stained glass and encaustic tile.

Jack did not watch the Speaker's Procession that began the day's sitting in the House of Commons. Instead he watched the men and women who for the first time witnessed the ceremony that daily occurred inside the Houses of Parliament.

He saw their awe, gazing wide-eyed at the Serjeant at Arms who bore the five-foot-long gilded mace that symbolized royal authority. But the wonder the spectators radiated was eclipsed by the raw emotion that coursed through Jack.

Rose Clarring had watched him orgasm. She had cried the tears Jack had not cried for Cynthia Whitcox.

Not when he had read about her death on the front page. Not when he had read about her funeral in the obituary.

Excitement sparked the spectators.

They saw the Speaker—trainbearer holding up the ceremonial

black silk robe—follow behind the Serjeant at Arms. Jack saw a finger-pinched postcard of a naked man fucking his fist.

A low rumble of restlessness filled the domed, octagonal hall.

The chaplain and secretary who trailed the trainbearer through the East door and into the Commons Corridor disappeared behind massive oak.

The two doors would not open for another three minutes.

Inside the House of Commons, the Serjeant at Arms secured the mace on the Table while the Speaker and chaplain knelt for Prayers.

But the spectators did not know what they could not see. And Jack did not see what could come of himself and Rose Clarring.

Yet he could not stop thinking of her.

The pain that had compelled her to approach him outside the Old Bailey Courthouse. The need that had turned her blue eyes black, watching him undress.

Her resolve to gain a divorce when a divorce was impossible to be gained.

The spectators marked the time: They faced the North door. Jack marked the time with them: He faced the East door.

Johanna of Navarre, Queen of Henry IV; Henry V; Katherine, Queen of Henry V; Henry VI; Margaret, Queen of Henry VI; and Edward IV gazed down at Jack.

For every king, there was a queen. Together they symbolized the foundation of the English Commonwealth: family.

Yet inside the Central Hall there was no queen for Edward IV. And Johanna of Navarre's king guarded the North door rather than the East.

Jack read the Bible verse that was inlaid inside encaustic tiles underneath the marble statues: *"Except the Lord keep the house, their labor is but lost that built it."*

"Prayers are over!" vaulted down the Commons Corridor and through the Central Hall. Doorkeepers simultaneously threw open the galleries.

The three minutes were up. The House was now sitting.

Feminine and masculine heels pounded encaustic tiles, clattered up stairs.

Memory slashed through Jack, the image of six women and five men.

While awaiting the judgment of Frances Hart, Rose Clarring had stood in the rear of the courtroom gallery between John Nickols, a man confined to a wheelchair, and Joseph Manning, the mustached founder of the Men and Women's Club.

Marie Hoppleworth, a spectacled woman, had rested her hand on John Nickols's shoulder. Joseph Manning had cupped the elbow of Ardelle Dennison, a coldly beautiful woman.

They had congregated as if they had the legal right to do so.

Men did not stand with women in the Houses of Parliament, Jack reflected.

Left hand tightening around a leather satchel, he pushed away from the wall, hat and umbrella secure in his right hand.

The male spectators climbing the stairs would publicly watch the machinations of England's most powerful club of men in the gallery while the female spectators privately observed through a brass trellis.

Unseen. Unheard.

Unrepresented.

"No, madam, I cannot accept a penny less."

Rose stared down at the letter clenched between her fingers.

The fifty-three-year-old butler came with perfect references.

She recognized the name of his last employers. She knew that his reason for leaving their employment was valid.

The employers had leased their townhouse and purchased a manor in the country. The butler did not want to leave London where his family lived.

Rose did not blame him. It was obvious he blamed her.

She was a notorious woman who belonged to a scandalous

club. No respectable servant wished to work in such a household without due compensation.

"Then I'm afraid we will not do, Mr. Tandey." The salary he demanded was outrageous. Carefully Rose smoothed the reference before folding it. Glancing up, she extended the letter with a steady hand. "Thank you for coming."

Curling his lips in dismissal, the man grasped the edge of the folded paper.

He would have no problem gaining future employment with a respectable household, that smirk told her.

Rose knew it. He knew she knew it.

He was the fourth such butler she had interviewed with a like mind.

Sniffing, the man tripped out of the drawing room.

Rose sat back in the too-soft, velvet-upholstered armchair and stared at blue damask.

Purple-blue eyes blackened by shadow stared up at her.

Is your husband here with you today? invaded the dead silence.

She squeezed her eyes closed to shut out the memory.

Jack Lodoun relentlessly pursued her. *Look in the gallery, Mrs. Clarring. Do you see your husband?*

No.

Why not?

He's not in the courtroom.

Is he waiting outside? squeezed her throat. *Shall we call him in?*

No, he's not outside.

Why isn't your husband in the courtroom with you, Mrs. Clarring?

"Because in Jonathon's eyes, I don't exist," Rose whispered, eyelids opening, dry eyes confronting the truth.

But she had not been able to say that, penned on all sides by strangers: the judge, the jury, the witnesses who gobbled up her every word.

She had not been able to say that there was no one to whom

she could turn for comfort, save for the other members of the Men and Women's Club. But they did not need her, either. They had found comfort in each other, one man for every woman, Rose the odd woman out.

Unbidden images blotted out the blue damask settee.

Red gold hair glinting. Ruby-tipped flesh glistening.

Rose had not known that a man's sex cried for passion. But now she knew.

She knew how Jack Lodoun needed to be touched. She knew where Jack Lodoun needed to be touched.

She knew to what depths Jack Lodoun had penetrated the woman he loved.

Jealousy for the deceased woman—more bitter than bile—flooded her mouth.

Four distant bongs permeated the faint rumble of carriage wheels.

The Houses of Parliament, she remembered, sat at four in the evening.

Rose stood.

Her stomach growled.

She realized she had not eaten since snatching a coffee and a pastry before visiting the employment office.

Afternoon sunlight danced on polished oak.

Rose walked in reverse the steps she had walked seventeen hours earlier.

Bronze, cherry and brass gleamed in the shadows.

A lone black cloak and bonnet occupied the foyer.

There was no sign of the man to whom she had opened her door, and from whom she had then demanded he open his trousers. It was as if the night before had never happened.

Rose buttoned her cloak and settled the black bonnet over her upswept hair.

For long seconds she studied her reflection in the oval, bronze-framed mirror that hung above the foyer table.

Sunlight gilded her blond hair and blushed her pale cheeks.

She was, indeed, a woman who deserved to be loved.

The thought did not banish the shadows inside her reflection.

Unable to hold the dark gaze inside the mirror, Rose reached into the top drawer of the foyer table for her reticule, grabbed instead last evening's edition of *The Globe*.

The drawing of a woman stared up at her, eyes black with lust.

Gentle blue eyes superimposed the charcoal eyes.

Did Jonathon look at the picture in the newspaper, she wondered, and see the innocent bride Rose had once been? Or did he see an adulteress, as Rose's father had seen?

Gentle blue bled into purple-blue.

Rose saw the gray-wigged, black-robed man who had shredded her reputation. Rose saw the bare-headed, black-suited man who had eviscerated her emotions.

Rose saw the naked man—light dancing on sharp collarbones, shadow pinching beaded brown nipples—who had gifted her with his sexuality.

Jack Lodoun had not once condemned her for wanting to be a woman rather than a mother.

Forcefully Rose crumpled the newspaper: It crunched.

Puzzled, she smoothed out the wrinkled print.

Cookie crumbs pelted the naked cherry table.

A smile streaked through Rose: Giles, the butler, had not forsaken her.

Warmth permeated the chill foyer.

Later she would clean up, but not now when the sunshine beckoned.

Tapping the remaining crumbs out of the newspaper into the palm of her hand, Rose grabbed her reticule out of the drawer and flung open the white enameled door.

"There you are, darling!" riveted her.

But the feminine voice was not familiar.

Rose surreptitiously glanced to her left at the mustard yellow house that adjoined her robin's egg blue house.

A woman in her thirties—Rose estimated she was close to her own age of thirty-three—stood on the stoop of the neighboring row house and hugged a woman who was comparably aged. Together, arms linked, they descended the short steps and crossed the sun-dappled street.

Sisters, perhaps. Or perhaps they were simply friends.

Laughter, pure and free from the taint of betrayal and scandal, trilled behind them. They disappeared behind a four-wheeled cab.

Relaxing, Rose popped an oblong crumb into her mouth: The oatmeal-coated raisin was still moist. She raised her hand—filling her mouth with cookie—and turned to lock the door.

Startled wings whirred up into the air.

"Hello, Rose."

The familiar voice stole the sunshine and dragged down Rose's hand.

Dryly chewing, swallowing—the raisins had inexplicably dried to the consistency of pebbles—Rose locked the white enameled door and turned with a smile.

A blue-bonneted woman stood at the bottom of the stoop. She was clearly in an advanced stage of pregnancy.

"Hello, Lucy," Rose returned, stomach fighting to reject the cookie crumbs it digested. "Should you be here, this late in your term?"

The twenty-seven-year-old wife of Rose's oldest brother—and mother to his three sons—smiled with maternal contentment. Gently she caressed the rounded curve of her abdomen that marked her fourth pregnancy. "The baby misses his aunt."

"He'll miss his mother more if Derek finds you out and about," Rose said dryly.

"Derek wouldn't dare hurt me," Lucy complacently returned, "for fear of you."

As if any of her brothers had ever heeded their older sister, all five of them taller than she by the time they reached puberty.

A reluctant laugh escaped Rose's tight throat. "I assure you, Derek has never been afraid of anything, least of all me."

"We're all afraid for you, Rose," snatched away her laughter.

Rose clenched the iron key inside her hand. "Lucy, I appreciate your concern, truly I do, but I assure you, I am perfectly well."

Lucy had never been reticent. "Rose, many women fear childbirth, but it's a small price to pay for what comes afterward."

Always a woman's life revolved around children and motherhood.

An image of Jack Lodoun flashed before Rose's eyes.

Stroking his penis. Loving his penis.

"Do you enjoy being with my brother?" she impulsively asked, metal key biting into her fingers.

"I love Derek," Lucy said, face glowing with happiness and pregnancy.

"But do you love what he does to you," Rose pressed, "to give you children?"

Shock widened Lucy's eyes.

Afternoon light glinted off the younger woman's dark curls, turning brown into red.

Red had glinted in Jack Lodoun's hair, Rose remembered. But not in his pubic hair.

"Lucy." Rose took a deep breath. "I will tell you what I told my parents: I love you, but what I do has nothing to do with you. Nor has it anything to do with my brothers. I am just now setting up house, and do not yet have servants or even furnishings." A small lie: She had basic furniture and linen only. "Much as I would like to entertain you, it is not yet possible. Please do not come back until I invite you."

Hurt wiped away the glow of Lucy's happiness. "What shall I tell Derek?"

"Tell him I love him."

The hurt on Lucy's face was not abated.

Rose descended the three steps—Lucy was four inches taller than she—and forced herself to reach out and lay her hand on her sister-in-law's rounded abdomen. A tiny foot slammed into her palm.

"And tell him," Rose said, keeping her hand over the baby instead of jerking it away as every muscle, every ligament inside her body demanded, "if this is a girl, that I expect him to name her after her aunt."

"It's not likely, after three boys." Lucy's nose, peppered with freckles, wrinkled down at Rose. "But if it is a girl, Derek wants to name her after me."

"Lucy Rose has a good sound, don't you think?" Rose suggested.

Lucy smiled, Rose's transgression forgiven, unaware that she herself transgressed. "Lucy Rose it is."

Rose dropped the iron key into her reticule and slid her hand through Lucy's arm. The kick that had imprinted her palm continued to pulse. "Now, let's get you home. We can stop and have an ice, shall we?"

Lucy grabbed Rose's hand and tightly caged her bare fingers. "Will you come home with me?"

Rose determinedly stared ahead at the future. "Of course."

"Will you stay and have a visit with Derek?"

Gently Rose squeezed Lucy's gloved fingers. "No."

Lucy was not deterred. "Derek talked to Jonathon."

A busy intersection loomed ahead, only two blocks away. There they could catch a cab, or an omnibus.

Rose forced her left foot forward. She *would* make the distance.

"What did Jonathon say?" she asked through stiff lips that curled upward in a smile while the palm of her hand burned and throbbed.

Chapter 8

Twin oak doors closed behind Jack. The snick of a lock glanced off his skin.

Perfumed pomade and expensive cologne clogged the corridor. To his left, darkness pressed against stained glass windows. Overhead, brass hall pendants flickered and hissed.

Two hundred and nineteen men shuffled forward—joking, boasting, politicking—each one familiar with the Noes Lobby, where men met to vote *no*.

There was no discussion of the private act upon which they were now called to vote: Their decision—as was Jack's—had been made before the third reading.

The body of men merged, MPs filing into a double row between two large Division desks. At the end of the corridor twin oak doors swung wide.

A masculine voice rang out: "Edward Limpton." It was immediately followed by another voice, more tenor than baritone: "Brian Dougby."

The two lines surged forward. Each exiting member spoke his name.

It was all that was required to vote no, and to destroy a woman's dreams.

Jack stepped up to the Division desk and saw not a scribbling clerk, but a nightgown-clad woman with dark nipples who had opened her door to a stranger.

The clerk glanced upward, pen poised. "Your name, sir?"

Rose Clarring would damn him and Parliament for this day.

Jack gave the clerk the vote for which he waited—"Jack Lodoun"—and strode through the double doors.

The chill air inside the House of Commons did not disperse the suffocating scent of men and power. Gleaming oak beams and green-leather-upholstered benches crowded his vision.

"Lodoun," carried after him . . . caught up with him. "Shall you join us for supper?"

"I have commitments," Jack lied, steps not faltering.

"Right-oh!" A hearty slap jarred Jack's bones. "Another time, old chap. Dougby, dear fellow. Go ahead! I'll catch you in the dining room."

But Jack had already exited the House of Commons.

In the Commons Lobby he retrieved his coat and hat, another MP among dozens more shelving their political agendas for a break outdoors. In the Central Hall MPs eager for press wooed reporters.

"Mr. Lodoun!" echoed inside the domed ceiling.

Jack kept on walking, wool coat slapping his thighs.

A man wearing a plaid reefer jacket—dark hair slick with macassar oil—stepped in front of him. "Yesterday you lost against James Whitcox in a civil suit. What do you have to say?"

Jack recalled that the lobby correspondent wrote for *The Pall Mall Gazette*.

"I have nothing to say," Jack said. And stepped around him.

The reporter followed. "You lost a criminal trial to Whitcox on the twenty-seventh of April. You then resigned your position as attorney general on the twenty-fourth of May. Did you resign so you could go against Whitcox in the civil suit?"

Jack's heels hollowly corroborated: "I have nothing to say."

"Is there a rivalry between you and Whitcox?"

"I have nothing to say," Jack repeated, gaze trained forward.

"How did you vote today in the act for Greffen?"

It was a matter of public record.

"I voted against it," Jack said.

"Why?" nipped his heels.

"The law did not support it," Jack said.

"Mr. Prime Minister," rippled inside the Central Hall.

Jack exited the West door underneath the blind justice of royals.

The reporter for *The Pall Mall Gazette* did not follow; he had bigger fish to pursue.

Jack entered St. Stephen's Hall and walked between the dead, clicking footsteps ricocheting off encaustic tile and stained glass.

Marble eyes bored into him.

He knew the name of each life-sized statue. He knew the legacy of each man.

Selden. Hampden. Lord Falkland. Lord Clarendon. Lord Somers. Sir Robert Walpole. Lord Chatham. Lord Mansfield. Burke. Fox. Pitt. Graham.

The *Descriptive Account of the Palace of Westminster* described them as "men to whom England owes her gratitude for their patriotism and public virtue."

Jack had read the booklet when he had been twenty-four years old. Jack had walked between the statues as a fellow MP at the age of thirty-four.

He had been one year older, Jack reflected, than what Rose Clarring's husband was now.

Jack pushed through heavy doors.

Rose Clarring leaned against a lamppost, face turned up to the dying sun.

Jack paused, cock flexing in recognition.

A mechanical clank pierced the monotonous grind of carriage wheels, a warning precursor: The three-quarter bells struck.

Rose Clarring's head jerked, gaze fixing on the three-hundred-and-fifteen-foot-tall clock tower that dominated the northwestern sky.

The wonder that illuminated her face, listening up close to the bells that could be heard throughout London, fisted inside his chest.

This woman wanted to experience passion. But Parliament did not recognize passion.

Letting go of the heavy door, Jack crossed the pavement, pigeons scattering, footsteps drowned by the deafening clamor of the Westminster Chimes. Inhaling the clean scent of springtime roses, Jack grasped her wool-padded elbow on the fourth refrain.

Cornflower blue eyes shadowed by pending night turned up to his. Inside their depths was the knowledge of his sexuality.

The testicles he had squeezed. The cock he had fucked.

The woman he had loved.

"It's very beautiful here," carried over the clear strike of a bell.

The warmth of her skin leaked into Jack's fingers. "Yes."

He had once thought so.

"You were drinking last night, before . . ." Her voice trailed off. Elbow tensing, she asked, "Do you at all remember . . . ?"

Heat licked Jack's cheeks and lapped a trail down to his cock. "Yes."

He remembered every word she had spoken. Every flicker of shadow inside her eyes, first watching him undress, and then watching him fondle his flesh.

"Did Mrs. Whitcox love you?"

The lingering quiver of a Westminster chime died. The singsong whine of carriage wheels permeated St. Stephen's Circle.

"Is that why you came to the Houses of Parliament," Jack asked, voice remote, devoid of the emotion she elicited, "to enquire about my former lover?"

"I didn't know where else to find you." Uncertainty wiped clean the sexual awareness inside her gaze. "Is this not a good time?"

No woman had ever met Jack outside the Houses of Parliament: The raw vulnerability he had felt inside her drawing room—dressing in cold, wrinkled clothing and cleaning up his ejaculate—crawled up his spine.

"We generally break for supper around eight," Jack said neutrally.

"You said you'd consider representation if I demonstrated that a woman's passion is worth a man's reputation."

Behind Jack, sharp footsteps and excited voices pierced the grating whine of passing carriages: The spectators, as well as MPs, were breaking for the evening meal.

"Yes," Jack said, voice distant.

He had said that.

"Did I?"

A muscle ticked inside his jaw.

He thought of the private act upon which he had just voted. He thought of the reporters who could at any moment exit St. Stephen's Hall, each of them familiar with Rose Clarring and the trial he had lost.

He thought of Father, and the carrot of Lord of Appeal in Ordinary that he had the night before dangled.

"I see," Rose Clarring said, shadowed face becoming a polite mask. His fingers involuntarily tightened around her elbow: She emotionally moved out of his reach. "I didn't mean to intrude on your time. Please accept my apologies."

But Jack couldn't let her go.

"Why didn't you buy a dildo?"

The harsh question underscored sharp heel taps and rousing laughter.

Rose Clarring had said she wanted to feel a man inside her body. Yet when visiting the Achilles Book Shoppe, she had purchased a French postcard instead of an object that would provide physical if not emotional satisfaction.

The stiffness of her elbow did not relax. "I wanted my vagina to be a special place for my husband."

But Jack was not Jonathon Clarring.

A tiny pulse beat against the palm of his hand.

Her need. Or his.

"Did he ever give you an orgasm?" Jack asked, knowing the answer, hoping he was wrong.

She searched his gaze for long seconds, as if seeking inside his eyes the man who had twenty-one hours earlier exposed his sexuality.

But Jack was not drunk this night. And this night belonged to neither Cynthia Whitcox nor Rose Clarring, but to the common good of England.

"We were children," she said finally.

Pain knotted Jack's groin, history repeating itself.

"So your husband never gave you an orgasm," he unemotionally surmised.

"I don't need my husband to give me an orgasm." The sharp click of footsteps receded. A feminine trill trailed behind the men. "I'm quite capable of doing so myself."

"By exciting your clitoris."

An external appendage.

Gaslight burnished a gold curl; shadow hollowed her eyes. "Yes."

"But you don't fuck yourself," Jack said flatly.

"No," she confirmed.

"But you want to divorce your husband."

"Yes."

"So that you'll be free to find passion."

The heavy rumble of a wagon rode the street.

"Yes," Rose Clarring said, acknowledging the needs Parliament did not.

"Yet you don't know what passion is."

Denial sharpened her voice. "I know it doesn't reside inside a woman's womb."

"Then where does it reside, Mrs. Clarring?" Jack studied her face in the flickering light of the lamppost: the pale slice of a cheek, the soft curve of a lip, the darkness of her pupils. "Inside a woman's vagina?"

"No," she said with conviction.

"You know that"—her flesh beneath her wool coat scorched his fingers—"how? Because you didn't orgasm when your husband fucked you?"

"Don't say that."

"That your husband fucked you?" Jack deliberately asked.

"My husband did not *fuck* me," Rose Clarring said tightly.

"But that's what you wanted him to do, isn't it?"

"No."

"You said you wanted to be fucked by a man, Mrs. Clarring," Jack said, purposefully pushing, fingers throbbing, unable to relinquish her. "You said you wanted to feel his sex buried inside your sex, thrusting deeper, and harder, and deeper."

"I said I wanted a man to take pleasure in the love we share," she riposted.

"You said you wanted to experience passion." The scream of a fire engine drifted over the Thames; the whine of traffic swallowed it. "How do you know, Mrs. Clarring, that passion isn't just a splendid fuck?"

She had not once refused to answer in the witness box. She did not do so now.

"I don't," she said finally. Lamplight leaping . . . falling. "I don't know."

Neither did Jack.

Fingers tightening around the soft wool protecting her elbow, he guided her away from the lamppost.

"Where are we going?"

Jack propelled her toward the busy street. "To find passion."

Stepping off the curb, he skirted a lumbering omnibus.

A passing Clarence cab sucked the air out of his lungs. An unseen wheel whipped the tail of his coat.

Pulling Rose Clarring closer—her hip intimately abutted the top of his thigh—Jack gained the opposite curb.

She stiffened, sighting the shop to which he directed her.

Jack jerked open the door to the Victoria Book Shop. A bell rang out; gaslight spilled onto the pavement, starkly illuminating her colorless face.

Rose Clarring did not step forward.

"This is why you came tonight, isn't it, Mrs. Clarring," Jack asked, feeling the rigidity of her bones throughout his entire body, "to find passion?"

Hot, painful color flooded her face. "I will not find passion inside a bookstore."

"You, of all women, know"—deliberately he called to mind the words she had spoken the night before, that he of all men knew a woman need not divorce one man to take another to her bed—"that not all bookstores are what they seem."

"Do you think, Mr. Lodoun," she asked tensely, "that I'll find passion in a dildo?"

"I think, Mrs. Clarring," Jack said intently, "that you cannot know the difference between passion and the pleasure afforded by a stiff prick if you have experienced neither."

Blackness swallowed her cornflower blue irises.

"Excuse me," leapt between them. "Sir . . . madam."

Gaze breaking away from Jack—dark, shamed color fading to twin circles of pink—Rose Clarring hastily stepped aside.

Cold air replaced the warmth of her flesh.

Jack opened the door wider.

He did not see the face of the woman who entered the store. He concentrated solely on the woman who stood opposite him.

"You're frightened," he said, echoing her words outside the Old Bailey Courthouse.

"This is a public shop." Rose Clarring stepped over the threshold. "Why should I be?"

Because Jack was frightened.

He had made an adulteress of one woman, and now she was dead. He had destroyed this woman's future, but he could not escape the need she evoked.

"Through here," he shortly instructed, reclaiming her elbow.

She did not outwardly protest his touch. The stiffness of her flesh seared the palm of his hand.

The Hour Chime obliterated the soft murmur of voices and the beat of Jack's heart: It was followed by eight bongs.

In nine more minutes the sun would officially set, ending the day and beginning the night. But Jack did not know what the night would bring.

A somberly dressed clerk stepped forward, blocking access to the door leading to the back of the shop. A sharp glance from Jack propelled him backward.

Jack's pupils ate up the darkness in the dimly lit room. Behind him, the door clicked closed.

He watched Rose Clarring's reaction to the secret sex shop that every parliamentary member knew existed but about which no one talked.

A junior MP—another conservative, five years younger than Jack—glanced upward, eyes widening at sight of a woman. Immediately his gaze was captured by Jack's.

They stared at one another for long seconds.

Jack knew the MP. Jack knew his wife.

Jack knew the MP liked young, virginal girls who were scarcely older than his thirteen-year-old daughter.

The junior MP glanced downward.

Dark pink stained Rose Clarring's cheeks. She did not bow her head to hide from male perusal.

Admiration—sharp and piercing—shot through Jack.

Cursorily he guided her forward through the dim aisles, fingers sliding from her elbow to span the small of her back: It was as rigid as her elbow. "Over here."

A glass display showcased a variety of sexual paraphernalia: cock rings. Nipple bobs. French chain cuffs.

"May I help you, sir?" enquired a timorous voice.

A clerk fixedly gazed up at Jack.

Jack glanced at Rose Clarring.

She stared down at the showcase.

The image of a man—of himself—squeezing his testicles and ejaculating into the air slammed through his thoughts.

Watching the curve of Rose Clarring's nose and cheek—all that was visible underneath the brim of her bonnet—Jack said, "We wish to inspect the dildos."

Nervously—gaze pointedly avoiding the woman who stood beside Jack—the clerk laid out a dozen phalluses: small ones . . . monstrous ones . . . glass ones . . . leather ones.

"Leave us," Jack said.

The clerk was only too happy to oblige.

Rose Clarring stared at the instruments that were designed for no other reason than to penetrate. "I did not come tonight to have sexual congress with you."

Jack ignored the sharp pang her denial inflicted.

"But you do wish to be fucked, do you not?" he pressed.

Her breasts rose and fell beneath the black wool of her cloak. "Yes."

"Then choose your prick, Mrs. Clarring."

Chapter 9

A muted cough broke the stillness, a caustic reminder they were not alone.

Men watched.

Her. Him.

Stiffly Rose Clarring reached for a small leather dildo that was hardly bigger than his middle finger.

"Take your gloves off," Jack said shortly. Her hand froze mid reach. "Feel what it is you're going to take into your body."

She peeled off black leather gloves—the jet-beaded reticule looped around her left wrist glinted black fire—and stuffed the gloves inside her coat pocket.

Rose Clarring had small, slender fingers.

Carefully, as if it were a loaded pistol, she picked up the narrow leather dildo that measured some five inches in length.

"That's for a woman's—or a man's—anus," Jack advised, the scent of roses burning his chest.

Instantly her gaze leapt up to his. "Have you ever . . . ?"

"Buggered a woman with one?" he supplied neutrally, the gazes of men crawling on his skin.

"Been the one in whom it was inserted?" she corrected him.

Invasive memory wormed through his body.

"Yes," he said reluctantly.

An inventive mistress had once introduced him to many erotic sensations.

Some of which he had shared with the woman he loved. Some of which he had not.

The cornflower blue eyes darkened. With curiosity, Jack saw; not repugnance.

A pulse leapt from the base of his spine and inched down his groin.

Freeing his hand from the electric heat her back generated, Jack reached for smooth glass.

It was both longer and thicker than the phallus she held.

"Try this one," he instructed, and plucked out of her unresistant fingers the small leather dildo.

Rose Clarring cradled the glass phallus in her left hand; it overflowed her palm.

Jack stepped closer to narrow the gap between their bodies so that other men would not witness her erotic exploration.

She traced the clear glass.

Phantom fingers feathered Jack's cock.

"Mr. Whitcox referred to these as widow's comforters," she said in a low voice.

The name of his lover's husband prickled Jack's skin.

He swallowed the objection that welled inside his throat.

He didn't want to know about James Whitcox. But he did want to know about Rose Clarring.

Still without looking at him, she said, "You accused Mrs. Hart and Mr. Whitcox of learning about passion by reading 'sexual perversions' in academic books."

Jack's judgment outside the courthouse stood between them.

"But, in fact, Mr. Lodoun"—there was no judgment inside her voice—"we studied your so-called sexual perversions *before* Mrs. Hart joined the club. It was quite educational, actually. Did you know, in ancient Greece the city of Miletus was known for making *olisbos*"—a short, manicured fingernail scraped Jack's glans—"dildos. By all accounts, it was quite a profitable enterprise."

Jack did know, but only because he had read it in the minutes of the Men and Women's Club.

"Many ancient treatises refer to artificial phalluses." She rimmed the blunt tip of glass, as if searching for the tiny urethra that spurts sperm inside a woman. "Even the Bible. But we never called them dildos. We never called the *membrum virile* a cock. We never applied what we learned to our own lives, or even to our own times. Then one Saturday Mr. Whitcox brought in French postcards."

The day Frances Hart had officially joined their club.

The secretary had recorded the April sixteenth meeting, but she had not described what it was that the pictures depicted.

"It was clear he had brought them for Mrs. Hart," Rose Clarring said, fingertip probing the smooth frenulum, "to show her the various sexual acts that excited him."

Jack remembered the postcard he had perused inside the Achilles Book Shoppe.

The thought of sharing the same sexual desires as James Whitcox—as he had shared the same woman—burned from his esophagus all the way down to his groin.

"In one of the postcards a woman held a dildo." She rotated the glass, turning the frenulum toward her palm. "It was the first time I'd seen a picture of one. Her legs were splayed; there was no question as to what she was going to do with it."

Left palm curling, Rose Clarring's slender fingers circled the girth of the phallus.

"I thought how odd," she continued in a low, distant tone, fingertips touching: thumb to forefinger . . . thumb to middle finger, "that a man would take pleasure watching a woman so fill herself."

An invisible hand tightened around Jack's penis.

"Have you ever watched a woman fuck herself, Mr. Lodoun?"

Rose Clarring addressed the dildo. Her question rocketed through Jack.

The answer was unwittingly drawn from him. "Yes."

"Did you enjoy it?"

Images divorced from emotion surged through him.

A woman's body. But he could not remember her features. The color of her hair. The scent of her skin.

"Yes," he said.

"This is smaller than you," she observed, fingers releasing the artificial phallus.

Jack did not answer: They both knew the size of his sex.

He waited for what she would next say or do, shoulder blades burning with the lust of the men who watched.

Rose Clarring set aside the glass dildo. Slender fingers hovered over a six-inch-long leather phallus . . . scooped it up and weighed it.

Jack's sex felt suddenly full and heavy.

"Miss Palmer purchased one like this at the Achilles Book Shoppe," she said. "So that she could experience the comfort of a man."

Jack visualized the thirty-two-year-old woman whose face had blushed purple when examined, but who had unflinchingly answered his every question.

She had the day before the trial informed the fashionable girls' academy at which she taught of her involvement with the Men and Women's Club. They had dismissed her, she had testified, to save their reputation.

The Times had printed the name of the academy, ruining both the teacher and the school.

Setting down the six-inch-long dildo, Rose Clarring's pale fingers skimmed over a glass phallus that was bigger around than Jack's wrist, settled on a leather dildo that approximated his own dimensions.

A pulse throbbed to life in the crown of his penis.

She could not span the circumference that he had the night before spanned.

"This is thicker than the one Miss Palmer chose," she noted dispassionately. And then, "Did the woman obtain an orgasm?"

The faceless woman who had taken an artificial phallus into her body while Jack watched.

"Yes," he admitted, breathing in the scent of masculine lust and springtime roses.

"The instrument she used . . . was it as large as this one?"

"I don't remember," Jack said, ridiculous pride that she found him "large" flushing his skin.

"In the Bible, Ezekiel calls dildos 'images of men.'"

Resting the brown leather in her left hand—beaded reticule clinking on the glass showcase—she placed a thumb at the base of the phallus and stretched out her right hand.

The shaft protruded several inches beyond her little finger.

Jack felt the brand of her splayed fingers run from the base of his cock to the tip of his glans.

Feathered bonnet rearing back—eyes devoid of color—Rose Clarring caught his gaze. "I'll take this one."

The phallus that was fashioned in his image.

"This is what you want inside you?" Jack asked tautly.

There was no hesitation inside her eyes, but neither was there desire. "Yes."

Jack had two heartbeats.

One inside his chest. One inside his cock.

"Are you wet between your thighs?" he probed.

"Yes," she said.

"Are you frightened?"

"Yes."

Jack knew fear; it was not fear that stared at him.

He took the leather phallus. "Wait for me in the main area."

She stood firm. "I will pay for my own purchase, Mr. Lodoun."

"You will give the clerk an apoplectic fit, Mrs. Clarring."

Bright laughter momentarily pushed away the darkness inside her eyes.

Jack saw Rose Clarring as she must have looked twelve years earlier, married to a man who made her laugh with happiness.

Immediately the laughter inside her eyes died.

Head tilting downward—black and white obscuring his vision—she reached into her reticule and produced three florins.

A curious sensation curled in the pit of his stomach.

Jack had never before accepted money from a woman. But Jack had never before met a woman like Rose Clarring.

He palmed the three florins. The silver was warm from her fingers.

"You will let me know if it costs more," she said firmly, tilting back her head to meet his gaze.

"Yes," Jack lied.

Every man in the back room watched her retreat: the waving of the white feathers that crowned her bonnet; the proud carriage of her back, swathed in black wool; the gentle sway of her hips, natural curves enhanced by a bustle.

The curling sensation inside Jack's stomach coiled into a knot.

For two years he had privately met with a woman behind closed doors, yet this woman publicly discoursed with him in a pornographic shop.

"Will that be all, sir?" the clerk asked, bolder now that he did not have to face a woman.

"A bottle of Rose's Lubrifiant," Jack added, following the disappearance of black-bustled buttocks and the closing of the back door.

"I say, old man," scraped Jack's nerves. "Wasn't that the cow in the paper? The one from that sex club you exposed?"

Jack glanced at the junior MP, an inch taller than he. The man's face was flushed with lust.

He, too, gazed at the door through which Rose Clarring had exited.

"I have no idea to whom you are referring," Jack said coldly.

Puzzlement clouded the MP's eyes; he glanced at Jack instead of after Rose Clarring. "That woman—"

"There was no woman." Jack held the younger man's gaze. "This room, sir, does not exist. If it should do so, then certain facts would of necessity come to light."

The MP's flush darkened.

He remembered the wife who bore his children. He remembered the young girls who satisfied his lust.

He heeded Jack's warning.

For the moment, Jack grimly thought.

Jack took the brown-paper-wrapped package from the clerk.

His pupils shrank, stepping through the door Rose Clarring had exited.

A sharp jangle serrated his skin.

Someone entered the bookstore. Or someone exited.

Slowly the blinding light dimmed to round gas globes.

Respectable men in bowler hats and women in conservative black cloaks with feathered bonnets complacently wandered short aisles in between tables piled high with books.

There was no evidence of the dark sexuality that lay behind closed doors.

Rose Clarring stood amid the respectable facade, back facing him, head tilted downward. Baby-fine wisps of gold hair clung to the nape of her neck.

Jack stepped closer to see what it was that had captured her interest.

She flipped back and forth a half page inside *Beauty and the Beast*, a Home Pantomime Toy Book, giving Beauty her beast, then taking away the beast. Giving. Taking. Giving. Taking . . .

Her fingers abruptly stilled. Turning—extending her naked hand—she smiled up at Jack. There was no smile inside her eyes. "Thank you."

Jack did not relinquish the package. "I'll hail you a cab."

The darkness inside her eyes flickered. Dropping her hand, she merely said, again, "Thank you."

Jack's hand curled around her elbow, fingers shaping soft wool and even softer skin.

A bell jangled, door opening before them . . . door closing behind them.

The night squeezed Jack's chest.

The third-quarter bell battered the streetlight: It was eight forty-five.

Night had fallen.

He glanced down at the woman beside him.

Waving white feathers and a black brim blocked his vision.

Jack needed to see Rose Clarring, but she did not glance up at him.

Tension hummed through her fragile bones that would snap so easily.

By him. By Parliament.

Reluctantly he focused on the street before them and the zigzagging line of bouncing carriage lanterns.

Jack raised his hand. A hansom passed him by.

The third hansom stopped, metal-secured reins jingling.

Rose Clarring stepped up onto the iron stair and turned—wooden platfrom creaking, harnessed horse snorting—to take her purchase.

Lamplight glanced off a pearl earring and revealed a sliver of cornflower blue.

Jack thought of Lord Falkland, one of the men whose statues he had passed in St. Stephen's Hall. He had died at the age of thirty-three, a bitter, defeated man, for all that he was honored by Parliament.

When it is not necessary to make a decision, it is necessary not to make a decision, the former statesman was often quoted as saying.

It was now time for Jack to make a decision.

He must let Rose Clarring go. Or he must follow where their need took them.

Dildo burning his hand through the brown paper wrapper, Jack stepped up onto the cab.

Chapter 10

The cab rocked. The iron bridge vibrated.

Rose Clarring did not speak. Neither did Jack.

She shifted, trying to avoid the press and grind of his hip. With every turn of the wheels, their bodies were thrown together while the dildo wrapped inside the plain brown paper frigged his fingers.

Vibrating iron became unyielding pavement.

"Do I owe you money?" sliced through the palpitating tension.

"No."

The truth.

"Won't you be late, when the House sits?"

"Perhaps," Jack evaded.

"I interviewed butlers today."

Jack turned his head and perused Rose Clarring in the darkness.

Shadowy light briefly illuminated the white feathers crowning her hat, turned a blur of flesh into a cheek and nose.

"Did you hire one?" he asked.

Would it matter? he wondered.

Would the presence of servants alter the events of this night?

His own servants had not interfered with his actions. But he had only ever brought one woman to his home.

"I did not meet their standards," broke through Jack's thoughts.

There was no accusation in her voice.

Jack wondered if on the morrow she would read *The Pall Mall Gazette*.

It was a paper with which she was familiar: John Nickols wrote for the daily journal.

"My sister-in-law visited today," vibrated over the whine of carriage wheels.

Rose Clarring had five brothers and five sisters-in-law, each one of them younger than she.

Fleetingly he wondered which sister-in-law had visited.

Jack searched the darkness, but he could not see in her face the emotion that resonated inside the cab.

"When?" he probed.

"Just after four in the evening."

When Jack had sat in the House of Commons, mind already decided on a reading he had yet to hear.

He braced his foot against the shuddering cab door. "Is that why you waited for me tonight?"

But Rose Clarring did not answer his question. Instead she said, "I felt the child inside her kick."

Jack's cock cried sudden tears.

There was no emotion inside his voice. "Does she know your husband is sterile?"

"No."

"So she believes you're responsible for your childless marriage."

"Yes."

For twelve years Rose Clarring had kept her husband's secret.

Out of love. Not out of political aspirations.

The cab tilted, right wheel dropping into a pothole.

Rose Clarring grabbed a pull; it did not stop her hip from crowding his.

Instantly the cab righted, taking away the hard press of her hip. The imprint of her softness continued to burn and throb.

She stared out the window, pale feathers waving back and forth. He stared at her, body rocking with the motion of the cab.

Light and darkness played across her skin, each passing streetlamp revealing another facet of Rose Clarring: a chin . . . an eyebrow . . . a pearl-studded ear . . . the taut line of a throat . . .

The dark silhouette of her bonnet abruptly turned; the shadowed whites of her eyes pierced the darkness.

"Have you ever before petitioned Parliament for a divorce?" grated his skin.

Suddenly unable to look at the woman who touched him with every turn of the wheels, Jack faced the large rectangular window.

"No," he said shortly.

"Did you ask Mr. Whitcox for a divorce?"

The cab sharply tilted to the left, turning onto a side street.

Jack's thigh muscles corded, heel and sole pressing and grinding into the door. "No."

"I'm sorry," penetrated his chest.

"For what?" he asked curtly.

"I'm sorry that when you ejaculated, I wasn't Mrs. Whitcox."

The emotion squeezing Jack's cock fisted inside his chest.

But he couldn't speak of his grief for another woman, not when desire for this woman knotted his groin. So he said nothing.

"My sister-in-law delivered a message from Jonathon."

Jack's head snapped toward Rose Clarring. She gazed outside the small side window instead of at Jack.

"What was it?" Jack asked, and did not know if he asked as a barrister, a member of Parliament or a man.

"He forgives me."

The emotion gripping his chest and his cock clenched his stomach.

"When you orgasm tonight, Mrs. Clarring," Jack's voice was harsh even to his own ears, "who will be with you?"

"You, Mr. Lodoun."

The cab slowed . . . halted . . . wheels rolling backward . . . forward . . . stopping altogether.

"You will be with me," she reiterated.

Rose Clarring did not wait for him to open the door.

"How much?" drifted down into the darkness.

The cabby answered, a Cockney rumble.

Rose Clarring reached over the roof to pay.

Flickering lamplight cupped her breasts.

The memory of a rock-hard nipple stabbed Jack's tongue.

He exited the cab at the same time Rose Clarring stepped down from the wooden platform, his weight stabilizing the loss of hers.

She did not acknowledge his presence, neither when she unlocked the night-darkened door, nor when he stepped over the threshold behind her.

Purposefully Jack closed the door and locked it, sliding the bolt hard and deep, like a cock fitting a woman's vagina.

Pulsating darkness cocooned them; it echoed the force of the penetration.

A small clink—a metal key hitting a metal coin—danced across his skin.

Jack searched the small table inside the foyer, purchase secure underneath his right arm. Straightening, he struck the tip of a safety match against a strip of powdered glass and red phosphorus.

White flame sparked.

Silently he lit the crystal sconce above the small table reserved for mail, but which was now empty of both mail and mail tray.

He wondered if she had yet changed her address at the post office.

Would she on the morrow return to her husband who claimed to forgive her, and thank God for His interference?

Methodically Jack removed his hat and coat, and hooked them onto the narrow brass coat tree beside the door. Rose Clarring's face, when he turned, was pale but composed. She solemnly handed him her bonnet . . . her cloak. Jack hung them beside his own hat . . . his own coat . . . hers black, his gray.

The lack of color in their lives corded muscles that were already stretched too tightly.

"Is there coal in the fireplace?" he asked shortly.

It was spring, but spring nights were even cooler than spring days. He didn't want her to suffer any more discomfort than what he could prevent.

"Yes." She stepped around him, topknot glinting gold in the light pouring through the gaslit sconce. Fine, fly away hair shadowed the nape of her neck. Inside the bronze-framed mirror above the small foyer table, lashes shadowed her cheeks. She pulled out the drawer to the cherry table—wood scraping wood—and stuffed inside it a black-beaded reticule. "I cleaned out the ashes this morning and filled it with fresh coal."

The duties of a butler. But now no respectable butler would work for her.

Jack remembered the spurt of his ejaculate. Immediately the memory was replaced by Rose Clarring's tears.

He strode down the hallway into darkness, ground glass and red phosphorus burning his fingers. Rose Clarring followed, heel taps piercing his vertebrae.

Inside the small drawing room Jack lit a heavy bronze lamp. The hiss of gas filled the pulsing silence.

Rose Clarring's gaze followed his motions . . . the taut splay of his thighs . . . the tensing of his shoulders . . . the reach of his fingers.

The damp coals in the fireplace slowly caught fire. Jack opened the flue—a sharp *clang* shot up the chimney—and hunkered in front of the small iron fireplace until a sheet of white flame coated the black coals and the fire crackled with heat.

Standing, dusting off his fingers, he placed the tin of safety matches on the mantel.

Jack turned.

He had known what was coming; he just had not known how it would come.

The sight of Rose Clarring unfastening her bodice—dark lashes shielding her eyes—ripped the breath out of his lungs.

"I know I'm not Mrs. Whitcox." A sliver of white chemise shone above working fingers; she released a second satin-covered button . . . a third . . . a fourth. . . . "I know how difficult this must be for you." Gaping black wool revealed the ever widening V of a pink satin corset until there were no more buttons to free. She peeled off the bodice, pale arms shedding black wool. "But I need you tonight." Dark lashes lifting—bodice falling to the floor—she captured Jack's gaze. Knowledge of how fully she was about to expose herself dilated her pupils until black devoured the light of blue. "I need you to see me, and not Mrs. Whitcox."

The dildo underneath Jack's arm burned through the wool of his coat and the cotton of his shirt.

He had the night before gazed at her naked desire until he could no longer watch, and had escaped in the arms of a woman who was now dead.

"I do see you, Mrs. Clarring," Jack said quietly.

He saw her pain. He saw her need.

He felt her utter aloneness throughout his entire body.

Gaze dropping, she unfastened the band of her black wool skirt. "I was very naive—like women are—when I married."

The skirt fell, a rustling slide of wool.

Jack stared at the lashes that fanned Rose Clarring's cheeks and the shadows that consumed her life, thirty-three, the same age as Lord Falkland.

"I thought love made babies," she said, gold gilding the tips of her lashes.

A soft thud pierced the hiss of gas, a bustle impacting wood.

"Not literally, of course." A soft swish—the slippery descent of a silk petticoat—scraped Jack's testicles. "I wasn't quite that ignorant." The pain shadowing her face was momentarily erased by wry self-mockery; a second swish resounded over the pop of embers, another petticoat liberated. "I thought when Jonathon ejaculated inside me, it was a gift, a special way in which a man demonstrated his love for a woman. And I liked it."

Gaslight flared; gold feathered a delicate eyebrow.

"Jonathon didn't give me an orgasm, but I enjoyed having him lie between my thighs"—A sharp snap pierced Jack's cock, the release of a corset spring latch—"and the intimate connection when he joined our bodies. I enjoyed feeling his love spurt deep inside me."

A second snap reverberated with remembered pleasure.

Rose Clarring taking a man's ejaculate. Jack giving a woman his ejaculate.

"I asked him, when he lay with me on Christmas Eve, why he no longer loved me." A third snap shot down Jack's spine. "He said making love . . . he never used the word *fucking*, Mr. Lodoun"—a fourth snap pierced Jack's chest—"he said making love to me was like a form of self-abuse. Children, he said, were a man's gift to the woman he loved. He no longer had anything to give me, he said. So we held each other while his ejaculate leaked from my body onto the sheet, and we cried." A fifth snap gripped Jack's throat. "When I woke up the next morning, he was gone."

A wave of memory crashed over Jack.

The harsh groan of masculine release. The sharp cry of feminine orgasm.

Jack's drowsy satiation. Cynthia Whitcox's kissing laughter.

She had left him after their shared pleasure, and he had never again seen her.

Not alive. Not dead.

White cotton abruptly blocked Rose Clarring's face.

Jack instinctively glanced downward.

Visually he followed the upward glide of a cotton chemise riding silk drawers . . . whispering across smooth flesh . . . clinging to upthrust breasts—pale hair glinted gold in the dark hollows of underarms—jerking free of a snagging hairpin.

Rose Clarring had small breasts, firm and round like the globe of a brandy snifter. Dusky pink nipples stabbed the air, hard with need as Jack's cock had been hard the night before.

He took no pleasure in her vulnerability.

Rose Clarring's closed eyelids slowly opened; her stark gaze pinned Jack. "I felt Lucy's unborn baby, and I needed to see you."

"Why?" ricocheted off the bare walls that were dressed only in shadows.

"Because you love another woman," she said, standing tall in ribbon-laced drawers, stockings and shoes. "And I love another man. But they are both dead to us. Yet we cannot share our loss with anyone."

Her unspoken words vibrated over hissing gas and popping embers: *Save for each other*.

He was a politician who had completely betrayed her. She was a woman who totally exposed herself.

Jack should walk out now, before she penetrated the special place she had saved for her husband: He could not.

"Take off the rest of your clothes, Mrs. Clarring." Jack's voice hardened; the package underneath his arm throbbed as if it were a part of his cock instead of a lifeless, soulless object designed for the sole purpose of fucking. "Let us discover where a woman's passion resides."

Chapter 11

"Do you mind if I sit down to take off my shoes and stockings?"

Rose Clarring asked for the same simple dignity she had granted Jack when he had stood before her clad only in his trousers, small-clothes, socks and shoes, body pulsing with his pending nakedness.

Silently gesturing toward the settee, Jack turned to give her a minute of privacy.

The small sigh of a depressing cushion slithered down his spine. The impact of wood—the heel of a shoe dropping onto the floor—clenched his groin.

Jack glanced about the small, bare drawing room, the size and shape typical of the terrace homes daily popping up to house the newly emerging breed of lower middle class.

Another thud of wood pierced his chest.

Jonathon Clarring's town house, Jack thought—deliberately distancing himself from the undressing that occurred behind him—was located in an older neighborhood, a wealthy community that combined elegance with practicality. But Rose Clarring—living separately from her husband—would no longer be able to afford the luxuries to which she was accustomed.

An almost imperceptible sigh abraded his skin, cushion plumping after being released of weight.

Black leather, oak wood and gilded metal leapt out at Jack.

The trunk from which she had twenty-three hours earlier produced the French postcard was shoved against a far wall. The dark blue velvet armchair in which she had sat while he stood fucking his cock faced the settee.

A slick slide of silk drawers pricked the hair on the nape of his neck.

Jack crossed the floor that was bereft of a rug—footsteps deafening over the pop of embers—and lifted the heavy chair, muscles cording with strain.

A low rustle wormed through his bones, a cushion depressing . . . a cushion shifting.

Jack set the velvet-covered armchair at the end of the settee, a heavy thud of wood impacting wood.

Pale flesh twisting on blue damask snagged his gaze.

Rose Clarring slid back on the settee, naked hips turning, heel digging into a cushion to gain purchase.

Heat licked Jack's cheeks and gripped his cock.

Slowly she lay back, round breasts plumping, right knee rising, left knee falling over a blue damask cushion.

An inverted arrow of dark gold pubic hair framed swollen, dusky pink lips.

Harsh, solitary breathing—Jack's breathing—sounded over the distant bong of Big Ben.

Rose Clarring exposed her sex as Jack had exposed his sex. The tiny fissure that was her vagina darkly shone between the folds of her vulva.

Eyes stripped of innocence caught his gaze.

Pearl earrings gleamed in the shadow of her hair.

A gift from her husband. Or perhaps a gift from her father.

Pearls for a virgin bride.

Tearing open brown paper, Jack held the dildo in his left hand while with his right hand he unstoppered the bottle of lubricant. Slowly, carefully, he directed the bulbous leather into the clear, slippery oil.

The crystal lip was far larger than the fissure of her vagina. Only the very tip of the dark leather fit inside the opening.

Jack set the bottle down by the bronze base of a hissing lamp. The sharp click of glass on wood reverberated over the crackle of burning coals. Walking to the middle of the settee—not quite touching her knee that angled off blue damask—he offered the dildo.

She gazed at the leather phallus for long seconds, dark lashes hollowing her cheeks. A glistening thread of lubricant slid down the thick shaft, as if the artificial glans was alive and cried with masculine need.

Slowly Rose Clarring reached up to take the dildo.

Electric heat jumped from her fingers into Jack.

Her gaze snapped upward, wide and vulnerable. Jack did not step back to afford her more privacy.

"I've always dreamed it would be Jonathon who would tutor me. That it would be he who introduced me to the delights of my vagina." Bitter cynicism twisted her lips and scoured Jack's skin. "But you are quite right, Mr. Lodoun. How can a woman expect a man to please her, when we women do not know what pleases us? When we do not even know if we are capable of taking pleasure in a 'stiff prick'?"

Wetness streaked Rose Clarring's cheek.

A matching tear leaked from Jack's cock.

"Perhaps this *is* all a woman needs"—her slender fingers tightened around the artificial phallus until they were white-tipped from the pressure—"and passion does not exist save in the minds of love-starved women."

They would both discover the answer before the night was over.

Brown leather protruding both above and below her fingers, Rose Clarring guided the dildo between the delta of her thighs.

The thick shaft divided dark blond public hair . . . was sandwiched in between the lips of a dusky pink labia . . . blotted out the small fissure of a vagina.

Jack stepped back and sank into the armchair.

The position afforded him a different perspective.

He could see the large artificial crown, the size of his own crown: It was shiny with lubricant. He could feel the collapsed opening of her vagina, unoccupied for eleven years: It glistened with unshed tears.

Brown leather notched pink flesh. Pink flesh swallowed brown leather.

The glans. The crown.

The shaft.

One inch . . .

Two inches . . .

Three inches . . .

The flesh of her vagina stretched to form a fragile ring around the piercing leather.

Four inches . . .

Five inches . . .

Six inches . . .

The brown leather could go no deeper for the grip of her white-tipped fingers.

Jack clasped giving velvet.

He couldn't see her clitoris or her labia for the column of her wrist. But he could feel the slick, wet embrace of the concealed lips. He could feel the hardness of her clitoris, as hard as his cock.

He could feel the raw invasion of her body, filled with hard, impersonal leather instead of the flesh of her husband, the man she loved. Journeying alone in pursuit of passion. Uncertain of what awaited her.

Jack dug his fingers into the soft velvet armchair, cock thickening and elongating. He hurt for the discomfort she was bound to be experiencing, celibate for so long. He ached for her to penetrate herself more deeply, to take two more inches, the full length of the dildo, the length of his own flesh.

The brown leather shaft slowly reappeared.

One inch . . .

Two inches . . .

Three inches . . .

The taut ring of flesh relaxed, skin less painfully stretched.

Four inches . . .

Five inches . . .

Six inches . . .

Jack saw the leather crown. Jack saw the leather glans.

They were slick with more than artificial lubricant.

Rose Clarring took six inches. Rose Clarring gave up six inches.

She took. She gave.

Giving Beauty her beast. Taking away Beauty's beast.

Shallow strokes. Deep strokes. Gentle strokes. Hard strokes.

Learning what it was that gave her pleasure.

Her left hand that gripped the edge of the settee curved over her lower abdomen, as if mapping the internal thrusts that cleaved it.

Jack's hand curved, shaping velvet into a tautly rounded stomach that pulsed beneath his fingers.

Swelling with entry. Collapsing with emptiness.

A ragged soughing of air accompanied the slick suction of flesh, her breathing matching his.

Jack witnessed the changes in her body—the darkening ring of her vagina that clung to the pistoning phallus; the glistening desire that coated hard brown leather—and could not breathe for the clasp of her sex.

Opening. *Closing.*

Giving. Taking.

A woman's desire no longer a beast, but a pleasure to be savored.

Pale motion grabbed Jack's attention.

Rose Clarring's left hand arched upward and grasped her left breast.

The pressure of her fingers crushed his cock.

A low moan rode the slap of leather.

Jack's gaze snapped upward.

Her face was taut, caught between the pain and the pleasure of orgasm. Dark red colored her cheeks and spilled down her chin.

Jonathon Clarring had not been with her in the past when she had needed him. Jack hoped, for her sake, that he was with her now. Jack hoped it was Jonathon Clarring her vagina welcomed. Jack hoped it was Jonathon Clarring's cock that brought Rose Clarring pleasure.

He wanted her to find the orgasm her husband had not given her. He wanted her to cry out to Jonathon Clarring in the passion for which she yearned.

She had said Jack would be with her. But she had no memories of Jack which she could draw upon.

Jack did not want her to be alone, not at that moment when men and women were at their most vulnerable.

An agonized cry broke over the wet suction of flesh and the harsh soughing of breathing and the crackling of burning cinders.

Jack waited, heart beating inside his cock, breath ripping in and out of his testicles.

Rose Clarring opened her eyes. Rose Clarring saw Jack.

Her pupils—the size of pinpricks—swelled until all he could see was blackness.

Pain eviscerated Jack.

He had not gotten what he had hoped for. Neither had Rose Clarring.

Unable to gaze at the stark loneliness inside her eyes, Jack glanced down at the pale fingers that rested against the mound of her vulva.

The thick base of the leather dildo stiffly protruded from the stretched ring of her vagina. A single teardrop of glistening liquid spilled onto the blue damask settee.

Jack stood up and walked to the doorway, heels hollowly clicking.

"Why did you answer me?" stopped him short. Her voice was husky with the tears she did not cry and the need she had not satisfied. "When I asked who you had loved?"

After he had told her he didn't feel compelled to share his private life with strangers.

"Because I, too," Jack said, "need someone to understand."

Chapter 12

Rose shoveled cold cinders into the ash dump.

Her muscles throbbed and ached.

Her right wrist. Her right arm.

Deep inside her pelvis where she had penetrated her body.

She breathed black dust.

No, not where she had penetrated her body, she corrected herself: Where she had *fucked* her body. While Jack Lodoun watched.

Her vagina no longer belonged to Jonathon.

Purple-blue eyes black with shadow stared up from the ashes.

But neither, Rose thought—over the acrid sulfur clogging her nostrils, she smelled the rich, masculine spice that was Jack Lodoun's scent—did it belong to her.

The sharp rap of a knocker scattered the pungent memories.

Hopefully, Rose grimly thought, the employment service had sent a butler who was a little less nice in his requirements.

Slamming shut the ash dump door—a gray cloud billowed up

the chimney—she backed up out of the fireplace and hung the shovel with the other fire irons.

Her hands—they were black. So was her frock.

Rose wiped her hands on the sides of her wool skirt and answered the door.

Her heartbeat quickened. Skipped a painful beat.

The man who stood on her stoop was as tall as Jack Lodoun. But he wasn't the man who had watched her cry out with orgasm.

Nor was it a perspective butler.

"You have soot on your face," Derek said, navy wool overcoat and pomaded blond hair impeccable in the late-morning sun.

Instinctively Rose brought up a hand to her left cheek.

A familiar glint of laughter lit up the thirty-one-year-old man's eyes. "Now you have more soot on your face."

"Derek." Lowering her hand, Rose clenched her fingers into twin fists. There was no wiping away the results of last night. "Fancy seeing you here."

The mischievous laughter died. "Thank you for bringing Lucy home."

"She shouldn't have come," Rose said, steadily holding the gaze of the man who shared the same hair color as she, but whose eyes were the pale blue of their mother instead of the cornflower blue of their father. "And neither should you have."

His clear eyes clouded. "I don't understand, Rose. You've always been so happy."

"Have I?" Rose asked, the ashes she had inhaled swelling inside her throat.

"Divorces are difficult to come by." Derek searched her gaze. "I hear they're frightfully expensive."

"I have my dowry," Rose said. Jonathon had set up a bank account in her name when they married; he had not touched her funds. "I'll manage."

"Why don't you talk to my solicitor—"

So that the solicitor could talk sense into Rose, Rose surmised.

"I have a barrister," Rose interrupted. "He's going to petition Parliament for a private act."

The cloud inside Derek's eyes darkened. "I see."

"I would invite you in for a cup of tea," Rose said politely, aching for the relationships her desire had tarnished, "but I'm afraid I don't have the makings yet."

"Lucy said you didn't yet have any help."

Because of the trial, his troubled gaze added. No one wants to associate with a disreputable woman. But Jonathon Clarring forgave her sins.

Why wouldn't Rose go back home to a husband who so obviously loved her?

"I have an interview shortly," Rose intervened before Derek put thoughts into words.

It was not a lie.

Any moment now, a man would arrive from the employment agency.

Gaze dropping away from hers, Derek lowered his blond head—gold where kissed by sunlight—and extended a newspaper. "I came to give you this."

Her oldest brother was the type of man who was comfortable in a roomful of strangers. It hurt to see him so uncomfortable with her, his only sister.

Rose ignored his outstretched hand. "I don't need to read any more reports of the trial, Derek."

One had been quite enough.

Derek rifled through the newspaper, folded it to a middle page. "You need to read this, Rose."

"Derek—"

Derek lifted his head: Pain dilated his pupils until his irises were a thin band of color. Leaning down, he kissed her cheek.

The clinging warmth of his lips penetrated her defenses.

Rose couldn't remember the last time Derek had demonstrated

his affection. She scarcely noticed the stiff newspaper he folded her fingers around until he stepped back.

"Read it, Rose." Reaching inside his outer coat, he slipped a monogrammed white handkerchief out of a navy, pinstriped frock coat. Carefully he wiped Rose's face . . . her forehead . . . her left cheek . . . her right cheek . . . her nose . . . her chin . . . eyes focusing on his work instead of meeting her gaze. Rose stood perfectly still, head tilted up for his ministrations, starched cotton a stiff abrasion, gentle fingers a soothing consolation. Abruptly his pain-darkened eyes met her gaze; his hand dropped, cool spring air replacing familial warmth. Derek added, "Please."

His retreating footsteps sharply clicked against the concrete pavement. Rose watched his gold head duck inside a Clarence cab.

Cynthia Whitcox had died underneath a four-wheeled Clarence cab, Rose remembered reading.

James Whitcox had joined the Men and Women's Club to find passion. Jack Lodoun rode two-wheeled hansoms to escape passion.

Two men grieving for one woman.

The cab pulled away, the clip-clop of solitary horse hooves as lonely in the day as it was at night.

The empty town house was dark after the brightness of the sun. The echo of her feet followed her into the small drawing room.

She sat on the blue settee, wool blocking the abrasion of damask.

The memory of cold, thick leather penetrated her.

Driving deep. Driving hard.

I, too, need someone to understand thrust home against her cervix.

Through a blur of tears Rose noticed a dark flaw in the blue damask.

The ache inside her pelvis deepened with the realization it was her desire that stained the settee.

The dildo that had precipitated the stain had cost four shillings sixpence. Jack Lodoun had left a shilling and sixpence on the table in the foyer.

Taking a deep breath, Rose stared down at the newspaper Derek had pressed into her hand. Quickly she scanned the headlines: "Parliament to Review Corn Laws" . . . "House of Westminster Plans Queen's Jubilee" . . . "Juror Accepts Bribe" . . .

Jack Lodoun leapt out at her.

The article, a small column—titled "Private Act Denied"—occupied the bottom, right-hand corner. It was dated Thursday, the second of June.

Yesterday's date.

Chill, damp foreboding feathered the nape of her neck.

She read the single-paragraph column:

> A private act for the divorce of Harriet Maria Greffen from Justin Dwight Greffen was rejected by Parliament. Mrs. Greffen lodged to sever her marriage and gain the right to remarry. The petition read before the House of Commons charged Mr. Greffen with drunken, disorderly conduct, assault and battery, and claimed irreparable alienation and disaffection between man and wife. Barrister, QC and Conservative MP Jack Lodoun was among the overwhelming majority who voted against the private act. Lodoun said: "The law did not support it."

Rose had the curious sensation of looking down at a blond-haired woman dressed in black.

She couldn't have read what she had just read.

Slowly she perused the article, analyzing word by word the first sentence, the second, the third, pausing on the fourth, a complex sentence.

Rose could not get past the subject: *Barrister, QC and Conservative MP Jack Lodoun.*

Long moments passed before she realized the pounding in her ears came from the front door instead of inside her chest.

Chapter 13

The nearly inaudible click of a closing door skidded down his spine.

Jack was no longer alone.

He stared down at the opened Hansard Report instead of at the man who invaded his privacy. "Put Walden in the conference room, Mr. Dorsey."

"Mr. Walden isn't here," the clerk said in his calm, quiet voice. "His secretary telegraphed he's running late. It's Mr. Stromwell, sir. He's waiting outside."

The black type blurred.

Jack saw not a Parliamentary motion, but Ezekiel 16:17: *Thou hast also taken thy fair jewels of my gold and of my silver, which I had given thee, and madest to thyself images of men, and didst commit whoredom with them.*

Face expressionless, he glanced up. "What does he want?"

"I don't know, sir; he didn't say." Sunlight slanted across navy wool carpeting and turned twenty-seven-year-old Nathan Dorsey's dark brown hair into bronze. Behind him, the discreetly closed door gleamed, honey oak streaked with gold. "Shall I tell him you're busy?"

Jack thought of Rose Clarring, alone in a row house with no servants. Jack thought of Blair Stromwell, calling Rose Clarring a slut.

"No," Jack said, the dull throb inside his groin seeking an outlet. "Show him in."

"Shall I bring brandy, sir?"

Had Jonathon Clarring drunk himself into a state of unconsciousness while his wife fucked herself with the image of Jack?

"Yes." Jack closed with a sharp thud the thick volume of Parliamentary motions. "The good Chairman of Justice likes his brandy."

"Very good. A courier just picked up the minutes to the Men and Women's Club, and I've sorted the post." The clerk crossed the carpet and proffered a clutch of letters. "The top one is from Mr. Seaton."

The solicitor who had referred Frances Hart's son.

Jack ignored the papers, white instead of brown, bearing words instead of a dildo. "I take it he won't be referring any more clients."

"On the contrary." No judgment shone inside the clerk's clear green eyes. "He asks you to plead a case before the Courts of Summary Jurisdiction."

A trial without benefit of a jury.

The judge trying the Hart case had been a Conservative: Had there been no jury, Jack would have won.

"For what situation?" Jack asked incuriously.

"Mr. Justin Greffen wishes to sue his wife for restitution of his conjugal rights."

The husband of the woman to whom Jack and two hundred and nineteen other MPs had denied a divorce.

Jack studied the twenty-seven-year-old man who stood before him.

He had hired Nathan Dorsey three and a half years earlier.

There was no knowledge of Cynthia Whitcox inside the younger man's eyes. Yet he had not once commented on the trials Jack had lost to James Whitcox.

On the day of Cynthia's death, he had cancelled Jack's appointments for the remainder of the week, before Jack had even been aware she'd died.

And now Jack was drawn to Rose Clarring, yet another man's wife.

The papers inside the clerk's outstretched hand remained steady.

Nathan Dorsey worked the way he lived: with dignity and reserve.

"Were you my client, Mr. Dorsey," Jack observed, gaze meeting the waiting eyes of his clerk, "I would argue that the steadiness of your hand is proof you're an honorable man."

No pride at being judged an honorable man flickered inside the clerk's eyes.

"Were you a plaintiff," Jack continued, "I'd argue that the steadiness of your hand is proof you're an inveterate liar."

No offense darkened the clear green gaze.

"How would you plead a case, Mr. Dorsey, in which your client is a liar, a drunkard, a profligate and beats his wife?"

Justin Greffen.

"I don't know, sir." The clerk was bluntly honest, his gaze as steadfast as his hand. "That's why I don't practice law."

Yet Nathan Dorsey—who had been called to the bar—knew the law better than most barristers: It was why Jack employed him.

"How would you plead a case," Jack pressed, "in which a plaintiff's only culpability lies in his inability to sire children?"

Jonathon Clarring.

Understanding dilated the clerk's pupils.

He had prepared Rose Clarring's file. He had watched her in the witness box.

He saw her now in Jack's gaze.

Her loneliness. Her vulnerability.

The clerk's pupils shrank to a small black dot.

"A woman," Nathan Dorsey calmly suggested, "may annul her marriage if the husband has been impotent for three or more years."

In the eyes of the law, sterility and impotence were often interpreted as one and the same.

"She doesn't want any aspersions on her husband's sexuality," Jack said flatly.

"Does the husband perform his conjugal duties?" the clerk quietly returned.

Heat edged Jack's cheeks at discussing Rose's sexual relations with another man. "No."

"Desertion is grounds for a separation."

"Desertion is defined by cohabitation, Mr. Dorsey," Jack said dryly, "not matrimonial intercourse."

"Perhaps a judge could be convinced differently, sir," the clerk suggested quietly, calmly, "if he believed a man willfully denied his wife a child."

Jack studied the clerk's clear green eyes for long seconds.

He did not have the ability to persuade a judge, Nathan Dorsey's gaze said, still ruled by the idealism of law rather than the reality. But Jack, who had long ago traded a conscience for position, did.

"She's no longer living in his house," Jack said neutrally.

The law required that a woman who petitioned the courts for a separation must live with her husband.

"Perhaps, sir," the clerk said, "the husband maintains another abode in which she may temporarily abide."

The thought of Rose Clarring residing in a property owned by Jonathon Clarring knotted his stomach.

"Perhaps." Jack took the letters. "Show the chairman in."

The clerk shifted in preparation of turning, as Rose Clarring had shifted her hips on the settee.

A single teardrop leaked into Jack's thoughts.

Would the club resume their Saturday meetings now that the trial was over? he wondered.

Rose Clarring was a passionate woman.

Would she on the morrow speak of sex using cold, clinical analogies while unabated need pulsed through her body, as it pulsed through his?

Had she even now returned to her husband who "forgave" her for wanting more than his children?

A portly man with thinning gray hair blackened Jack's threshold.

The clerk shut the door, closing in a man who had sacrificed everything with a man who offered everything.

"Lodoun, old chap." Stiff white collar pushing up a roll of fat, Blair Stromwell plopped down into the burgundy leather wing chair opposite Jack. He slapped two newspapers onto the edge of the crowded oak desktop. Settling back onto tufted leather, he pulled out a cigar from a dark brown wool frock coat. "Want one?"

Jack concealed his distaste. "No."

"Ah, the Bible." The older man affably nodded toward the black, leather-bound book that peeked out from underneath the mound of letters. "Interesting reading, that. I'm particularly fond of Job: 'The eye also of the adulterer waiteth for the twilight, saying, No eye shall see me: and disguiseth his face.' "

The spring sun warming Jack's hair turned winter cold.

Puffy lids concealed Stromwell's gaze: He had short, spiky lashes.

A match sparked.

"In the last three years you've lost"—Gray smoke billowed out of the senior MP's thin mouth and curled up around a veined, bulbous nose. Without warning, the spiky lashes lifted and pale brown irises made translucent by the sun pinned Jack—"five trials to James Whitcox, what?"

Blair Stromwell knew his record as well as Jack.

"Yes."

"Those are the only cases you've lost," the older man stressed. A plume of acidic smoke pelted Jack's face. "Ever."

Jack was not expected to answer, so he didn't.

The older MP blew out the burning match.

"A sterling record, nonetheless." The razor-sharp acuity inside his eyes slid behind complacent affability. Leather squeaking—bulk shifting—the chairman leaned forward and dropped the blackened matchstick into a ruby-faceted ashtray. "One in which to take pride."

The dull pain pulsating inside Jack's groin traveled upward and lodged inside his left temple.

"Are you here to commiserate my losses, Chairman, or congratulate my wins?" he asked flatly.

"You're not like Whitcox, old boy." A gray ring of smoke circled the chairman's balding head, dissipated like the fragile trust of a woman. "He's a barrister; you're a politician. Whitcox's kind don't care about the values of this country. Now I remember his father—"

A man who had also held the position of attorney general.

"What can I do for you," Jack coldly interrupted, "that couldn't wait until this evening?"

When the House of Commons sat, Jack implied.

The cordiality inside the senior MP's eyes vanished.

A soft knock bounced off oak cornices and beige silk-swirled walls.

Stromwell did not look away from Jack; Jack did not look away from Stromwell.

The door opened, a waft of cool breeze.

"Your brandy, Mr. Lodoun." The clerk's voice cut through the pulsing silence. "Mr. Chairman."

Liquid splashed. Crystal glinted.

When the clerk moved to set down a gold-rimmed decanter, Jack waved him back.

The door quietly clicked shut.

Scooping up a snifter, the chairman assessed Jack for long seconds. "You didn't return to the Commons last night after supper. Had you done so, you would have been there when the Prime Minister read a petition from those shrieking sisters and canting brothers. This evening we take a third reading. As a party Whip, it's my duty to ensure that the Conservative party members attend this reading, and that we stand united. We do not support women's suffrage. Do we?"

Jack cupped his brandy snifter, round like Rose Clarring's breasts. Unlike flesh, the glass was cold and brittle. "Have I ever been disloyal to the party?"

"Sixteen months ago Lord Salisbury was forced to stand down."

"Six months later he was back in office," Jack said.

"Only because the liberal party was divided."

"Lord Salisbury is Prime Minister because Gladstone didn't listen to public opinion," Jack sharply corrected.

"Which brings us back to you, Lodoun."

The tension dancing on Jack's skin focused on the senior member of Parliament.

The chairman paused, deliberately swallowing amber liquor, brown eyes shining over the crystal rim.

In the distance the first-quarter bells struck: It was two fifteen. Outside the closed door to Jack's office a smaller chime rang.

The chairman lowered the snifter, brandy-wet lips glistening, as if coated with a woman's sex. "We allow the members of our party many liberties, as long as they're discreet." A sweeping motion of his hand trailed gray smoke. "Some men's wives, you'll agree, fairly beg to be fucked."

The throb in Jack's groin and his left temple spread to his chest and his testicles.

"But we do not soil our own backyard." The pale brown eyes studied Jack through a billow of gray smoke. "The core of this country is patriarchal. Marriage and children are our God-given rights. Poor. Rich. A woman and a child are properties that any man can acquire. It's what brings men together. It's what unites this country: men."

Leather squeaked.

Stuffing the cigar—brown like the dildo Rose Clarring had stuffed into her vagina—between wet lips, the chairman reached out and tossed a newspaper across the desk.

Jack instinctively glanced down.

His name snared his gaze.

"When you take family matters out of the hands of men," sliced through the coldly slanting sun, "you endanger our entire way of life. What would become of us if women had the same rights as men? Soon they'd want to serve in Parliament. Women are not the same as us, dear boy; men reason, women feel."

An image of Rose Clarring's cornflower blue eyes stripped of innocence stabbed through Jack.

He knew with sudden clarity that she had read *The Pall Mall Gazette*.

Jack had forced her to confront her dream of passion. Then he had reduced it to a solitary act of satisfaction.

While he watched. And said nothing. His flesh weeping the tears she did not.

And now she had read his quote, not realizing the machinations of Parliamentary law.

"That's not to say they're less deserving of justice," shouldered aside Jack's thoughts. "It's simply that they cannot be trusted to act on reason. And that is what the law is, Lodoun: reason. No one needs to understand that more than does a Lord of Appeal in Ordinary.

"Now *that*, in *The Pall Mall Gazette*, is what we want to see from you in the future." Leather squeaked; *The Standard*—the leading Conservative paper—crashed down on top of *The Pall Mall Gazette*. "Not this."

The reporter for *The Pall Mall Gazette* had privately questioned

Jack's motivation in stepping down as attorney general. The reporter for *The Standard* publicly speculated that there existed a personal rivalry between Jack Lodoun and James Whitcox.

Jack had made allies in Parliament, but he had also made enemies.

If a reporter should dig, he would unearth dirt.

"Do you understand, Lodoun?"

Jack glanced up from the two papers.

A clear warning blazed in the translucent brown eyes.

The Conservative party would allow no more indiscretions, those eyes conveyed.

No more affairs. No more controversy.

No more losses.

"Perfectly," Jack said.

The pounding throb inside his temple dissipated.

Jack perfectly understood what he had to do.

Chapter 14

Afternoon sunlight burned Rose's dry eyes.

"Mrs. Clarring, I'll be going now!" wafted up the stairs on a pungent wave of lye soap and beeswax polish.

The employment agency had sent a housekeeper instead of a butler. She and Rose had cleaned until they had nothing more with which to clean.

"Very well, Mrs. Dobkins." Blindly Rose tucked the duvet more firmly beneath the mattress. Sparrows squabbled outside the bedroom window. "I'll see you tomorrow morning."

A faint murmur was swallowed by a clicking closure.

The housekeeper was gone.

Rose collapsed on the edge of the bed.

A telltale creak rang out over the squeal of the bedsprings, the step of a foot on a stair.

It was too heavy to belong to Mrs. Dobkins.

Knowledge of whom the step belonged to resonated throughout her entire body.

Rose closed her eyes against the light that papered the naked walls.

Another creak pierced the solitude, the top stair. Wooden heels irrevocably advanced down a narrow wooden corridor.

The footsteps stopped; their impact did not.

Images seared the backs of Rose's eyelids.

Jonathon Clarring. Jack Lodoun.

Neither her husband nor her barrister was the man she had thought he was.

The innocence they had stolen was a palpable pain.

But she could not speak of her hurt. So the man who stood in her bedroom doorway spoke of his past.

"James Whitcox has never lost a trial," carried on a scrabble of talons and the flutter of wings.

The images of Jonathon and Jack Lodoun were joined by the forty-seven-year-old barrister and fellow club member.

"Three years ago, neither had I. When I came up against him on the bench, I wanted to learn more about my rival: I started with his wife."

Rose had no image of Cynthia Whitcox.

"I'd seen her at social events—we travel in the same circles, the men who create law and the men who practice it—but only in passing. I knew she'd be attending a court function, so I attended. She wore a red silk gown."

Behind Rose's closed eyelids, a woman materialized beside the three men: She wore a red dress, but she had Rose's face.

"She didn't want me at first. But I didn't care." Neither regret nor remorse colored the implacable voice. "I saw her, I wanted her, I pursued her, and I won her. Just as Jonathon Clarring pursued you."

But Rose had not been married. And Jonathon had wanted her babies, not her body.

"It wasn't that difficult," stung her skin, truth more painful than nettles. "Whitcox didn't love her. Theirs was an arranged marriage.

You were quite fortunate in that respect. Imagine marrying a man—a man you didn't love—and lying in his bed waiting for him to take your virginity, sexual intimacy a matter of legal consummation."

But Rose could not imagine another woman's marriage when her own marriage consumed her every breath.

"She hadn't shared a bed with Whitcox for twelve years. Like you, she saved her vagina for some imaginary lover. She was tight, like you were tight."

The pinching vulnerability she had felt—stretching herself with a dildo—inched through Rose's pelvis.

"I taught her how to take and give the pleasure Whitcox had not." In his voice were reverse memories, the penetrator rather than the penetrated. "She was my wife more than she had ever been his. Even though she had borne him two children. Even though English law recognized him—and only him—as her lawful husband. But Whitcox married her. And Whitcox buried her. And now she's gone."

Rose stared at flickering darkness.

"You asked if Cynthia loved me," squeezed her chest.

And then Rose had asked if she had yet demonstrated that a woman's passion was worth a man's reputation.

So that he would petition Parliament for a divorce.

A divorce he had never had any intention of petitioning.

"I believe she did." Her pain bled into his voice. "But I will never know why. I will never know if she loved me simply because I gave her splendid fucks."

Rose's eyelids snapped open.

Jack Lodoun filled the doorway, head and shoulders framed by sunshine and shimmering dust motes.

He snared her gaze, eyes so purple in the clear light of day it hurt to look at him.

Purposefully, he added, "Just as you will never know if Jonathon Clarring married you because you come from a fertile family."

For one long second she was immobilized by the pain inside his eyes.

A pain with which she had lived for twelve years.

Afraid of asking. But more afraid of knowing.

The clip-clop of four hooves permeated the silence. The grind of carriage wheels trailed after the lone horse.

Both bound.

The horse to the carriage. The carriage to the horse.

No release for either until they made the long journey home.

"But you asked the wrong question, Rose Clarring."

The hair on the nape of her neck prickled a warning.

"Last night, in the cab," he expounded, too-purple gaze holding hers, "you enquired if I had asked for a divorce. But you should have asked: What would I have done *if*—upon asking—James Whitcox had refused to divorce her?"

Rose didn't need to ask: The answer was clearly visible in the taut stretch of his cheekbones and the hard line of his mouth.

"Nothing," he emphatically stressed. "I would have done nothing. Parliamentary law is very specific: A woman may divorce her husband if he is a bigamist, if he commits incest or if he deserts her. Whitcox was guilty of none of those crimes. Nor is your husband.

"Every day I wonder if Cynthia would still be alive had I asked Whitcox. But I didn't. Nor could Cynthia have won a divorce. And neither can you." Jack Lodoun was illuminated by the sun; there was no light in the future he painted. "But a separation doesn't require Parliamentary approval. I can win you a separation in the Courts of Summary Jurisdiction."

Rose struggled to reconcile the man who so obviously hurt with the MP who had voted to deny a woman the right to a divorce, simply because the "law did not support it."

Only one thing was clear: "You didn't win Mrs. Whitcox a separation."

"I didn't offer to procure her one," he flatly returned, pupils a stark black dot.

Yet he now offered to procure one for Rose.

"I will be unable to remarry. Jonathon will be unable to remarry." The white band of flesh where Rose's wedding band had marked her finger throbbed. "Of what use is a separation?"

"You will gain full legal control over your person."

"So Jonathon can't lock me away in an insane asylum, you mean," Rose said. "As your client attempted to lock away Mrs. Hart."

There was no apology inside his eyes for the man he had represented and the lives he had destroyed.

"Nor," he added, "could he sue for restitution of his conjugal rights."

The truth burned like acid all the way down to her empty, aching vagina. "My husband has no interest in claiming his conjugal rights."

"But he has the legal right to force you to live in his home," Jack Lodoun riposted.

An empty house that would never be filled with the laughter of Jonathon's children.

Rose swallowed, reality a bitter pill. "If Jonathon came to you, could you win him a private act?"

"Yes."

"Because London believes I'm an adulteress," she essayed, back straight, coiled metal sharp underneath the softness of the mattress.

"Yes."

"But I couldn't divorce *him* on the grounds of adultery."

"No," danced and shimmered inside the sunlight.

"So if Jonathon will not divorce me, I will live the rest of my life alone." Rose gripped the quilted duvet inside her fists and forced out the words. "Unless I take a lover."

There was no compassion inside his gaze, only the hard reality of Parliamentary law.

"Yes," he said.

"A husband can sue his wife's lover for"—the polite euphemism for adultery scraped raw her throat—"criminal conversation."

It was not a question.

"If I were legally separated, and I should take a lover," Rose asked, dying a little inside that her need for passion had brought her to this, contemplating the very act of which Jack Lodoun had publicly accused her, "would Jonathon be able to sue him?"

He murdered the brief spark of hope. "Yes."

The loneliness she had felt—penetrating herself with a cold, lifeless phallus while the man who stood before her watched—washed over her.

"What man would want me"—her fingernail snapped a thread—"*knowing* the price he could ultimately pay?"

"I want you."

Emotion swelled Rose's breasts.

"*You* want me, Mr. Lodoun?" she quizzed, light stinging her eyes.

"Jack. My name is Jack," Jack Lodoun replied. "And yes, I do want you."

"Because you watched me fuck myself with a dildo," Rose said, deliberately vulgar, hurting, with no legal recourse to rectify her hurt.

"And you watched me fuck my cock," he countered.

Inside his eyes she saw a man stroking his penis and a woman engorging her vagina.

"You needed me to see you, Rose." His gaze would not let her look away from the nakedness they had revealed to one another. "But I need you to see me, too. I am a man who desires you, but I'm also a member of Parliament. I told you divorce was out of the question."

Outside the courthouse, he had told her.

But Rose had not wanted to believe him.

"Parliament is not going to break the vow you do not have the courage to break yourself," sliced through flesh and pierced hope. "If you want passion, you will pay for it."

Rose wanted to protest: She could not.

She *did* want Parliament to liberate her so she wouldn't have to choose between fidelity and passion.

The impossibility of what she wanted shone inside his eyes.

He had said every situation he accepted affected his career.

"What would happen," Rose asked, fingers cramping, "if you were brought to trial for criminal conversation?"

"I'd lose my position in Parliament."

The question shot out of her mouth, the question he had asked the night before: "*Why?*"

He did not pretend to misunderstand her.

"I don't want you to be alone when you orgasm."

"But you don't love me," Rose said, sounding like the naive woman she was, full of dreams that had no basis in either law or reality.

"And you don't love me," he returned unapologetically.

Chirping flirtation infiltrated the silence, a mating sparrow fleeing pursuit.

A dull thud killed the chase, feathered body crashing into the window.

The bird had mistaken glass for air.

"If you could go back in time," Rose suddenly asked, "knowing the pain that would come . . . would you still seduce Mrs. Whitcox?"

"If you could go back in time," Jack Lodoun flatly parried, "knowing that Jonathon Clarring would contract the mumps . . . would you still marry him?"

Memories flitted through her thoughts.

The warmth of Jonathon's kisses. The gentleness of his embraces.

The joy of his laughter.

Rose had two perfect months of love before the mumps had taken her husband away from her.

"Yes," she said, finally. "I would."

Rose would not change one minute of the precious time she and Jonathon had spent together.

His purple-blue eyes mirrored her answer.

He would not change the past, his gaze said. But was she willing to pay the price for passion?

Four distant bongs echoed inside the barren bedroom, Big Ben announcing the sitting of the House of Commons.

Jack Lodoun turned. Jack Lodoun departed.

The squeaking descent of footsteps filled the empty bedroom.

It was Rose's decision, those footsteps said. It was Rose who would bear the consequences of her decision.

Rose and Jonathon.

And Jack Lodoun.

Chapter 15

The clock tower glowed against the blackening sky, two dark hands poised to advance.

A minute. An hour.

Silently Rose counted down the seconds that would catapult copper and gunmetal into motion: *fifty-one, fifty-two, fifty-three, fifty-four . . .*

Heat penetrated her elbow; the curving pressure of familiar fingers clenched her abdomen.

She lowered her head and met the unfathomable gaze of Jack Lodoun.

He lived with pain. He lived with guilt.

The price of passion.

"I want you, too, Jack Lodoun," Rose said. The brim of his bowler shadowed his eyes and nose; lamplight sharply delineated his lips and chin, bottom lip fuller than the top, chin caught between light and darkness. "And I will pay the price."

Vibrating chimes pierced the air.

The first strike of Big Ben ripped through Rose's chest. The second strike cupped her right cheek. The third strike brought Jack Lodoun's shadow-darkened face closer, red-gold hair glinting. The fourth strike enveloped her in liquid heat.

He kissed her, lips petal soft.

Her breath rasped inside her throat.

It had been so *long. . . .*

Rose gazed into his eyes until she could no longer stare into their darkness for the bittersweet waves of sensation that rolled over her with each strike of Big Ben.

A man's scent. A man's touch.

A man's taste.

The warmth of his hand and the heat of his kiss dissipated on the ninth bong.

"I'll try not to hurt you," forced open her eyes.

The motionless bell continued to vibrate the night.

Rose gazed up at Jack Lodoun. "I'm not Cynthia Whitcox."

She didn't need to be wooed and coaxed into his bed.

Underneath the brim of his hat, the darkness in his gaze glittered. "And I'm not Jonathon Clarring."

He was not a gentle man. Unlike her husband.

Truth compelled Rose to speak. "I'm glad."

His eyelashes closed for a long second, as if her confession brought him pain. Shadow hollowed out his cheeks.

Approaching footsteps snapped open his eyes. His fingers that clasped her elbow pulsed in time to her vagina. "Would you like supper?"

They had lived alone for too long.

"What I would like"—Rose paused a heartbeat before initiating intimacy—"Jack, is for us to go home."

Footsteps veered, heel taps receding. Masculine laughter drifted, faded into the careen of grinding wheels.

The impenetrable blackness that was Jack Lodoun's gaze bored into Rose.

"Last night . . . when I got to my town house . . ." A long, tapered finger branded her cheek. ". . . I fucked my fist."

The imagery his words conjured was explicit.

"When you reached orgasm," Rose queried, breasts swelling, chest hurting, "who was with you?"

"You, Rose Clarring." Her presence had not been entirely welcome. "You were with me."

Rose blinked away scalding moisture. "I purchased a tin of machines."

The chemist had blushed with the shame of which she was curiously devoid.

His hand dropped. "I have my own."

"I meant what I said," Rose said, and did not know why: There could be no lasting relationship between the two of them. "I don't want any man's child."

"And I meant what I said," Jack Lodoun returned, turning, firmly cupping her elbow. "I want nothing more than to share the pleasure of your body."

Pleasure rattled on the wheels of an approaching Clarence cab, dual lamps a bobbing blur of light.

Pinching fingers dug into her skin. Jack Lodoun did not hail the cab.

Still tied to the past.

A dusky black horse—breath steaming the night—raced toward them. A shadow slashed through the darkness, the slice of an umbrella and a swinging satchel. The horse pulled to the curb, head shaking in protest, reins jingling.

Jack Lodoun secured Rose's elbow when she stepped up onto an iron stair. He followed her into the black cavity of the hansom cab—hip abridging her hip—and closed the door, sealing them in darkness.

The pulsation inside her vagina spread to her hip.

The cab lurched forward.

"Do you have to return to Parliament tonight?"

His gaze touched her breasts. "No."

The pulsation inside her hip spread to her breasts. "Do all MPs break for supper?"

"Yes." His gaze touched her lips. "Why?"

The pulsation inside her breasts spread to her lips. "I've not seen that many men."

"Not everyone leaves the building. There's a dining room inside. A tunnel leads to St. Stephen's Club, for those who wish to dine there. As for the others"—the shrug of a shoulder abraded Rose's shoulder; the grating crunch of wheels on pavement turned into the hard vibration of wheels crossing an iron bridge—"House members have private entrances."

Unrelieved darkness framed Jack Lodoun.

"But you don't use them?" Rose asked.

"I prefer the St. Stephen's Hall entrance."

Rose had never been inside Westminster Palace. But she didn't want to think about the place that legislated the lives of women.

"I stretched myself," she offered. "Before I came to you."

"With the dildo?" His dark gaze probed hers, hip rubbing and grinding her hip while underneath her the hard leather bench rubbed and ground her vulva.

"I wanted to be"—Rose swallowed—"I didn't want you to have to stretch me."

As he had stretched the woman he loved.

The hard vibration of iron became a grating crunch of pavement.

Passing lamplight set afire the hair framing Jack Lodoun's lean face and illuminated a chiseled lip. "Did you orgasm?"

The left wheel dropped into a pothole.

Rose grabbed a leather pull. "No."

"Why not?"

The climax she had not precipitated suddenly throbbed inside her vagina, open and vulnerable now, penetrated by a hard prick if not by passion. "I didn't want to be alone."

Her hand that was clenched inside her lap independently lifted.

Rose's breath caught inside her chest.

"When you stretched yourself"—Jack Lodoun peeled off her leather glove—"did you insert it all the way in?"

Chill air inch by inch embraced her fingers. "Yes."

"Did you imagine it was my cock that stretched you?"

Inch by inch.

"Yes."

He pressed the palm of his hand against the palm of her hand: Instantly the heat throbbing inside her hip, breasts and vagina spread to her fingers.

"Was I gentle?"

Heat licked her cheeks. "No."

"You weren't gentle last night." His breath feathered her cheek, cooler than her skin. "Did you hurt yourself?"

"A little," Rose admitted. The muscles inside her lower abdomen constricted in memory of burning invasion. "At first."

"When you stretched yourself this evening"—naked fingers slid between her naked fingers—"were you tender?"

The intimate connection swelled her breasts until Rose had no room inside her body for oxygen.

"Yes," she said.

She was tender still.

"Will I hurt you?"

Rose closed her eyes against the stark touch of his hand and the finality of her actions; darkness pulsed against her lids. "I don't know."

She did not lie.

Rose did not know how much this man would hurt her. She did not know to what extent her actions this night would hurt others.

She only knew that she would pay a price for her pleasure. As Jack Lodoun continued to pay for his.

"You said you enjoyed sex," she managed.

"Yes."

Rose attempted to pull her thoughts away from his fingers that bound her, and his hip and shoulder that ground into hers. "What do you most enjoy about it?"

"Touching." Fingers hugging her fingers—a separate pulse beat in each of her five knuckles—Jack Lodoun rested their clasped hands on her thigh. Their combined heat penetrated the wool of her dress. "Holding."

Jack Lodoun outwardly appeared cold and untouchable. His simple desire for tactile contact squeezed a part of her that was neither her heart nor her womb, yet was connected to both.

"Will you stay the night?" Rose asked.

"Yes."

The tears that had earlier scalded Rose's eyes tightened her chest.

"I hired a housekeeper today," she offered, needing to share more than just the pain of desire.

"She let me in, earlier," tickled her cheek. "Will she be there tonight?"

The cry orgasm had forced out of her reverberated over the grind of wheels.

Rose could not imagine engaging in physical intimacy with this man while another person resided in the same house.

"She has her own family to care for," she shakily explained, "so she'll be going home in the afternoon. She'll be back tomorrow morning. She said she'd bring a cook and a maid with her."

"Did she have good references?"

It was so ridiculous, discussing domestic help when his linked fingers were melting the flesh off her bones.

"Her references were well enough."

Not perfect. But Rose had given up the right to expect perfection.

"Will the cook and maid be living in?"

The cab turned. Rose clung to the leather grip.

Hard muscles and grinding, vibrating wood sandwiched her hip and shoulders.

The cab straightened. The pressure of Jack's fingers remained hard and binding.

"No," she said.

They, too, had families of their own.

"Will you allow me to win you a separation?"

Rose stiffened in rejection. But she could no longer deny the precariousness of a woman's legal standing.

Frances Hart had won liberation from her son, but only because the man beside her had withheld evidence.

"Yes," Rose said, hand tightening around the darkness that embraced her fingers. And then, because it could no longer be avoided, she asked: "Why didn't you offer to procure a separation for Mrs. Whitcox?"

The cab abruptly halted, wheels rolling backward . . . forward.

"Whoa, Bessy," penetrated wood and glass. "Whoa there, I say."

The heat that suddenly crushed her fingers evaporated into chill night air. Cool leather weighted her palm, the glove he had earlier removed.

For a long second she didn't think he'd answer.

But then he did.

"For the same reason I didn't ask James Whitcox for a divorce," he said.

Jack Lodoun had needed Rose to see him. Rose did indeed see.

Chapter 16

"You loved Parliament more than you loved Mrs. Whitcox," Rose Clarring deduced.

"*Power,*" Jack bluntly corrected. "Not Parliament."

Inside the cab window, two pale images framed swivelling equine ears.

Rose Clarring. Jack Lodoun.

A woman who betrayed her husband. A man who had betrayed his lover.

Metal jangled. The cab rocked.

"I chose power," he repeated.

Jack would live with the knowledge of the choice he had made for the rest of his life. And so would Rose.

Standing—umbrella and satchel weighting his right hand—he threw open the cab door. Digging out a florin from his coat, he tossed it upward.

Deft fingers caught the tumbling silver; immediately the cabby—age and face indiscernible in the dual lamplights of the hansom—settled back and bunched a scarf over the lower half of his face.

Turning, fingers throbbing as if they were his cock, Jack held out his left hand.

The incurious eyes of the cabby prickled his skin.

He had seen Rose Clarring. He now possessed her address.

Reporters would pay handsomely for the cabby's information.

Pale, slender fingers reached out of the flickering darkness and firmly clasped his fingers.

Sensation fisted inside Jack's chest.

Rose had such small hands.

She stood, eyes momentarily glinting blue in the lamplight. Turning—the platform stabilized by his weight—she stepped down off the cab into darkness.

Jack followed, platform tilting, groaning, no one to offset his actions.

The blue of the row house was black in the night.

Head bowed—blond hair bleeding into black wool—Rose unlocked the door.

Jack stepped into unmitigated blackness and turned the bolt.

The finality of their actions echoed inside the foyer.

Gas hissed. Blue light sparked. White fire flamed.

Rose lit a crystal sconce; a bronze-framed mirror and a cherry table leapt out of the darkness.

Jack leaned leather burgundy against clawed brass. Straightening, he hooked his umbrella on the narrow coat tree and shrugged out of his coat.

"I don't have brandy," reverberated off the naked expanse of wood flooring and empty walls; a small hand offered a black cloak, "but there's wine, if you'd like. . . ."

Rose's voice trailed off uncertainly.

Jack accepted her cloak and hung it beside his.

He didn't want wine. He wanted her to hold him.

He wanted her to accept what he could not.

"Wine will be fine," Jack said, hooking her black bonnet onto the coat tree beside his gray hat.

Retreating heel taps clattered down the hallway.

The Noes Lobby was carpeted; Jack's passage between the Division desks had made no sound when he had voted—not for law but for the party.

The tie knotting his throat tightened like a noose.

Grabbing the tin of matches out of the top drawer of the small foyer table, he climbed the narrow stairs.

The first door opened into a rectangular room empty of furniture. Jack tried the second door.

White porcelain gleamed.

The small bathroom smelled of Rose.

There was no gas upstairs. He lit an oil-filled sconce.

Nickle-plated pipes gleamed in the flickering light. A damp pink towel draped a circular curtain ring.

Jack's stomach clenched, realizing Rose had showered before visiting him.

He lifted the wooden lid on the toilet.

A stair creaked in warning.

Unfastening four of five trouser buttons, Jack pulled out his semiswollen flesh and aimed it downward.

Approaching heel taps clicked.

Water splattered water.

The sharp heel taps abruptly halted.

Out of the corner of his eyes Jack glimpsed Rose, black-clothed body framed by dark walnut.

In her two hands she held a bottle of wine and two water glasses.

She did not turn away. Jack did not stop urinating.

"I opened the wine," she said quietly.

Her interested gaze danced up and down his vertebrae.

Jack shook himself before unfastening the last trouser button. "I'm going to shower."

He didn't want to go to her smelling of politics.

Jack jerked the porcelain pull; the toilet loudly flushed in the silence.

Still Rose did not turn away.

Releasing the front closure of his suspenders, Jack hooked his thumbs into the band of his trousers and smallclothes.

"I'll get you a clean towel," she said, watching the two layers of wool slide over his hips.

Her gaze latched onto his cock.

He grew longer. He grew harder.

"This is fine," Jack said, stepping out of his trousers and smallclothes. Straightening . . . shirttail bunching around the base of his shaft . . . he grabbed the towel she had earlier used and brought it to his face. "It smells of you."

"I don't . . ." Uncertainty hitched her voice. "In what way?"

Jack tossed the towel into the plain, white porcelain sink, heavy sex swinging. "It smells like roses."

"It's the soap," she offered.

Gaze snaring Rose's gaze, Jack shrugged out of his jacket. Securing the bottle of wine between her breast and her left forearm, Rose stepped over the threshold and extended her right hand for gray, pinstriped wool.

The sharp feeling he had felt earlier while standing on the cab gauging her small hand squeezed his chest until he struggled to breathe.

This woman could lose her liberty. For no other reason than taking his body into hers.

Jack said neutrally, "Then I'll smell like roses, too."

A welcome scent over the stench of greed and power.

Rose accepted each article of clothing: waistcoat, shirt—his sex sprang free—vest. Dropping down the lid to the toilet, he sat—engorged cock dangling inside the commode—and peeled off his shoes and socks.

"When you . . ." Rose hesitated; Jack stepped into the shower, her gaze branding his buttocks. ". . . fucked your fist last night, did you touch yourself like you did the other night?"

A tear of excitement was squeezed out of his swollen glans.

"Yes," Jack said, pulling the curtain closed.

Metal hooks sliding around a circular metal rod scraped his skin.

"Do you like it when a woman touches you like that?" breached the curtain.

The water was cold. His cock was hot.

"Yes."

"Had a woman ever watched you before?" Rose asked over the stinging drone of the shower.

Hot water invaded the cold. Gray steam spiraled upward like cigar smoke.

Jack reached for the soap dish embedded in the tiled wall. "No."

The truth.

No woman had ever seen his naked emotions.

"I'm glad I was the first, Jack."

The scent of roses grew with each lather of his hands. "Are you, Rose?"

Would she still be glad come the morning?

Raining water greeted his question.

Jack showered off the soap: Rose was gone.

Emotion knifed through him.

Rose had collected his trousers, smallclothes, shoes and socks, and laid down a towel in their stead. Protecting him from the danger of slipping on wet tile.

But who would protect Rose?

Roughly Jack dried and draped the two towels—one blue, one pink—over the curtain ring.

No personal artifacts cluttered the white marble-topped washstand.

Jack opened the top side drawer.

Various jars, a toothbrush and tin of toothpowder gleamed in the shadowy depths.

The second drawer contained the comb he sought; it lay on top of a stack of washcloths beside a silver-plated mirror and hairbrush.

A gold hair shone in the flickering light.

He was overcome by the need to know Rose.

The bottle of Rose's Lubrifiant occupied the third drawer, pushed between wood and thick towels. The top towel bulged with a familiar shape.

Jack remembered Rose's utter loneliness when she had climaxed.

He did not know if he would see the same terrible solitude in her eyes when she came with his cock buried deep inside her. But he could hope that tonight would be worth the pain that the morrow would bring.

Jack returned the comb to the second drawer.

Engorged cock feinting the air, he walked naked to the bedroom at the end of the narrow corridor.

An oil lamp lit an iron bed. A rose-quilted duvet and a white sheet were turned down in readiness.

The bottle of wine waited on a walnut nightstand, two mismatched water glasses carefully arranged in front of it.

Pale movement snared his gaze.

Rose squatted in front of a small iron fireplace.

White cotton hugged her hips and buttocks. Gold and shadow streaked her shoulder-length hair.

Jack had told her she was a very pretty woman. He had lied: Rose Clarring was a beautiful woman.

His gray, pinstriped frock coat hung from an oval mirror. His trousers and smallclothes were neatly folded on top of a scar-pitted chest.

Bare feet silent, Jack padded across the wooden floor and reached into the inner pocket of his jacket.

His fingers closed around cold metal. Her fingers imprinted the small of his back.

"May I?" Rose asked.

Straightening, turning . . . spine tingling . . . Jack gave her the small, silver-plated condom holder: It fit in the palm of her hand.

"This is much more attractive than a tin bearing Queen Victoria's likeness," she huskily observed.

Above the silver holder, light and shadow caressed the tops of her breasts, plunged inside the low-cut white cotton chemise. Dark nipples edged the square neckline.

"Gladstone's image is quite popular, too," Jack said, hands fisting to prevent himself from taking more than she offered.

Rose glanced up. "I would think the likeness of Mr. Gladstone would wilt any erection."

The image of the dour queen chased away that of the stern statesman.

"I assure you, not nearly as quickly as the thought of begetting nine children," Jack said dryly.

The budding smile faded from her eyes.

She tilted her head downward, gaze hidden by the fan of gold-tipped lashes. A small snap exploded the silence.

Jack glanced at the silver holder she had opened, and the six compartments that each held a condom.

Carefully Rose selected a rolled sheath. "Have you ever wanted children?"

Silently Jack took the condom holder out of her hand and snapped it closed. "No."

"Why not?"

Jack envisioned his parents, mother worn-out from childbearing, father a bantam rooster, ruling his roost.

They resembled the queen and the former prime minister, he thought.

Cynicism curling his lips, he tossed the condom holder onto the bed. "I never fancied procreating for God and country."

Heat jolted up his urethra.

"Do you have brothers to carry on your name?"

Was Jonathon Clarring the last of his line?

"Yes," Jack said, watching Rose's somber face as she explored his cock.

A sharp nail traced blood veins that throbbed inside his eyes.

"You watched me in the bookshop."

Jack watched her now.

Testing his weight. Measuring his circumference.

Outlining the taut ring of his foreskin.

Her lashes flickered. "Did you feel my touch, Jack?"

"Yes," he said.

Each probe. Each glide.

"Your skin is so soft here." A small fingertip—smooth and gentle instead of rough and blunt—spread the slick lubrication of his desire over his glans. "Softer than leather."

Fighting off a wave of vulnerability, Jack reached up—carefully cradling her face between his hands—and gave her unimpeded access to his body. "I'm not a dildo."

Just a politician.

. . . *and didst commit whoredom* . . .

"I'm not experienced." Head tilted downward—gaze hidden by the fan of her lashes—Rose positioned the condom. "But neither am I an ignorant bride."

Gritting his teeth, Jack concentrated on the baby-fine hair that clung to his hands and her cheekbones that pulsed against his palms rather than the rubber that slipped and slid and the fingers that struggled to harness him.

"I know what I want, Jack."

Firmly she gripped the base of his shaft with her left hand. Rubber ballooned over his glans.

"What do you want, Rose?" Jack asked, his heart beating inside his cock.

"You." Shadow licked her lips. Rubber pinched his frenulum. "Like this. Hard. Erect. Wanting me."

The truth weighed more heavily than the blood that pulsed inside his cock.

She had said she would pay the price. But she did not yet know the cost.

Rubber squeezed Jack's chest.

"I'm not a dildo," he repeated, fingertips digging into soft hair and warm skin, independently seeking the essence of Rose Clarring. "When you take my cock inside you, you will lose all your legal rights."

"Exactly what rights will I be losing?" she countered, gaze lowered, face solemn. "The right to sleep alone each night?"

"A woman charged with adultery forfeits custody of her children and maintenance from her husband," Jack said bluntly.

"I don't have children." Rubber banded the base of his cock and trapped pubic hair, a sharp pang. A soft finger immediately freed the sensitive hair. "And I don't need my husband to support me."

The heat of Rose's hand was replaced by chill air, cock clothed in rubber while Jack stood naked.

"I know what you are, Jack."

Jack had once thought he knew what he was: He had proven himself wrong.

Ten heartbeats imprinted his chest.

Her right hand. Her left hand that still bore the mark of matrimony.

A sharp nail scraped his nipple.

Jack fisted his fingers in Rose's hair and pulled back her head.

He stared at the dark valley between her breasts. He stared at her lips that did not smile.

He met her gaze, black orbs ringed by cornflower blue. "What am I, Rose?"

"You're my lover, and you're in pain." Her fingers tightened in his chest hair, taking the pain he gave her, but giving pain in return. "I want to give you comfort."

"What if you find," Jack asked, glans crying for the solace she offered, "that fucking my cock is no different than fucking a dildo?"

Chapter 17

"Then at least I'll know."

Jack did not know which would hurt Rose the most, fucking without passion or finding passion with a man she did not love.

"And when you do?" Jack asked. An ember popped, small explosion skidding down his spine. "Will you return to your husband?"

Light defined a golden eyebrow; shadow fingered an oval cheek.

"No," Rose said finally, with finality. "I will not go back to Jonathon."

Jack remembered the silence inside his town house each time Cynthia had returned to James Whitcox.

But Rose was not Cynthia.

Lowering his head, he grazed her lips with his.

She smelled differently, of roses rather than bergamot.

Jack opened his mouth, tongue probing.

She tasted differently, of need rather than desire.

Rose opened her mouth.

She kissed differently, sharing the price of pleasure.

Jack had taught Cynthia Whitcox how to kiss. How to fuck. He now knew a man could not teach a woman how to love.

A moist tongue touched his tongue.

Breath rasping his throat, Jack closed his eyes and explored Rose.

The sharpness of hard enamel. The softness of slick muscle.

The sensitivity of a textured palette.

Rose sucked in his breath, unused to a man kissing her with his tongue.

Jack didn't want to tutor another woman.

He sucked in her tongue.

Smelling Rose. Tasting Rose.

Willing Rose to take him, as he would take her.

Tentatively she explored his mouth.

The muscles underneath his tongue. The ridged slope of his palette.

Jack had the curious sensation of drowning in Rose.

A finger flicked his nipple.

Jack's cock jerked, reaching for Rose.

"Jack," filled his mouth.

He tasted her lips that were slick with his saliva. "What?"

"Do you ever lie awake"—hot, moist breath expanded his lungs—"aching to be touched?"

Every night he lay awake, aching.

Jack pressed his lips into the bridge of flesh formed by cheek and nose; underneath the softness of skin he found a steady thrum: It matched his heartbeat. "Yes."

"When you lie there, alone"—Rose experimentally pinched his nipple between her thumb and forefinger—"do you touch your breasts?"

Jack inhaled the scent of springtime roses. "No."

"I do," seared his chin.

The image of Rose poised on the brink of orgasm—small hand grasping her breast—flickered behind his closed eyelids.

"I roll my nipples like this"—the twisting motion of a thumb and forefinger knotted his testicles—"and pretend my fingers are a mouth."

Jack's lips independently sought fluttering eyelashes . . . the feathery protrusion of an eyebrow . . . the warm indentation of a temple.

"But they're not a mouth, Jack."

Her solitude pulsed against his lips.

"Fingers don't kiss," Rose whispered.

Shoulders stooping, head bending—resisting his hand that clenched in her hair to hold her close—Rose brushed his nipple with her lips.

Jack's heart constricted.

"Fingers don't taste."

Liquid heat licked him.

Jack cradled the back of her head, flyaway hair clinging to his skin.

"Fingers don't love."

A wet furnace enveloped him.

Jack's body curved over Rose.

"I know you don't love me," Rose said, mouth a wet kiss over his drumming heart, "but I would rather lose everything I have than endure one more night of loneliness."

Jack opened his eyes and stared down at a knitted blond brow and a straight nose, all that he could see of Rose's face.

The need to give her the love her husband did not was a visceral pang.

"When I lie alone at night, aching"—he curved his fingers, shaping fragile bone, there a vertebra. Reaching down, he fisted his hands into soft cotton—"I touch my cock."

"Last night . . ." Rose straightened, chill air biting his wet nipple. "Did you pretend it was I who touched you?"

As she had earlier pretended it was his cock that stretched her.

Jack jerked up the cotton he fisted, forcing up Rose's arms.

"I didn't want you to touch me," he said, brutally honest, chemise fluttering to the floor.

He still didn't.

Rose did not hide her body, nipples hard, shadow-caressed hair tumbling to her shoulders.

The pain his words caused twisted his stomach.

Jack clasped soft skin that would bruise so easily—all he need do was sink his fingers into her waist a little more deeply—and lifted. Simultaneously he turned.

A startled cry was answered by a popping ember.

Her legs flailed: a hard knee . . . stubbing toes. Sharp fingernails carved his biceps.

Jack sat her down. Flesh slapped wood.

The chest of drawers gave her height, aligning her sex with his sex.

Her breasts—small, perfect breasts that she had milked to replicate the love of a man—rapidly rose and fell.

Holding her gaze—watching her startled surprise transform into sexual awareness—Jack stepped between her thighs.

The crown of his cock notched the opening to her vagina. The admission of her loneliness continued to burn his chest.

"I wanted you to fuck me"—Jack slid his hands down over her hips . . . between her thighs . . . in between the hard wood of the chest, a cushion of wool trousers and the softness of feminine buttocks—"like you fucked the dildo."

Rose gripped his shoulders, fingers blistering his skin; her flesh . . . stretched from his likeness . . . swallowed his glans.

The thin ring of blue surrounding her pupils disappeared.

Purposefully Jack fed her images of raw sexuality to overcome the pain of his occupation.

"Your sex is a dusky pink, like your lips." Bending, Jack tasted the flush that stained her cheek. Rose jerked her head back from the unfamiliar caress. He breathed against her skin, drying the wetness of his saliva. "When you fucked yourself, it ate the leather." Pretty pink swallowing base brown. "Last night . . . in my thoughts . . . it was *my* cock that made a mouth of your vagina."

Rose turned her face into his; moist heat serrated the bridge of his nose.

The simple intimacy—a woman's breath, a woman's touch—clenched his groin.

"Do you want to know what you did, Rose"—an electric lick seared his cheek; Rose tasted him, as he had tasted her—"while I fucked you?"

Slick lips moved against his skin, as hot and wet as the lips that embraced his cock. "What did I do, Jack?"

"You took me like you took the dildo. Hard. Deep. All the way inside until I kissed your womb." Lifting his head—holding her gaze—Jack dug his fingers into the softness of her buttocks and fed her his cock. "Like this."

He watched Rose take the reality of a man instead of the image of a man.

He watched her pain, becoming an adulteress. He watched her pleasure, taking a lover.

He filled her until his pubic hair meshed with her pubic hair and the wetness of her desire leaked onto his testicles.

The ragged hitch of her breath sounded over a wafting chime.

"You breathed . . ." Leaning down, Jack licked the dusky pink rose that blossomed inside her cheek. Eyelashes shielding the hurt he caused, Rose turned her face upward for his caress. ". . . my breath."

The breath that belonged to another woman.

Lips sliding across rose-scented flesh, Jack kissed Rose, his tongue filling her mouth as his cock filled her vagina.

Her flesh fluttered around him.

"You ached from me, and for me," he whispered inside the wet heat of her mouth, "and you fought to take more of me."

Holding her buttocks, Jack fucked Rose until the chest of drawers rocked underneath them and he felt her hurt, tender still from the dildo with which she had stretched herself.

"Jack." Fingernails stabbed his shoulders; inside her eyes blue uncertainty diluted black need, teetering between pleasure and pain. "Jack."

But he could not stop the pain their actions this night had catalyzed.

"You cried out for me to fuck you deeper . . . and *harder* . . . and deeper until my cock was a part of you," Jack whispered raggedly. "And I did, Rose." Jack fought for air. "I fucked you until my cock became you. And you cried." Jack's cock cried for the hurt he caused. "You cried for me."

While the memory of another woman's cries chased his ejaculation.

Holding Rose's gaze that was suddenly devoid of color, Jack angled his hips so that the thickest part of his penis pushed against the most sensitive part of her vagina. Giving her pleasure to counteract the coming pain.

He tunneled in, pushing apart the flesh that he stole from her husband. He tunneled out, leaving behind the tears of the woman he had betrayed.

The wooden chest legs *tap-tap-tapp*ed with each thrust. A wooden rail dug into his knuckles with each withdrawal.

He fucked her deeper . . . and *harder* . . . and deeper until all that stood between them was a thin sheath of rubber.

Jack saw her pending orgasm, black pupils shrinking to tiny pinpricks. And then Jack felt her orgasm, ballooning flesh swallowing him.

No cry of pleasure filled the void of illicit sex.

Rose closed her eyes and shut him out, fisting fingers and vagina hurting him.

Jack buried his face in the rose-scented hollow of her neck and shoulder and thrust so deeply he kissed her womb and came, hot sperm shooting into a rubber casing.

A pulse frantically beat against his lips; it did not slow with the ebbing of her contractions.

Lungs laboring, sweat stinging his cheeks—afraid of what he would see when he gazed at her face—Jack slid his hands out from underneath her buttocks and lifted her onto his still-ejaculating cock.

Her legs limply embraced his thighs.

Jack wanted to comfort her: He knew he could not.

Shrinking cock plugging her vagina, Jack carried her to bed, each breath she exhaled scorching his skin.

Planting a knee on the mattress—metal coils squealing, her sex nipping his—he let her go.

Gold hair threaded with brown shadow spilled across cotton that would never again be innocent white: She had taken pleasure in a man who was not her husband.

Crystalline liquid glinted in the shadow of her temple.

Rose did not open her eyes when he left the bed, mattress lurching upward.

Tugging off the condom that flaccidly dangled like a foreskin, Jack padded down the barren hallway and flushed the sheath down the toilet.

Rose lay where he had positioned her, flushed breasts rising and falling, nipples beaded, eyes closed.

She was not asleep.

He could feel her breath as if it were his own. He could feel the emotions coursing through her body.

Betrayal. Grief.

Need that did not die.

They were his emotions.

Jack stood beside the bed, cock wet from his sperm.

Cold.

Aching.

Alone.

Abruptly her eyes opened. They were a clear cornflower blue. "I'm not a doll, Jack."

He thought of the men in her life—husband, brothers and father—who had shielded her from the dangers of a man's sexuality.

"I know what you are, Rose," Jack returned flatly.

"A whore?" she suggested, voice equally flat.

"A woman in pain."

The cornflower blue shrank. "Can you take away the pain?"

He would not lie.

"No."

Five bongs permeated wood, glass and sorrow.

"I ache," Rose said on a sixth bong, dark eyes filling with tears.

A seventh bong closed his lids against the dull throb that inched up from his cock and swelled his chest.

"I ache from you, Jack," reverberated over an eighth bong. A ninth bong carried: "And I ache for you."

A final tenth bong sounded over a combusting ember, Parliament still in session.

Slowly Jack opened his eyes.

Rose slid her right knee upward, left leg fanning outward. Sharing with him her ache for intimacy.

The inverted arrow of gold hair that framed her vulva glistened with the wetness he had created. The dark fissure between the swollen, dusky pink lips was an open portal.

Stretched for him. And then by him.

The tears her vagina leaked burned his eyes.

She still wanted him. *Knowing* the price she would pay.

Jack lay on cool, crisp cotton—mattress and springs sharply dipping with his weight—and cupped her soft hips that had never been stretched by a child.

He could see her: Her swollen glans peeped out of a fleshy

prepuce. He could smell her: The sweetness of roses blended with the spice of sexual arousal.

Rose had said he didn't love her—and he did not love her as he had loved Cynthia Whitcox—but Jack could no longer deny the need she evoked.

He kissed her portal that he had rubbed raw with friction and licked away her pain.

Small hands cradled his head.

Jack licked a wet line between dusky pink lips and kissed her hard little glans, dark red like his glans.

Her fingers fisted inside his hair.

Jack licked until sharp, cacophonous cries pierced the harsh soughing of his breathing and the hard little glans that pulsed in rhythm to his heartbeat slipped back inside a snug prepuce.

She had cried tears for her husband. Now she cried out the name of her lover.

Invisible fingers crushed his testicles.

Blindly he sought her vagina, fluted tongue probing the mouth he had made.

Gentle muscles fluttered around him.

Kissing him. Tasting him.

Loving him.

Innocent of sin. No matter that the law said otherwise.

Jack pushed up her body and braced his forearms on either side of her narrow shoulders.

His naked cock pulsed against her naked pelvis.

Blue eyes probed his gaze . . . solemnly studied his mouth.

A soft fingertip burned his chin. "You're wet."

"From you, Rose," he bluntly returned.

Her gaze slid upward.

Jack brushed her lips with his, sharing with her the pleasure her husband had not. "This is what your orgasm tastes like."

Uncertainty shadowed her face, was overcome by curiosity.

Rose opened her mouth and tasted the tongue he fed her.

Pleasure-pain blackening her eyes, she threaded her fingers through his whiskers. "What are we going to do, Jack?"

She was a woman who loved another man. He was a man who loved another woman.

"I'm going to suckle your breast until your heart pounds against the tip of my tongue and you come," Jack said.

The yearning inside her eyes hurt him where a man should not be able to hurt.

"And then I'm going to fuck you, Rose, until my cock becomes a part of you, and you cry for the pleasure I give you."

The tears she had cried for her husband moistened her eyes.

A trembling finger rimmed his ear. "What will you do, Jack, when I cry for the pleasure you give me?"

He would not lie.

"I don't know."

Jack didn't know if he could ever let go of the woman his love had killed.

Chapter 18

Chirping agitation awoke Rose to unfamiliar heat.

It weighted her breast. It anchored her abdomen.

It rode her thighs.

Images burst behind her eyelids.

Brown hair black with water. Purple-blue eyes black with need.

A muffled bong scattered the memories: Three more bongs followed.

Eyes opening, Rose stared at the pink-and-gray shadows that painted the ceiling.

The night was over. Now it was morning.

The feminine scent of roses vied with the masculine smells of spice and musk.

Hand drifting upward, she lightly traced soft hair, a sideburn that became wiry whiskers. Prickly morning stubble encroached either side of the wiry hair.

A sudden gust of hot breath serrated the valley between her breasts.

Jack Lodoun sighed. Jack Lodoun snuggled closer.

Moist heat kissed her hip, elongating flesh achingly familiar.

Tears burned her eyes.

She was an adulteress in deed as well as thought.

Rose slid out from underneath Jack.

His arm hooked her waist, refusing to let her go.

The sensation that knifed through Rose was sharper than the loneliness induced by a passing carriage.

Slowly Jack relaxed in boneless sleep. Equally as slowly, Rose peeled back the covers and sat up.

A pinching ache stabbed through her pelvis.

Carefully she slid off the bed—the spring coils softly squeaked—and padded down the dawn-streaked hallway.

Every step reminded her of Jack Lodoun.

His circumference. His length.

Firmly she closed the bathroom door.

Blackness cocooned her.

Rose found the tin of matches Jack had left by the sink.

White porcelain gleamed.

Rose touched the flaming match to a black wick.

Nickle-plated pipes leapt out of the darkness. Blue and pink towels cast dual black shadows.

The tears burning her eyes clogged her throat.

Jack had neatly hung up the towels she had laid out for him.

Rose relieved herself and gently padded dry tender flesh with a Bromo tissue.

Jack had twice flushed a condom down the toilet, the gurgle of pipes wafting down the hallway. Rose tugged a ceramic pull.

She held still for long seconds, willing the flush not to awaken him.

Jack had touched a place inside her body that she had not known existed, and she did not know what to do.

Habit came to her rescue.

She twisted a white enameled tap. Water gushed out of the nickle-plated spout.

Rose scrubbed her hands before grabbing up the toothbrush and tin of powder from the cabinet drawer. Vigorously she brushed her teeth, salty powder replacing the taste of musky spice. Leaning over the sink, she cupped cold, clear water and rinsed out her mouth.

The reflection inside the mirror snagged her gaze.

The woman's breasts were elongated, left nipple dark and ripe like a sun-kissed grape dangling from the vine.

Straightening—shutting off the cascading water, fingers dripping liquid diamonds—Rose touched her nipple.

Remembered sensation jolted through her.

The hot suction of Jack's mouth. The sharp edge of Jack's teeth.

Irresistibly she reached between her legs.

The valley between her labia was fever hot.

Rose reached farther back, sliding fingers plunging inside a hot, wet mouth.

The heat gripping her fingers grasped her left hip.

Rose jerked upright.

Purple-blue eyes riveted her.

Inside Jack's gaze was the knowledge of her sexuality.

Her breasts she had squeezed. Her clitoris she had caressed.

Her vagina he had caught her exploring.

He had smelled her. He had tasted her.

There was nothing this man did not know about her body.

A wave of vulnerability crashed over Rose.

"I didn't mean to wake you," she politely apologized, as if they met in public, two strangers fully clothed.

The heat clasping her hip dissipated.

Jack stepped around Rose. "You have noisy birds, Mrs. Clarring."

Rose followed his motions through the trail of sounds he created:

the sharp clip of the wooden toilet seat banging a metal water pipe . . . the splatter of water.

Uncertainty—raw and jagged—streaked through her. She twisted on the faucet and rinsed off her toothbrush. "I'm sorry."

The toilet flushed.

Moist heat nestled in the small of her back. At the same time purple-blue eyes pinned her gaze.

"Are you?" he asked, voice neutral.

He was a full head taller than she.

She studied his chin—dark with stubble—that reached above the top of her head. She studied his mouth—bottom lip full, top lip chiseled—that had shared with her the taste of her orgasm. She studied his nose—break invisible in the flickering light—that had nuzzled her cheek and temple.

"No." She squarely met his gaze. "I do not regret our night together."

Hard, prickly heat caged her ribs.

Between one heartbeat and the next, Jack plucked the toothbrush out of her hand.

Tapping toothpowder into the palm of his right hand—his left arm lifting up her left breast—he dipped the toothbrush into the cleaning powder.

Briskly he brushed his teeth.

He had white teeth, eyeteeth a little longer and sharper than the others.

Pain flared through her.

She had never seen Jonathon brush his teeth.

With each brushing motion Jack's chest hair prickled her back and his penis prodded her buttocks.

Intimacies shared only with lovers.

Leaning to the side of Rose, Jack rinsed out his mouth.

The roar of cascading water abruptly died.

Arms that glinted with red-and-gold fire banded her breasts. The weight of his chin clenched her womb.

Jack stared at her for long seconds before dark lashes lowered and fanned his cheeks.

Icy water dripped from his hand and trickled down her hip.

Memory overrode the wafting chirp of sparrows.

He had churned her vagina until the sound of her wetness had rode the pop of embers and perspiration glued their bodies. He had thrust until the squeal of springs matched the soughing of her breath and the bedcovers slithered to the floor. He had pounded until she had begged him to fuck her deeper, *harder*.

And he had.

Rose had cried out his name with each splintering spasm of orgasm.

"When you suckled my breast"—she spoke past the tightness in her chest—"did you feel my heartbeat?"

The dark lashes fluttered open. "When I fucked you, did my cock become a part of you?"

She would not lie.

"No."

His chest that rhythmically swelled and ebbed against her shoulder blades stilled.

"I felt the machine"—unfeeling, desensitizing rubber—"not your cock."

Blackness ate up the purple inside his eyes. "Would you like my naked cock inside you, Rose?"

"Yes." She needed to overcome the memories of the past. "I would like to feel you ejaculate inside me."

His eyes closed.

He had enviably long lashes.

She reached up and clasped the hard band of his arms: There was no delicate way to ask, so she mimicked his bluntness.

"Will you"—Rose swallowed *love me*—"bugger me?"

The long lashes lifted: The desire that blazed inside his eyes nearly blinded her. "I don't want to hurt you, Rose."

But he would.

"The price of passion, Jack."

He closed his eyes and tightened his arms until the bathroom shrank and all that existed was Jack Lodoun: his scent, his heat, the prickly texture of his hair and skin.

A slick tear slid down the dark crevice between her buttocks.

The arms holding her abruptly loosened. Leaning down, Jack opened the third drawer.

Shock rippled through her.

Jack straightened. His gaze caught hers in the mirror.

"After I showered, I needed a comb."

Rose held his gaze.

The darkness inside his eyes squeezed her womb. "And then I needed to know you."

So he had rummaged through her drawers.

Rose bit her lip at this unexpected invasion. "Shall we go to the bedroom?"

His eyes assayed her in the mirror. "I want to watch you."

She had not seen Jonathon in the dark: She had only felt the wetness of his ejaculate and his tears.

And then he had left her.

"You're much taller than I." Suddenly, acutely aware of what she requested, she asked: "Will it not be uncomfortable for you?"

There was no light inside his eyes. "I'll manage."

"Will you?"

This man had touched her. But she had touched him, too.

Gold and red danced on either side of his face; his lashes lowered. "Yes."

She forced out the question: "Do you regret last night?"

Solid glass rolled on marble, the crystal stopper.

"No."

There was no regret inside his face, but neither was there evidence of the desire that had moments earlier blazed inside his eyes.

A gurgle of liquid danced on her skin.

On her wedding night she had lain in the dark, heart drumming inside her chest. Rose felt that same mixture of anticipation and apprehension.

"What are you doing?" she asked tensely.

"I'm pouring oil into my hand," he said.

The faint whisper of flesh rubbing flesh permeated the silence.

Rose had no vision of what he did outside the field of the mirror.

The dark lashes flickered, his eyes seeing what she could not.

"Now I'm lubricating my cock."

Out of the corner of her eyes she glimpsed a hand.

Glass impacted marble.

Five fingers cupped her stomach; they were slippery with oil. His head that glinted red and gold in the light lowered, forehead bridging the top of her head. At the same time he touched her there, where she had never before been touched.

Hot air gusted her scalp. "Now I'm lubricating you."

Without warning, his head lifted.

His gaze, darker than night, snagged her gaze. "Now I'm loving you."

He penetrated her.

One finger.

A plugging tip . . . a stretching knuckle.

Rose sucked in chill air.

"When I'm inside you like this, Rose"—the darkness of his gaze pierced her chest—"I *am* loving you."

Another betrayal of the woman he loved.

"When I stretched myself last night," she volunteered unevenly, "I thought about you."

The long finger slowly withdrew.

The stretching knuckle . . . the plugging tip.

"In what way?"

He rimmed her.

Beguiling. Soothing.

"I thought how alone you looked, when you said you needed

someone to understand." Rose breathed deeply, body both beguiled and soothed. "I wondered what you were thinking about, sitting in the House of Commons."

The soothing tip of his finger became the fullness of a knuckle.

"I thought about you," he said unexpectedly, dark gaze intently mapping the effect of his penetration.

A sudden weakness liquefied her bones. "What did you think about?"

"I thought of your pride in the bookstore," Jack said. One finger probed deep between her buttocks; three hard knuckles dug into the softness of her cheeks. "When you wouldn't look away from the men who looked at you."

The slippery descent of his finger was overlaid by the prickly discomfort Rose had felt in the bookshop, her sexuality judged by strangers.

"I thought of the desire inside your face"—one fingertip became two; they crowded her lungs and heart—"when you touched the leather dildo."

The memory of the length and the girth of the artificial phallus dissolved into the length and the girth of his two fingers that lodged deeply between her buttocks.

"I thought of the pain inside your eyes"—the two fingers slipped out of her; inside the dark eyes staring at her she saw the squeeze of her muscles, trying to keep him inside—"when you said you thought love made babies."

He shifted, body unseen but felt.

Suddenly he was only inches taller instead of a head taller.

His gaze—lower, no less acute—did not move from hers.

Slick, blunt flesh licked her. Notched her. Pierced her.

"I thought of the tears you cried"—Jack's slippery fingers spanned her lower abdomen, hitching her closer; at the same time the long, thick glide of his penis stole her breath—"when you took the dildo from my fingers and acceded that passion may not exist."

Rose's head snapped back, cheek impacting bristly skin.

There was no rubber barrier separating his flesh from her flesh.

This was Jack.

His penis that cried tears of desire. *His* chin that was coarse with beard stubble.

His need that matched her need.

"I thought of how vulnerable you were"—he notched his penis so deeply inside her that she could feel the prickle of his pubic hair and the leathery pouch of his testicles; his left arm banded her breasts—"when you cried out in orgasm."

But Jack was not a dildo.

He had tried to warn her the night before. But she had not listened.

"I didn't know it would hurt this much" was wrenched from her throat.

"This?" vibrated her vertebrae.

Slick fingers molding her stomach—as if he could feel his flesh buried inside her flesh—he tunneled so deeply between her buttocks that they were one body, and Rose couldn't breathe for his penis that filled her and the tears that dammed her throat.

"When you're inside me like this, Jack"—the burning stretch of his sex and the intensity inside his eyes dissolved both flesh and bones—"I feel loved."

Another betrayal of the man *she* loved.

Rose curved his slippery fingers around her womb.

The need to comfort Jack superimposed the need to be comforted.

"You asked why I now wanted a divorce," she volunteered.

"Yes," Jack acknowledged.

Red-and-gold fire licked his arm that banded her breasts; lifting up her left hand, Rose sank her fingers into the living flame, right hand firmly pressing his fingers around her lower abdomen.

"For many years I blamed myself for Jonathon's pain." His

heartbeat pounded inside her throat; five matching heartbeats tattooed her womb. "He didn't love me like I needed to be loved, so I thought I must be responsible."

The pain of the past was dulled by the flesh that filled her.

"I joined the Men and Women's Club in the hopes that I could reach Jonathon." Rose swallowed sudden tears. "Or that I could at least learn to accept our situation."

Light flamed his hair. Shadow shuttered his eyes.

"Then Mrs. Hart . . . purely by accident"—her voice husked, the memory of the red-haired woman overlapping the burning reality of Jack—"interrupted a club meeting."

The heart beating inside her accelerated.

"She said she believed there are women who may want more out of marriage than what their husbands are capable of giving to them"—Jack's dark eyes gauged the involuntary clenching of her buttocks, stubbornly clinging to a man to whom she brought only pain—"just as she believed there are men who may want more than what their wives are capable of giving."

Jack's nostril's flared; simultaneously his chest expanded, wiry hair prickling her heart.

"She said . . ." Rose forced herself to breathe over the burning length of his penis that crowded her lungs ". . . she didn't believe either are at fault."

Jack did not physically move. His sudden distance cramped her stomach.

"When I received your subpoena"—Rose held him close with her hands and her body—"I realized I no longer had a reason to stay with my husband."

Memories flickered inside his gaze: Wanting. Taking. Losing.

"You loved a woman, Jack," Rose said, throat cording at the pulsating emotion that leaked from his body into hers, "to the best of your ability."

Pain spasmed his face.

"You are not responsible for the death of Cynthia Whitcox."

The first hot spurt of his ejaculate filled her chest. The second hot spurt scalded her eyes.

Jack closed his eyes on the fifth and final spurt.

Chapter 19

Jack watched Rose sleep until a muffled knock climbed the stairs and invaded the bedroom.

He had showered. Dressed. Now he would leave her to awaken alone, filled with his ejaculate.

Just as her husband had left her.

Bright chirps mocked the regret that pinched his testicles.

Rose's cheek was flushed in the morning sunlight. A bruised nipple peeped above the sheet that smelled of roses, sweat and sex.

Jack reached out, needing to touch her.

A knock halted his hand.

Quietly he exited the bedroom and closed the door, shielding Rose's naked sexuality from curious eyes.

His heel taps dully echoed in the bare corridor.

Dissipating wisps of steam roiled inside the bathroom.

The top stair creaked. The middle stair creaked.

Jack opened the front door just as a third knock vibrated the enameled wood.

A woman in her fifties—shorter than Rose but more stout—glanced up, hand raised.

There was no surprise in her canny eyes.

Behind her a tall, thin woman and a woman of middle height with a generous waistline stared at him with wide eyes.

They recognized his face. They comprehended by his damp hair and unshaven face where he had spent the night.

"Mrs. Dobkins." Jack stepped back, hand gesturing for the trio to enter. "Ladies."

"Mr. Lodoun."

The use of his name confirmed that the three ladies had, indeed, recognized him.

"Are you the cook?" he addressed the most sturdy of the two nameless women.

"No, sir." The tallest of the trio stepped forward. "I be Mrs. Finley, the cook."

"And I be Mrs. Brown, sir." Jack glanced at the woman of medium height who spoke. "All-around maid."

The three women were clean, but their clothing was worn: Clearly they needed this position.

Jack did not have time for subtleties.

"You know who I am."

Barrister of the Queens Counsel. Member of Parliament.

"Yes, sir."

"And you know who Mrs. Clarring is."

Knowledge of the newspaper articles shimmered inside their eyes.

"Yes, sir," the cook and maid chorused.

"And we know who we be, Mr. Lodoun," the housekeeper tartly interrupted.

Jack assessed the short woman who stood no taller than four feet nine inches tall. "And who would that be, Mrs. Dobkins?"

"Women who be grateful for the opportunity to work."

Jack held her gaze. "You understand, then, what will happen if word should leak out that I am a visitor in this house."

"If word leaks out"—the housekeeper did not glance away from the authority he deliberately radiated—"it'll not come from our mouths."

A faint smile twisted his lips: Rose had chosen well.

"Mrs. Clarring is sleeping." Jack did not know what—or even if—Rose had eaten before meeting him outside the Houses of Parliament. "She'll appreciate a hearty breakfast when she awakens."

"The cupboards are bare." The housekeeper held her ground. "And she ain't got no dishes."

The untouched bottle of wine and the two mismatched water glasses flitted through his mind.

Jack reached into his pocket and pulled out his wallet. He peeled off a twenty-pound note.

"Buy what you need in order to cook and serve her breakfast." Rose had only brought the one trunk from her husband's home. "No doubt she'll want to shop for the rest."

"Aye." Grudging respect shone inside the housekeeper's eyes. "We can do that."

"Very good," Jack said dismissively.

The cook and maid followed the housekeeper, their steps clattering on the wooden floor.

A series of bongs trailed their retreat: It was eight in the morning.

The courthouse closed at noon on Saturdays.

Jack could only hope that Jonathon Clarring did not act first.

"Mrs. Dobkins."

Jack's voice barreled down the narrow corridor.

The three women turned, eyes hidden by shadows and the brims of black bonnets.

Rose had said they would not be living in.

"I do not want Mrs. Clarring to be alone in this house during the day. Make certain that every single person who walks over this threshold is known." Frances Hart's butler had made the mistake of allowing the madhouse doctors into her home; it had almost cost her freedom. "If Mrs. Clarring doesn't know who they are, do not let them enter. Is that clear?"

The housekeeper's voice rang with authority. "We won't let no one take Mrs. Clarring."

They could only circumvent a court order; they couldn't stop it.

Neither could Jack.

The three women turned in unison.

"Mrs. Dobkins."

The housekeeper paused, back stiff. "Yes?"

Rose smelled of roses. So, too, did Jack.

"Add to your shopping list a toothbrush and unscented soap."

He could shave at work, but he often met with clients outside his office.

"And a shaving kit," Jack appended.

The bed sagged, rolling Rose against a warm body. Gentle blue eyes stared down at her.

I forgive you, Rose.

An angry sparrow catapulted Rose upward.

The bedroom was empty.

She clutched her breast, heart racing, soft nipple hardening at her touch.

Musk filled her nostrils.

Over the scent of man and sex wafted the aroma of baking bread.

Sudden comprehension flashed through her.

Jack had opened her door to the housekeeper, and then he had walked out. His absence was a palpable void.

A distant chime announced the quarter hour, but it did not inform her of which hour.

Resolutely Rose jerked back the covers and sat up.

A soft knock pierced the aching portals between her thighs and buttocks.

"Mrs. Clarring?"

The housekeeper's voice squelched the ridiculous hope that it was Jack who had knocked.

Rose clenched cool cotton and firm mattress. "Yes, Mrs. Dobkins?"

"Mr. Lodoun thought ye'd like a bit o' breakfast; it'll be ready shortly." The older woman's voice was matter-of-fact, as if every day she received instructions from a man who was not her employer's husband. "Should ye like a tray, or shall ye come downstairs?"

Glass impacting marble slammed through her memory.

Jack had set the bottle of Rose's Lubrifiant on the bathroom cabinet.

Had the housekeeper seen it?

Rose reached for black wool. "I'll take breakfast downstairs, Mrs. Dobkins."

"Very well, ma'am."

Hurriedly she pulled on the bodice and skirt she had worn the night before, wool abrading sensitized skin. Without the bustle, it dragged behind her.

The marble counter in the small bathroom was bare.

Quickly Rose opened the bottom drawer.

A crystal stopper glinted.

"Should ye like assistance, Mrs. Clarring?"

Sucking in moist air, Rose shut the drawer. "No, thank you, Mrs. Dobkins." Standing, turning—fingers fisting to prevent them from independently combing back her tangled hair—she asked: "Did you bring the cook and maid we discussed?"

"Indeed, ma'am." White light flared; the housekeeper stretched to light the sconce above the sink. "Cook is preparing breakfast. Mrs. Brown is cleaning baseboards."

Light illuminated white marble and a nickle-coated spout.

Above the sink, a gray ribbon of moisture streaked the bathroom mirror.

Jack had showered before leaving, Rose realized.

"What time is it?" Rose asked.

"Nearly ten, it is." The housekeeper straightened—she was several inches shorter than Rose—and blew out the blackened match. A starched white cap topped her head. "Shall I start ye a shower?"

Rose was suddenly, painfully aware of the slippery oil between her buttocks and the masculine musk that clung to her skin.

"No, thank you," she said shortly. "I can do that."

"That Mr. Lodoun is a bit of a tartar." The eyes that gazed up at Rose were shrewd. "I expect he's the same 'atween the sheets."

Shock bolted through Rose.

She opened her mouth to rebuke the housekeeper for her familiarity. Immediately she remembered the frigid condemnation inside the eyes of her husband's butler.

There was no judgment inside the housekeeper's canny eyes.

"Cook will keep yer breakfast hot," the older woman said brusquely. "Take as long as ye like in the shower; it'll do ye good."

Rose's mouth snapped shut.

"Thank you, Mrs. Dobkins."

Firmly she locked the door behind the housekeeper. Dropping the blue towel onto the tile, Rose twisted the hot and cold water cocks. Stinging water scoured her skin that felt raw and abraded.

Rose tried to remember how she had felt the morning after her wedding night: She couldn't. She had never experienced the degree of intimacy with Jonathon that she had experienced with Jack.

Snatching up the pink towel off the sink, she briskly dried—inhaling deeply the faint scent of spice—and threw on last night's skirt and bodice.

The bedroom was filled with the chatter of sparrows. Black wool and more black wool filled the scarred chest.

When she had married, she'd worn gay colors.

Fleetingly Rose wondered at what point she had changed.

After Jonathon started drinking? Or after she realized he only drank when he was at home, alone with her?

Rose screwed on pearl earrings—the only jewelry she had brought with her—and made her descent.

"Ma'am." A woman of medium height and appearance materialized at the foot of the steps; a white cap concealed her hair. "Would ye like breakfast now?"

"That would be most welcome," Rose said. "You are Mrs. Brown, are you not?"

"Aye, ma'am, an' it please you." The maid—unlike the housekeeper—flushed with shyness. Or perhaps she flushed with the knowledge of Rose's illicit affair. "I'll get yer breakfast."

"Please tell Cook I would like to meet her," Rose called after the fleeing woman.

It dawned on Rose she had no dining room furniture.

The drawing room was chill and dark. The velvet armchair guarded the fireplace instead of sitting at the foot of the settee in voyeuristic readiness.

There was no sign of the two men her adultery would most affect: Jonathon and Jack.

Rose inanely realized that the two men in her life both had names that started with a *J*.

"Mrs. Brown, help me move this trunk and we'll make a table for Mrs. Clarring," called Rose to attention.

The housekeeper and the maid lifted the heavy leather-and-brass trunk and moved it in front of the armchair. A third woman—the cook, no doubt—carried a cloth-covered tray.

"Mrs. Finley, put the tray here," the housekeeper directed. "Mrs. Clarring, if ye'll be seated."

Rose gingerly sat, too-soft velvet molding her buttocks.

Irresistibly she remembered the cradle of Jack's pelvis.

A clearing throat brought Rose to the present.

The three women—housekeeper, maid and cook—stood side by side, patiently waiting.

Rose surveyed the breakfast tray: A steepled white linen cloth jutted out from a white china cup.

"The plate and cutlery are new," she observed.

"Yes, ma'am," The tall woman—the cook—spoke up. Rose draped the napkin over her lap and picked up a shiny fork. "I purchased them this morning, along with other necessities."

"I see." The scrambled eggs were moist and surprisingly flavorful. Rose swallowed. "That was very thoughtful of you. You are Mrs. Finley?"

"Yes, ma'am, if you please."

Steam rose from a small white pot. Rose poured a fragrant cup of tea.

A creamer, sugar bowl and a saucer of lemon slices occupied the far corner of the tray.

She knew how deeply Jack filled her body, she thought with a curious pang, but she did not know how he took his tea.

"Breakfast is quite delicious, Mrs. Finley." Rose added a cube of sugar to her tea. "If you'll give me the bill, I'll reimburse you."

"Mr. Lodoun paid for it, ma'am."

Rose froze, teaspoon creating a dark swirl.

"Mr. Lodoun?" she repeated. Carefully she tapped the teaspoon against delicate china and balanced it on the edge of the matching white saucer. "Exactly what did Mr. Lodoun say and do this morning?"

While she lay sleeping, dreaming of another man.

"He gave us a twenty-pound banknote and told us to buy what we needed to prepare ye breakfast." The housekeeper bluntly spoke up. "He told us to watch over ye during the day, to not let anyone ye don't know enter the house."

As if Jonathon would cause her harm.

But he could.

Because of men like Jack.

"And then he told us to buy a toothbrush and a bar of unscented soap."

A hiccup of laughter caught in Rose's throat.

"And then," the housekeeper grimly concluded, "he said we should purchase a shaving kit."

Correctly holding the knife and fork—spine erect, vulva throbbing—Rose sliced off a sliver of ham. "As you said, Mrs. Dobkins, a bit of a tartar."

"Shall we go over the menu, Mrs. Clarring?" the cook anxiously asked, all three women so obviously in need of employment.

It wasn't that difficult lanced through Rose.

Love-blind. Love-starved.

Every woman had a weakness.

Chapter 20

"I can't, Dr. Burns." Tears streaked the woman's face; an angry lesion cracked the corner of her mouth, the manifestation of pernicious anemia. She was thirty-one years old; she looked fifty-one. "I've been birthin' since I was fifteen. I can't birth another bairn. I just can't."

Pain and poverty were bleak counterpoints to the bright sunshine streaming through slanted blinds.

Before the trial, Sarah remembered, it had rained. After the trial, the wind had chased away the clouds.

The pain and poverty had remained, a London staple.

"Then you shan't, Mrs. Wilkins." Reaching over the sturdy wooden table that served as her desk, Sarah clasped rough red hands and answered the younger woman's plea. "You shan't."

The woman's relief was immediately overcome by guilt.

Her fingers—twice as small as those of Sarah—turned and gripped her hand so tightly Sarah fought not to wince. "I love me childers, Dr. Burns."

"I know you do, Mrs. Wilkins."

Sarah had long ago learned that the love of children and the consequences of bearing children were two separate issues.

"I don't regret birthin' 'em."

"Of course you don't," Sarah soothed.

"But I 'ave nine bairns alivin'. An' I'm so tired." Fresh tears bubbled up inside the woman's red-rimmed eyes. "I can't do it agin."

She was physically and emotionally exhausted; years of pregnancy and nursing had depleted her body of iron. She would die: If not while giving birth, then afterward, feeding the child from her body when she herself did not have enough to eat.

Still, Sarah had to ask: "Have you told Mr. Wilkins?"

"He wouldn' understand."

Many men didn't understand the toll their physical demands made on women.

"Then we won't ask him to give more than he's capable of giving," Sarah said.

The words eerily echoed the woman for whom she had been subpoenaed.

"I can't pay right away," redirected Sarah's thoughts.

The small office—white walls cracked; pine woodwork chipped—was ample evidence that many of her patients couldn't pay their fees "right away."

"Don't you worry about that, Mrs. Wilkins; we'll work out something." Sarah was merely thankful the woman had come to her instead of a local butcher who would have mutilated if not killed her outright. "But if we're to keep you safe, we need to do this soon."

A wafting polka filled the sudden lull of grinding carriage wheels.

The harsh lines of guilt that etched the young-old woman's face suddenly eased.

"Monday," she said, pulling free her hands.

"Monday," Sarah confirmed, letting her go.

The thirty-one-year-old woman walked out of the small office—shoulders squared, spine straight—and shut the door behind her.

Sarah did not know if she'd be back or not. Sometimes women chose their own options: arsenic; the path of a carriage; the Thames. All Sarah could do was hope she would make the right decision.

She closed the file on Mrs. Wilkins and dropped it into a wooden crate.

A hesitant tap pierced the monotonous whine of carriage wheels. The soft click was accompanied by a draft of stale air.

"Miss Days," Sarah acknowledged, riffling through papers, "do you have Mrs. Maloney's chart?"

But it wasn't the secretary who answered.

"I'm sorry, Dr. Burns; Miss Days said I should come in."

Abruptly reduced to a six-foot-one-inch-tall, thirty-four-year-old spinster instead of a sexless, ageless physician, Sarah jerked upright.

Eyes the color of cornflowers snagged her gaze.

The small office suddenly pulsed with the secrets the members of the Men and Women's Club had publicly revealed, and the secrets they privately hoarded.

"Hello, Mrs. Clarring," Sarah said, acutely aware of the fashionable woman who stood five feet tall and of her own ungainly stature swathed in a wrinkled white frock coat. Stethoscope throttling her throat, she hid her embarrassment behind bluntness. "What are you doing here?"

"I wanted to commend you on your testimony." Sincerity radiated from the painfully pretty woman from whom Sarah had sat across for two years, yet with whom she had never become friends. "I don't think the jury would have reached the verdict they did had it not been for you."

Sarah was not used to praise: There was very little to be had for a woman who worked in a career dominated by men. All she could think to say was: "I did no more than what any of us did."

Concern darkened Rose Clarring's eyes. "Have you lost many patients because of the trial?"

Esther Palmer and Thomas Pierce—fellow members of the club—crowded the small office.

The newspapers had reported that both the teacher and the banker had been dismissed from their positions before the trial. Their reward for confiding in their employers.

"No," Sarah gruffly answered. "My patients have neither the money nor the time to read the papers."

Sarah knew that was not the case with the members of the prosperous middle-class society to which Rose Clarring belonged.

She had once been envious of the petite woman. She could no longer hold her beauty against her.

"Sit down, Mrs. Clarring," Sarah briskly instructed. Mentally she reviewed the patients who waited outside: Their health was not critical. Surely they wouldn't begrudge her a few minutes with a woman she wished she'd befriended. "Would you like tea?"

"No, thank you." Rose Clarring quietly closed the door, white egret feathers waving above a stylish black hat. "I won't keep you long."

The scent of roses infiltrated the acrid scent of antiseptic.

Incongruously Sarah compared the thirty-three-year-old woman to the thirty-one-year-old woman who had just left.

Outwardly, there was no comparison: Rose Clarring had no children, and her clear, unlined skin shone with good health. Yet both women walked with purpose.

"How may I help you, Mrs. Clarring?"

Rose Clarring did not answer. Instead, she sat with a graceful flair that Sarah—tall and big-boned—had never been able to cultivate, and asked: "How is Mr. Addimore?"

Hot blood flooded Sarah's face, remembering the past meeting in which she had confessed her desire to be small and vulnerable, and George Addimore had confessed his inability to maintain an erection.

She knew that Rose Clarring also remembered the meeting.

Sarah resisted the urge to hide the unlikely relationship budding between herself and the accountant: They had all been through too much to lie to one another.

"He lost his position at the accounting firm," she said matter-of-factly.

After the trial.

The family-owned business would not chance their respectable clients being corrupted by a man who belonged to the "Club of Dreadful Delights," as *The Times* had labeled the Men and Women's Club.

"I'm so sorry, Dr. Burns."

The regret on Rose Clarring's face warmed Sarah.

Sarah wanted to ask if she had suffered at the hands of her husband, but the privacy within which each club member had cloaked themselves for two years halted her.

"He's opening his own office; he'll manage," Sarah said. It had been three days since the trial ended. Impulsively, she asked, "Have you heard from anyone?"

The regret inside the blue eyes deepened. "No."

Sarah pictured the London Museum and the elegant boardroom in which they had weekly held their meetings. "Do you think we'll ever meet again?"

"I don't know," Rose Clarring said honestly. "I like to think so. But we're not the same people we were two years ago. I'm not certain what we could offer one another now."

Friendship, Sarah thought.

But the club members who had banded together in the gallery as a group had walked out of the courtroom as couples.

All save for Rose Clarring: She had walked alone.

Sarah and George Addimore had been among the last members

to be called to witness. Sarah suddenly needed to know: "Did you hear Miss Fredericks testify?"

One of the two women who had refused to accompany them to the Achilles Book Shoppe, and whose mother was dying of syphilis.

"No." A sudden smile lit Rose Clarring's eyes. For a brief moment Sarah saw the friend the petite woman would have been, if only Sarah had possessed the courage. "But you would have been quite proud of Miss Hoppleworth. Did you know she was certified to teach at university?"

"No," Sarah said. "I didn't."

"She said she preferred being a student over a teacher because she liked to learn." Admiration mingled with amusement inside the bright blue gaze. "Mr. Lodoun asked if she learned much in the club. She said yes, indeed. When he asked her to provide an example, she replied, 'I am now learning about law.' "

Sarah visualized the thirty-six-year-old secretary who wore silver-framed glasses.

"When Mr. Lodoun asked why she voted Mrs. Hart into our society," Rose Clarring continued, "she said it was because of her honesty. He dismissed her, but Miss Hoppleworth protested she hadn't answered the question to her satisfaction. The judge intervened, instructing her she had answered the question to Mr. Lodoun's satisfaction, and therefore, to the satisfaction of the court. 'Consider this another lesson in your study of the law, Miss Hoppleworth,' he told her."

Sarah could not restrain herself: She laughed, a hearty bray of uninhibited jocularity. The shocked quietness emanating from the waiting room sobered her.

"I am certain you gave a credible presentation, too, Mrs. Clarring," she awkwardly offered.

The smile lighting Rose Clarring's face faded. "I believe we all discovered of what we're made, Dr. Burns."

The Daily Herald had called her a child murderess, for blocking the conception of her husband's children.

Sarah suddenly wanted to comfort this woman who stood thirteen inches shorter than she, but she didn't know how. So she spoke with the mannish bluffness she had learned in medical school: "Jack Lodoun is a right bastard for suggesting the things he did."

Her words did not have the hoped-for effect.

"It would be fruitless to blame Mr. Lodoun for what he said inside the courtroom." Rose Clarring glanced down at her lap, round hat hiding her expression. "Like us, he did what he had to do."

"And what if Mrs. Hart hadn't won her liberty, Mrs. Clarring?" Sarah returned, remembering all the men who had made her studies difficult, simply because she was a woman. "Would you still say he was not to blame?"

One second Sarah stared at black felt and white feathers; the next instant she gazed into Rose Clarring's eyes. "Without Mr. Lodoun, Dr. Burns, would you have had the courage to turn to Mr. Addimore?"

There was steel inside fragile cornflowers, Sarah thought.

And truth.

Without the subpoena, George Addimore would not have offered his arm, and she would not have walked down a London street with a man three inches shorter than she.

"No," Sarah admitted. And then, on a restless wave of impatience that penetrated the cracked wall, she said: "You didn't come to this part of town merely to compliment me, Mrs. Clarring." She repeated: "What can I do for you?"

The purpose Sarah had seen in Rose Clarring's posture blossomed inside her eyes. "You are an excellent physician, Dr. Burns: I would like your advice regarding preventive checks."

A series of bongs penetrated the whine of carriage wheels and the inaudible motion of fidgeting bodies: It was twelve noon.

Sarah—taller than those who had mobbed the Old Bailey Courthouse—abruptly identified the gray-coated man and black-cloaked woman she had glimpsed on the corner of Old Bailey and Newgate: Rose Clarring and Jack Lodoun.

Promptly the vision was replaced with the postcard of a man fondling his penis.

He had told me that . . . that having intimacy without the hope of having children is like . . . is like what this man is doing, Rose Clarring had confessed during the meeting in which the club members had too late shared their emotions as well as their intellect.

And now Rose Clarring had found a man with whom she could share the intimacy for which she yearned.

Sarah wanted to warn her that she was not a widow like Frances Hart: A husband could inflict far more harm than either a son or a father. Sarah wanted to caution her that Jack Lodoun was not James Whitcox: But they had both seen that during the trial.

Sarah asked, simply, "What would you like to know?"

Rose Clarring matched her bluntness: "Is the Mensinga diaphragm as effective as a condom?"

"I don't know," Sarah truthfully replied, face ridiculously hot: Rose Clarring was consulting her as a physician, not as a woman. "But I believe that a Dutch cap is."

"What is a Dutch cap?"

"It fits over the cervix."

"Does not a diaphragm also fit over a woman's cervix?"

Standing—chair shooting backward—Sarah rounded the sturdy table. Stepping behind Rose Clarring—wood creaked; she could feel the younger woman's gaze following her—she grabbed a pamphlet out of a plain pine case crammed with books and papers.

The page she needed was dog-eared.

Silently she proffered the pamphlet.

Rose Clarring looked for long seconds at the two black-and-white illustrations.

"A Dutch cap can be left in position for several days," Sarah gruffly expounded. "Unlike a diaphragm, it fits directly over the cervix."

Glancing up—cheeks rouged with the heat that seared Sarah—Rose Clarring asked: "Can you measure me for this device?"

"No." The contraceptives that were most effective were not affordable to those who most needed them: Sarah had neither the necessary equipment to make such a measurement nor the caps. "But I can direct you to a gynecologist who can."

A whistle shrilled over the careening traffic, a bobby charged to protect the morals of London as well as the physical safety of her citizens.

Taking a deep breath—woman to woman—Sarah added, "And I will give you a pill to take if your monthly courses should ever be late."

Chapter 21

A twelfth bong faded into the wafting grind of carriage wheels and the snick of a turning lock.

The outer door to the suite of offices had been breached.

Jack stared through thick glass at the city of London.

He did not see what he needed, view obstructed by ever-heightening buildings.

An almost inaudible click was chased by a draft of cool air.

Jack did not face the opening door. "How many people inhabit our great country, Mr. Dorsey?"

It was a rhetorical question: Jack knew the answer.

"At the last census, sir, we were twenty-five million, nine-hundred-seventy-three thousand, five hundred and thirty-nine."

"And how many of those are women?" Jack asked.

Jack did not know the answer.

"Thirteen million, three-hundred-thirty-four thousand, five hundred and thirty-seven," the clerk calmly responded.

"More than half," Jack said neutrally.

"Nearly fifty-four percent, sir."

A majority, yet the majority did not rule.

Dark motion caught Jack's eye.

In the distance a pulley elevated a scaffold up the front of a brick building, one storey at a time. A man—arms like matchsticks—clung to invisible ropes.

The Saturday edition of *The Daily Herald* reported that a window washer had yesterday plummeted to the pavement and died.

He envisioned Rose Clarring standing on the scaffold.

"Do you support the women's movement, Mr. Dorsey?" Jack asked.

"I don't know, sir."

The clerk's ambivalence was shared by both men and women, statesmen and civilians.

When it is not necessary to make a decision, it is necessary not to make a decision.

"Seaton rang while you were out," Jack said. The pulley stopped, scaffold swinging, man clinging. "I refused the Greffen situation."

"I'll send a letter extending our regrets," Nathan Dorsey replied quietly. "Did Mr. Olsen make his eleven o'clock?"

"Yes." Jack swivelled the leather chair around and faced the clerk. Slanting sunlight divided them. "He offered me fifteen hundred pounds if I would support his appointment to public office. Has Jonathon Clarring petitioned for the restitution of his conjugal rights?"

There was no surprise on the junior man's face, either at the fact that Jack had been offered a bribe or at the change of subject. "No."

So why didn't Jack feel relieved?

"Which judge is most receptive to a writ of separation?"

"The Honorable Arthur Bellington."

Jack was familiar with the name but not the man.

"He's granted more separations than the other judges?"

"Yes."

"How many children does he have?"

"Eight."

Gladstone, the former prime minister, had eight children: A Liberal, he staunchly argued against divorce.

"Is the judge open to bribery?" Jack asked.

"The court clerks say he's a conscientious man."

Jack could be said to be a conscientious man. So, too, could James Whitcox.

They were both diligent at their work.

"Did you find any records of a separation that had been granted to a wife who lived apart from her husband?"

"No."

Jack *would* win Rose a separation. But he did not know how.

"Did you talk to Frowt?" he pressed.

A private investigator.

"Yes, sir. He said he'd compile a report on Mr. Clarring as soon as possible."

Nathan Dorsey had done all he could do; now it was up to Jack.

"Go home, Mr. Dorsey," Jack said flatly.

"The letter to Mr. Seaton—"

"Will wait until Monday."

Neither relief nor regret marked the clerk's face. "Very good, sir."

The clerk's departure was a clicking closure.

First inside his office. Then inside his suite.

The dull throb inside Jack's thighs and back was a pulsing reminder he no longer straddled the fence of ambivalence.

Standing, he locked his satchel inside his desk.

Brass winked.

Jack retrieved his coat and hat from the heavy, ornate coat tree.

He remembered the small brass coat tree that dominated Rose's foyer.

She had said she didn't regret their time together. But she had been naked in his arms. Regret, he thought, would occur when—fully dressed—she faced Jonathon Clarring inside a courtroom.

Jack locked the door to his office, and then the door to his suite. Gunmetal—the same metal as the hour hand on Big Ben—blackened the corridor. A push of a button catalyzed grinding gears and coiling cables.

"Good afternoon, Mr. Lodoun." The opening cab revealed a navy-uniformed man; he did not smile. "Splendid day, sir."

Would Rose still want splendid fucks, Jack wondered, if Jonathon Clarring offered her the intimacy she needed?

Jack stepped into the dully lit elevator. "Quite splendid, Mr. Applebaum."

The drop of the lift brought home the fact that Jack did not know the man Rose loved.

He knew the pain Jonathon Clarring caused Rose. But he did not know the face that Rose carried in her mind while Jack occupied her body.

The cab opened to blinding light.

"Good evening, Mr. Lodoun," trailed after him.

Jack pushed through a heavy glass-plated door. The noon sun warmed his face even as a cool breeze batted his hat.

A hansom waited at the front of the queue in the cab stand: Jack stepped up onto the iron rail.

"Where t', gov'nur?"

Where could Jack find the knowledge he needed?

There was only one place that came to mind. "The London Stock Exchange."

The cab door obliterated both light and air. A faint scent filled the dark cavity, sweeter than soap.

His cock hardened in realization of what he smelled: Rose's skin; Rose's sweat; Rose's sex.

He wondered if Jonathon Clarring would recognize her scent.

The London Stock Exchange monopolized the greater triangle formed by the streets of Throgmorton, Bartholomew, Threadneedle and Old Broad. Carriages clogged the busy intersection. Men and women crowded the pavement, bowler hats bouncing, bonnets bobbing. Footsteps irrevocably marching forward.

Jack tossed the cabby a florin.

Inside the newly expanded building light poured through a glass-domed ceiling.

Men and women congregated around a rectangular column. Men formed circles in front of a bank of elevators.

Impervious to the consequences of his actions—he a man who lived for the public—Jack punched a bronze button.

Metal clanged metal, a cab descending a wire cable. Metal slammed metal, the elevator door opening.

"Which floor, sir?" cheerfully enquired a burgundy-uniformed man.

He did not recognize Jack. *And why should he*? Jack ironically thought. This was the world of finance, Jonathon Clarring's world.

Jack stepped into the cab; his reflection inside a bronzed mirror stepped toward him. "Whichever floor where I can find Jonathon Clarring."

"That'll be the fifth, sir."

The elevator opened onto luxurious burgundy carpeting. Crystal wall sconces flickered in artfully subdued shadows.

"That way, sir," the lift man offered, pointing.

Jack stalked his quarry.

A third mahogany door sported a bronze nameplate.

Silently he turned a white porcelain doorknob. Silently the door swung inward.

A woman with dull brown hair twisted in a loose topknot leaned over a typewriter; she jerked upright in surprise. "May I help you?"

Jack stared at the young woman for long seconds: She was in the latter stages of pregnancy.

Blushing a painful crimson, she glanced downward, clearly embarrassed by her condition.

The dull pain inside his thighs and back traveled up to his chest.

"I'm here to see Jonathon Clarring," Jack said, voice expressionless.

He did not know if he hid his emotion, or if he had no emotion to show.

The young woman glanced up: There was no knowledge of his identity inside the hazel eyes that shone with good health and pregnancy. "I'm afraid Mr. Clarring has no appointments today, Mr. . . . ?"

This was a game Jack was not going to play.

"Blair Stromwell referred me," he said, giving the name of the Chairman of Justice, a man known by all of England.

The woman's eyes widened in recognition. "Of course. Perhaps Mr. Clarring can spare a few moments. If you'll be seated . . ."

"Of course," Jack echoed.

He remained standing.

Flushing darker yet, the young woman hurried from behind the secretarial desk, blue wool skirts swishing. Briefly she knocked on a massive mahogany door before opening it and slipping inside Jonathon Clarring's office.

A faint murmur leaked through the crack.

Instantly the door opened wide.

The pregnant woman—Jack estimated her between seven and eight months—pressed her back against the mahogany wood; awkwardly she gestured. "If you'll step through here, sir."

Jack stepped over the threshold.

Sunlight illuminated the spacious office, glanced off expensive bronze and crystal. It silvered fine brown hair that was devoid of gold or red highlights.

It took only a second for Jonathon Clarring to recognize Jack.

"Close the door, Mrs. Jacobson."

There was no emotion inside the sky blue eyes.

Not of a man's grief, for the children he could not sire. Not of a man's betrayal, married to a woman who had in the eyes of the public cuckolded him.

The door closed behind Jack with a soft thud.

"Have you now come to subpoena me, Mr. Lodoun?" Jonathon Clarring asked.

Jack studied the man who had spurt his "love" inside Rose.

Jonathon Clarring was thirty-three; Jack was forty-four. Jonathon Clarring was smoothly shaven; Jack's long sideburns fanned out into side whiskers.

The two men had nothing whatsoever in common, save for one woman.

"I've come on behalf of your wife," Jack said.

The pain that flashed through Jonathon Clarring's eyes almost buckled Jack's knees.

The younger man—Jack wondered if he had ever looked that young—leaned back into dark mahogany leather and closed his eyes.

The wafting whine of carriage wheels interspersed the sharp cries of street vendors.

Jack pictured Jonathon Clarring proposing to Rose with the demand for children. Jack pictured Jonathon Clarring bedding Rose—both of them children still—on their wedding night.

Jack pictured Jonathon Clarring visiting Rose on the eve of Christmas, hoping for a miracle baby.

The image of the pregnant secretary laid down between husband and wife.

Jack harshly asked: "Is it yours?"

"I am sterile." Jonathon Clarring opened his eyelids. Jack stared into blue eyes that contained neither greed, nor malice, nor hunger for power. "As you know."

Jack swallowed fleeting disappointment, no less bitter for its passage.

It would have been so much simpler if Rose were the one who was sterile, and Jonathon Clarring had impregnated his secretary.

He remembered the words with which Rose had battered him.

"Do you imagine the child is yours when you fuck your secretary?" Jack asked.

"I have not, nor will I ever touch Mrs. Jacobson." Jonathon Clarring did not flinch at Jack's deliberate crudeness. "Can you say the same about my wife?"

Jack would not lie. "No."

Pain dilated his pupils; Jonathon Clarring remained calm. "I will not divorce Rose."

"Even though you know she's fucking another man?" Jack goaded, wanting to pierce the calm and find the man who had made Rose laugh with happiness.

"Rose is my wife, sir," he merely said. "Regardless of what you may think of me, I insist you speak with the respect she is due."

"Rose is my lover," Jack reciprocated. "And I have nothing but respect for her. It is you, Clarring, I question."

"I have told you everything you need to know."

As her barrister, but not as her lover.

Jack asked, simply, "Why?"

"I have no doubt my wife has told you the answer," the younger man returned stonily.

But Jack was not referring to his lack of sexual attentiveness.

"Why won't you divorce her?" he elaborated.

"She's my wife."

Jack understood James Whitcox. He needed to understand Jonathon Clarring.

"Does it excite you, thinking about your wife with another man?" Jack asked.

Emotion flitted across Jonathon Clarring's unlined face; he was so young Jack wanted to weep.

"No," he said.

He spoke the truth.

"Do you fuck your fist," Jack probed, "imagining the sexual acts she performs with another man?"

"No."

Again, he spoke the truth.

"Do you get hard, Clarring, thinking of another man filling your wife with his seed?"

The calm inside the blue eyes splintered.

"I love her," ricocheted off crystal and bronze.

Jack had succeeded: He saw the man who had dreamed and laughed, but whose dreams and laughter had been stolen by the mumps.

Rose had said the love Jonathon Clarring bore her was each day killing him: Jack now saw the pain she had seen, living with him for twelve years.

"I love her," Jonathon Clarring repeated. The unadulterated pain inside his eyes dulled but still remained. Calmly, quietly, he asked, "Can you say the same?"

". . . 'Sam'wiches! 'Am sam'wiches! Fresh 'am . . . !" filled the silence . . . fled the silence.

By Jack not answering, he betrayed Rose as surely as did her husband.

"You've forced her to live alone for twelve years, Clarring," Jack said instead. "Those are not the actions of a man who loves his wife."

The pain Jonathon Clarring had inflicted upon Rose shone inside his eyes. "What I do or do not do is strictly between my wife and me, sir."

Jack's nipple burned with the memory of Rose's kiss.

"What kind of a man, Clarring, forces the woman he loves to seek love with another man?"

"What kind of a man, Mr. Lodoun, humiliates a woman in a court of law and then takes her as a lover?"

Jack would not apologize for his actions in a courtroom.

"I did what I had to do."

"As did I," Jonathon Clarring returned.

Underneath the pain in his sky blue eyes, Jack read castigating guilt—an emotion with which Jack daily lived—and a determination that chilled his bones.

Jack did not know Jonathon Clarring, but he did know that the man who gazed at him now was not the boy with whom Rose had fallen in love.

"Why won't you give Rose her freedom?" Jack pressed. And wondered anew: *Would* James Whitcox have granted Cynthia Whitcox a divorce?

"I will answer your question," Jonathon Clarring offered, as if they were two businessmen, he a stockbroker and Jack a client, "if you will answer mine."

Jack's loyalty remained with Rose.

"Which question is that?" he asked neutrally.

"Does my wife love you?"

The past juxtaposed the present.

James Whitcox confronting Jack. James Whitcox questioning Jack.

Did she love you?

Jack had not answered James Whitcox. But he answered Jonathon Clarring.

"No," he said flatly.

There was no triumph in Jonathon Clarring's gaze, only that grim determination that filled Jack with foreboding. "Who does Rose love?"

Pain knifed through Jack. His pain, not that of Jonathon Clarring.

Rose had said she felt loved when Jack was inside her body, but she had been very clear from the outset: "You."

But Jonathon Clarring had already known the answer to his question.

"I have always known my wife would take a lover, Mr. Lodoun," jolted through Jack.

A pulse beat inside his temple. A matching pulse pounded inside his cock.

Inside the younger man's eyes burned the knowledge of Jack and Rose's carnal love.

A love he desired, Jack saw, but which he deliberately suppressed.

"Just as I have always known it is I to whom she will return." Between one blink and the next, the dark desire inside Jonathon Clarring's eyes died. "And that, sir, is why I will not divorce Rose."

Chapter 22

"Shall I bill your address, Mrs. Clarring?"

Gaslight danced on the woman's hair, turning dark brown into auburn red.

Incongruously Rose remembered that light had reflected off the gynecologist's balding head.

Three men now knew her intimately.

Rose took a deep breath. "I'll pay now, thank you."

"That will be"—the comparably aged woman squinted down at the gynecologist's hastily scrawled notation—"three . . . four . . ." A surprisingly throaty laugh escaped her. She flashed up a rueful smile at Rose. "I keep threatening to send him back to school to learn how to write so others can read his script. That will be four shillings one pence, please."

Rose dug out a half crown and two shillings from her reticule and neatly lined up the silver coins on the wooden desk. "I appreciate you taking me in like this."

She had arrived just as the doctor was seeing the last patient for the day.

"Not to worry." Gold flashed on the woman's ring finger; Rose instinctively thumbed over the bare spot on her left hand. "My husband enjoys his work. We're taking the children to the Zoological Gardens, but they don't feed the lions and tigers until four, so it worked out well." Head rising—gaze warm—she extended her hand. "I think you and your husband will quite enjoy the cap, Mrs. Clarring."

But it was not for her husband.

Rose had the odd sensation that this woman who glowed with the love she bore her balding gynecologist would understand the need that had brought Rose and Jack together.

She stuffed the receipt, a threepence coin and two copper pennies into her reticule. "Thank you, Mrs. Reynolds."

Sunlight streaked the corridor outside the dark cherry door that locked behind her. Before her a black runner marched downward into a lighted stairwell.

The small rubber cap—cheaper than a leather phallus—squeezed her cervix.

Inexplicable fear stabbed through her: She could not take those stairs.

Rose pressed a finger-smeared button beside a white-enameled lift.

The grumble of metal coiling around metal instantly responded.

A dark shadow climbed enameled mesh.

"Smashin' outside," the lift man cheerfully observed through painted wire.

"Indeed, it is," Rose responded politely.

The lift halted, a jarring clank. Simultaneously, the darkness behind the wire moved: A gate slammed open.

Shadow turned into a red uniform topped by auburn hair: "Goin' down?"

The lift man was a boy . . . a very handsome boy who could barely be more than sixteen years of age.

"Yes." Rose dubiously stepped up four inches into the wire cage. "Thank you."

The boy slammed shut the metal gate; mottled light shone through the wire mesh. "This be me first day on th' job 'ere."

The elevator dropped: Rose's stomach dropped with it.

"You're doing very well," she lied, fingers slipping through cold wire and tightly gripping.

"Ain't just nobody they 'ire t' wear this uniform. I be a man now, m' da says." The lift came to a jarring halt. He threw back the gate to unfiltered sunshine and stepped aside. Frank admiration glowed in his clear, young face. "Got me a break comin' up. Buy ye a cuppa?"

Unbidden pleasure rushed through Rose. It had been a long time since a man had flirted with her. Even longer since one this young had done so.

"Perhaps another day," she said gently.

Gingerly unlatching her fingers, she prepared to step down five inches; instantly a white-gloved hand appeared, steadying her.

"Sure," the boy said, cheer undiluted by rejection. "Ye're just lettin' me down easy-like. M' da told me 'bout ladies like ye. Th' pretty ones 're always taken, 'e said. 'Mind yer 'eart, boy,' 'e said, 'else they'll steal it away an' leave ye wi' nuthin' but a great bleedin' 'ole in yer chest.' "

Rose gained the tiled floor on a lilting laugh.

For a second she didn't recognize the source of the laughter; abruptly she realized it had come from her.

Breath catching inside her throat, she glanced up at the junior-aged gallant who held her hand.

Fleeting memories joggled her thoughts.

A Sunday rather than a Saturday. A swaying boat rather than a caged lift.

A sky so blue it had hurt to look at it.

Or perhaps it had been Jonathon's eyes she had gazed into.

"Someday, sir," Rose said, blinking into focus bright green eyes that sparkled in the sunshine, "a pretty young woman is going to come round and knock you off your feet."

A young woman who believed that love precluded adultery. As Rose had once believed.

He winked, warm fingers gently pressing before releasing her hand. "Can't be as pretty as ye."

"You're a shameless flirt." Rose reached inside her reticule and retrieved a threepence coin. "But a charming one. Enjoy your break."

"Awww, ye don't 'ave t' do that, ma'am." He pocketed the silver coin. "But I thank 'ee. May'ap ye'll be back later? I be off at five."

Rose remembered the uncomplicated days of laughter and courtship, when love and sexual satisfaction had in her naivety gone hand in hand.

She gazed up at the boy poised on the threshold of manhood, his natural advantage enhanced by the five-inch lift of the cab. "Do you know, I am tempted."

His thin young face flooded with undisguised pleasure. "Really?"

Rose smiled. "Really."

" 'Ey!" he called behind her. "I'll be 'ere! M' name's—"

The revolving door cut off the boy's name. The sincere admiration in his eyes followed her out onto pavement that sparkled in the sunshine.

Pulling on black leather gloves, Rose rounded the corner of the quiet off-street. Immediately she was swallowed in a sea of prodding umbrellas and bouncing bustles.

This was the heart of London, the business district.

The crush and rush was oddly exhilarating. They didn't care who she was—those faceless, nameless men and women who pushed and shoved to get where they wanted—and neither did Rose.

Breathlessly she stepped out of the human locomotion into the path of the London Stock Exchange. The massive building formed a triangular island surrounded on all sides by a clamoring sea of noise and motion.

Back stiffening, Rose stepped inside the financial palace. Instantly London receded.

Fractured light illuminated a black-and-white diamond-patterned marble floor.

Rose glanced up, heels hollowly echoing: The tall, domed ceiling was glass.

A clutch of men wearing dark wool coats and felt bowler hats leaned against a rectangular column, voices a rumbling murmur. Rose did not recognize their faces: They could be clients or stockbrokers.

Regret danced on shimmering rays of sunshine: The London Stock Exchange was as much an enigma as the Houses of Parliament.

Squaring her shoulders, Rose determinedly followed a line of black diamonds.

A man wearing a dark gray hat and coat detached from a bank of bronze elevators and strode toward her, heel taps louder than hers.

Rose slowed . . . footsteps faltering . . . womb clenching in recognition.

Underneath the flapping gray coat the man wore black.

They were not the same clothes he had worn the night before, she thought on a painful surge of tenderness.

And then there was no room for thought.

Jack Lodoun stepped in front of Rose, a head taller than she, so close she could smell warm wool and the distinct aroma of spice and roses. Underlying the three familiar odors was the unmistakable scent of his flesh, a scent that could not be manufactured or duplicated.

"What are you doing here?" Rose asked, mouth so dry she could not swallow.

Deep between her buttocks she felt the faint presence of his ejaculation.

"What are you doing here?" he rejoined, voice expressionless, face clean of stubble, eyes darkly shadowed by the brim of his hat.

"I came to see my husband."

"So did I."

The rubber cap squeezing her cervix palpitated, as if it possessed a heartbeat.

Rose forced out the words. "What did you say to him?"

"I told him I was your lover," he said unapologetically.

Rose had the curious sensation that the floor tilted.

"No," she said. Or maybe she only thought she spoke.

She had not wanted Jonathon to learn this way. Not from the man with whom she had cuckolded him.

Rose stepped around Jack.

Only to find her way blocked by Jack.

"He won't divorce you," he said flatly.

"You had no right," she said, corded silk cutting through her leather glove. And again stepped around him.

Only to again be blocked.

"I'm your barrister." Shimmering sunlight framed his shadowed face. "I have every right."

"The fee I pay determines your rights," Rose lashed back.

Rights jolted up to the glass-domed ceiling.

The gazes of men crawled on her skin like electricity. The pain that blossomed inside Jack's eyes cramped her stomach.

"Don't go to him," he said. "Stay with me."

"He's my husband."

And Jack had hurt him.

"And I'm your lover."

And Jonathon had hurt Jack.

But she had not vowed to love Jack. She had not betrayed Jack in the most fundamental way a woman could betray the man she loved.

Rose stepped around the barrister. He did not stop her.

The ornate bronze lift on the far right was open.

Hurriedly she crossed the marble floor, reticule swinging, bustle bouncing, heel taps echoing.

If only she could walk faster. If only she had not flirted with the lift boy.

"Afternoon, ma'am." A burgundy-uniformed man heartily welcomed Rose. "Which floor?"

Every direction in which Rose stared she saw her ignorance reflected inside a mirror.

Rose had never asked Jonathon the simple question of what floor he worked upon. Nor had Jonathon volunteered the information.

Now it was too late.

"I'm here to see Jonathon Clarring," she said, gloved fingers fisting, unable to stop the cycle of pain she had instigated.

"Popular man today, is our Jonny," the man said. "Fifth floor is what you want."

Tears pricked Rose's eyes: She had never known anyone to call her husband anything other than Jonathon.

The cab seamlessly halted, directed by an experienced man instead of a boy. Slamming metal drove home the urgency spiraling inside her.

Jonathon was slipping away. But she could not yet let him go.

Rose stepped onto plush, burgundy carpeting.

"Third door to the right, ma'am," trailed after her.

She did not recognize Jonathon—an unassuming man in both dress and manners—in the opulent decor.

Crystal sconces flickered in the windowless corridor. White porcelain doorknobs gleamed.

Brass bore Jonathon's name, at last a sign of familiarity.

A soft *tat-tat-tat* permeated the mahogany door.

Heart pounding—hands swimming inside the leather gloves—Rose turned the porcelain doorknob.

A woman busily typed on a large nickle-plated typewriter; she did not notice the opening door.

The tears burning Rose's eyes swelled her chest.

She was young, the woman who typed Jonathon's letters. And she was quite, quite pregnant.

Her skin glowed with youth and happiness.

Rose estimated her age to be twenty-two.

Had Rose's womb accepted Jonathon's seed on their honeymoon, Rose distantly thought, she would have been in the advanced stages of pregnancy at the age of twenty-two.

Without warning, the rhythmical *tat-tat-tat* died.

Hazel eyes—neither brown nor green—caught Rose's gaze. The young woman smiled, a pretty smile. "Hello. May I help you?"

There was no recognition inside the shining face.

Her father's office, Rose remembered, was papered with photographs of his wife and children.

There was nothing inside the waiting room to remind a client—or Jonathon—of his wife.

Rose gripped her reticule. "I'd like to see Mr. Clarring, please."

"I'm afraid Mr. Clarring is not available right now." No guile marred the young woman's innocence. "Would you like to make an appointment?"

I would like *to see my husband.*

The desperate demand lodged inside her throat.

Rose could not let this pregnant young woman announce her. Impulsively she crossed the room and opened the door that could only lead to Jonathon's office.

A slender, navy blue shoulder slipped through a matching door behind a large mahogany desk.

"Miss . . . Missus," called behind her, pregnancy slowing down the secretary. "You can't go in there. . . ."

Rose ignored the young woman, her entire being focused on the man who would not face her, not in his home, nor here in his office.

"Jonathon," tore out of her chest.

His name slid through the crack.

Jonathon closed the door on Rose with a quiet, definitive click.

She could not let it end this way.

Rose crossed thick carpeting that sucked at her feet and wrenched open the door through which he had disappeared.

For one fleeting second she fully saw his back, light brown hair and navy frock coat black with shadow.

"Jonathon, please don't walk away from me," chased down the dimly lit corridor. "Talk to me. *Please*."

A door opened—light cut through the shadows. The door closed, taking with it the light.

Please bounced off wood leeched of color; it was swallowed by flickering darkness.

"Ma'am." The secretary had decided upon a safe form of address. Feet heavily navigated the quagmire of carpeting behind Rose. "Ma'am. You can't go there." The heat of two bodies suddenly crowded Rose's spine, mother and child. "That way goes to the trading pit. Ma'am, please come back."

Rose abruptly became aware of her right hand that reached out for a man who in every way possible had rejected her. Clenching her fingers into a fist, she dropped her arm and turned around.

The young woman was taller than Rose by several inches. Swollen breasts that would suckle a baby heaved up and down in distress.

Rose dragged her gaze upward.

The secretary's face was so pale she could see tiny blue veins pulsing underneath her eyes. Clearly she did not understand what she had just witnessed.

"It's all right," Rose said numbly. "I merely wanted Mr. Clarring to"—what exactly would a client want from Jonathon?—"to reconsider my stock options. It's all right, really. Please don't get excited. I'm leaving."

Uncertainty flared inside the young woman's eyes. "Should I ring someone to help you?"

The secretary was concerned for *her* health.

Laughter worked up inside Rose's throat. Distantly she realized it was hysteria. Tightly she clamped down on the laughter.

"I should be asking you that question," Rose said gently, the eldest child. A "little mother," her mother had always called her. "Shall you be all right? I didn't mean to alarm you. Shall I ring for assistance?"

A healthy flush colored the woman's too-pale cheeks. "Oh, no, ma'am. I'm fine, really."

Rose allowed the pregnant secretary to escort her back to the waiting area.

Settling behind her desk—typewriter monopolizing the wall to her right—she reached for a black leather diary. "Shall I make an appointment?"

"No." Hazel eyes shot upward; uncertainty resurfaced within them. "I'll ring," Rose assured the pregnant woman; she was curiously devoid of emotion. And then, "Are you sure you're all right?"

"Yes, ma'am." Her sudden smile blinded Rose with its youthful sweetness. "Thank you, ma'am."

Rose took one step at a time. Exiting the office. Closing the door. Walking down the corridor.

A lift waited, cab open.

Rose simultaneously saw the different facets of Jack Lodoun: Face dominated by darkness. Left profile streaked with a fan of red-gold hair. Right profiled nose wearing his past. Thick brown-red hair shone below dark gray felt and hugged the base of his skull.

"Can you operate this?" she asked evenly.

There was no purple inside Jack's eyes. "Yes."

"How did you gain control of it?"

"I bribed a lift man."

Rose stepped inside.

Gray coat flapping, Jack expertly notched the metal gate. Gently the cab lurched . . . descended.

"Have you ever fucked inside a lift?" she asked incuriously.

It should not be possible for his eyes to grow any darker. "No."

Rose reached out and pressed a bronze button. The cab halted in between floors.

"Fuck me, Jack."

Chapter 23

"I don't have any condoms."

Jack's voice mirrored Rose's lack of desire.

"Perhaps, Jack, I was wrong when I insisted I would fuck no man without a machine." Bronze metal and mirrored glass closed around her; the open shaft below the cab yawned beneath her feet. "Perhaps I'm not in need of protection."

"Or perhaps, Rose"—his eyes underneath the gray hat were devoid of light—"you'd like a child to give to your husband."

"No." Pain nipped at her womb. "I told you I'd never go back to Jonathon."

"But you did, Rose." There was no accusation inside his voice; the stark knowledge of the choice she had made hollowed his cheeks. "You did."

"So now you won't fuck me?" she asked, attempting whimsy, falling short.

"Is that all you want from me?" Uncoiling cable snaked through bronze and glass: People going up, people going down, impervious of the man and woman who were stalled between floors. "A splendid fuck?"

The danger of their position—suspended over an elevator shaft—danced on her skin.

"Isn't that what you want, Jack?" Her dangling reticule weighted her right arm; the cutting cord was curiously painless. "For me to fuck you? Like I fucked the dildo?"

"I don't have any condoms," he repeated.

She had not seen the silver condom holder when she had vacated the bedroom that smelled of Rose and Jack and the sex they had shared.

Would the maid find it?

Or had it disappeared, like her brief laughter thirty minutes earlier?

"I visited a gynecologist," she reluctantly confided.

His nostrils flared. "You're wearing a diaphragm?"

Had the woman he loved worn a diaphragm?

"A Dutch cap," she corrected.

Obviously he knew what it was that guarded her womb. Like a Chinese trap, deterrents of contraception said of feminine protective devices.

Jack reached for his trousers, gaze holding hers. "Lift up your skirts."

Rose lifted her cloak, skirt, and two petticoats over her knees . . . up to her waist. She leaned against the mirrored wall like the prostitutes she had seen portrayed in lurid newspapers. "Like this?"

But Jack did not answer.

One second he was across the cab—red, swollen sex jutting out from a black vent—the next instant hard fingers tunneled underneath the four layers of wool and lifted her off the floor.

The breath was momentarily knocked out of her lungs.

Rose looked down into his eyes, as she had looked down at him inside the courtroom.

But he had not then been her lover.

A renting wave of emotion slammed through her. "Jack."

She was sandwiched between hard glass and equally hard man.

It hurt.

Her wire bustle that dug into her buttocks. His fingers that dug into her waist.

The pain Jonathon had caused her. The pain she had caused Jack.

The fingers pinching her right waist disappeared.

Rose dropped, body listing.

For one terrifying second she thought the lift had snapped a cable.

Instantly she released her skirts and grabbed Jack's shoulders, reticule a swinging pendulum, fingers digging into three layers of wool. Simultaneously Jack found her, sharp knuckles jabbing into her tender vulva, the head of his penis as big as a fist.

Reason assured her the lift was not dropping. Reason did not stop the slide of crunching wire and bunching wool.

Inch by inch Rose slid down the cold, impersonal mirror that reflected their union.

She was not wet with desire, but she was slick from the lubricant the gynecologist had used when examining her.

Jack gorged her vagina—inch by inch—until he could go no deeper and her eyes were even with his nostrils that flared with each gusting breath.

The painful stretch of her body dilated his pupils.

"What do you want, Rose?" he rasped.

"I told you what I want," Rose insisted. She was fully clothed: She had never felt so naked, with only their sexes touching. "I want you to fuck me."

It was the only form of love they would ever be able to share.

Body shifting—Rose's breath snagged inside her chest; she could not breathe for the twin pressure of glass and groin—Jack crowded his hands between her thighs and lifted up her buttocks.

Rose sucked in hot, moist air. "Jack."

Her pain flared inside his eyes.

"That's all you want from me?" he breathed into her mouth, chasing the words with his tongue. "A fuck?"

The triple penetration of his penis and his tongue and his breath pierced the very core of Rose.

"Yes," she gasped, jerking back her head. Hard glass blocked her escape. "That's all I want."

Splendid fucks.

"What about what I want, Rose?" He held open her buttocks and her thighs and thrust so deeply the wire bustle fused her lower spine and he stabbed her heart. "Don't you want to know what I want?"

"What *dif*ference—" He thrust again, *hard*, wire gouging, wool scratching the insides of her thighs. She gasped, throwing back her head. "Oh, my dear God!"

The ceiling was mirrored.

Rose stared up at a man who wore gray, and a woman who wore black.

Beaded jet winked in the dim light. Black gloves clutched gray-shrouded shoulders.

"I want you to want me"—the black-bonneted woman with the beaded reticule and gloved hands surged upward; at the same time Rose was split apart—"for *more* than a splendid fuck."

Rose could feel a wetness pooling inside her vagina that had nothing to do with the lubrication from the gynecologist and everything to do with the man who was her lover.

"I want you to take my cock," Jack said, voice gritting. A hard thrust cleaved Rose in half. "And love the jizzum *I* give you."

The next rending thrust snapped down her head.

Jack's face was rock hard with purpose.

He would not stop thrusting. The pain would not stop hurting. The pleasure would not stop building.

"I want you to want me *more* than you want your husband," convulsed her womb.

Rose's arms locked around Jack's neck. His penis—fist-sized crown pulsing like a heartbeat—lodged inside her chest.

A grating cry ripped her throat. At the same time ejaculating sperm scalded her pelvis.

"God," licked her temple. Five fingers dug into her left buttock; Jack ground his sex so deeply inside her she could not tell if it was her pubic hair that pricked her pubes or his. At the same time a hard hand wormed out from between her thighs and tunneled up the back of her bodice, fingers spanning her corseted spine. "Rose. Rose."

Jonathon had never called out her name. Now he never would.

And now Jack was leaving her, each hot spurt shrinking the connection of their flesh.

"I'm sorry." Throat tightening to fight back tears, Rose turned her face into prickly soft whiskers. "I'm sorry."

"It's all right," scraped her cheek.

But it wasn't.

"I wanted the pain to go away." A stubble that had escaped his razor pricked her top lip. "Just for a moment."

"I know." The timbre of his voice vibrated her skin. "I know."

Because of his love for another woman.

"Your cock *is* a part of me, Jack."

Wet heat licked her jaw.

"And I value your pleasure." Her vagina fluttered in the aftermath of orgasm. "More than I can say."

"Rose," laved her cheekbone.

Her admission had not brought Jack the comfort she had hoped.

"You're not wearing the same clothes you wore last night," she said, gulping air.

Clothes that she had folded for him. And upon which he had loved her.

Hot breath gusted her forehead . . . her right eyebrow. "I changed at the office."

But her lover's office was as unfamiliar to Rose as had been her husband's office.

Struggling to breathe—crushed between wool-padded muscles and unyielding glass—Rose latched onto a subject that involved just the two of them. "How much did you give the lift man?"

"Ten pounds."

"You gave my housekeeper twenty pounds," she said unevenly.

Lips softer than sunshine grazed her left eyelid. "I wanted to feed you my cock, not your breakfast."

Laughter worked up inside her chest, was halted by her too-tight throat.

"I gave a lift boy threepence today," she whispered.

A hot tongue flicked the corner of her eye. "Why?"

"He said I was a pretty lady." She clenched her vagina to keep Jack inside her, softening crown a kissing bud. "And he asked me to join him for a cup of coffee."

"Cheeky bastard," scraped her forehead.

Rose blindly turned up her head, following the warmth of his lips. "He made me laugh."

Jack stilled, gusting breath catching . . . slowing.

An image of the pregnant young secretary flashed behind her eyelids.

Rose tightened her arms, bracing herself against more pain. "Is the child his?"

"No," resonated against the bridge of her nose.

Rose did not know if she was glad or regretful.

Her fingers with a will of their own worried a stiff collar, searching for more of Jack, touch frustrated by cotton and leather. "He wouldn't see me."

The soft knob of his penis jabbed her on a sudden intake of air. "What do you mean?"

"There's a door inside his office that leads down to the"—Rose struggled to remember what the secretary had called it—"traders' pit."

Soft lips branded her temple; the brim of a hat collided with the crown of her hat.

"He must have heard my voice," Rose said, the hurt Jonathon had inflicted muted by Jack's flesh. "When I went into his office, he walked out. When I followed him, he escaped through another door."

His naked flesh slipped free of her naked flesh.

Reluctantly Rose released the comforting warmth of Jack's neck. At the same time he let her go: her buttocks . . . her spine . . .

Silk drawers peeled away from her sliding thighs, wool trousers a rough abrasion.

Her shoes impacted a tiled floor, heavy skirts dropping over her hips. Warm liquid trickled down the inside of her left leg.

She stared up into eyes that leaked purple pain.

"He'll have to confront you in court," Jack said.

But she could not say what she needed to say in a room filled with strangers.

Rose glanced downward.

Jack had unfastened all but the top button of his trousers. The bold red crown of his penis was now a bluish bud that shyly peeped out of a shiny-wet prepuce.

Irresistibly she reached out—his flesh was slippery, soft even through butter-soft leather—and tucked him inside pink wool.

A damp circle darkened the front of his smallclothes.

The wetness did not all come from him.

Rose spoke past the sudden lump inside her throat. "When I married Jonathon, life was so simple."

She fastened a wooden button, the slitted hole tight, gloves a black hindrance.

"I thought when a man and a woman loved one another," Rose said, "they would live together happily ever after."

Metal cable coiled around a metal gear, a lift rising above them.

Rose fastened a second wooden button, leather-covered knuckles brushing wool-protected flesh. "I thought love was all that mattered."

The front of his smallclothes tented, sex reaching for her.

"You're not a simple man, Jack," she acknowledged ruefully, heart twisting inside her chest.

Always Parliament would stand between them.

She fastened a third button, gloved fingers finding the rhythm of masculine dress.

"But I do know one thing," Rose said, firmly closing the V of black wool.

Jack's voice was guarded. "What?"

Rose fastened the fourth and final button. Carefully she tucked a roll of white shirt inside the band of his trousers and smoothed the wrinkles out of a pearl gray silk waistcoat before stepping back.

She would not hide from the truth.

Rose met his gaze. "I do want you more than I want my husband."

Dark color edged the tautly stretched skin over his cheekbones.

The rift Jack had created loomed between them.

"But I need to talk to Jonathon."

"Why?" he asked harshly.

For better or worse, she had been married for twelve years.

"I need to say good-bye," she said.

Jack searched her gaze for long seconds before he lowered his lashes; the brim of his hat shadowed his face. "He believes you'll go back to him."

Rose breathed deeply. "I can't."

The pain had to end.

Reaching inside his frock coat, Jack pulled out a crisply folded white handkerchief. Lashes lifting, gaze veiled, he asked. "May I?"

Rose irrepressibly remembered the care with which her brother had cleansed her face and the familial closeness she had felt.

"Yes," she said, needing Jack, but also wanting Jack. "Please."

Jack leaned forward until he filled her vision: Eyes dark underneath the gray brim of a hat; hair that glinted with red fire even in the dim lighting of the lift. At the same time surprisingly cool air crawled up her legs.

"I've only ever loved one woman, Rose." Starched cotton shaped by masculine fingers slipped inside the vent of her drawers and swiped dry her inner thighs. "I never thought I'd want another woman. But I want you."

Tears burning her eyes, Rose reached out and straightened his black-and-gray-striped tie. "I know you do."

"No, Rose." The flesh-contoured handkerchief slipped between her thighs, seeking admission. "You don't know."

She parted her left leg . . . her right leg, granting him the same access to her sex that he gave to her.

Abrasive cotton swirled around the portal of her vagina . . . reached up inside her vagina.

Rose involuntarily abandoned his neckcloth and gripped the lapels of his coat.

"I will not allow you to live alone for the rest of your life." Gently, firmly, Jack swirled the handkerchief deep inside her. His gaze penetrated her far more deeply than his fingers. "I will stay with you for as long as you want me."

Rose closed her eyes against the pain and the pleasure that was Jack Lodoun. "And you'll love me when you fuck me."

"And I will gladly pay the price."

Slowly, methodically, he cleaned her. She could feel his gaze mapping her every reaction: internal . . . external.

The fullness inside her vagina traveled up into her chest.

"Would you want me, Jack," Rose asked, lashes lifting, fingers tightening, throat swelling, "if I should terminate a pregnancy that resulted from our union?"

He kissed her eyelids closed. "Yes."

Unable to stop the pending loss, Rose held her face still for the moist press of his lips.

Jack withdrew from her body: fingers . . . lips. Warm wool slithered down her legs.

Rose opened her eyes and studied the man she had taken as her lover. "You called my name."

It reverberated inside the cab.

Her name. His name.

Lashes lowered, Jack folded the handkerchief with which he had cleansed her and thrust it into his trouser pocket. "Yes."

Rose felt the presence of Cynthia Whitcox.

"Do you cry for her?" she asked impulsively.

Jonathon had cried over the loss of his children. Did men cry over the loss of a woman?

Jack's lashes slowly lifted; his voice, when he spoke, was as expressionless as his eyes. "No."

He lied: He cried every time he ejaculated inside her.

Rose took a deep breath.

She had set out with three objectives this day: to visit Sarah Burns, to confront her husband, and to shop. While Jonathon had thwarted her second goal, she could yet accomplish the third.

Chapter 24

Men did not rule in the domain of women.

"There, Madame Clarring." Careful hands lowered a hat onto guinea-gold hair. "It is *très* chic, *non*?"

Rose angled her head; mottled sunshine laved an oval cheek. The pearl that hugged her earlobe glowed as if it were alive. "It's very purple."

"It is heliotrope, madame." Slender, clever fingers straightened a primrose bow, fluffed a tuft of white feathers. "*Très* fashionable. You are an attractive woman. This hat"—she expertly curved the brim—"shows off your face . . . *comme ci* . . . while the ostrich feathers give you height, *non*?"

Inside the mirror, cornflower blue eyes snagged Jack's watching gaze. "Do you like it?"

Jack thought of the pain Jonathon Clarring, her husband, had caused her in the past. Jack thought of the pain that he, her lover, would bring her in the future.

"A beautiful hat for a beautiful woman," Jack said truthfully.

Rose flushed with pleasure. "I'll take it, Madame Benoit."

"Excellent," the milliner said, French accent slipping. Quickly the thin, energetic woman caught herself. "*Maintenant*, a chapeau for the simple pleasures of summer. *Oui*?"

"Madame Benoit," drifted up to the front of the shop. "Do you have any more of the dark gray cocks' plumes?"

"*Un moment*, Madame Gerard," the milliner called out.

Nimble fingers quickly replaced plush heliotrope with gold straw.

To Rose, the milliner said, "You have *beaux yeux*, madame."

Beautiful eyes.

No vanity at the compliment shone inside Rose's eyes.

Reaching into a bulging white apron, the milliner produced a spool of bright blue ribbon. "I wrap the ribbon round like this. . . . See how it brings out the color? Monsieur"—the milliner's voice subtly chilled—"if you will be so kind as to hand me that spray of flowers. . . ."

Jack sharply glanced upward.

Brown eyes captured his: They were filled with condemnation.

She knew Jack, the milliner's gaze said. She knew the pain he would inflict.

It was obvious she had read about the trial.

Her disapproval, Jack curiously noted, did not extend to Rose.

Instantly the woman's animosity disappeared. A thin finger pointed toward a table beside Jack.

Silk flowers covered the wooden surface: white orange blossoms . . . purple irises . . . pink primroses . . . red roses . . .

Unerringly Jack selected a sprig of silk cornflowers. Impulsively he added a purple-blue spray that resembled periwinkles.

The woman's brown eyes flickered. "*Très bien, monsieur*."

"Thank you, madame, that is very attractive." Inside the mirror Rose gazed at Jack rather than the silk flowers the milliner stuck into the band of blue ribbon. "Can you make it up while we wait?"

"Certainly, madame."

Plucking off the straw hat, the milliner disappeared in a rustle of wool.

Muted murmurs carried over the whine of carriage wheels.

"She recognized you," Rose said in a quiet voice.

"Yes," Jack merely said.

He was oddly untroubled by the thought.

"When will you petition the courts?" carried over the quiet murmurs behind him.

But Jack did not have an answer.

"How did you come by your earrings?" he asked instead.

Shadow kissed her face. "They were a gift."

He held her gaze inside the mirror. "From whom?"

"My father."

The pain Jack had caused dilated her pupils.

"Why did you visit him?"

Jonathon Clarring.

"I needed to see the man you married," Jack said.

A man who had filled her with his sperm.

Now Jack's sperm resided inside her body.

Jack had fucked only one other woman without benefit of a condom.

A sharp jangle pierced his spine: Grinding wheels, plodding hooves and raucous voices invaded the shop. Immediately the door closed, dulling the cacophony of civilization.

"Bonjour, Madame Hallsburn!" wafted from the back of the shop. "I'll be with you shortly."

"Good afternoon, madame . . ." drifted away from the front of the shop.

Rose's gaze did not veer away from Jack. Jack did not look away from Rose.

Sexual awareness glimmered inside her eyes.

"In which place did you prefer ejaculating?" she unexpectedly asked.

Before him men and women strolled past the window. Behind him three women concentrated on the makings of hats.

Or perhaps not.

"Your vagina," Jack said, voice equally quiet, acutely aware of the public setting in which they privately discoursed.

"Why?" Rose asked curiously.

The memory of her flesh embracing his naked flesh rubbed raw his nerves.

"I wasn't alone when I came."

He had felt disjointed and vulnerable when he had buried himself between her buttocks, taking his pleasure while she gave him absolution.

"I came alone last night," she observed.

"I breathed your scent; I swallowed your taste. You came in my hands, against my tongue." Jack held her gaze. "You were not alone, Rose."

Inside the mirror, light played on her face while darkness swallowed her eyes. "You didn't cleanse away all of your ejaculate."

Hot blood seared Jack's cheeks at the imagery of her vulva swollen and wet, dripping his sperm; a matching band of heat ringed his cock. "Can you feel the Dutch cap?"

"Yes." She matched his sexual curiosity. "Could you, when you were inside me?"

"Not with my cock," Jack replied, gaze unwavering. "What does it feel like?"

Her face was solemn. "When I left the doctor's office, I was afraid to take the stairs for fear I'd dislodge it."

So she had taken a lift. And a young boy had made her laugh.

Jack squelched a spark of jealousy. "And now?"

"I think it may be permanently affixed to my cervix."

A purely masculine laugh shot out of his throat.

"*Ici*, madame," stanched his laughter. "Should you like to look at more hats?"

"No, thank you, Madame Benoit." Rose stared at Jack's reflection instead of the milliner. His stomach clenched, seeing the feminine appreciation inside her eyes. "Just these two, please."

He wanted to pay for her purchases; he had learned his lesson at the bookshop.

Shoving a hatbox underneath his right arm, he thrust open the shop door; overhead a bell jangled. At the same time Big Ben hailed the hour.

"Look, Mama, it's Mrs. Clarring!" wafted over the dual bells.

Jack's gaze snapped toward the two women walking toward them.

For one second he caught their gazes; they glanced away on the second bong.

Rose stepped over the threshold, carrying the second hatbox.

She, too, had heard the two women speak her name.

"Hello, Mrs. Witherspoon," Rose said politely. "Miss Witherspoon."

The two women—one a matron, one a debutante—walked past her.

Jack glanced down at black felt and white feathers that danced on a sun-warmed breeze, all that he could see of Rose. He wanted to tell her it would get better: He didn't. Because it wouldn't.

Instinctively he found the curve of her elbow; a familiar pulse pounded against his fingers. "Where to now, Madame Clarring?"

Rose did not move for long seconds. Resolutely she squared her shoulders. "My dressmaker is just down the street."

Jack shortened his steps to match Rose's steps.

"You don't have to do this, Jack."

Jack leaned his head downward to hear over the grind of wheels and the clip-clop of hooves. "Do what?"

"I know what people are saying; I don't need you to protect me."

Jack could not stop gossip, any more than he could stop the careening wheels of a Clarence cab.

"I'm not here as your protector."

Rose halted, face turning upward into the sunshine. "Then why are you here?"

Faint lines—Jack wondered how often she had laughed in the last twelve years—fanned outward from her eyes.

"I smell you, Rose, the scent of your skin, your sex. I still taste you on my tongue." His fingers tightened around wool, and underneath that, fragile flesh and bone; releasing her elbow, Jack jerked open a glass-plated door. The chatter of women, the whispers of fabrics and the rustling of paper tumbled onto the London street. "I want to be with you."

The pained pleasure inside her eyes squeezed his testicles.

He would never bring Rose the happiness that Jonathon Clarring had briefly given her, but neither would he condemn her to a life of loneliness.

Rose stepped over the threshold.

All sound abruptly ceased on a closing jangle.

"Mrs. Clarring!" trilled a feminine voice that possessed neither warmth nor sincerity. The milliner had not judged Rose: The expensively gowned woman with elegantly coiffed graying blond hair who hurriedly approached them did. "What a surprise!"

"Hello, Mrs. Cambray," Rose said evenly, head tilting to stare up at the woman who stood five inches taller than she. "I'm sorry to drop in on you like this. Is Mrs. Throckenberry available?"

"Yes, of course." Cold eyes raked over Jack. Recognition flared inside the frigidly disapproving gaze. "Please step in here."

Her unspoken *away from respectable customers* knotted Jack's shoulders.

The windowless antechamber was cramped with a pink velvet settee, a pink-striped armchair, a round table smothered in lace and ruffles, and racks of fabric samples.

In its unchecked femininity it was as harshly judgmental of women as the uncompromising masculinity inside the House of Commons.

"Miss Williams," the proprietress called out in the palpating silence, "bring refreshments." Lowering her voice, she pointedly asked, "What will you have, sir?"

Rose sat on the pink velvet settee, seemingly impervious of the insult the older woman issued. Jack settled beside Rose, his hip notching her hip.

Her heartbeat pounded inside his groin.

"Brandy," he said, voice expressionless.

"Certainly." The woman's lips thinned, forced to address a woman publicly accused of adultery. "What will you have, Mrs. Clarring?"

Setting the hatbox on the table between the settee and armchair, Rose peeled off her gloves. "I'll have the same, please."

"Certainly," the woman grimly repeated. "I'll send in Mrs. Throckenberry."

Rose reached up to take the heavy tome the older woman extended, hip and shoulder nudging his hip and shoulder. "Thank you."

The silence inside the shop exploded with the closure of the door.

Jack moodily glanced down at Rose, unable to see her face. "Do you enjoy brandy?"

Rose opened the thick, cumbersome book. "It can be quite fortifying."

Black-and-white illustrations of women with rosebud lips and exaggerated bustles posed on finger-crimped paper. Outside the closed door whispers raged across the shop.

"I'm behaving badly." Rose abruptly glanced up. Her hip chafed his hip. "I should not have requested brandy."

There was no sign of the feminine curiosity or the sexual awareness that had earlier shimmered inside her eyes.

"Why did you?" he asked neutrally.

She glanced downward, face dissolving into black felt and white feather.

"I've never been shopping with a gentleman," she evaded.

Nor did she now: Jack had never claimed to be a gentleman.

"I've never been shopping with a woman," he admitted.

Black felt and white feathers became a pale white face and searching blue eyes.

Rapping knuckles overlapped muted whispers. Without waiting for permission to enter, a dark-haired girl pushed open the door, charged voices rushing past her: *Mrs. . . . How dare . . . Poor Mr. Clarring . . .*

Rose's pupils dilated with pain.

Jack's lips tightened into a thin, hard line.

This was the gossip with which she would live every day of her life.

Blushing a painful red, the dark-haired girl—younger than Jonathon Clarring's secretary—proffered a silver tray: Dark amber liquid sloshed inside crystal glasses. "Mrs. Clarring."

Head lowering—hat shielding her face—Rose grasped a short, crystal stem; Jack felt the shifting of her hip throughout his body. "Thank you, Miss Williams."

The young woman extended the tray to Jack. "Sir."

Jack scooped up the second glass.

The door softly closed. Pinching the stem as if it were a wineglass, Rose raised her snifter.

Her thoughts were on the other side of the door.

"Cup it," Jack instructed over the pulse of gossip that throbbed like a heartbeat through the thin walls. "Like you cupped my cock."

Rose glanced up, startled awareness flickering inside her eyes. "I beg your pardon?"

"Warm the brandy between your fingers"—Jack embraced brittle glass instead of the flesh he ached to touch—"until it's the same temperature as your body."

Eyelashes shielding her gaze, Rose's palm curved around her snifter, fingers smaller than his, more vulnerable than his. "You make drinking brandy sound sensual."

He saw in the shadows on her face the years of neglect she had experienced, married to a man who chose the oblivion of alcohol over the comfort of her arms.

"It can be," he said, deliberately drawing Rose's attention away from the pain of the past. "Bring the glass up . . . like this . . . and slowly inhale."

Jack held the rim of the snifter level with his chin.

Rose imitated his motions.

"The first smell is called the *montant*." Harsh alcohol burned his nose. "Now gently swirl your glass."

Rose carefully swirled her snifter, amber liquor sloshing.

He felt again the gentle caress of her fingertip, swirling his ear while he suckled her breast.

Her heartbeat had tattooed his tongue.

"A fine brandy—like a woman," Jack said, cock aching for her and from her, "has a special bouquet. Swirling releases the true character of the liquor. Inhale it"—he raised the snifter to his lips; above the glass he caught her gaze—"like this."

Rose raised her snifter. Her nostrils delicately flared.

"A fine brandy," Jack continued, "will have a fruity or floral aroma."

"I don't smell anything other than alcohol," Rose said, a woman of reason but also a woman filled with emotion.

Jack raised his glass and swallowed. Rose duplicated his movements.

"That's because," he said calmly, lowering his glass, watching her swallow, "this isn't a fine brandy."

A strangled laugh filled the narrow mouth of the snifter. Quickly, she replaced the glass with her fingers and patted dry her lips.

Jack knew her laughter wouldn't last.

"I can't change what I've done to you, Rose."

Rose glanced up, feathers dancing, laughter dying. "What do you mean?"

Chapter 25

"I've made you an adulteress." A soft knock brought home his point. "Every day you'll be judged." Jack remembered the tear he had licked from the corner of her eye, holding her inside the suspended lift while grinding cables coiled and recoiled around them. "But every day I'll fuck you until the pain goes away."

Inside her gaze he could see a question forming.

"Just for a moment," Jack added.

Always the pain would be waiting in the wings.

A turning click warned Jack of the coming intrusion.

"Hello, Mrs. Clarring!" fell on a sudden lull of gossip. "Sir."

For a long, charged second Rose assessed Jack. Head suddenly tilting higher, she smiled, a smile that was filled with both warmth and sincerity. "Hello, Mrs. Throckenberry."

"I'm sorry to keep you waiting." A gangly, ginger-haired woman—older than the girl who had served their drinks, but younger than Rose—perched on the pink-striped velvet armchair opposite the settee. Instantly she stood. "I'm sorry. Do let me take your cloaks."

"No, thank you, we're fine," Rose assured her.

The ginger-haired woman sat. "I see you've been to Madame Benoit's." Leaning forward, the woman pried off the top of the hatbox. "May I?"

"Certainly," Rose said.

Jack silently took Rose's snifter: He couldn't protect her from gossip, but he could protect her from cheap brandy. Leaning forward, he set both glasses onto the lace-covered table.

"How exquisite!" Purple flashed in his peripheral vision: The ginger-haired woman held up the heliotrope hat. "I know just the dress to compliment it." Reaching over the table, she flipped through the fashion book. "There . . . isn't it splendid?"

Jack had only ever seen a finished frock. Curiously he studied the black-and-white illustration.

Rose dismissed it out of hand: "It has fur—"

"It can be removed," the dressmaker hurriedly assured her. "Both the dress and the mantle are made of heliotrope *faille française*, and are quite versatile. They may be worn in spring, summer and fall. The mantle is of a darker heliotrope, and has bead and chenille ornaments on the front and the back, with heliotrope-colored beads on the shoulders. With your figure and your hair, you'd be positively smashing, Mrs. Clarring. I've often thought . . ."

Jack alertly glanced up.

The woman's face matched the pink of the settee. Her eyes were sincere: There was no pettiness inside them.

"What I mean to say, Mrs. Clarring, is that I think you're a beautiful woman. You've been nothing but kind to me, and I deeply regret the reception you've received today."

"Thank you, Mrs. Throckenberry." Rose was forgiving: Jack was not. "The dress is beautiful. How soon can I have it?"

The ginger-haired woman was not pretty; her smile transformed her face. "I should think in a week."

A date for Rose's hearing would be forthcoming in the next week, Jack thought.

"Is that another hat?" The dressmaker's eyes caught Jack's gaze: Her beautiful smile evaporated. "May I see it, sir?"

"Certainly," Jack said evenly, echoing Rose.

Gaze sliding away from Jack, the ginger-haired woman efficiently lifted the hat from the box.

"This is quite charming, Mrs. Clarring. If you'll turn the page . . ."

Rose studied fashion plates. Jack studied Rose.

Her fingers tracing a panier . . . Her breasts straining her cloak . . . Her hand reaching for a fabric sample . . . Her voice deciding upon a pattern . . .

She was animated in a way he had never before seen a woman.

Jack realized *this* was the picture of femininity that Parliament held: A woman taking pleasure in simple material comforts. A dress. A home. A child.

They didn't see that underneath the silk and lace their flesh pulsed with the need for love.

But Jonathon Clarring knew, Jack thought.

The dressmaker gathered together her notes. "We'll start work immediately, Mrs. Clarring."

"I have a new place of address, Mrs. Throckenberry." Rose reached into her reticule and withdrew a card. "Please send the bill here."

"Yes." The ginger-haired woman smiled. "Of course."

The dressmaker disappeared in a swirl of skirts: She did not close the door.

"When you're inside me"—Rose addressed Jack, but she stared at the empty chair—"does it ease your pain?"

Jack stared down at black felt and white egret feathers. "Yes."

"Did you like it"—her black cloak tented, breasts rising on an inhalation—"when I suckled your breast?"

The emotion she engendered squeezed his testicles.

"Yes," Jack said.

"I ache from you, Jack." Rose glanced up. "But I ache even more to feel you inside me again."

Her admission of desire squeezed a tear from his glans. Shifting, hand raising—knee pressing into her thigh—Jack skimmed her cheek that was softer than silk. "Rose—"

"Excuse me, Mrs. Clarring, sir," shattered their private moment.

The dressmaker's voice was stiff and angry.

Jack braced himself, hand dropping. Knowing what was coming.

He could give Rose moments of pleasure, but always the pain would return.

Rose glanced away from Jack, innocent still of what he had done to her. "Is anything the matter, Mrs. Throckenberry?"

"Mrs. Cambray said we cannot bill your new address."

Shock blackened Rose's eyes.

"She said . . ."

Jack waited, focused solely on Rose.

"She said she would be happy to bill your husband's address." The dressmaker's voice shook with embarrassment. "Or if you prefer, you may pay now."

Emotion chased away Rose's shock: pain . . . anger. Realization of what she would endure for a lifetime suddenly transformed into resolve.

"Please instruct Mrs. Cambray to join Mr. Lodoun and me immediately," Rose said evenly.

"Yes, ma'am."

The door swished half-closed.

Rose stared past Jack for long seconds before confronting his gaze. "You never asked Mrs. Whitcox if she wanted a divorce."

"No," he said, knee throbbing, cock aching.

"Because of this."

"Yes."

She would have become a pariah to the society she loved.

"You were afraid she didn't love you enough to agree."

The truth but not the whole truth.

"But you were even more afraid," Rose said, blue eyes black with pain, "her love wouldn't survive the scandal."

And now he would never know.

"Yes," Jack said flatly.

He smelled the proprietress, a rush of expensive perfume and pettiness: She smelled much like Blair Stromwell.

"Is there a problem, Mrs. Clarring?"

Staring eyes burned his knee, mentally photographing the image of Rose and Jack to fuel more gossip.

"Indeed not, Mrs. Cambray." Rose slowly glanced away from Jack. "I wished to express my congratulations."

"Indeed." The older woman's voice was nonplussed. Insincerely, she added, "Thank you."

"Your establishment must be quite prosperous," Rose continued calmly, face pale, chin high.

The older woman's voice bloated with pride. "Yes, we do quite well."

"You must do so well, Mrs. Cambray, that you will not miss the business of seven women."

Jack could feel the proprietress's smugness draining like pus.

"You do realize, I'm sure," Rose said, "that if you refuse my business, you also refuse the business of my mother and my five sisters-in-law."

"I am so sorry, Mrs. Clarring," the proprietress stiffly apologized, "if we have in any way led you to believe we do not value your patronage."

There was no rancor on Rose's face, only the quiet determination of a woman who refused to be judged. "Then you will send my bill to the address with which I provided Mrs. Throckenberry."

"Of course." Outside the open door malicious whispers rose and fell. "I will speak to Mrs. Throckenberry: She must have misunderstood my words."

"Thank you, Mrs. Cambray." Rose nodded her head in dismissal; dusky pink edged her cheekbones. "I was certain it must be a mistake. Please tell Mrs. Throckenberry to choose whatever accessories she feels will complement my wardrobe and to send them with the hats next week. You are very fortunate to have her; should you not, I believe we should have to take our business elsewhere."

"We deeply value Mrs. Throckenberry, Mrs. Clarring. As we do you and your family. Good day." Jack felt the proprietress's gaze. "Mr. Lodoun."

The defeated woman exited in a rustle of silk: Her scent lingered.

Rose had gambled and won.

This time.

Standing—cold embracing his knee—Jack extended his hand. "What would you have done if she'd said au revoir?"

Rose's naked fingers clasped his naked fingers; she stood in a rush of wool. Roses and Rose replaced the scent of perfume and greed. "I would have regretted the loss of my frocks."

"And would she have lost six additional customers?" Jack asked alertly.

Had Rose lost her family, as well as her husband?

Sadness dimmed the triumph in her eyes. "We'll never know, will we?"

Reaching up, Jack grazed her cheek with his forefinger, offering her a moment's respite. "I ache for you, too, Rose."

Briefly she closed her eyes and leaned into his touch.

Silence fell inside the shop, the proprietress murdering one rumor at a time.

Rose abruptly pulled away from Jack and hooked her arm through his. "Shall we go?"

The sunshine celebrated Rose's victory, dancing and bouncing on glass and metal harnesses.

Stoically Jack watched a four-wheeled Clarence cab pass him by.

A dark profile shone within.

Jack did not know if it was a man or a woman he glimpsed.

Slashing motion captured his gaze.

Rose hailed a hansom cab, black beaded reticule winking and waving.

Somberly he gazed down into cornflower blue eyes.

There was no judgment inside Rose's gaze.

"You did not make me an adulteress, Jack," she said firmly. "You made me your lover."

The acrid scent of horse and sweat stung his eyes.

Hand seeking, he found the anchor of Rose's spine.

He felt the bunching of muscle, her leg lifting. Her back stretched, arm reaching for the splashboard.

"Pantechnicon on Motcomb Street," drifted over the whine of wheels.

Jack followed Rose. Her scent and her heat filled the cab.

"What are we shopping for?" he asked, lungs constricting at her nearness.

The cab leapt into the stream of traffic.

"I have an empty house that needs to be filled with furniture."

Jack had a house full of furniture: He had not chosen one piece of it.

A small square of light glinted off a pearl earring.

"I shouldn't have mentioned you by name," Rose suddenly apologized.

"She recognized me," he said neutrally.

Rose's likeness had in several papers been coupled with Jack's photograph.

"Surely it won't matter what a few shopkeepers say." The cab lurched. Rose grabbed a leather pull. Jack braced his foot against the door. "Will it?"

"No," Jack lied.

Turning, Rose half stood and slid down onto the floor between his knees, dark hat and waving feather obscuring her face. "I want to feel you come in my hands, Jack, against my tongue."

Jack's heart gorged his cock. "You don't have to do this, Rose."

"But I want to." Hands bumping and grinding with the motion of the cab, Rose freed the second button fastening his trousers. "Inside the elevator, your cock pulsed inside me like a heartbeat. I want to taste your heartbeat, Jack."

Vulnerability charged through him.

Jack grasped her hands; her fingers continued moving. "I've been inside you, Rose."

The third button slithered free, his sex hardening with each twist of her fingers.

Rose rocked between his thighs with the motion of the cab. "I know, Jack."

She had tasted herself on his tongue, but she had never before taken a man's cock into her mouth.

Jack instinctively braced his foot more solidly to hold his body still against the shuddering motion of wood and leather.

"I don't want you to be repulsed by my scent," he said, forcing his fingers to release her.

Rose freed the fourth button. "Why would I be repulsed by the scent of our sex?"

Small hands found him. . . . Cool air kissed him.

Jack's head snapped back against the leather seat.

The hansom chased a Clarence: The four-wheeled cab could not outrun the two-wheeled cab.

"When I got up this morning"—warm breath blurred the top hat that whipped free of the Clarence cabby—"I smelled like this."

Jack closed his eyes, hands gripping the leather bench.

"Of roses, my scent." Warm lips grazed his cock. "Of spice, your scent."

Two women danced behind his eyelids: Cynthia Whitcox in red; Rose Clarring in black.

"Of musk"—a rasping tongue tasted the tears his cock cried and swallowed the woman in red—"our scent."

Hot liquid crawled down his cheek.

"I wanted you, Jack, the first moment I saw you," Rose whispered. Four distant bongs pierced wood and wool, flesh and bones. "For more than a splendid fuck."

Chapter 26

The glint of crystal and amber-colored brandy filled the darkness.

Across from the glass-topped desk, Jonathon could make out the shimmering outline of a woman.

She sat in a brown leather wing chair. She cradled a snifter of brandy against her stomach.

She talked. He listened. Unable to respond.

Now Rose was gone. And still the pain gnawed at him, every day swallowing another chunk of his life.

"Mr. Clarring?"

Jonathon was abruptly aware of where he was—his office, not his den at home—and the incessant hum of wheels that wafted up from the busy street below.

"Yes?" he asked alertly, head lifting.

A woman's head peeked around a mahogany door. "I stayed late to finish the letters you dictated this morning. Shall you sign them now, or wait until Monday?"

Pain stabbed through Jonathon.

The hazel eyes of the twenty-two-year-old woman were filled with so much vitality it hurt him to stare at her.

"Come in, Mrs. Jacobson," he said quietly, averting his gaze. "I'll sign them now."

The secretary reluctantly pushed open the door.

Afternoon sunlight slanted across thick burgundy carpeting, picked up gold highlights in her dull brown hair, and sharply delineated her extended abdomen.

She was embarrassed by her pregnancy. Jonathon thought she was beautiful.

Waddling slightly—hands holding a sheaf of papers in front of her to hide her condition—Elda Jacobson crossed the burgundy carpeting. She halted beside his desk, so close he could touch the rounded abdomen she strove to conceal.

Jonathon accepted the sheaf of letters, eyes focusing on the neat black typing instead of her gaze. "Sit down, Mrs. Jacobson."

"Thank you, Mr. Clarring, but I'm perfectly well, really I am."

Jonathon wondered what Rose would look like, swollen with child. Would her face glow with pregnancy, like the secretary's face glowed?

Would it bring joy back into her eyes?

He reached for a heavy silver pen. A shadow caught his gaze: It punched the front of the secretary's gown.

"Mr. Jacobson and I are ever so thankful to you, Mr. Clarring." The secretary's youthful enthusiasm spilled over Jonathon. "I don't know what we'd do now, if you had cut me off."

A woman was expected to retire out of sight of society once she was pregnant. As if carrying a man's child was something shameful.

"I appreciate the fact that you've stayed on, Mrs. Jacobson." Jonathon focused on the letter, and the pen that he suddenly clutched. "You're quite the most accomplished typewriter I've ever had."

"Thank you, Mr. Clarring." The wafting voice of a vendor

faintly cried out; it was instantly swallowed in the whining careen of afternoon traffic. "I appreciate you saying so."

Another shadow punched out the secretary's dress.

Jonathon paused, pen poised over a scribbled C, breath coming more quickly.

Surely the movement could not be what he suddenly suspected.

Dragging his gaze away from the secretary's abdomen, he finished his signature and laid aside the vellum paper.

"Did you take on that gentleman Mr. Stromwell recommended?" crawled down his spine.

Forcefully Jonathon concentrated on separating the second and third letters. "No."

"I'm glad," the secretary confided. "He made me a bit uncomfortable. It was his eyes. Purple, they were. Like purple ice."

Jonathon had not noticed the color of Jack Lodoun's eyes.

He had always known Rose would one day take a lover. But he had never thought he would meet with the man vis-à-vis.

Blindly he affixed his signature.

"A woman came after he left." The scent of wool and powder drifted over Jonathon; out of the corner of his eye he saw the secretary scoop up the signed letter. "She was quite pretty. She said she was a client, but I've not seen her before."

Jonathon reached for a third sheet of vellum paper.

He remembered the woman Rose had once been, as innocent and vibrant as the young secretary. When he had gazed at her in white organza with rose blossoms crowning her guinea-gold hair, he had thought she was the most beautiful woman God had ever created.

Jonathon still thought so.

"What was her name?" he asked, head bent over his work, knowing the answer.

"She didn't say." The scent of wool and powder washed over him, the secretary scooping up the third signed letter. "In her way, she was quite as frightening as the gentleman with the purple eyes. I told her you weren't available, and she marched right into your office. You must have just left to go down to the pit: I heard her call out. Did you hear her?"

"No," Jonathon lied. *Jonathon* reverberated inside his ears; it was chased by *please*. He reached for a fourth letter.

"Her eyes were quite striking, too," the secretary said, unaware of the fact that she talked about Jonathon's wife. "Blue as freshly picked cornflowers, they were. They'd make beautiful babies, she and the man with the purple eyes. Do you know her?"

Sharp quill slashing across vellum paper—lashes hiding the tears that suddenly blurred his vision—Jonathon quietly repeated, "No."

"Shall I ring security should she come again?"

Of one thing Jonathon was certain: "She won't be back," he said, and extended the fourth and final letter.

But Jonathon could hope.

Jack Lodoun did not love Rose like Jonathon loved her.

Jonathon could hope that the MP would do what was best for her.

The shadow punched out of the secretary's abdomen.

An uncontrollable yearning gripped Jonathon.

"Is that the baby?" he asked compulsively.

"He's very active today." A soothing hand rubbed the swollen abdomen. Distant bongs carried on a whine of traffic. "Mr. Jacobson says he's going to kick his way out one of these days."

"Does it hurt?" Jonathon openly gazed at her pregnancy. "When he kicks?"

"It's a bit of a jar." Sudden laughter reverberated inside Jonathon's ears. "That was a big one. You should feel it. . . ."

The secretary's voice died off in sudden embarrassment.

Jonathon tore his gaze off her abdomen and glanced upward. Her youthful face was crimson, the glow of pregnancy replaced with a flush of shame.

"I'm sorry," she said, exuberance stilted.

"There's no need to be," Jonathon said in all sincerity. "Your condition is perfectly natural."

She gazed at Jonathon for long moments, understanding slowly blossoming inside her hazel eyes, eyes the color of rich earth and fertile grass. "You don't have children, do you, sir?"

"No." Jonathon braced himself against a fresh wave of pain. "My wife and I were not so blessed."

Shy uncertainty flickered inside her gaze. "Would you like to feel the baby?"

Jonathon could not keep the hunger out of his eyes. "I don't want to presume."

"But you wouldn't be, Mr. Clarring. You've been so kind to me." Long fingers reached out; they were swollen now, as they often were. Warmth clasped Jonathon's fingers. Brought up his hand. Curved his palm over the round expanse of an abdomen. "Babies are such a joy, I think."

Rough wool abraded his fingers. Underneath the padding of cloth he could feel the warmth of skin. And underneath that a flutter . . . a kick.

Jonathon jerked back; his hand was held firm.

"There," Elda Jacobson said, generously sharing the life she carried within her, and the simple joy she took in motherhood. A joy of which Jonathon had cheated Rose. "That's a good one. Do you feel that, Mr. Clarring?"

A tiny foot—there was no mistaking the shape—sharply kicked the palm of Jonathon's hand.

Over the whine of traffic wafted four bongs.

"Yes." Tears scalded his eyes, feeling another man's child. "I do feel it, Mrs. Jacobson."

"Sometimes I can't sleep for his kicking." The warm, comfortable hand held him close. "There's another one. Do you feel it?"

Warmth seeped through Jonathon's body, a peace he had never before experienced.

He felt a kick. He felt a flutter. He felt another kick, a tiny imprint on his soul.

Jonathon pressed his hand more firmly against rough wool, feeling the future. Within Elda Jacobson's abdomen the seed of hope grew.

Chapter 27

One moment Rose drifted on a sea of roses, spice and musk; the next instant she was aware of staring eyes.

Her eyelids snapped open.

Jack stood beside the bed. Dark hair devoid of color slashed his forehead, blanketed his chest and nestled his sex.

The pale bud of his crown peeped out of an umbrageous hood.

Slowly Rose's gaze traveled back up his body. Greenish gray shadow pitted his cheeks.

"It's raining," he said.

Rose abruptly became aware of the now-familiar ache between her thighs and the steady patter of pelting water.

Jack had slept the night in her arms. Now Sunday had dawned and stolen the sunshine.

Rose flipped back the covers. "Then come back to bed."

The mattress dipped, propelling Rose sideways in a squeal of metal coils. "Do you still ache from me?"

Rose turned into the arm that slid underneath her, body bonelessly melding with his, left arm and leg anchoring his waist and thigh. "Yes."

Warm fingers cupped the back of her head and pressed her face into tightly curled chest hair. "Do you still ache for me?"

The heat prickling her legs and face lodged behind her eyes. "Yes."

Warm fingers swept heavy hair off her forehead. "Go back to sleep, Rose."

The gentleness of his touch squeezed her womb.

Over the steady drum of his heartbeat rain rhythmically slashed the window.

With a will of its own, her hand followed an arrow of prickly hair.

His sex—soft and warm—stirred in greeting.

"I think he likes me," Rose murmured sleepily.

A warm fingertip rimmed the curve of her ear. "I think you're right."

Gently she cupped twin sacs: Inside the leathery pouch hard flesh—round like two jack's balls—shied away from her fingers.

Twelve years earlier she had not understood how mumps could destroy a man's seed. She now understood the physical properties of reproduction, but she still did not understand how a man's sterility could destroy a marriage.

Throat tight, Rose husked, "Do they get cold?"

Jack cupped her hand. "Not when you're holding them."

The steady thrum of his heart and the warmth of his fingers and the patter of rain merged.

Growling motion woke her.

It took Rose a long second to identify the sound.

Slowly she released the testicles she protected—instantly the heat cupping her fingers dissipated—and pressed her hand against Jack's stomach, muscles harder than hers, but no less mortal.

A smile tilted her lips. "You're hungry."

"The growl, madam"—the timbre of his voice vibrated against her ear—"arose from your stomach."

"A hungry mouth, Jack."

One second she lay on her side; the next she was on her back staring up into shadowed eyes.

Fingers slid into the wetness their satisfaction had created.

The pain and the pleasure of his penetration dilated her pupils.

"How many fingers?" she asked.

"Three." Gently he explored her vagina. "I think the cap *is* permanently affixed to your cervix."

The memory of his laughter contracted her vagina.

"Perhaps," she said.

She would find out Tuesday.

The half pain, half pleasure that filled Rose was mirrored inside his eyes. "Did you like the taste of us?"

"Yes," she said, swallowing past the tenderness that swelled her throat. "Very much."

The three fingers filling her vagina slipped free, an audible slurp over the dull patter of rain.

Holding her gaze, Jack traced her lips, coating them with their essence.

Her nostrils flared, scenting him . . . her . . . them.

Lashes shielding his eyes, he leaned closer, breath a soft fan, and delicately licked her lips . . . in between her lips. Tasting the flavor she had earlier tasted. Simultaneously he found her underneath the sheet.

"Four fingers," he whispered.

Gently fluted to fill her.

Rose turned her face into beard stubble and wiry whiskers and held him until a wave of pleasure so intense it was pain passed over her.

Curiously she followed his arm.

His hand disappeared inside the heat that radiated from her body, thumb tucked against the prickly wetness of her vulva.

"Shall I feed you, Jack?" she asked, throat tight, tightening her arms.

Warm lips bussed her cheek.

She could not stop the withdrawal of his fingers. Her hands that embraced his shoulders were as ineffective as her vagina.

The mattress tilted forward; Jack swung his legs over the edge of the bed, springs voicing the protest she did not. "I shall feed you, Madame Clarring."

Rose stared at the shadowy indentation of his vertebrae. "You're going to prepare breakfast?"

Jack stood and flipped back the covers. The chill, nipping air was offset by his challenge: "You don't think a man can feed a woman?"

Rose solemnly took the hand he offered. "I have no doubt whatsoever, sir, that you can feed me."

The left corner of his mouth quirking—damp fingers firmly closing around her fingers—Jack effortlessly pulled her up and out of bed.

He trickled out of her.

Jack stared down at her thighs, half smile fading.

Flushing, Rose reached for a black pile of wool.

A long, narrow foot kicked her skirt and bodice under the bed. "There's no need to dress."

The clasp of his fingers clenched her womb and chased away the cold.

Feeling like a truant schoolgirl—a naked one, at that—Rose padded down the corridor with Jack.

"I have to"—how ridiculous to be embarrassed—"I have to wash."

Jack saw through the partial lie. He merely said, "I'll find the kitchen."

Rose quickly relieved herself. Snatching up a washcloth from the second drawer, she hurriedly cleansed her inner thighs and vulva.

Her naked breasts bobbed with the descent of each stair.

Watery gray light streaked the downstairs corridor.

Jack had indeed found the kitchen.

Overhead gas globes brightly illuminated the oblong room.

Jack peered inside the icebox, testicles dangling between his legs. A spotted enamel tea kettle heated on a flaming gas burner.

Tears filled her eyes.

Never in the twelve years she had slept alone—nightly fantasizing what sharing her life with a man might be like—had she imagined this type of intimacy.

Irresistibly she crossed the chill tiled floor and cupped his right buttock.

His skin was warm; a patch of hair prickled her fingers.

Jack straightened, a wire basket of eggs and a jug of milk in his hands. Slowly his gaze roamed over her body . . . her thighs, cleansed of his ejaculate . . . her abdomen, that was still filled with his ejaculate . . . her left breast, nipple dark and swollen from his suckling. Vivid purple eyes caught her gaze. "Grab the butter and cheese, and I'll make us an omelette."

She had not cried when rent with pain; she would not cry with pleasure now.

Scooping up a cheese and a crock of butter, Rose closed the icebox. "Where did you learn to cook?"

"There are more lawyers running around London than chimney sweeps." Jack opened several cabinet doors before finding what he needed. "My practice didn't immediately take off, as I had envisioned. It was a matter of learning how to cook over a single gas burner or going hungry."

Rose grated cheese, vision blurred. "Didn't your father help?"

"I have three brothers and five sisters." Jack whisked eggs and milk. "He put me through university. Even had he been so inclined, he didn't have the finances to indefinitely support me."

Pungent cheddar burned her nose. "You and your father aren't on good terms?"

"My father believes that a man who is left-handed has a serious flaw in his character." A wooden spoon banged a cast-iron skillet. "Whereas, I believe that a man who impregnates a woman in the name of God has a serious flaw in his character."

"Yet, Jack"—Rose rinsed off the cheese grater, water thundering over slashing rain, popping gas and sizzling butter—"you sit in Parliament surrounded by men who share the beliefs of your father."

"I never said," Jack said evenly over the angry hiss of semiliquid eggs poured into hot butter, "my father's estimation of my character wasn't correct."

Twisting off the faucet, Rose grabbed up the bowl of grated cheese.

Her nipple stabbed his arm.

Jack glanced down. There was no emotion inside his purple-blue eyes.

"Did you know your left testicle hangs down longer than your right?" Rose asked.

Bright purple light glinted down at her. "No doubt another symptom of my flawed character."

"No doubt," she agreed solemnly.

Between one blink and the next, Jack bent down and kissed her, clinging lips hotter than sizzling butter. The next instant he retrieved the bowl from between her fingers and dumped the grated cheese into the skillet.

Turning, opening a cabinet door—naked breasts lifting upward with the stretch of her arm—she found two white china plates with matching cups and saucers. "Cook purchased two table settings yesterday."

The thoughtful actions of both the cook and the man who now cooked fluttered Rose's heartbeat. Whimsically, she asked, "Shall we eat in bed and make a mess of the sheets?"

"We only need one plate." A warm hand fleetingly cupped her left buttock . . . reached over her head and plucked white china out of her fingers. "And we've already made a mess of the sheets."

Rose turned into a solid wall of hair-studded skin.

She could smell him. Taste him still on her tongue.

His heartbeat pounded against her stomach, his penis an intimate connection.

Throat cording, Rose threw back her head. "I didn't know it could be like this, Jack."

Lips branded her forehead. "I didn't, either, Rose."

Steam shrilled over the pop of grease and the drum of rain.

Grasping his naked hips—harder than hers, narrower than hers—Rose closed her eyes and leaned into his kiss.

A sheet of water slammed into the kitchen door.

They would pay for this moment of happiness, it warned.

But not today, Rose thought.

"Shall I make tea?" she asked, corded throat taut.

"Please."

Please *don't turn away* echoed over the pounding precipitation. Words she had spoken to Jack outside the courthouse. Please *don't walk away from me* chased the earlier plea, words she had spoken to Jonathon.

The hurt she had felt upon the two disparate occasions melted in the heat of naked skin.

"How do you take it?" Rose asked, chest aching.

Chapter 28

Jack carried up the omelette-laded plate. Rose carried a sloshing cup of sweet, lemony tea, gray steam spiraling upward into greenish-gray light.

Rain relentlessly slashed the solitary bedroom window.

Soundlessly—afraid of disrupting their intimate companionship—she deposited the cup and saucer on the nightstand.

Rose held the plate while Jack positioned the two pillows and sat back against the iron headboard. Jack held the plate while Rose climbed onto the bed and straddled his thighs.

Hair-studded skin prickled her vulva. His dark eyes squeezed her chest.

Carefully he forked a bite of egg into her mouth. Just as carefully Rose chewed and swallowed.

His gaze—watching her chew . . . watching her swallow—clenched the muscles deep inside her abdomen.

Her vagina—stretched by her position—remained open, a hungry mouth waiting to be fed.

Unable to bear the intensity inside his eyes, Rose took the fork from between his fingers. "Have you ever purchased a French postcard?"

A distant rumble of thunder permeated the drum of rain.

"Yes."

"I didn't realize men and women did the things they did . . ." Rose said, escaping his gaze by concentrating on slicing through egg and cheese. Silvery steam and the pungent aroma of cheddar wafted upward. ". . . until I visited the Achilles Book Shoppe."

"Were you disgusted by what you saw?"

"No." Rose tested the temperature of the egg with a flick of her tongue. Lashes lifting—his eyes were almost on a level with her own—she extended the fork. "Surprised."

He opened his mouth, gaze stark, and accepted the food she fed him.

Carefully Rose maneuvered between two rows of white teeth. "Intrigued."

His lips closed around the tines.

Slowly Rose tugged free the utensil. "Aroused."

His pupils dilated, the darkness of desire blending into the darkness of the day.

"But I wasn't disgusted," she reiterated.

Hard flesh surrounded Rose's fingers . . . took from Rose the fork.

His lashes lowered. Metal scraped china.

Lashes opening—gaze pinning hers—Jack offered the fork. "Open your mouth, Rose."

"It is open, Jack."

She had not realized a woman's body could be so open to a man.

A look of near-pain hardened his face. He leaned forward, mattress dipping.

His lips were hot, his tongue hotter yet.

He kissed her mouth open while her vagina leaked desire onto his thighs and lethean rain pelted glass.

"Keep your mouth open," vibrated her tongue.

Sharp, pointed metal entered between her lips.

She was suddenly, acutely aware of the damage that could be inflicted with the forked tines.

A single jab could pierce the back of her throat.

"Close your mouth," Jack said, voice a dark rasp.

Rose closed her lips tightly; egg and sharp cheddar replaced the taste of Jack.

Slowly he pulled out the fork, metal dragging against her inner lips.

The gentle scrape pierced her thighs.

"Which postcard most surprised you?" he asked, gaze fastened on her lips.

She remembered the blunt heat of his penis, pressing against the back of her throat. She tasted again the salty spurt of his sperm.

She knew that he, too, remembered the cab ride to the furniture store.

He had come in her hands, against her tongue.

"I think I was most surprised when I first saw a postcard of a woman spanking another woman," Rose said unevenly. It was on the tip of her tongue to add that the card had been brought to a club meeting by James Whitcox: She swallowed the name. "I hadn't realized that men took pleasure in a woman's pain. The bookshop possessed a wide selection of such cards, with both sexes featured. I realized then that it wasn't a woman's pain that titillated men, but the idea of inflicting pain."

"Pain is a form of power: It can be titillating for both the administrator and the recipient," Jack said enigmatically. And fed her another bite. Fork deeply entering her mouth. Like his sex. "Which postcard most intrigued you?"

Metal dragged between her lips, squeezing out of her vagina another trickle of desire.

Rose swallowed. And took from him the heavy silver utensil.

"I think it would be the one in which a man was being pleasured by two other men. One man knelt before him, kissing his sex," she said, sharp tines cutting. The image of Jack, naked—sex reaching—superimposed itself on the shadowy V of omelette. "Another man—I could only see his hands and forearms—stood behind him and caressed his nipples. The man who was being pleasured held out his arms and gazed at the camera, as if saying, 'See how splendid is man.'" Lashes lifting, she offered Jack the fork. Sincerely, she added, "I think you're a splendid man, Jack."

He took the fork deep into his mouth. He clamped his lips around the tines.

He let her see the naked need that she evoked in him.

"Which postcard most aroused you?" he asked.

Rose offered Jack the last bite. "One that depicted two men and a woman."

"Ménage à trois," he said, holding her gaze.

"Yes," Rose said, experiencing again the curious blend of need and longing that had fluttered inside her womb when gazing upon the postcard. "Have you ever engaged in the act?"

But Jack didn't answer. Instead he took the fork from between her fingers and set the plate onto the nightstand.

China thudded. Metal clanged.

Warm hands clasped her hips and tugged her forward, hair-studded thighs scraping her vulva.

She was not a doll, diminutive though she was. But Jack had never treated her like a doll.

For the first time in many years, Rose felt like a woman.

Her thighs embracing his hips. His sex nestling between her sex lips.

A curl of his chest hair ringed her nipple.

"What did you imagine when you looked at the third post-card?" he probed, the hard intent of desire softened by greenish-gray shadow.

"I thought how fortunate a woman would be"—Rose threaded

her fingers in his hair; it was thick and baby-fine—"to have the love of two men."

The white surrounding a pupil glinted in the gloom. "You have three mouths, Rose."

But only one of which her husband had been interested.

"Here," he whispered.

A scalding tongue licked the seam of her lips and laved her womb.

"Here."

A tapered finger dipped into her open vagina and prodded her heart.

"Here."

Fingertips feathered the indentation at the top of her buttocks.

Jack's gaze was dark and stark. "Which two did you imagine that the men filled?"

"My vagina and between my buttocks." Her vagina nipped his finger. "If you were one of the men in the postcard, which mouth would you fill?"

"All three," he promptly returned.

"You have filled all three."

"Not at once."

"If you had three cocks, Jack"—the yearning Rose felt for Jack clenched her vagina—"I would gladly take you in my every orifice."

"I do have three cocks."

Closing her eyes, she leaned her forehead against his.

"My tongue." Moist heat seared her chin. "My prick." Hard, pulsing flesh flexed between her nether lips. "My fingers."

He dipped a tantalizing inch into the dark crevice between her buttocks.

Jack invited her to reenact her fantasy. But he far superseded insubstantial flights of fancy.

"Where would you first fill me?" she asked, breath quickening, rain unceasing.

"Your vagina."

Jack lifted her buttocks. Rose guided his penis.

She took his sex deep inside her sex until he kissed her womb and her perineum cushioned his testicles.

"Your arse."

A tapered fingertip breached her buttocks.

Rose clasped his neck, her gaze holding his.

Inside his eyes she saw the fragile barrier that separated his penis and his finger.

Stretching. Ballooning.

A curious expression that was neither pain nor pleasure carved his face.

"Your lips."

He filled her lungs with his breath and her mouth with his tongue. At the same time he gave her a second finger.

His oxygen snagged inside her throat.

"Do you like being filled with three cocks?" licked her lips.

With each breath his chest hair prickled her nipples and his pubic hair tickled her clitoris.

The pain and the pleasure that was Jack contracted her womb. "Yes."

"Is this how you imagined it would feel?"

The tears leaking from her vagina burned her eyes. "This is exactly how I imagined it would feel."

He probed within her, touching a place deep inside her body where a man should not be able to touch a woman. "Do you feel loved?"

Cold rain pelted the window. Gray shadow weighted the air.

"I have never felt as loved, Jack," Rose said truthfully, his heart pounding inside her body, "as I feel now."

Chapter 29

Morning had dawned.

Jack had to leave, but he couldn't.

Rose bonelessly slept on his shoulder, thigh sandwiching his thigh.

He traced soft skin; underneath flesh was sharp bone.

Rose buried her cheek into the palm of his hand. Jack buried his face in Rose.

Smelling her. Smelling him.

Smelling the unique scent their sex created.

Warm fingers tangled in his whiskers. "It's Monday."

Jack nuzzled a shell-shaped ear. "Yes."

"I like your whiskers," Rose whispered against his cheek. "How long have you grown them?"

His sex reached for the comfort of her sex.

"I thought they befitted a member of Parliament," he thickly volunteered. "I grew them when I first stood for office."

"When was that?"

"Ten years ago."

Two years after her husband had contracted the mumps.

"I wish you didn't have to go," she murmured.

But Sunday was over. And Monday had dawned.

"I have an arraignment at eleven."

Her combing fingers tightened. "It's raining."

"I know," Jack said, accepting the pain.

"But you don't have an umbrella."

He had left it in his office, prepared for sunshine.

"I'll manage."

For the first time in forty-four years, he wondered if he would.

He wanted this woman, but she belonged to another man.

A slamming door vibrated the bed.

"The servants are here," she said. Pelting water underscored their loss of privacy. "We're not alone."

Jack felt the invasion as deeply as Rose. "No."

"When will we have a court date?"

"I don't know."

Jack had needed to see her husband. But by confronting him, he had compromised his position as her attorney.

"What did you mean, yesterday," seared flesh and bones; her fisting fingers once again became a comb, "when you said you hadn't thought it would be like this, either?"

But Jack could not answer. He was not yet ready to confront the consequences of their weekend.

Twisting, he flipped their bodies so that he lay between her thighs, forearms caging her narrow shoulders.

Soft, moist flesh sandwiched his hard flesh.

A pulse that matched his heartbeat throbbed against his glans.

Rose stared up at him, the tension of sexual need replacing the compliance of sleep.

"Love me, Rose," Jack said tautly.

He did not want to fail her. But he could see nothing but failure.

A sharp clang pierced two floors, an iron skillet impacting an iron burner.

Gaze holding his, she reached between their bodies—Jack lifted his hips—and grasped his cock.

"When I take you inside me, Jack," she murmured, vagina kissing his glans, swallowing his crown . . . Jack lowered his hips; her pupils dilated, embracing the full length of his shaft, "I am loving you."

But Jack wanted more.

Metal coils squealed. Thunder rumbled low and angry.

Jack took more.

He swooped down and took her cry of orgasm. He gave her his cry of orgasm in return.

He rolled over onto his side and held her—one body, one heartbeat—until her sobbing breath quieted and his cock slipped free.

The sheets were wet with their sex and sweat.

"Will you meet me tonight at the Houses of Parliament?" he asked raggedly, cradling the back of her head.

Sharp fingernails dug into his shoulder blade. "Shall I bring you supper?"

Jack thought of the reporters, always hungry. Jack thought of the position of Lord of Appeal in Ordinary, soon to be available.

Jack tasted her temple, damp with perspiration. "Please."

Warm fingers massaged away the half-moons her fingernails had made. "What would you like?"

"You, Rose."

Moist heat gusted his cheek; damp pubic hair tickled his glans. "Roasted or *flambeaux*?"

"Spitted," he said bluntly, moist cock hungrily reaching.

"In which mouth?"

"All three."

His name—the cry of her orgasm—had vibrated his tongue and his cock and his fingers.

Her lashes fluttered against his cheek, briefly caught on the stubble of his beard. "I still taste you."

The admission squeezed his chest. Jack squeezed her buttocks. "I'm glad."

But the courts did not care about a woman's satisfaction.

"I have to go," he said regretfully.

Her clasping hands lowered, pulling his hips forward until the glans of her clitoris kissed his glans. "I know."

He should not ache with desire; he did.

Faint voices pierced the bare wooden floor. They were chased by a three-quarter chime.

Jack did not want Rose walking in the rain.

"I'll send a cab for you tonight." Quickly—afraid he'd give in to the temptation that was Rose—he extricated her hands and bussed her lips. "Go back to sleep."

She did not protest his departure. Chill air nettled his skin.

Hurriedly he dressed. He just had time to brush his teeth and shave.

Jack pulled open the top drawer in the bathroom cabinet.

Emotion . . . part tenderness, part possessiveness . . . reamed him: His toothbrush and razor set beside her personal artifacts.

The blade in the razor was new: He nicked his neck.

There was no time for pain.

He dried his face, surrounded by Rose.

Wool abraded his cock, his thighs, his buttocks, every place Rose had touched him.

The top stair creaked.

Each descending step built the unease that thrummed through his temples.

Dark peripheral motion snagged his attention. "Mrs. Dobkins."

The housekeeper turned and gazed up at him. "Mr. Lodoun."

She was not in the least afraid.

Neither was Rose.

But she should be.

"Remember," Jack curtly instructed, "no one enters this house except with Mrs. Clarring's approval."

"Aye, I remember."

Jack resisted the urge to visit the drawing room and the kitchen.

The house would not be the same when he next saw it.

Icy rain pounded the brim of his hat and trickled down his collar.

Rose followed Jack.

Her smell. Her taste.

The muffled clank of a muffin boy's bell vibrated the air.

Another hansom trotted by, wheels spraying muck and water.

There were no vacant cabs.

A billboard-plastered omnibus pulled in to the curb, wood creaking, leather reins wetly slapping.

Grimly Jack stepped up into the dark enclosure.

Damp wool and perfume leadened the air. Streaming water patterned finger-smeared windows.

With each stop men and women entered the front and exited the back. Men talked politics and sex. Women talked economy and children—

" 'E don't last no longer than a sneeze. . . ."

—and sex.

Jack stepped off the bus into driving rain.

A sea of sexless black umbrellas parted before him.

"Good morning, Mr. Lodoun." The navy-uniformed lift man eyed Jack in surprise. "Left our umbrella at home, did we?"

Jack remembered the vulnerability inside Rose's eyes: He had pleasured her, and then he had left. Jack remembered the laughter inside Cynthia's eyes: She had pleasured him, and then she had left.

"Yes," Jack lied, stomach coiling with the ascension of the cab.

"Good morning, Mr. Lodoun." Nathan Dorsey sat at his desk,

dry and dignified, rifling through a manilla folder. A mug of steaming coffee sat at his elbow. "Did you have a pleasant weekend, sir?"

Jack would not describe the time he had spent with Rose as "pleasant." She had alternately eviscerated him with her passion and humbled him with her generosity.

"Quite pleasant, Mr. Dorsey," Jack said. Fleetingly he wondered if Rose had gone back to sleep. Or did she lie awake between sheets wet with their sweat and their sex, thinking of her husband to whom she had yet to say good-bye? "We're running late, I'm afraid. I rode the omnibus."

The clerk followed Jack into his office, a vigilant shadow. "Apparently Mr. Thaddens rode an omnibus, also; tonight he's reading a petition to grant the city more monies to expand services."

Jack derived from this piece of information that the House of Commons's "Order of Business" had arrived.

"He's won a vote." Jack hung his dripping coat on a hook beside his umbrella. "Arrange for a cab to pick up Mrs. Clarring tonight at seven."

"Yes, sir. You have time for a shower and a change, if you like," the clerk calmly suggested. "We can go over the briefs in a cab."

Hot water did not diminish the chill caused by leaving Rose.

Quickly he toweled dry and dressed in dry clothing.

A quarter chime penetrated water, brick and wood: It was fifteen minutes after ten o'clock.

Motion sounded behind the bathroom door.

Jack turned the brass knob. "Mr. Dorsey—"

Slashing rain framed a balding head. Thick cigar smoke curled upward in the gloom.

Jack stiffened. "Chairman."

"Lodoun, old boy." Blair Stromwell sat in Jack's chair, an overt gesture of the political power he wielded. "Young Mr. Dorsey was kind enough to brew coffee. Come join me."

"Another time," Jack said shortly. "I have a court arraignment."

The affability slid out of the older man's eyes. "You do have a penchant for other men's wives, Lodoun."

The heat of the shower crystallized on Jack's skin: The junior member of Parliament had not been able to keep his mouth shut.

For a moment, he felt the same sick helplessness he felt when confronted with a Clarence cab, unable to stop the past.

"You're in my chair." Jack's voice was toneless; emotion coiled inside him. "And you're mingling in my business."

"When you fuck a whore, Lodoun, that's your business." Dark smoke circled the senior MP's head. "When you fuck another man's wife and cram her down the public's throat, that's our business."

Anger had a color: It was gray like cigar smoke.

"I have voted for the party," Jack coldly returned. "I will not live for the party."

No more.

"We have stated our position on the matter of marriage," Blair Stromwell countered.

The rule of men rather than the rule of law.

"For ten years we've groomed you." Water like worms crawled down the glass framing the Chairman of Justice. "We are not going to allow you to upset our ambitions because you can't keep your cock out of other men's wives."

A jagged streak of lightning momentarily blinded Jack.

"You will cease this disastrous liaison," Stromwell warned, "or you will regret it."

Jack knew the power that the older MP exercised: He had in the past deliberately courted it.

The lightening faded: Jack clearly saw the Chairman of Justice.

"Get out of my office." Jack's dislike was mirrored on the older man's face. Crossing the carpet, he jerked open the door. Out of the corner of his eye he glimpsed a familiar silhouette. "Mr. Dorsey. Do not ever again allow Mr. Stromwell into our office unless he makes an appointment." Holding the pale brown gaze, he deliberately mimicked the Chairman of Justice's question three days earlier. "Do you understand?"

Chapter 30

"Is breakfast to yer liking?" the maid anxiously asked, plump cheeks a raw red. She did not meet Rose's gaze. "Mrs. Finley will prepare ye something else, if ye like."

It was obvious she had heard the creaking bedsprings.

The embarrassment Rose should feel would not come.

"This is perfect, Mrs. Brown." Rose spread strawberry jam on evenly browned toast. "Pantechnicon will be delivering furniture this afternoon. Please inform Mrs. Dobkins that I would like the house thoroughly cleaned before the delivery. If you or Mrs. Dobkins or Mrs. Finley would like any of the old furniture, please do take it. Pantechnicon will take away the rest."

"Oh, that'll be lovely, Mrs. Clarring." The maid's appreciation overcame her embarrassment. "Thank ye! Shall ye be needing anything more?"

"No, thank you."

The maid's departure was followed by a burst of activity.

A reverberating knock froze the fork between the plate and Rose's mouth.

It was too early for the furniture to be delivered.

Muted voices drifted down the hallway. The door abruptly slammed shut.

Hot steam lazily curled upward in the greenish-gray morning.

Rose now knew how Jack took his tea. But it was not Jack who walked the corridor.

Brisk heels *tap-tapp*ed wood. Harried footsteps—those of the maid—followed.

Rose set down her knife and fork, heartbeat accelerating.

First came a shadow. Then came the visitor.

Blue eyes snared her gaze.

Rose's heart skipped a beat.

"Mrs. Clarring—"

"It's all right, Mrs. Brown," Rose interrupted. "You may go."

The familiar blue eyes studied Rose for long seconds. "You *are* having an affaire."

It was not a question.

"Yes," Rose confirmed.

Five days earlier she was not, but she most certainly was now. Rose had showered: Jack continued to occupy her.

The blue eyes—her mother's eyes—suddenly filled with tears. "You were so happy when you returned from your honeymoon. You glowed with love and joy. But week by week your happiness faded. I kept telling myself I was imagining things. But I knew I wasn't. Then I told myself you'd be happy again when you had children. But you didn't have children. Then I told myself you'd tell me if something were the matter. But you didn't."

Because it wasn't her secret to tell, Rose wanted to say.

But Jack had seen through the lie.

"I couldn't," Rose said.

She had not been able to admit her husband had married her

only for the children she could give him. She still could not admit it to her mother.

"This man with whom you're having an affaire . . . can you talk to him?"

"Yes."

Rose had never talked as openly to another person as she had talked to Jack.

The blue eyes that her brothers had inherited but which Rose had not closed on a spasm of pain.

Rose had to know: "Did Jonathon send you?"

Her mother opened her eyes. "No."

"Has he talked to you?"

"No."

"He talked to Derek," Rose said.

And Jack.

But all Jack had relayed of the conversation was that Jonathon would not divorce her, and that he believed she would return to him.

What exactly *had* the two men discussed?

"What did Jonathon say?" her mother asked, blocking further speculation.

Rose blinked back sudden tears. "He said he forgives me."

Understanding flooded the older woman's eyes. "And Derek told you."

"Lucy did."

"Lucy is a prat."

The tears stinging Rose's eyes burned her chest. "Derek said he didn't understand why I had left Jonathon, because I'd always been so happy."

"Derek is a prat, too."

Rose had never heard her mother use vulgar slang.

She looked at the woman instead of the mother.

"Why did you name me Rose?" Rose impulsively asked.

"Because it wasn't Susan," Susan Davis returned frankly.

Laughter pushed up inside Rose's throat; tears pushed it back down. "I can't win a divorce, Mother."

"So our solicitor said."

"You and Father saw a solicitor?"

"Your father still sees the little girl whose hurts he kissed away," Susan said pragmatically. "He isn't ready yet to see a woman who must make her own way in life. I consulted with our solicitor earlier this morning."

Rose remembered cornflower blue eyes—her eyes, masculine instead of feminine—clouded with hurt.

"What will Father say when you confirm that I"—*have a lover* caught in her throat—"am having an affaire?"

"Are you ashamed of your actions?"

Rose felt many emotions when she was with Jack, but shame was not one of them.

"No."

The rift Rose had created between husband and wife flickered inside Susan's eyes. "Your father loves you, Rose: He will not turn away from you, any more than will I."

Rose glanced down at her nearly empty plate, and saw not the remains of egg, bacon and tomato prepared by the cook, but the omelette prepared by Jack. "Would you like breakfast?"

"What I would like, Daughter"—Rose glanced up at the sudden determination inside her mother's voice—"is to see your new house."

"Certainly." Rose patted her mouth with the folded napkin. "This, as you can see, is the drawing room."

For one brief second gold and red glinted in front of the iron fireplace.

No memorabilia adorned the room, but already it contained so many memories.

Room by room Rose showed off the small row house: the dining room . . . the kitchen and the scullery that was being cleaned by the cook . . . the upstairs bathroom . . . the two empty bedrooms that were being cleaned by the housekeeper and the maid. She did not show the bedroom that was filled with the scents and sounds of her and Jack. Nor did her mother request to see it.

The middle step squeaked, Susan preceding Rose down the stairs. "Your help seems competent."

"Yes, they are."

Inanely Rose wondered what Giles would say of the odd trio of women.

Susan stepped down off the last step and turned. Their eyes were level. "You have a lovely home, Rose."

It wasn't—the row house was tiny in comparison to Jonathon's and her parents' town houses, and desperately needed paint and furnishings—but Rose flushed with pride. "Thank you."

"Did Jonathon hurt you?" arrested the spurt of pleasure.

Rose did not look away from her mother's searching gaze. "Not in the manner you mean, no."

The need to know more was a palpable pain in the pale blue eyes.

Susan took a deep breath. "Will you humor your mother and allow her to take you shopping?"

Rose had never seen uncertainty inside her mother's eyes: She saw it now.

"She, too," Susan said, "is having a bit of difficulty adjusting to the fact that she can't kiss away your troubles."

A blue flash of light aureoled the older woman; immediately she was engulfed in greenish-gray gloom.

"I'd like that," Rose said. "The furniture won't be delivered until later this afternoon. I'll just tell Cook I'm leaving."

Rain as sharp as needles pricked her skin. A dull flash of lightning streaked the sky.

"You kept the cab waiting," Rose noted, tilting the umbrella to protect her face and hat.

"I'm punishing your father," carried over the steady drum of water. "The more money I spend, the more quickly he'll get over the sulks."

Clear laughter rang out over a rumble of thunder.

It was so absurd, to hear her mother talk as if her father were a little boy.

A surprisingly strong arm pulled Rose into a maternal embrace. Soft lips—feminine instead of masculine—burned her forehead. "It's been so long since I've heard you laugh, Rose."

The needling water stung Rose's eyes.

She lifted up her head and kissed her mother's rain-dampened cheek, inhaling the familiar scents of love and lilac. "It's been a long time since I felt like laughing, Mother."

"He makes you happy."

Her lover.

"Yes."

The feminine arm tightened, offering warmth as well as safety.

One second Rose was a sexual woman; the next instant she was a little girl.

"I love you, Mother." She clung to the older woman, rain trickling down her collar. "I'm sorry I've hurt you and Father."

Rose had not realized how strong was a mother's love: The arm holding her squeezed her lungs empty of air.

Watery laughter abruptly pierced the pounding rain and freed Rose. "Why are we standing here getting wet when we have a cab!"

Laughing for no reason whatsoever, Rose linked arms with her mother and raced down the steps to the Clarence cab. No sooner did they settle on opposite benches than the four wheels lurched forward.

"You'd like Mrs. Hart," Rose said, closing her umbrella.

"She certainly sounds like an interesting lady." A flurry of water droplets pelted Rose. Susan propped a rain-slick umbrella against the right door. Green and gray shadow erased the age that marked her face. "What was the club like?"

The Men and Women's Club.

"It was a discussion club."

"What did you discuss?" Susan asked with genuine interest.

They had discussed so many things over the course of two years.

Not once had they touched upon the unbearable tenderness sexual intimacy engendered.

"Prostitution," Rose said. She thought of John Nickols, crippled because he had investigated a ring of child prostitution. "Darwinism." Rose thought of Ardelle Dennison, the woman who would not conduct meetings outside of the museum in which she worked. "Malthusianism." Rose thought of Louis Stiles, a man who buried his nose in a sketching pad but who did not show his sketches.

Rose suspected she would never see his drawings.

"I didn't know about contraceptives when I married your father," drew Rose away from the uncertain future. "It seemed as if every time we were intimate, I conceived. But that was the way it was supposed to be. Or so I thought at the time. I love you and your brothers dearly, but I have to agree with our queen: I rather felt like a rabbit. After Jason was born, your father admitted there were machines to prevent pregnancy. I got so angry—that he hadn't told me before—I didn't speak to him for a month."

It had never occurred to Rose that her parents might use contraceptives.

Rose did a quick calculation.

But it should have, she realized.

Her mother had been thirty when she had given birth to Rose's youngest brother. Three years younger than Rose was now.

"I didn't know"—Rose swallowed embarrassment, and did not know if it stemmed from her past ignorance or from the present realization that her mother gave every indication of enjoying sexual relations and might even now be tender and swollen, as was Rose—"you and father employed contraceptives."

"Your father would have died of an apoplectic fit had I told you. He still would." The amusement infusing the older woman's voice died. "These are different times, Rose. I won't pretend to understand what you're going through . . . nor can I say that I wholeheartedly approve of your actions . . . but I do admire your strength. You were always the bravest of my children."

Rose stared through rain-streaked glass. "You called me a 'little mother.' "

"You were a little mother to the boys."

The riveting drops of water grew faces.

Jonathon. Jack.

"I will never have children, Mother." The Dutch cap squeezed her cervix. "By choice."

"I had no choice in the matter, Rose." There was no condemnation inside her mother's voice. "I don't know what I would have done had I been given one. I trust you to make the correct decision for your happiness."

The faces of her husband and her lover blurred. "Are you trying to make me cry, Mother?"

"Absolutely not." The denial was unsteady. "It is my sole intention today to cosset you and spend your father's money."

Rose had been shopping at Whiteley's Department Store many times. Never had she enjoyed it more than walking arm in arm with her mother.

"This china pattern is very pretty, Rose."

"Please, Mother: no roses."

"The bird of paradise, then . . .

"Look, Rose: This shade of blue matches the bird of paradise; it would be lovely on your dining room walls."

"Yes, it would. And the crimson paint for the drawing room . . ."

". . . Rose, what are you looking at?"

A naked woman carved in white marble held a bearded head in one hand and a pan flute in the other.

"She killed him," Rose said, eyes filling with explicable tears. "She killed Bacchus."

The god of wine and ecstacy.

"Rightfully so." Susan drew Rose away. "Look at those wicked ears. Oh, now, this Oriental vase would be lovely on your mantel. . . ."

The rain had not ceased during their shopping.

Rose hailed a cab. Conversely, she wanted to wave away the hansom that stopped and wait for a Clarence.

"Mother, why don't you take this cab"—rain streamed down her neck—"and I'll hail another. There's no need for you to see me home."

"Nonsense." Susan stepped up the stair and into the dark cavity of the hansom. Reluctantly, Rose followed. "Of course I need to see you home."

Memories of Jack lurked inside the cramped, dark corners: There she glimpsed an oblong shadow, the wrapped dildo with which she had penetrated herself. There was the outline of two hands, his naked fingers lacing her naked fingers.

Rose made the transformation from cosseted daughter to sexual woman.

Whiteley's would be delivering everything from china to linen. Contractors would paint on Wednesday.

"Please let me reimburse you for the purchases." The Oriental vase—protectively wrapped in brown paper—weighted Rose's lap. With difficulty she folded her umbrella, wire ribs locking with wire ribs. Water sprayed her face. "Father *will* have an apoplectic fit."

"Your father"—calmly Susan untangled the two umbrellas, feminine hip pressing into Rose's hip, lilac scent infusing the gloom—"will thank me, when he comes to his senses." Without skipping a heartbeat, she asked, "Do I know him?"

Jack.

"No."

Rose did not lie.

Her parents would no doubt recognize his name from the papers, but they did not move in the same circles in which Jack moved.

Neither did Rose.

Nor could she ever, a lover instead of a wife.

"Would I like him?" Susan probed.

The housekeeper thought he was a tartar. Dr. Burns had called him a bastard.

Please reverberated over the drumming rain and the watery grind of wheels.

"I don't know," Rose said truthfully.

Rose knew from personal experience that Jack could be both a tartar and a bastard.

"Do *you* like him?"

"Yes." The carriage wheels ate up the road. "I like him very much."

"Does he love you, Rose?" crowded the gloom.

She had held Jack's testicles while he slept: She was now filled with his sperm.

"Like Jonathon loves me?" Rose asked, bittersweet emotion tinging her voice.

"*Does* Jonathon love you?"

Always Rose would remember Jonathon with smiling eyes framed by a blue sky.

"I believe so," Rose said.

Sadness filled her mother's voice. "You love him still."

"Yes."

The hip pressing Rose shifted. "I will tell your father. . . ."

Rose turned her head and studied the eyes that were ageless in the shadowy light. "What will you tell him, Mother?"

How could she possibly justify to her father why Rose committed adultery?

"I will tell him," Susan said on a deep breath, "you have met a man who has given us back our daughter."

But Rose was not the same woman who had married Jonathon.

The cab halted too soon.

"I have to let you go," Susan said regretfully.

"Yes," Rose said. She had a house waiting to be transformed into a home. "Will you and Father come visit"—would Jack be interested in meeting her parents?—"me?"

"Certainly," Susan said dryly. "He can see for himself what his stubbornness cost."

Smiling, Rose unfurled her umbrella and reached for the cab door. "Thank you, Mother."

"I was wrong, Rose," halted her.

Water pummeled the umbrella. "About what?"

"You did the right thing when you testified." Rose stared at the bulleting rain. "In the end, that is what matters: That you do the right thing. Regardless of the consequences."

Rose exited the cab and slammed shut the door.

Big Ben sounded over the drumming rain: It was four o'clock. Jack would be taking his seat in the House of Commons.

The hansom lurched forward, horse hooves a muffled clop.

Rose juggled the vase and the umbrella. Out of the corner of her eye, she saw a cab door open.

There was no reason for her heart to start hammering: She hurried down the pavement.

"Rose," stopped her at the foot of her stoop.

She threw her head back at the pain that knifed through her chest.

It had been so long since he had spoken her name.

Slowly she lowered her head, opened her eyes and turned around.

Rain hammered her umbrella . . . the pavement . . . the man's umbrella.

"Jonathon," Rose quietly acknowledged.

Chapter 31

Jack knew Rose did not wait for him the moment he stepped outside St. Stephen's Hall.

Black sheets of rain battered the flickering streetlamp.

Emotion surged through him.

Fear. Rage.

Not again.

A hansom cab waited in the circle, horse stoically enduring the cold and wet: The cabby huddled underneath an umbrella.

Steps muffled—rain pounding his umbrella like fists—Jack closed on the cab and stepped up onto the platform.

"'Ere now." The cabby alertly came to life. "What d'ye think ye're—"

Jack jerked open the door.

A pale orb dominated by two fathomless eyes stared up at him.

Rose's housekeeper. Not Rose.

Rain slashed Jack's exposed neck. "Where is she?"

"She didn' come home."

The cab shuddered underneath his feet.

"Whoa, there!" the cabby shouted, voice wetly ringing over a roll of thunder. "I say whoa, damn ye!"

"Where did she go?" Jack asked, voice distant.

"She went shoppin' wi' her mum." The housemaid's voice sounded as distant as did Jack's. And then, as if he did not know the woman's name, she added: "Mrs. Davis."

"What time did she leave?"

"Around eleven, Cook said."

Jack had been in court for an arraignment. But Rose had known that.

I have always known Rose would take a lover, rumbled on a roll of thunder. *Just as I have always known it is I to whom she will return.*

"What time did she say she'd be back?" Jack asked tonelessly.

"She said furniture'd be comin' in the afternoon," the housekeeper said. Hard, cold rain punctuated each syllable. "She said she'd be back before it was delivered."

"What time was it delivered?"

"Thirty minutes after four."

A quarter chime rang out: It was fifteen minutes past eight.

Rose had said the housekeeper had her own family to take care of.

Water crawled down his collar. "Why are you here, Mrs. Dobkins?"

"I be a woman of my word, Mr. Lodoun: I said we wouldn' let no one take Mrs. Clarring."

"What makes you think someone took her?"

"Cause I saw 'em do it."

Lightning split the sky, turning pale skin and dark eyeholes into a guilty woman.

Jack wanted to shout. Jack wanted to weep.

Instead he harshly asked: "Who took her?"

"Git in the cab, Mr. Lodoun, an' I'll tell ye." A piercing clap of thunder vanquished the lightning, leaving behind a pale shadow that suddenly sounded old and tired. "Ye ain't gonna do 'er no good by standin' in the rain an' catchin' yer death."

Jack had heard that tone of recalcitrance in both men and women who had witnessed violence: The housekeeper would not talk until she regained a semblance of control.

Bending—simultaneously folding his umbrella—Jack stiffly stepped into the cab.

The close air smelled of damp wool and unfamiliar woman.

Slamming shut the door, Jack said: "Tell me what you saw."

A wool-padded shoulder dug into his arm: Simultaneously words tumbled into the night.

Jack didn't want to see the housekeeper's words: Vivid images slashed through his mind.

Rose. Jonathon Clarring.

Two strange men.

"The first man must've called out t' 'er, 'cause she stopped in front of the stoop."

Jonathon Clarring would have called her name, Jack grimly thought. That's all it would have taken to get her attention: for him to simply acknowledge her.

"She stood there fer long seconds," the housekeeper said over the relentless drum of water, "wi' the rain comin' down, an' then she turned. The other two men 'ad split up, one goin' left, the other right. When Mrs. Clarring turned t' face the first man, they sneaked up in the rain."

The sun had been shining, Jack remembered, when Cynthia had died.

A brisk October rendezvous.

Had she seen the cab before it struck her? he wondered.

"I didn't know 'ow t' contact ye, so I waited," the housekeeper said. "And then a cabby came t' the door an' said 'e was t' pick up Mrs. Clarring. So I told the cabby I was 'er an' came in 'er place. 'Oping it would be ye. Or someone else who could help 'er."

Because the police couldn't.

But neither could Jack.

"Go home, Mrs. Dobkins."

Another time, another woman flooded his mind: *Go home, Mrs. Clarring,* Jack had told Rose outside the courthouse.

But she had not listened.

Jack wondered if she now regretted her decision.

"It be my fault." The pale eyes gleaming in the darkness winked out of view. The shoulder crowding Jack hunched, arm circling, hand digging. "Mrs. Brown an' Mrs. Finley don' deserve t' be discharged. They work 'ard. It would be a 'ardship fer 'em t' lose this position."

You are not responsible for the death of Cynthia Whitcox, Rose had adjured.

"How long did you stand watching?" Jack asked hollowly.

"It 'appened so quickly." The arm and shoulder chafing his arm stilled. "A minute, mayhap."

"You're not at fault," Jack said.

But words did not absolve guilt.

"Go home, Mrs. Dobkins," he repeated, reaching into his pocket. He pressed a half crown into the housekeeper's gloved fingers, hand smaller than Rose's hand. "Mrs. Clarring would want you to take care of her home."

And so did Jack.

"Will she be all right?" the housekeeper gruffly enquired.

"I don't know," Jack said flatly.

"Are ye all right?"

Jack pushed open the door and exited the hansom.

One goal drove him forward in the numbing rain.

"Where ye be goin', mister?"

What are we going to do, Jack?

Jack gave the cabby the address he had requested.

Tears slithered down the windows, danced in passing streetlamps.

Do you cry for her?

Would Jack cry for Rose?

Long seconds passed before Jack realized the cab was no longer moving.

No light illuminated the ground floor. A window on the second floor shone like a beacon.

Through the glass and the rain, a dark silhouette blocked the flickering light.

Heart skipping a beat, Jack stepped out of the cab. "Stay."

"It's rainin' like piss," the cabby protested. "I ain't waitin' in this bloody weather fer God 'imself."

God would not pay in sterling silver.

"I'll give you a night's fare," Jack bit back.

He did not wait for the cabby to accede; he stepped off the platform into a river of racing water.

A pale, oval face in the upstairs window peered down at him.

Every muscle inside his body clenched in recognition.

Jack was suddenly, painfully alive, cold and rain scouring his skin.

A gas lantern feebly lit the front door.

Jack pounded on wood, water sluicing down his hand and underneath his cuff.

No one answered.

The woman in the window spurred him on.

"Open this bloody door!" Jack suddenly shouted. He could not be this close to Rose and lose her. "Goddamn you, Clarring! I know you're in there! Open this bloody fucking door!"

But Jack could not force open the door.

And the law would not force Jonathon Clarring to relinquish his wife.

" 'Ere now!" crashed through the violence that gripped Jack. "Just who do ye think ye are? This be a respectable neighber'ood. Git on wi' ye!"

Jack shook off the hand that banded his arm: It did not loosen.

Two men had grabbed Rose, one on either side. She hadn't struggled, the housekeeper had said. But it had not been the two men who had paralyzed her, Jack realized. Jonathon Clarring had taken the fight out of Rose.

She loved Jonathon Clarring. And he had betrayed her love.

Jack wanted to beat the bobby bloody with the raw emotion that coursed through him.

"Let go of me," he coldly enunciated through gritted teeth.

"Not 'til ye git in that cab an' get on," the helmeted man belligerently returned.

But Jack couldn't get on.

I need to say good-bye.

But he couldn't say good-bye.

Not to Cynthia. Not to Rose.

But he had to say good-bye: He could not help Rose when ruled by emotion.

Jack took a deep breath, inhaling heavy, wet moisture overlaid by garlic and onions, the bobby's breath.

"Let go of me," he repeated more quietly. "And I'll leave."

"I've a mind to take ye down to gaol."

The bobby's desire for violence danced on raindrops.

Jack voided his face of all expression and stared down into eyes that were dark pits screened by slashing silver.

Uncertainty replaced the bobby's bullishness.

"Git on wi' ye." Jack staggered at a forceful push; quickly he regained his balance, hands fisting to prevent himself from reciprocating. "I'll be keepin' me eyes open fer ye, that I will."

Jack did not look back.

Rose's watching eyes followed him.

The step up onto slippery iron. The water-streaming platform that tilted with his weight.

The rigidity of his body, fighting not to turn and meet her gaze.

Jack gave the cabby two silver crowns.

The hansom did not wait when Jack next stepped down.

Dimly he realized he had left his umbrella inside the escaping cab: He did not feel the cold and rain that kept on falling.

The town house was larger than the one owned by Jonathon Clarring. Unlike at Jonathon Clarring's house, the owner answered the door.

Jack stared into the eyes of James Whitcox. "I need to know."

Chapter 32

"How did you find my address?" James Whitcox feinted.

There was no emotion inside the shadow-darkened eyes.

The two men could be facing one another over the bench in a court of law. In a sense, they were: Tonight would result in a woman's liberation or perpetual confinement.

"I've known the address since you purchased this house," Jack replied, rain dripping off the brim of his hat. "My clerk is as good at ferreting out information as your clerk is at hiding it."

"Yet you lost."

In court.

"I didn't prosecute to convict the defendants," Jack said flatly.

It was as close as he would ever come to apologizing for his actions inside the courtroom.

He had argued to prove he was a better man. A better barrister.

A better husband.

He had failed.

James Whitcox's voice was equally flat. "What do you need to know?"

Every night he lay awake, wondering: "How did she die?"

The woman who had been James Whitcox's wife and Jack Lodoun's lover.

Lightning flashed, turning shadow-blackened eyes into hazel. "It was in the papers."

Every newspaper in London had printed the story: "Barrister's Wife Struck Down by Clarence."

But the papers had not detailed what Jack needed to know.

"Did she suffer?" Jack asked, icy water trickling down his cheek.

Brows snapping together, James Whitcox closed his eyes.

Jack imagined Rose had worn the same look of pain when Jonathon Clarring had called out her name.

Perhaps, even, she had closed her eyes against the safety of her door that was only three steps away.

Lashes abruptly lifting, James Whitcox opened the door and stepped aside.

Jack entered the home that the barrister had purchased for another woman.

His house was much like Jack's house: the best that money could buy. Unlike in Jack's house, the crystal chandelier that illuminated the foyer was electric.

A woman with tousled red hair and a wrinkled green frock stood at the foot of a marble staircase, hand to her throat. "Mr. Lodoun."

Jack took off his hat; water spilled onto veined marble. "Mrs. Hart."

James Whitcox purposefully blocked Jack's view of Frances Hart, the woman he loved. "I'll be up shortly."

Inside his voice was the tenderness Jack had not been able to publicly express to the woman he had loved.

A whispered, "Will you be all right?" drifted upward to sparkling crystal.

"Yes." James Whitcox briefly leaned forward. Jack could not see the kiss, but he felt it, a man's promise. "It'll be all right."

Frances Hart climbed the marble stairs. Jack followed James Whitcox.

The tap of their heels diverged, Frances Hart going up, James Whitcox and Jack laterally advancing.

Whitcox stepped underneath white enameled wood; Jack stepped over the threshold behind him and closed the door.

The masculine den looked unused, black leather chairs unworn, mahogany wood freshly stained, green Oriental carpet bright and unspoiled.

Silver glinting in crisp chestnut hair, the forty-seven-year-old barrister leaned over a lacquered Chinese table: glass clinked, liquid gurgled. Turning . . . meeting Jack in the center of the room . . . he offered a brandy-filled snifter.

James Whitcox was two inches taller than Jack. He wore a white shirt that was open at the neck; it had been hastily tucked into black wool trousers. Hair that was thicker and darker than the hair that matted Jack's chest showed through the V of starched cotton.

Jack had a curious sensation of déjà vu.

"She knows," he said, cupping brittle glass.

Frances Hart.

The hazel eyes were expressionless. "About you and my wife, yes."

Familiar emotion churned inside Jack.

"Does she know about the women you fucked while you were married to Cynthia?" he bit out.

"Yes."

"Does she know you didn't love the mother of your children?"

There was no apology in the cold hazel eyes, but neither was their condemnation.

James Whitcox had not loved his wife. But Jack had not loved her enough to seek a divorce.

"Yes," Whitcox said. Regret flickered inside his eyes. Or perhaps electric light flickered, just as did gaslight. "She knows."

Jack drank brandy, swallowing the useless anger.

"Tell me." He lowered the snifter and met waiting hazel eyes. "How Cynthia died."

"The coroner said the wheel severed her spine." Whitcox lifted his arm; dark hair protruded from underneath a starched white cuff. His gaze, when he lowered the snifter, was stark with the death of the woman they had shared. "He said she didn't suffer."

But no one would know her final moments.

Neither Jack nor James would know if she had been frightened. They would not know if she had called out in her fear, or even to whom she would have called.

They would never know if she had welcomed death to end the lies and subterfuge. Or if she had fought death to gain a final opportunity to say: *I'm sorry.* Or, *I love you.*

Jack's throat tightened. "Was she disfigured?"

Cynthia had been self-conscious about the stretch marks left from pregnancy: She had thought they made her undesirable.

"Her face wasn't," Whitcox said, remembering damage Jack had not seen.

Still Jack could not say good-bye.

"What did she wear"—his fingers tightened around fragile glass that could so easily break; in his right hand soggy felt yielded cool water—"when she was buried?"

"She wore red," serrated Jack's control. "She requested in her will that she be buried in her red silk ball gown. So that is what I buried her in."

Jack turned away from the probing hazel eyes and downed the remainder of the brandy.

The scalding heat stinging his eyes traveled down his esophagus.

It was a good brandy—a Napoleon brandy—flavor fruity and floral, body soft and smooth. Rose would enjoy it.

But Rose was locked up inside her husband's house. A living reminder of every dream Jonathon Clarring had ever dreamed.

Jack had been attorney general: He knew of what men were capable.

Good men. Gentle men.

Men who made women smile with happiness.

I need your help, Rose had said.

But Jack could not help her.

Jack stared at the door he had closed.

"I need your help." The word Rose had five times spoken pushed through the barrier of masculine pride. *"Please."*

Chapter 33

Frances fell into wakefulness.

James caught her, prickly heat spooning her back and thighs.

Over the creak of metal springs rain pummeled the windows.

She cupped James's tunneling hand and shaped it around her breast. "It's late."

Warm fingers molded her flesh; at the same time hot, moist air combed her hair. "It's early."

Pale marble gleamed in the darkness: The ashes inside the fireplace were cold and dead.

When Frances had slipped into bed, alone, blue-and-yellow flames had illuminated the night.

The hour was indeed early.

"I dreamed of you," she murmured.

Semierect flesh nuzzled her buttocks. "Did I give you an orgasm?"

The desolation Frances had felt in her dream invaded her voice. "You lost."

Because of Jack Lodoun.

"You won, Frances." Warm lips seared her scalp. "No one can ever take that away from you."

But she would not have won had it not been for one man.

Thunder rattled glass.

"What did he want?" she whispered.

But James did not answer.

Three bongs penetrated rain, brick and wood.

Frances remembered the first time she had awoken in James's arms.

I have you, he had said. *Stay with me.*

Frances could not imagine being anywhere else.

"Rose Clarring and Jack Lodoun are lovers," James said finally.

Shock crowded out the bittersweet memories of their past. "For how long?"

James pulled Frances closer, chest hair prickling her back, pubic hair tickling her buttocks, his sex a solid reality. "She approached him after the trial, hoping he would petition Parliament for a divorce."

Frances did not know of divorces.

Men and women in the country lived in the same cyclical pattern as the land they tended: They married, they bore a fruitful harvest, they died.

But Rose Clarring was a London woman. Unlike Frances.

"Did he agree?" she asked.

"No," James said, sighing voice ruffling her hair.

The pain Jack Lodoun had caused buffeted their home.

"He said such hurtful things to her," Frances said.

"I've done far worse than accuse witnesses of adultery, Frances," James said, fingers apologetically kneading her breast.

And he would do so again.

Because of the law.

Frances spoke past the sudden tightness inside her throat. "Does he love her?"

The man who had loved James's wife.

"The very fact that he came to me tonight suggests he feels very strongly toward her."

Slowly the heat James radiated relaxed the stiffness of her muscles.

"Why did he come?" she asked, breath a silvery plume in the chill dampness.

"He wanted to know about Cynthia's death," James said, voice suddenly devoid of emotion.

Frances soothed his wrist, his skin a prickly consolation.

Rain steadily pelted the window: life following death.

Fleetingly she thought about the man to whom she had been married for thirty-four years, and who now rested in the land he had all his life farmed.

"And he asked me to help liberate Mrs. Clarring," James added, soothed by her touch as she was by his.

"What do you mean"—puzzlement replaced the memory of their deceased spouses—"liberate her?"

"Mrs. Clarring moved out of her husband's home on the day of the trial." James curled around Frances, his calves warming her feet. "Yesterday he abducted her off the street."

As Frances could have been abducted. And would have been had the lunatic men caught her.

Now Rose Clarring—a woman who had testified on Frances's behalf so that she might gain liberation from a son—had lost her own freedom to a husband.

Tears scalded Frances's eyes. "You said once a woman is incarcerated inside a lunatic asylum, there's no hope for liberation."

"Nor is there. But he hasn't committed her," James replied. *Yet* slammed into wood, brick and glass. "He took her to his home."

A home to the husband. A prison to Rose Clarring.

"If she were free," Frances asked, "could she divorce her husband?"

Warm fingers stroked her hip. "Not as the law currently stands."

"Because she's a woman," Frances said, remembering the pain she had felt upon discovering her son had signed a lunacy order. Because *she* was a woman.

"Yes," James agreed.

Frances grasped his wrist; a pulse throbbed against her middle fingertip. "Not even you could win her a divorce?"

A man who had never lost a trial.

"Not even I, Frances."

She stared into the cold darkness of morning: Heat blanketed her back, her buttocks, her thighs. The fingers that had explored her every crevice protectively curved around her breast, silently offering comfort.

But Rose Clarring had no one to comfort her.

"I remember the first time I met Mrs. Clarring," Frances said.

James had one by one introduced Frances to the members of the Men and Women's Club: They had not all been receptive to a forty-nine-year-old widow who had been educated in a one-room school.

"She smiled, and offered to show me her favorite London sites." An offer Frances had yet to accept. Wet heat trickled down her temple. "There was such sadness inside her smile, James. Can you liberate her?"

"I don't know," vibrated her vertebrae.

Regret tinged Frances's voice. She repeated: "Because she's a woman."

Reluctantly, he said, "Because she's a wife."

Frances refused to believe that the law would not help a woman simply because she was a man's wife.

"Surely there must be something you can do for her?"

"Tomorrow I'm going to file a writ for habeas corpus."

Frances knew the pain that the law caused, but she did not know the law. "I don't understand."

"Every English citizen—man and woman—is obliged to appear in court when summoned," James explained, lips and breath a warm caress. "If the Queen's Bench will approve the writ, Mrs. Clarring's husband will have to bring her to court, and the judges will then determine if he has the right to detain her."

Frances listened to James's body as well as his words. "You don't think they'll approve it."

"A judge's decision is a public affaire." James's voice was neutral, what Frances had learned was his barrister's voice. "They may be persuaded by certain things."

"Like what?"

"If a furor were created, they might not wish to vote against popular opinion."

Anger at the law that James loved whipped through Frances. "A woman forcibly taken off the street and imprisoned isn't a cause for a furor?"

"If it were brought to the public eye," James calmly returned, "yes."

"The newspapers," Frances assayed, anger arrested.

"Yes, but we have to move quickly." Heat penetrated tangled hair and burned her scalp. "For example, if we should create a disturbance outside Mr. Clarring's house, it would quickly draw attention from a variety of newspapers."

Frances thought of the women who marched for suffrage. "Like a demonstration, you mean."

"Yes."

"How many people would be needed to garner the necessary amount of attention?"

"However many could be gathered."

"Is this what you and Mr. Lodoun discussed?"

"It's one of the things we discussed."

Always there would be secrets between them: He was a man, but he would always be a barrister.

How much more difficult it would be for Rose Clarring and Jack Lodoun, he both a barrister and a member of Parliament.

"I could do that, James." Frances wanted to help the woman who had lost so much because of her. Heart skipping a beat, she twisted free of banding arms and sheets, springs squealing, mattress dipping. "I could talk to the members of the club. Surely they will want to help."

"Many have lost their positions, Frances." Brandy-scented breath caressed her lips. James was a familiar shadow, hazel eyes a slash of black. "Their lives aren't the same."

Because of her.

"This isn't about me, James; it's about Mrs. Clarring."

"They may not agree to see you."

"But I have to try."

Gentle fingers pushed heavy hair off her forehead. "I don't want you to be hurt anymore, Frances."

"I have you to comfort me." Frances slid her right hand in between a soft pillow and warm flesh; James lifted his head to give her access. She looped her arms around his neck. "Mrs. Clarring doesn't deserve to be incarcerated."

"No, she doesn't." The body that had spooned her was now all hard angles. "A demonstration might even convince Mr. Clarring to let her go."

He did not sound hopeful.

"James."

James grasped her hips and pulled her closer, his nestling sex so achingly intimate it brought fresh tears to her eyes. "What?"

Frances pressed her forehead to his lips. "Only a desperate man, surely, would abduct his wife."

His lips burned her skin. "Yes."

"What if, by us drawing public attention to Mrs. Clarring's plight, he hurts her?"

"There is no guarantee, Frances, that he won't hurt her, no matter what course of action we take."

Or do not take.

The unspoken words hung on humid air.

Every day, Frances thought, James must chose between action and inaction, liberation and imprisonment. Life and death.

"Why isn't Mr. Lodoun lodging the writ?" she asked, throat tight.

"Because the investigation would reveal that he's Mrs. Clarring's lover."

"You were my lover," Frances reasoned, the heat of his lips and his sex and the vulnerability of women squeezing her chest.

"It wasn't in Lodoun's best interests to reveal that information; had he done so, the judge would have dismissed your trial."

And Frances would have been turned over to the custody of her son. Just as Rose Clarring could be turned over to her husband.

A prisoner for the rest of her life.

"Will not an investigation—regardless of who is her barrister—reveal that Mrs. Clarring and Mr. Lodoun are lovers?"

"If so, we will just have to work that much harder."

There was no certainty inside James's voice.

But he always won, Frances thought. But he had not won in her dream.

"What will they do," Frances asked, "after you liberate her?"

Rose Clarring would still be married to another man.

"What you and I did"—hard fingers dug into the softness of her hips—"after you were liberated."

Frances tightened her arms. "*Is* love enough, James?"

"More binding than gold, Frances."

Happiness should not be painful.

Raising her head, she kissed the corner of his mouth, stubbly with a morning beard. "Where is Mr. Lodoun?"

James turned his face into hers and kissed the indentation between her nostril and cheek, his lips soft, the surrounding skin a prickling abrasion. "Procuring an affidavit."

Cold, stark images flashed behind her lids.

Jack Lodoun clutching a burgundy leather satchel, eyes glittering like purple ice. Jack Lodoun dripping water, eyes jet-black with loss.

"Come into our home, James," Frances urged.

Where there was no pain.

Body shifting . . . bed dipping . . . James reached for the nightstand.

"I prepared myself earlier," Frances said.

With the lubrication that her body no longer produced.

Had Jack Lodoun not knocked on their door, she would now be filled with James and sound asleep in his arms.

Unaware that a woman had been imprisoned, simply because she was a woman.

James loved Frances until their two sexes became one. Frances held James until their bodies became two, one man and one woman.

She must soon let him go, but not yet.

Threading her fingers through his sweat-dampened hair, she asked: "What did Mr. Lodoun do when you told him about your wife's death?"

James tasted her lashes. "He cried."

The tears James had once said barristers did not cry, but which James had cried after the trial when he had filled her body so full she had overflowed with his love.

"Silently," she whispered.

Like a cleansing summer rain.

But not all summer gales were gentle: Rain destroyed as well as replenished.

James's muscles tensed underneath her fingers, readying to leave her so that he could prepare for a court session he did not believe he would win. "Yes."

Chapter 34

"If this isn't a matter of life or death, I'll—" A sexagenarian man—white nightshirt tucked into black trousers; head covered by a blue nightcap—appeared through the opening door; he stopped short upon glimpsing Jack's face. A thin lip curled in recognition. "The master and mistress are not at home."

Clearly he had read the papers.

"If they love their daughter"—Jack stuck his foot into the closing door; he had long ago lost the ability to be hurt by the emotions of men—"they are at home."

"Come back in the morning"—the door blocked the butler; his voice snaked through the crack—"and I'll ask if they'll see you."

Four waterlogged bongs permeated the rain.

The sun had risen fifteen minutes earlier. But the rain blocked the sun.

"Their daughter has been abducted," Jack said brutally. "If they love Rose, they will see me *now*."

The door swung wide, sucking in rain and cold. "How would the likes of you know about Mrs. Clarring?"

The way to the parents lay through the butler.

"Because I am the man who made Rose Clarring an adulteress," he said bluntly.

The butler—Jack judged him to be in his early sixties; his eyes were sharp and clear—assessed Jack for long seconds before stepping aside. "Come in."

Jack stepped over the threshold.

"Stay on the mat," the butler tersely instructed, as if Jack were an errant five-year-old boy instead of a forty-four-year-old man who was a member of Parliament. "I won't have you mucking up my floors."

Jack did not underestimate the power of a butler: He stayed on the mat.

The house that Rose had grown up in was not rich, but it was prosperous.

A gaslit chandelier sputtered overhead; teardrop shadows splotched the oak floor.

Back ramrod straight, the butler hurried up graceful oak stairs and disappeared into blackness.

A muffled knock climbed down the steps; it was chased by muted voices.

A man in his late fifties and a woman in her early fifties hurried down the stairs, flapping shades of gray turning into brown velvet and pink silk night robes.

Bare feet padded across the oak floor.

Rose had inherited the color of her mother's hair, Jack thought, chest tightening. But she had inherited her father's eyes.

Cornflower blue blazed with fear that erupted into anger at sight of Jack. "What the devil do you mean knocking up my household in the middle of the night?"

"Sam, hush." Pale blue eyes snagged Jack's gaze. "You told

Giles that our daughter has been abducted. That's impossible, sir: I dropped her off in front of her house at four."

Twelve hours earlier.

"Three men apprehended her before she made it to her door," Jack said.

"If you saw men taking my daughter," Susan Davis said forthrightly, "why didn't you stop them?"

"I didn't see it," Jack said. "Her housekeeper did."

"My daughter isn't a rich woman, Mr. Lodoun." Masculine censure pummeled Jack. "Who would abduct her?"

Jack held Susan Davis's gaze. "Her husband."

"How would the housekeeper know"—pale blue eyes searched Jack's gaze—"if it was Jonathon?"

There were no pictures of Jonathon Clarring inside Rose's home, her gaze said. Nor had Jonathon Clarring's likeness appeared in the papers.

"I saw Rose in his house," Jack said flatly.

"And why shouldn't she be in his house?" Samuel Davis challenged. "It's her home."

Shadow flickered inside Susan Davis's eyes.

"Where did you see her, Mr. Lodoun?" she asked quietly.

"She was standing in a window. On the second floor." Jack forcibly blocked the vision of Rose. "Looking down at me."

"And you just *assumed* he abducted her?" Samuel Davis jibed. "Is that the only evidence you have?"

"Mr. Davis, I am assuming nothing: The housekeeper witnessed your daughter's abduction," Jack countered. "When I knocked, no one would answer the door."

"It's four in the morning: What do you expect?"

"It was nine in the evening."

"Rose is Jonathon's wife," Samuel Davis returned. "Why would he abduct her?"

"Because he *is* her husband," Susan Davis replied, her eyes filling with a woman's knowledge rather than knowledge of the law. "And because he can. Can't he, Mr. Lodoun?"

Jack would not lie.

"Yes," he said bluntly.

Women had few rights; wives even fewer.

Pain took away the blue in her eyes. "My daughter knew this was a possibility when she left him, didn't she?"

"Yes."

The price of passion.

"Were you having an affaire with her before the trial?" Susan Davis asked.

Before Rose had left Jonathon Clarring.

"No."

"Did you seduce her?"

"Of course he seduced her," Samuel Davis said contemptuously. "How else would Rose have anything to do with this man?"

Jack ignored the father and focused on the mother.

He thought of Rose's needs that had drawn her to him. He thought of his needs that had drawn him to Rose.

"She's my lover, Mrs. Davis," Jack said.

And he ached to hold her.

"Yes," Susan Davis said after long seconds, "I see."

"As do I," Samuel Davis remarked; he draped a brown velvet–covered arm across Susan Davis's pink silk–clad shoulders. "Come along, Susan. We'll look in on them later today: Everything will be fine."

"Sam, *please*," Susan Davis said to her husband. To Jack, she asked, "Why are you here, Mr. Lodoun?"

"You and Rose went shopping."

"We went to Whiteley's," she confirmed.

They had been together from eleven in the morning until four in the evening, the housekeeper had said.

"You must have talked about many things," Jack said neutrally.

The man who was her husband. The man who was her lover.

"Yes."

Susan Davis did not volunteer the topics they had discussed, guarding well her daughter's confidence.

"In a few hours James Whitcox"—the anger with which Jack had lived for three years fluttered inside his stomach—"is going to petition the Queen's Bench for a writ of habeas corpus. In order to do so, he must present proof that Rose would not voluntarily return to the home she shared with Jonathon Clarring. Will you sign an affidavit, Mrs. Davis, that Rose would not of her own free will return to her husband?"

"Absolutely not," shot down Jack's spine. Samuel Davis reiterated: "I absolutely forbid it. There's no need to 'liberate' our daughter. Jonathon is our son-in-law; he's not going to hurt Rose."

Light and shadow flickered inside Susan Davis's eyes.

"Do you know that for a fact, Mr. Davis?" Jack challenged, deliberately fueling Susan Davis's doubt. "That your son-in-law is not going to harm your daughter?"

"A man cannot abduct his wife," Samuel Davis returned. "They are one in the eyes of God. Jonathon vowed to love and cherish Rose. Susan, this *man* made our little girl an adulteress. I know what you said earlier, but you're wrong. This man cannot make Rose happy. He's jealous because she's chosen Jonathon over him. Let it be."

Susan Davis closed her eyes.

"You are the last person, Mrs. Davis," Jack pressed, "who talked to your daughter."

"This is for Rose and Jonathon to work out, Susan," Samuel Davis adjured.

"If we do not liberate your daughter, Mrs. Davis," Jack countered, "your son-in-law can have her committed to an asylum—this very morning—and there will be nothing we can do to help her."

Susan Davis opened her eyes: They were not the same color as Rose's eyes, but the black pain inside them was identical, forced to choose between two people whom she loved. "Tell me how my son-in-law took my daughter, Mr. Lodoun."

Without Susan Davis, they could not procure a writ.

Jack used all of his descriptive abilities to describe what the housekeeper had relayed.

Tears boiled up inside the pale blue eyes made black with pain and spilled down parchment white cheeks. "Rose has such slender arms."

Jack knew more than anyone how fragile Rose was, both physically and emotionally.

"You said she dropped her umbrella."

"Yes," Jack said, watching Susan Davis struggle to regain control, Rose's future dependent upon a mother's strength.

"She commissioned painters to paint her home. She wanted a crimson drawing room. I purchased an Oriental vase to sit on her mantel." Futilely wiping away tears—left cheek . . . right cheek—Susan Davis asked: "Did she drop it?"

The package to which the housekeeper had alluded.

"Yes," Jack said.

Fleeting regret sliced through him, that he would not see the vase Rose's mother had chosen for their home.

"Did it break?" she asked.

A question formed inside her eyes, a mother's plea.

Would Rose break?

When . . . *if* . . . she was liberated, would they—like "all the king's horses, and all the king's men"—not be able to put her back together again?

But Jack had no answer.

He did not know of what Jonathon Clarring was capable. Nor did he know how long it would take the judges presiding over the Queen's Bench to reach a decision.

"I don't know," Jack said truthfully.

Chapter 35

The snick of a lock jerked Rose awake.

Greenish-gray light illuminated a rose-patterned wall.

Memory flooded her consciousness.

Eyes the color of a blue sky.

But the sky had rained.

A rose-enameled door opened.

"Jonathon?" Rose asked, throat tightening.

But Jonathon was not alone.

Rose scrambled upright in bed, cotton nightgown and cotton sheets tangling.

Fear constricted her heart.

A tall, gray-bearded man accompanied Jonathon; he carried a black leather satchel. A tall, sturdy woman dressed in brown wool trailed behind the gray-bearded man, graying hair tucked up into a white cap.

Rose incongruously thought of Twiddledee and Twiddledum in *Through the Looking Glass*.

"Don't be frightened, Mrs. Clarring." The gray-bearded man—Rose judged him to be in his late fifties—set down his satchel on the nightstand beside the bed. He smiled. "I'm Doctor Weinberger, and this is Nurse Williams."

The smile did not reassure Rose. Neither did the stern-faced woman who nodded in greeting.

Rose was not prepared for this development of events.

If Jonathon thought she was ill, why hadn't he summoned their family physician?

"I assure you, Dr. Weinberger," Rose said, heart tripping, "I am quite healthy."

"That is not what your husband claims, Mrs. Clarring."

There was suddenly not enough oxygen inside the bedroom for four people.

"Dr. Weinberger, you saw my husband unlock the door." Rose struggled to keep her voice calm and rational. "I am being kept here against my will: Please help me."

The doctor's smile did not change. "That is why I'm here, Mrs. Clarring." Glancing down, he opened his satchel. "To help you."

Rose clutched the neck of her nightgown. "What are you doing?"

The doctor pulled out a stethoscope. "This won't hurt, Mrs. Clarring."

What did this man know of a woman's pain?

Her husband had *abducted* her.

"I don't want you to touch me."

"I'm simply going to listen to your heart and lungs." The doctor sat on the edge of the bed, mattress depressing: Rose tilted sideways. "Be so kind as to unfasten your gown."

Rose remembered that Dr. Burns—a physician rather than a lunacy doctor—had confided she had once signed an order to commit a woman to an insane asylum.

The girl had never been the same, Dr. Burns had shamefacedly confided.

"I am not insane," Rose said, calm fleeing.

Too-soft fingers imprinted the back of her hand that clutched her nightgown.

Rose recoiled from the doctor's touch.

"Of course you're not insane, Mrs. Clarring." The doctor's fingers were confident: One by one he released the tiny buttons holding together the top of her gown. He repeated: "Don't be frightened."

But she was frightened.

Each released button further invaded her privacy.

She wanted to slap the stethoscope from the doctor's hand. She knew that such an action would only corroborate a diagnosis of lunacy.

Cold metal seared her sternum.

"Breathe deeply, Mrs. Clarring."

Rose took a shaky breath.

"Very good," the doctor praised. As if she were a child.

Or a deranged woman.

"Lean forward. . . . Yes, like so." He invaded the back of her gown, body-warmed metal pressing between her shoulder blades. He smelled of damp wool, Macassar oil and strong cologne. "Breathe deeply. . . . Very good, Mrs. Clarring."

Without warning, Rose was free of both the doctor and his stethoscope.

The mattress sprang upward, relieved of extra weight.

"Is there someplace where I may wash up, Mr. Clarring?"

"Through here," Jonathon said, familiar voice bringing a lump to her throat.

Rose quickly fastened her gown, hands shaking.

The stern-faced nurse rummaged through the doctor's satchel: She pulled out a hard leather case.

"What is that?" Rose asked.

But the nurse did not answer.

Cascading water drowned out the thud of hard leather impacting even harder wood.

Glass shone in the shadow of black leather: A perfect rose for a perfect honeymoon.

"Jonathon." Rose addressed her husband's back; his navy wool jacket was crumpled. Rose had never before seen her husband in a state of dishevelment. She took a deep breath to slow the drumming of her heart. "Why are you doing this?"

Light flared: Phosphorus burned her nose.

The nurse leaned over the nightstand and lifted up the globe of the rose-colored lamp. Simultaneously, the rush of water stopped.

Jonathon still did not turn around and look at her.

"Mrs. Clarring." The doctor stepped out from the bathroom. "Your husband is concerned about the fact that you have not conceived a child."

Rose stared in shocked silence at the pale brown hair that overlapped Jonathon's white collar.

Surely she could not have heard what she had just heard.

"He brought me here to examine you," the doctor continued affably. "I know how embarrassing the coming minutes will be for you, but if you will roll up the hem of your nightgown, it will be over quickly. I promise to be as gentle as possible."

Out of the corner of her eyes, she saw the doctor open the flat case the nurse had deposited on the night table: Metal gleamed obscenely in the bright glare of the flickering lamp.

Gray smoke lazily drifted up from a rose-shaped bowl; a blackened match shone through pale pink glass.

"There is no need for this, Dr. Weinberger." Rose squeezed her thighs together; her flesh, stretched for and by Jack, pulsed with burgeoning anger. "My husband knows full well why I do not have children."

"Your husband mentioned that he had mumps, Mrs. Clarring, but not all men who contract mumps are rendered sterile."

The doctor's prognosis eerily mimicked Jack's statement six days earlier.

. . . *Mumps don't always make a man sterile,* he had said.

Rose had felt naked and alone when answering Jack: Rose now felt utterly violated.

The doctor stood over Rose. "Assist her, Nurse Williams."

The nurse flipped back the covers.

Rose's gown had ridden up to her thighs. Cold air lapped her naked skin.

"How *dare* you!" Rose said, outraged.

Between one convulsive breath and the next, the bed dipped in a squeal of springs.

Rose involuntarily fell backward into the depression the nurse made.

A surprisingly strong arm clasped Rose across her breasts that heaved up and down for oxygen; at the same time an equally strong hand grasped her shoulder and pressed her torso down into the nurse's lap.

"There's no need to be afraid, Mrs. Clarring," the nurse said, stale breath washing Rose's face, "I'm right here."

Rose would *not* let this happen.

Her knees automatically lifted and bent to give her scrabbling feet purchase.

Cold metal slipped inside her.

Rose froze.

"Hold still, Mrs. Clarring; this will just take a minute. . . ."

Rose stared up at the ring of light circling the ceiling.

"I didn't think, Jonathon"—her eyes were so dry they burned; a matching burn spread deep inside her—"you could hurt me any more than what you did yesterday: I was wrong."

"Mr. Clarring, were you aware that your wife is wearing a Dutch cap?"

"No," Jonathon replied, voice muffled.

Rose more sensed than saw the movement of the doctor: straightening . . . turning . . . bending over the bed.

Metal navigated through the metal speculum.

What one doctor had given, another doctor took away.

Rose clenched her fists; the antiseptic smell of the nurse churned her stomach.

"A Dutch cap has no lasting effect on a woman's ability to conceive." The hard metal slipped free of her aching vagina. The doctor straightened. "You're very fortunate, Mrs. Clarring: I see no abnormalities in either your vagina or cervix. I believe if you refrain from these Chinese traps, you stand an excellent chance of becoming a mother."

"Dr. Weinberger."

Jonathon spoke, but not to Rose.

Not to the woman who had held him in her arms while he cried his tears and she leaked his seedless sperm.

Arm and hand relaxing, the nurse slid out from underneath Rose.

"Yes, Mr. Clarring?" the doctor asked.

Rose did not move.

"I am understandably upset at my wife's duplicity," Jonathon said, but it was not the Jonathon she had married. "I think it will be some time before I can bring myself to touch her again. We were recently intimate. Is there any chance that she can still become pregnant, now that there is nothing to block my sperm?"

Chapter 36

Jack stepped into the office of James Whitcox.

A large teak desk was sandwiched between a high-backed, black leather chair and two smaller chairs. Glass-fronted bookshelves framed the wood and leather. Black leather hugged the far wall. Above the sofa, rain slithered down thick, uncurtained glass. Two wing-backed, brown leather chairs faced a black marble fireplace. A smaller teak desk guarded a second wall of glass-encased bookshelves.

Both furniture and books were well used.

This was where James Whitcox had spent his time while Jack had spent time with his wife.

"Mr. Tristan." Jack nodded at James Whitcox's clerk, also a man who had been called to the bar, but who, like his own clerk, did not practice law. "You know Mr. Dorsey."

The two men—one black-haired and twenty-five, the other brown-haired and twenty-seven—nodded cordially.

Big Ben tolled nine bells.

Rose had been in Jonathon Clarring's house now for seventeen hours.

There was no time for finesse, so Jack was brutally frank. "Whitcox is on his way to petition the Queen's Bench for a writ of habeas corpus."

"Yes, sir," Avery Tristan said, voice expressionless. "Mr. Whitcox rang."

"So you know Mrs. Clarring is being held by her husband."

"Yes, sir."

"And you know of the relationship between Mrs. Clarring and myself," Jack said flatly.

"Yes," Avery Tristan said.

Nathan Dorsey said nothing.

But he had already known.

"Mrs. Clarring—because she is now residing inside her husband's domain—may now officially file for a separation," Jack said.

Burning coals snapped inside the marble fireplace.

Jack wondered if Rose was warm. Jack wondered if Rose was safe.

Jack wondered if he would ever again see Rose.

"Mr. Dorsey suggested that because her husband does not perform his conjugal duties"—Jack closed his eyes against the desire that had briefly sparked inside Jonathon Clarring's eyes; opening them, he confronted brown eyes so dark they appeared to be black—"we file on the grounds of desertion. The court, of course, cannot command a man to perform matrimonial intercourse. However, because he deserted the marriage bed, we can argue that he has willfully deprived Mrs. Clarring of her womanly right to bear children, and plead that she be granted the right to live separately.

"In view of recent events, however, we may now plead Jonathon Clarring has treated his wife cruelly and unforgivably." Jack glanced over dark brown eyes and caught Nathan Dorsey's green gaze. "It is our job today, gentlemen, to write a petition that will leave a deciding judge in no doubt as to where his duty lies.

"A habeas corpus will grant Mrs. Clarring temporary liberation: We must permanently remove her from Jonathon Clarring's custody.

"Whitcox and I are in agreement: Because of my relationship with Mrs. Clarring, the petition cannot be filed in my name. You, Mr. Tristan, will lodge it on behalf of Whitcox and Mrs. Clarring. Mr. Dorsey is familiar with the judges and their clerks: He will accompany you to the courthouse."

Chapter 37

"My lords." James addressed three men who wore scarlet robes and bob-wigs. They were not jurors: They were judges of the High Court of Justice and bore the rank of Knight Bachelors. Hand-picked by the Prime Minister and appointed by the Queen, the law—and the law alone—was their conscience. "I would like to express my gratitude to this court for addressing this extraordinary writ. The Magna Carta Libertatum is the Great Charter of Freedoms. This charter provides that no man or woman be unlawfully detained or imprisoned. Yet, my lords, that is what has happened to Mrs. Rose Clarring."

Intrigue illuminated the faces of the three men who sat on the Queen's Bench.

James briefly paused before continuing: "Mrs. Clarring—due to reasons outside the purview of this court—no longer abides in the house of Mr. Jonathon Clarring, her husband.

"Yesterday, on the sixth of June . . . when returning from a shopping excursion with her mother . . . Mrs. Clarring was forcibly abducted. The man who abducted her, my lords, was her husband."

The curiosity lighting the three men's faces switched off.

They weren't interested in the physical and emotional trauma of a man's wife: They were interested in the law.

"Mrs. Clarring," James said, deliberately impressing upon the three judges Rose Clarring's vulnerability, "is a petite woman. She stands five feet tall. When her mother dropped off Mrs. Clarring in front of her home—Mrs. Clarring's home, my lords, not that of her husband—it was raining. She carried an umbrella in one hand, and a vase—a gift from her mother, purchased at Whiteley's that very day—in the other.

"Mrs. Clarring did not notice that a cab was parked at the curb. She did not see that a man stepped out from the cab and followed her."

James addressed the middle judge—a sixty-three-year-old husband, father and grandfather—appealing to the gray-bearded man instead of the bewigged adjudicator. "That man, my lord, was her husband.

"He called out to her when she reached the foot of her stoop.

"We do not know what went through her thoughts when she heard his voice, because she is not here to tell us. We do know, however, that she turned around to confront him.

"But he was not alone, my lords."

Jack's gaze penned the judge to the far right, a fifty-three-year-old bewhiskered husband and father who had a recently married daughter. "While Jonathon Clarring disembarked from his cab, a cab across the street discharged two men.

"Jonathon Clarring deliberately acted as a decoy to prevent Mrs. Clarring from entering the safety of her home. While he distracted and engaged his wife, the two men—one on either side—grabbed her upper arms."

Sweat crawled underneath James's wig; it forged an itching, burning path.

He imagined how he would feel were Rose Clarring Frances Hart, imprisoned against her will with no legal hope for liberation.

Impulsively he lifted up his left forearm; slick black silk parted around his elbow and pooled on top of the counselor's table. Simultaneously, cool air plunged inside his black wool court coat.

"If I may direct your attention, my lords."

The three judges instinctively glanced downward, curious men as well as appointed adjudicators.

"Mrs. Clarring's upper arms are no bigger around than my wrist. My fingers, great sirs, would completely wrap around her arms"—James circled his wrist above the thick black turnback cuff that identified him as a Queen's Counselor—"just as they now do my wrist.

"When extreme pressure is applied to the upper arms, it paralyzes the lower arms."

Lowering his hands, James snagged the gaze of the judge on the left. He was the youngest, a forty-five-year-old husband and father with five daughters: one a debutante, two in school, two in the nursery, all of whom would one day marry and be subject to the dictates of their husbands.

"These two men," James stressed, "gripped Mrs. Clarring so tightly that she lost the use of her arms. She dropped her umbrella and the vase with which her mother had gifted her.

"She had no means of protection: not from the pounding rain. Not from the brutes who accosted her. *While* her husband watched, these two men bodily lifted her by the arms and carried her across the street, where they forced her into the waiting cab.

"Jonathon Clarring stole Rose Clarring's liberty." James laid flat his hands on cool oak. "I urge this court to approve a writ of habeas corpus ad subjiciendum."

The faint drum of rain filled the silence.

The fifty-three-year-old bewhiskered judge was the first to speak. "Do you understand what you are asking of this court, Mr. Whitcox?"

"I am asking you to issue Mr. Jonathon Clarring a summons to bring Mrs. Rose Clarring to this courtroom," James said evenly.

"You are asking this court to come between a man and his wife," the bewhiskered judge sharply returned.

"The Magna Carta does not exclude protection from unlawful detention because a woman is a man's wife," James calmly rebounded. "Jonathon Clarring forcefully and with forethought captured and abducted Rose Clarring. Had his actions been legal, a policeman would have escorted her to her husband's home, and Mr. Clarring would not have needed to hire men to forcibly take her into his custody.

"But he did not have a court order that would allow him to take her into his custody. Mr. Clarring did not take legal action. Instead he waited outside her home until she was alone and had no one to help her. She was three steps away from her front door. He deliberately detained her so that the two thugs he had hired could and did with brute force seize her. His actions are not sanctioned by English law."

"Do we have witnesses to corroborate this so-called abduction, Mr. Whitcox"—the middle judge spoke, a man who hoarded his powers, both judicial and marital—"or is your theatrics based purely upon speculation?"

"The abduction was witnessed by Mrs. Clarring's housekeeper." James curtailed a spurt of anger: They did not want emotion, these men who held Rose Clarring's fate in their hands, but emotion was her only defense. "I have her affidavit, my lord."

"May we see it?" the middle judge asked sardonically.

"Certainly," James said. "I also have here an affidavit from the mother."

A court usher passed on the proffered documents.

The middle judge cursorily read the top letter. "The housekeeper—Mrs. Dobkins—claims Mrs. Clarring didn't struggle."

"It's difficult to struggle, my lord," James said dryly, "when one's arms are immobilized by men who are twice as large as oneself."

"The housekeeper made no reference to calls for assistance." The middle judge passed the two affidavits to his right; he did not read the letter from the mother. "Did Mrs. Clarring not call for Mrs. Dobkins to come to her aid?"

"The housekeeper witnessed the abduction from an upstairs window," James replied. "It was raining: She heard no sounds."

"You said he called out to her, Mr. Whitcox, 'to distract and engage her," the youngest judge quoted. "Are you now saying the housekeeper did not hear him call out?"

"Why else, my lord, would Mrs. Clarring have turned round, if her husband had not called out to her?" James reasoned.

"Perhaps she was expecting him," the middle judge said.

"So we don't really know that Mrs. Clarring was taken against her will," the bewhiskered judge to the right remarked, looking for a way to resolve his moral responsibility as a husband and father with his role as male adjudicator.

"The affidavit from the mother clearly states that Mrs. Clarring—during the shopping expedition—said she would not go back to her husband," James said.

"Mrs. Clarring is a woman, Mr. Whitcox," the middle judge pointedly remarked. "Women are known to change their minds."

"If Mrs. Clarring is with her husband by choice, we will agree that is where she should be," James said. "We ask the court to grant a writ of habeas corpus in order to determine whether or not she has been unlawfully detained."

"You said Mrs. Clarring does not live in her husband's abode." The youngest judge studied the letters. "Is she legally separated from him?"

"No, my lord."

"Then she belongs in her husband's custody," the middle judge adjured.

"The law grants Mr. Clarring the right to sue his wife for restitution of his conjugal rights," James responded. "The law does not give him the right to forcefully seize and detain her."

"Are there warrants on Mr. Clarring?" the fifty-three-year-old judge to the right asked, still searching for a way to resolve moral responsibility and judicial authority. "Has he in the past been charged with cruelty?"

"Mr. Clarring has no warrants, my lord, but that does not mean Mrs. Clarring's life is not in grave peril." James remembered Frances's words only seven hours earlier, his sex nestled between the lips of her sex, her forehead branding his lips. "Only a desperate man would take the drastic steps that Mr. Clarring has taken."

"At what time did this so-called abduction occur, Mr. Whitcox?" the youngest judge asked, imagining where his wife and daughters had been the previous day while another woman was snatched away only three steps from her door.

"Mr. Clarring seized Mrs. Clarring at four in the evening," James replied.

Rose Clarring had been taken while Jack Lodoun sat in the House of Commons.

Memory sliced through James.

His wife had been killed while he read a brief in the House of Commons, unaware she and the absentia Jack Lodoun were lovers.

"What proof do we have that she is in the custody of her husband?" the bewhiskered judge asked.

"She was seen through an upstairs window."

"Did no one knock on the door to verify whether she is being 'forcefully' detained?" the middle judge asked sarcastically.

James stoically met the senior High Court judge's gaze. "No one has been allowed admittance, my lord."

He had attempted to gain entrance prior to appearing in court: No one had answered the door, although he could tell there was activity inside.

"Did you see her?" the bewhiskered judge asked.

"No," James said truthfully.

"Who *has* seen her?" the middle judge barked.

"Her mother," James lied, unable to mention the man who was Rose Clarring's lover.

"What do you want us to do, Mr. Whitcox?" asked the youngest judge who had five daughters.

James had done all he could do.

"I ask only that you give Mrs. Clarring due process," he said. "And that you expeditiously grant her liberty—as directed by the Magna Carta—to determine where she wishes to dwell."

Chapter 38

"Jane!" The familiar voice marched up the stairs and knifed through her chest. "You have a visitor!"

Her heartbeat ridiculously quickened, anticipation mocking the pain that cleaved her.

Quickly stuffing folded chemises into a dresser drawer, she cursorily glanced in the mirror—no hair escaped the severe bun in which it was drawn up—before hurrying down worn stairs.

The visitor wasn't the man Jane Fredericks had hoped to see.

Two women—one dying of syphilis with graying brown hair, the other vibrant with good health and dyed red hair—sat on a faded, yellow brocade sofa.

"Mrs. Hart," Jane said, voice brittle.

"Hello, Miss Fredericks." The forty-nine-year-old woman with the absurdly youthful hair and fashionable green frock glanced up from the suede gloves she was peeling off. "I'm afraid I've made a mess of Mrs. Fredericks's floors."

"Nonsense." It hurt Jane to see her forty-six-year-old mother smile as if she were not day by day slipping away. "Jane, dear, sit down and entertain your guest while I make a pot of tea."

Jane wanted to grab her and say the hired woman would do it, but the hired woman did not work on Tuesdays.

Her mother's absence weighted the air.

Jane perched on a floral-patterned armchair opposite the faded yellow sofa.

Rain hammered the mullioned windows and crawled down the glass in squirming rivulets.

Jane imagined what it must be like, lying underneath mud with only worms for company.

"You didn't tell Mrs. Fredericks about the trial," dropped into the stilted silence.

"She doesn't read the papers," Jane said, reluctantly gazing at Frances Hart. "I saw no reason to distress her."

"Your mother is a lovely woman."

"My mother is dying," Jane said flatly.

"Your mother is very much alive now." The compassion in Frances Hart's voice flayed Jane's skin. "Don't bury her before she's dead, Miss Fredericks."

"I should be gay, then." Jane blinked back tears, spine straight, anger churning her stomach. "And be happy that she'll soon be dead, like you're happy now that your husband is dead."

Jane had intended to wound the older woman who dressed like a trollop. So why did her words hurt Jane?

The pale eyes darkened. "You're very young, Miss Fredericks."

The barrister—Jack Lodoun—had similarly remarked on her age. She was the youngest member of the Men and Women's Club, he had noted. And Frances Hart the eldest.

"I'm twenty-seven," Jane said.

"I will tell you what a very wise woman once told me," Frances Hart unexpectedly offered.

But Jane didn't want to hear words of wisdom from this woman who was alive and healthy, living in sin with a man to whom she was not married, while her mother was dying because of the bonds of matrimony. So she kept her mouth closed.

"She said," Frances Hart said, "'Death is no reason to stop living.'"

Death.

Living.

"How can a woman live with a man who is murdering her?" burst out of Jane's throat.

She stiffened her spine—too late to take back the words—daring the older woman to jeer at her lack of control.

No condemnation shone inside the pale green eyes, neither at the knowledge Jane's father had infected her mother with a dreadful disease, nor at Jane's outburst.

"If your father had contracted influenza, and passed it on to your mother," Frances Hart reasoned, "would you still blame him?"

"Of course not," Jane said scornfully.

"Did your father deliberately give your mother syphilis?"

"It doesn't matter if he did it deliberately." Bitterness welled up inside Jane. "He would not have contracted it had he been faithful to my mother."

Frances Hart glanced down at her damp gloves. A crystalline raindrop glittered on the green ribbon banding her straw hat: It shone like a diamond, pure and free of human corruption. "I came for your assistance, Miss Fredericks."

Jane had nothing to offer this woman.

"I do not think I shall be able to help you, Mrs. Hart."

The older woman raised her head, pale green gaze catching Jane's gaze. "I do not seek aid for myself."

"Mr. Whitcox"—the barrister with whom Frances Hart lived in carnal sin—"is quite capable of helping himself."

"It is Mrs. Clarring who needs our help, Miss Fredericks."

Jane pictured in her mind the quiet, reserved woman who was six years her senior, and from whom she had for two years sat across. Immediately the image was replaced by the postcard of a man touching his sex.

A postcard Rose Clarring had purchased at a pornographic shop.

It had hurt to see the image of what it was that had infected her mother. But it hurt even more to know that Jane had gazed upon a man's sex and wanted to feel every inch of it inside her.

Deliberately she banished both the image of the postcard and the desire it had generated. "Why would Mrs. Clarring need my aid?"

"You are a suffragette."

Jane bristled defensively; it had been a point of contention among the members of the Men and Women's Club for two years. "Yes, I am."

"You believe in the emancipation of women."

Jane flushed with guilt, but did not know why she felt guilty. "Yes."

"Mrs. Clarring is being held inside her husband's house," Frances Hart said.

Shock reverberated over a roll of thunder.

"Why would her husband do that?"

"Mrs. Clarring left him."

Outrage flared through Jane. "And so he feels it is his right to imprison her?"

The pale green eyes were uncomfortably astute. "Mrs. Clarring took a lover."

Jane's mouth snapped shut.

Rain pounded wood and glass.

"Does he still have the right to imprison her, Miss Fredericks?" Frances Hart gently queried.

"She was unfaithful," Jane said coldly.

Just as her father had been unfaithful.

"And so she deserves to suffer?" Frances Hart countered.

Jane envisioned the hard white syphilitic tumor on her mother's neck.

Every day it grew.

Jane's voice was emphatic. "Yes."

Someone had to pay for the pain.

"Even though," Frances Hart asked, "she confided in us that her husband is not intimate with her?"

Jane remembered that her parents had slept in separate bedrooms. Before the syphilis. Jane remembered the single bed her parents now shared.

They had not laughed when they had been healthy. Now they frequently laughed.

"My mother doesn't deserve to die," Jane said tightly.

"Your father is dying, too."

Every day.

"Are you suggesting it's my mother's fault that he went to another woman?"

"I'm suggesting, Miss Fredericks," Frances Hart said over the punishing rain, "that we often do not understand why men and women do the things they do."

"And understanding *why*," Jane sneered, "magically makes the pain go away?"

Memory flitted through the pale green eyes. "We none of us live without pain, Miss Fredericks."

There had been no pain before her father had been unfaithful.

Jane abruptly remembered the icy silence at the dinner table each night while she exuberantly chatted about women's suffrage and the changes she would someday wrought.

But now was someday.

There had been no pain before her father had infected her mother, she now realized, but neither had there been love.

The words leapt unbidden out of her mouth, three years of accumulated emotion. "But how can you live with pain?"

Her mother and father would die, and Jane did not know how she would survive their deaths.

Frances Hart leaned forward; comforting fingers squeezed her hand. "By living."

But now Rose Clarring suffered, *because* she had lived.

Jane withdrew her cold hand from Frances Hart's warm fingers and sat back in the chair. "How do you think I could aid Mrs. Clarring?"

Straightening—hurt flickering inside the older woman's eyes—Frances Hart asked: "You are familiar with marches and such, are you not?"

"Yes," Jane said, throat taut. "Of course."

Jane had marched many times in support of women's suffrage.

Frances Hart solemnly asked: "Will you help arrange a demonstration to liberate Mrs. Clarring?"

One woman.

An adulteress.

Jane heard again her self-loathing, unable to control the ache to experience physical love: *We will never, ever escape servitude if we do not sublimate our desires*. Jane felt again the bite of John Nickols's mockery: *Miss Fredericks, you are prepared to attack anyone who has not liberated your fair sex, yet you yourself have done nothing to advance your cause.*

Jane thought of the intimate glances her mother and father shared when they didn't think she was looking.

Chapter 39

"You must eat lunch, Mrs. Clarring."

Rose ignored the nurse who had held her down on the bed, and whose gaze now burned twin holes in her spine.

In the street, a rain-blurred carriage halted.

Her heartbeat escalated.

Was it another doctor? she wondered.

Her heart skipped a beat.

Was it Jack?

Had he come back?

Rose planted her palms against cool glass.

"You must eat for the baby, Mrs. Clarring."

The gray-bearded doctor had said a man's sperm could live inside a woman's body for several days. The balding gynecologist had advised her it was safe to remove the Dutch cap eight hours after sexual intercourse.

Who was right?

Rose's fingers fisted against the glass. "There will be no baby, Nurse Williams."

Please, God.

"God works miracles." The scrape of metal on china pierced her spine. "You should pray that He do so now."

The aroma of sharp cheddar and eggs overpowered the asphyxiating odor of chicken fricassee.

Pain is a form of power, Jack had said. *For both the administrator and the recipient.*

The anonymous carriage lurched forward in the rain.

Rose stared down at four black umbrella tops.

"Do you have children, Nurse Williams?"

"I have six children, Mrs. Clarring."

Maternal pride reverberated over a rumble of thunder.

"Do you have daughters?"

Metal ground into china.

"Two."

The pride in the nurse's voice was dimmer.

"You don't love your daughters?" Rose queried.

Never once had Rose felt less loved than her brothers.

"Of course I love my daughters."

Rose abstractedly watched the four black umbrellas that restlessly shifted, as if waiting for another umbrella to join them.

"Would you do this to them?" Rose asked.

"I've nursed them many a time through the years."

"Would you stand guard, Nurse Williams, while their husbands imprisoned them?"

China clattered; the pouring of fragrant tea blended in to the steady pound of rain. "You are a very fortunate woman, Mrs. Clarring."

Very fortunate.

Rose had experienced passion.

Another black carriage pulled to the curb. The four umbrellas bobbed after it, like black tops.

"How am I fortunate, Nurse Williams?" Rose asked incuriously.

"Your husband is a wealthy man."

"So that entitles my husband to hold me here against my will?"

"I read about you in the papers, Mrs. Clarring."

Raindrops kissed her knuckles, soothing little busses.

Jonathon could not hold her prisoner indefinitely, they promised.

The raindrops lied.

Her husband could have her locked away forever. And there was nothing anyone could do.

Because of men like Jack.

Rose spoke past the tightness of her throat. "Did you think my picture was a good likeness?"

"Pretty is as pretty does, I always say." China impacted china. "We get what we deserve."

Cynthia Whitcox had not deserved to die.

But she had.

"Did my husband deserve being sterilized by mumps?" Rose countered.

"You're not fooling anyone, Mrs. Clarring: We've read the newspapers. We saw that disgusting device with which you polluted your body. You're an adulterous woman. Thankfully, you've spared your husband illegitimate offspring. He's been more than generous. If it were up to me, the likes of you would be thrown in gaol with the other harlots who taint our fair city."

The black carriage pulled away. The four umbrellas had begat two more.

"Do you know how many men it takes to subdue a woman, Nurse Williams?"

"I wouldn't know."

Liar, Rose thought. This was how she made her living, stealing other women's pride and dignity.

"Two men, Nurse Williams." Black bruises cuffed her upper arms. "It takes two men to subdue a woman."

Rose had not cried out when they had carried her to the cab.

She had known Jonathon had the legal right to incarcerate her, but she had not thought he would do it.

Another carriage pulled up to the curb across the street.

"Do you know how many women it takes to subdue a woman, Nurse Williams?"

"I wouldn't know," the woman repeated.

The six black umbrellas bobbed toward the carriage.

"Neither do I," Rose said flatly. "Get out."

"My position is to look out for you."

Rose abruptly pivoted, wool skirt and flannel petticoats swirling.

The nurse sat behind an oak drum table that had been transformed into a dining table. Steam drifted upward from rose-patterned china. Behind the white-capped woman pink roses climbed the wall.

Pretty is as pretty does.

"I said," Rose said slowly, clearly, "get out."

"You're being irrational, Mrs. Clarring."

"If you do not get out," Rose said, gritting her teeth, "we will see how many women it takes to subdue another."

"Your manner now proves, Mrs. Clarring, that you are a danger to yourself." Smug superiority weighted the nurse's face: She was eight inches taller than Rose, and had forcibly immobilized Rose, her expression said. "I will not leave."

Rose had felt many emotions in her life. She had never before felt rage.

She felt it now.

"Then I will leave," she said abruptly.

Wariness replaced the nurse's smugness. "What are you doing?"

Rose slammed shut the pink enameled bathroom door: The lock turned with a satisfying snick.

Slowly she slid down painted wood, physically barring entrance to the bathroom: Wool, horsehair bustle and more wool humped in the small of her back.

Rose sat on the floor, cold tile imprinting a bared buttock.

Darkness pressed against her eyelids.

She could not cry.

Rose heard again the clatter of a wooden-handled umbrella striking wet concrete; it was chased by the dull shatter of porcelain.

She had not felt the ice-cold rain stabbing her skin. She had not felt the pain of being physically lifted off her feet.

The pain Jonathon had stolen from her had blossomed inside his eyes.

Now he stole her privacy.

A faint chime penetrated the barricade that was her body: Westminster Chimes announced the half hour. Or the three-quarter hour.

She had been inside the bathroom for fifteen minutes. Or thirty minutes.

She imagined living like this for the rest of her life: caged, like an animal.

"Mrs. Clarring." Rose felt the sudden pounding of flesh against wood as surely as if the nurse struck her spine. "Open this door."

"'No, no, I won't let you come in, not by the hair on my chinny chin chin,'" Rose murmured.

A giggle worked up inside her throat.

The thought of her youngest nephew—warm and drowsy from his nap—burst her laughter.

He loved the story of the *Three Little Pigs*. Perhaps even now he was enjoying the tale.

A low growl punctuated the pounding knocks.

Rose's stomach.

But Rose did not have Jack to feed her.

The tears that had not come earlier burned her eyes.

She had not been able to stop the examination, but she would not cry.

Rose stood by the simple expediency of climbing up enameled wood with her hands.

A lock, she discovered, made the same sound opening as it did closing.

The nurse jerked open the bathroom door; greenish-gray light invaded the cocoon of darkness.

"I have decided I am hungry after all, Nurse Williams." Rose calmly stared up at the older, taller woman in her dismal brown wool and frigid white cap. "Be so good as to step aside."

The nurse was flabbergasted.

A smile tugged up Rose's lips.

The smile died thirty minutes later when she resumed her post.

A small army of black umbrellas patrolled the pavement across the street. But it was not they who arrested Rose's attention.

A cab pulled up to the curb directly underneath her window: The first occupant was hidden by a black umbrella. The second occupant carried no umbrella.

Rose's heart rushed up into her throat.

Chapter 40

"Did Mr. Whitcox succeed?" The pounding rain throbbed inside Marie Hoppleworth's ears, a living, pulsing drum of retribution. Metal bit into her thigh. She carefully angled her umbrella, shielding two bodies instead of one. "Will the constable set her free?"

"We'll shortly know," John Nickols grimly returned.

Marie glanced down at the thirty-eight-year-old man with whom she had verbally sparred for two years, but who now intimately knew every nook and cranny of her body. "Will your paper print her story?"

"Adultery. Abduction. Why wouldn't they print it? The only ingredient that's lacking is murder." John looked out through the slashing rain and deepening gloom. "There's a reporter from *The Globe*; there's one from *The Daily Herald*. If press is what Whitcox wants, press is what he's going to get."

One moment the Clarring household was a prison; the next moment it flung open its door.

The ribbed tip of an umbrella collided with Marie's umbrella.

"Is that him?" demanded a familiar feminine voice. "Her husband?"

Marie glanced at thirty-two-year-old Esther Palmer, the mathematics teacher who had lost her position at Mrs. Beasley's Academy for Girls.

Her face was calm but shuttered.

Marie wanted to ask the woman if there was anything she could do to help, but this wasn't about the fallout from the trial.

Or perhaps it was.

Marie did not know why Jonathon Clarring had abducted his wife. All she knew was that he could murder Rose Clarring, and quite likely be let off with the time he had spent in gaol awaiting trial.

"I can't see," she briskly said.

"I see him," a familiar masculine voice volunteered.

All Marie could see of thirty-year-old Louis Stiles—a man who stood six feet seven inches tall—was a dark woolen coat and the leather-bound sketch pad he clutched between ink-stained fingers.

"What does he look like?" Marie curiously asked.

"We don't know what Mrs. Clarring's husband looks like," John flatly intervened, voice hollowly vibrating underneath the domed umbrellas. "So even if it were he standing in the doorway, we wouldn't know."

Another cab pulled up and discharged four women: Their numbers added to the growing crowd.

Tension gathered.

It was wet. It was cold.

Women and men restlessly milled about to keep warm.

"He's moved aside," Louis Stiles suddenly commented.

The constable and unknown man stepped over the threshold.

The door closed, sound obliterated by the hammering rain.

"Who do you think is with the constable?" Marie asked tensely.

"No doubt a representative of the Queen's Bench," John replied, voice equally tense.

"She's looking down at us," intruded a third masculine voice. "Do you think she knows we're here?"

"How could she, Mr. Pierce?" Marie asked the thirty-one-year-old man who was a virgin still. "All she can see are these great black umbrellas. She probably thinks we're all congregating at a neighbor's wake."

Marie refused to believe that they might in the near future be attending Rose Clarring's wake.

"He won't hurt her, will he?" Esther Palmer asked.

The husband.

But they didn't know what Rose Clarring's husband was capable of doing.

"The jury liberated Mrs. Hart," Louis Stiles unexpectedly reassured the teacher. He was a virgin, too, Marie thought. Or perhaps not . . . There was a decisiveness in his voice that had not been there before the trial. "The constable will surely liberate Mrs. Clarring."

"A husband is not a son, Mr. Stiles," thirty-four-year-old Sarah Burns gruffly advised. "Unless the constable is commanded by his superiors to do so, he will not interfere between man and wife. Hello, Miss Hoppleworth. Miss Palmer. Mr. Nickols. Mr. Pierce."

"Hello, Dr. Burns." Marie's fingers tightened around the grip of her umbrella: This woman more than anyone knew how easy it was to incarcerate women. "Mr. Addimore."

"We got here as quickly as we could," thirty-seven-year-old George Addimore said. There was a solemness about his eyes and mouth that was new. "Do we have any news yet?"

"No," John said shortly. "We believe a representative from the Queen's Bench is inside now."

"That's positive, surely," George Addimore said. "For how long?"

"Just a few minutes."

"What thoughts do you think are going through her mind?" Thomas Pierce asked.

Seven pairs of eyes assessed the rain-shrouded woman who stood in the upstairs window.

"What would you be thinking, were you abducted and imprisoned?" Marie asked.

"I'm not a woman," Thomas Pierce said.

"Even men, Mr. Pierce," Marie said, "feel the sting of betrayal."

"I was merely stating, Miss Hoppleworth," Thomas Pierce calmly expounded, "that I don't know what I would be thinking were I in Mrs. Clarring's shoes, because a man cannot be imprisoned by a woman."

"There are many types of prisons, Mr. Pierce." Marie stiffened at the cool, feminine response. "I assure you, women imprison men every day."

John glanced past Marie to the woman who had noiselessly joined them. Mockingly, he asked, "Would you march to liberate me, Miss Dennison?"

"Would you march to liberate me, Mr. Nickols?" twenty-nine-year-old Ardelle Dennison evenly returned.

The mockery on the face Marie had mapped with her fingers melted in the rain. "Yes."

"Likewise."

For long seconds John studied the woman Marie could not see; suddenly his glance slid sideways. "I see you and Miss Dennison no longer suffer from extenuating circumstances, Mr. Manning."

The excuse the two had used for not joining in club excursions held outside the museum.

"No," thirty-five-year-old Joseph Manning—the founder of the Men and Women's Club—imperturbably returned. "We don't."

"I thought," Sarah Burns said over the pelting rain and drumming tension, "that if anyone should ever be imprisoned, it would be me."

"Why?" Esther Palmer enquired.

"While we debated Malthusianism, Dr. Burns has all along been distributing literature in her office," George Addimore proudly explained.

It was clear that he and Sarah Burns were seeing one another.

The dull pounding of hooves and grinding wheels permeated the spatter of voices and falling rain.

A darkly cloaked woman exited from a hansom cab: Immediately she joined a group of welcoming women.

"She asked what I feared," John said harshly, referring to Rose Clarring.

Memory weighted the rain: Seven women and six men facing each other over a twenty-foot-long conference table. Rubber condom slapping wood . . . ivory cock ring rolling on gleaming mahogany . . . postcards cutting through the silence.

It occurred to Marie that the meeting to which John referred had led each of them here.

They had brought to the club an object expressing their deepest fears and desires.

Each of them, she now saw, had acted upon those desires.

They had come together in the trial because of a subpoena. They came together now because they had confronted their fears.

Esther Palmer spoke over the drum of rain. "I didn't think it would come to this."

A public trial. Reputations destroyed. A woman incarcerated.

"Neither did I," Marie said.

"Nor I," Ardelle Dennison admitted.

"Do you regret being a part of the club?" the founder of the Men and Women's Club asked the mathematics teacher, voice oddly yearning.

Marie saw Joseph Manning and Ardelle Dennison as they had weekly appeared underneath the unforgiving glare of gaslight: She with perfectly coifed brown hair and amber eyes; he with a pencil-thin black mustache and gunmetal gray eyes.

They were beautiful in a hard, cold way.

Standing in the rain—gathered together for the benefit of Rose Clarring—they appeared neither hard nor cold.

"No," Esther Palmer said finally, narrow shoulders visibly stiffening with resolve. "I don't."

Irresistibly Marie stared upward: The window was empty.

"I wonder if Mrs. Clarring does?" Thomas Pierce asked.

Marie knew that he, too, stared up at the empty window.

"If only she had taken a lover, like the newspapers accused her," Esther Palmer said.

"She did," Sarah Burns volunteered.

Marie wondered what type of man Rose Clarring—elegantly feminine yet quietly reserved—would take as a lover.

She glanced up at the doctor. "Did Mrs. Hart tell you that?"

Frances Hart had merely informed Marie that Rose Clarring had left her husband on the day of the trial, and had been abducted by him five days later: She had assumed Frances Hart had relayed the same information to the other club members.

"I saw her with Jack Lodoun outside the courthouse," Sarah Burns said.

"You must be mistaken," Marie denied.

"I don't think so, Miss Hoppleworth," the doctor replied. Her brown eyes—color blackened by the rain and gloom—were dull with worry. "They were . . . absorbed . . . in each other."

Marie had focused solely on John before and after the trial: She had not noticed the other members.

"I don't think it's regrets with which Mrs. Clarring is now grappling," Louis Stiles suddenly said.

But he didn't know that.

They might never know.

The reporter from *The Globe*—head bent against the rain—sloshed across the pavement that ran cold water. Two men parted from the sea of black cloaks and umbrellas: They followed.

Marie recognized the reporter from *The Daily Herald* that John had earlier pointed out.

"I have to go," John said, a reporter now instead of the man whose body had joined with her body. "Stand back; I don't want to hit you."

Battering water separated Marie and John.

Quickly he unfurled his umbrella; water cascaded over a dome of black. Twisting, he wedged the straight wooden handle in a specially crafted holder on the back of his wheelchair.

Every day he lived in fear, he had confessed during the meeting that had changed their lives.

He could be pushed in front of a carriage. He could be knocked over, unable to regain his mobility.

Rain blurred Marie's vision. Or perhaps it was moisture that fogged her spectacles.

Marie wanted to protect John.

But he didn't need her to protect him; he simply needed her to love him.

Clenching her hands into fists, she watched him wheel his chair through the lake that was the street.

Distant bells slogged through the damp and cold: An hour passed, three o'clock turning into four.

The occasional bark of masculine laughter drifted through the rain, men poised to report on a woman while inside the house men decided the woman's fate.

"Everything is prepared," ricocheted through Marie.

Her gaze snapped away from the rain-sluiced door that remained closed and the man who adjoined it, black umbrella lower than the others. "What is prepared, Miss Fredericks?"

The twenty-seven-year-old woman stood beside Thomas Pierce: She looked as grim as the waning day. "We will take shifts. Fresh suffragettes will come every eight hours, so that someone will be here day and night."

"You've done a commendable job, Miss Fredericks," Thomas Pierce said sincerely.

Jane Fredericks stared up at the man who had been a junior executive in a bank, but who was employed no longer.

Marie glanced away from the painful intensity on the younger woman's face: Not everyone had yet confronted their fears.

"What is taking them so long?" Ardelle Dennison suddenly snapped.

"They're men," Sarah Burns rejoined.

And men ruled.

The cold and the rain knotted Marie's chest.

"Look!" cried out a woman hidden inside a circle of black. "I see something!"

Hope surged through Marie. It was chased by fear.

She didn't want to think about what could happen if Rose Clarring was not liberated, yet she could think of nothing else.

The door opened; immediately it was filled with a black umbrella.

The body it domed was clearly masculine.

"Free Rose!" hurtled through the rain.

It came from Jane Fredericks.

All of the passion the young suffragette denied herself was captured in the shout.

"Free Rose!" Marie joined, remembering the county orphanage in which she had been raised, and the men who had abused the forsaken girls and boys.

Simply because they could.

"Free Rose!" enveloped Marie, a jarring chant comprised of male voices as well as female; suffragettes as well as members of the Men and Women's Club.

The emerging black umbrella was joined by four more.

Volleying voices rode the rain.

They had waited to see if the constable would liberate Rose Clarring: They got their answer.

Chapter 41

Jack could not stay away. Sitting in the gallery, face expressionless, he listened to the judgment of the Queen's Bench.

"On Tuesday, the Sixth of June, Mr. Whitcox did hereby charge the Queen's Bench with the serious task of summoning Mrs. Rose Clarring to this court to determine if her husband, Mr. Jonathon Clarring, has the lawful custody of her.

"A writ of habeas corpus is a powerful tool of liberty. It is not to be used lightly, nor is it meant to come between the unique relationship enjoyed between a man and his wife.

"Marriage is a sacred bond. A man vows to protect his wife and the sanctity of their union. We, the courts, grant him the supreme authority to do so.

"Mr. Whitcox charged that Mr. Clarring unlawfully detained his wife.

"To this charge, we say nay.

"Justice Coleridge *In re* Cochrane unequivocally determines that 'there can be no doubt of the general dominion which the law of England attributes to the husband over the wife.'[1] While 'the forcible detention of a subject by another is prima facie illegal, yet where the relation is that of husband and wife the detention is not illegal.'

"Justice Coleridge allowed that Mr. Cochrane could 'confine Mrs. Cochrane in his own dwelling house, and restrain her from her liberty, for an indefinite time, using no cruelty, nor imposing any hardship or unnecessary restraint on his part.'

"Had Mr. Clarring used undue force or cruelty against his wife, he could rightfully be charged with assault. Mr. Clarring acted wholly within the law when seizing Mrs. Clarring.

"Mrs. Clarring is a member of a notorious club that has recently featured in our papers. This group of men and women have encouraged her to commit acts contrary to the laws of marriage and to leave the sanctity of her husband's home. They took Mrs. Clarring from him. 'Prima facie he had a right to regain possession of her' and to remove her from those who would interfere with his custody.

"'If there were a prima facie case of cruelty, that would certainly entitle' Mrs. Clarring to apply for a ruling. But Mr. Clarring has made every provision for his wife: He has employed a nurse to tend her. A physician has attested to her good health.

"We will not issue a writ of habeas corpus that would only serve to 'unsettle the lady's mind, and make her believe that the court was going to do what the court will not do—remove her from her husband's custody—upon no ground whatsoever, except that she does not like to live with him.'

"Mrs. Clarring," the justices of the Queen's Bench concluded, "is where the law says she should be, and where she will stay as long as her husband says she will."

A sharp order ricocheted off brass and oak.

Black silk shimmered in flickering gaslight: James Whitcox rose.

Jack remained seated.

The three justices stood, silk robes glistening like red blood.

James Whitcox turned—gray periwig framing sharp cheekbones—and caught Jack's gaze.

There was neither victory nor defeat inside his gaze.

He was a barrister of the Queen's Counsel, he silently communicated, but he was not a member of Parliament.

Rising, Jack exited the courthouse.

Chapter 42

Rose lay on her side and stared at the rain-splattered window.

A dull roar of voices interwove with the incessant drum of rain.

Snatches of words pelted the glass: *free . . . rose that . . . woman's plight. Free the rose . . . dies . . . liberty.*[2]

Meaningless words.

Free . . . *liberty*.

A constable had entered Jonathon's house. The constable had exited Jonathon's house.

She had told him she was being held against her will. He had closed the bedroom door and locked it behind him.

This, then, Rose thought, was what Jack had meant when he'd said she would lose all rights by taking him as a lover.

"How much is Jonathon paying you, Nurse Williams," Rose asked, voice expressionless, "to live in his house and eat his food and spy on his wife?"

"Mr. Clarring is a generous man," the older woman merely said.

Rose had once thought so.

Abruptly she sat up, metal springs squealing, horsehair bustle biting.

The crochet needle winking in the flickering light of a lamp stilled. "What are you doing?"

"I'm going to relieve myself, Nurse Williams." Dark emotion coiled through the cold void of shock. "Would you care to watch?"

The nurse's gaze snapped downward; the needle resumed winking.

Rose firmly closed the bathroom door and located a tin box of matches.

Light flared.

Pale skin shone in the darkness.

A woman's hand . . . a woman's face.

Rose lit the pink crystal sconce and watched a blue line of fire crawl toward her fingers.

Did you feel my touch, Jack?

Yes.

Heat singed her skin.

The pain did not touch her.

Rose dropped the sputtering match into the toilet.

A distant bong seeped through rain and wood: The fifth bong drowned the fluttering light.

Rose had been a prisoner for forty-nine hours.

A fullness stretched her lower abdomen.

Forcefully she tamped down the dark emotion that swirled underneath the calm void: It was urine that swelled her stomach, not a baby.

The dark emotion refused to be ignored.

She could be pregnant with her lover's baby, it screamed. While the husband she loved held her a prisoner.

Dr. Burns had given Rose a pill to take should she be late with her monthly courses, but Jonathon—along with her liberty—had taken away her reticule.

Desperately she glanced about the flickering bathroom, seeking an emotional anchor.

Everywhere she looked she saw Jonathon.

Sky blue eyes that cried her tears. Brown hair made black with shadow.

I think it will be some time before I can bring myself to touch her again.

Rose acknowledged what she had not been able to acknowledge twenty-three hours earlier.

Jonathon had known when he called out to her just three steps away from her door that she was using a contraceptive.

But how could he?

Pain ripped through her stomach.

How could a man do to her what he had done?

Her gaze landed on the empty box of Bromo tissues.

Rose automatically opened the oak cabinet underneath the pink marble sink.

Three boxes of tissue were neatly stacked, exactly as she had left them one week earlier.

But she was not the same woman she had then been.

She did not know to what extent she had changed over the course of forty-nine hours: She only knew that a vital part of what made her a woman had been violated.

A muffled rap wormed through pink enameled wood.

Rose did not need to exit the bathroom in order to verify it was not Jonathon who knocked on the bedroom door.

He was not going to confront the past. And Jack was not able to liberate her.

The law did not support it.

Lifting up her skirts, Rose relieved herself.

Over the trickle of urine she heard the clicking closure of the bedroom door. The flush of roaring water obliterated further sound.

Rose mechanically washed her hands.

Soapy bubbles swirled down the dark drain of memory.

Dr. Weinberger had washed his hands with this same bar of soap. But the laudanum another doctor had prescribed for menstrual discomfort resided inside the top drawer.

Rose dried her hands and retrieved the brown bottle. Burying her hand and the bottle in the loose folds of a round lower skirt, she exited the bathroom.

Roasted beef wafted through the damp musk of rain: It had been a servant bearing dinner who had knocked.

The nurse in the rigidly starched white cap sat at the round table free of memorabilia, before her a plate filled with beef medallions, scalloped potatoes and green peas. Rose sank down in the waiting armchair opposite the nurse to a matching plate full of food.

Twin dishes of tapioca pudding completed the setting.

It was a familiar meal, one Rose had often eaten while Jonathon—buried inside his den—drank himself into a state of unconsciousness.

The nurse bowed her head and said grace: "For what we are about to receive, may the Lord make us truly grateful. Amen."

Rose was not grateful: She did not bow her head.

Rough, red hands poured aromatic tea into rose-patterned china cups.

Steam veiled the air between them.

Silently Rose waited until the nurse reached for a heavy, silver-plated fork.

Fingers clenching around cool glass, she asked, "Does not cleanliness go with godliness, Nurse Williams?"

Her voice was oddly jarring, as if it came from another woman.

And it did.

That other Rose—silently hurting in her solitary world—would not do what Rose now planned.

The nurse's hand paused.

Purposefully Rose met the gaze that for one brief second seemed oddly vulnerable, like a child reprimanded when reaching for candy. "Please wash your hands before eating at my table."

Ugly red splotched the older woman's face.

Rose thought for one sickening second she would not obey. Reluctantly the nurse rose from the makeshift dining table.

Rushing water drowned out the steady patter of rain.

Laudanum contained alcohol: The flavor would be unmistakable in tea.

Rose dumped tincture of opium over the medallions of beef, clear liquid thinning brown gravy.

Without warning the roar of gushing water died.

No sooner did Rose recork the bottle than the nurse returned.

"Thank you," she said, pushing the laudanum in between a silk-covered cushion and the silk-upholstered frame of the chair.

The nurse did not reply. Face splotched with angry red bites of embarrassment, she snatched up her knife and fork.

Rose smoothed a white linen napkin over her lap. More slowly, she lifted up the heavy silver utensils and sliced off a sliver of beef.

"This tastes odd," the nurse said, frowning.

Calmly Rose chewed and swallowed before replying, "Beef bourguignon can be an acquired taste."

"French."

The word expressed both contempt and intrigue.

The look on Ardelle Dennison's face when George Addimore had brought an ivory cock ring to a club meeting had been identical to the expression the nurse now wore.

"Yes," Rose said.

"There's nothing better than good English beef," the nurse righteously claimed, curiously forking up the remaining medallion.

"It is English beef," Rose calmly explained. "It's merely braised in burgundy wine and seasoned with garlic and onion. . . ."

Rose described how beef bourguignon was prepared while bite by bite the nurse devoured plain beef that was prepared with nothing more exotic than lardons, salt and pepper.

And tincture of opium.

An ingredient with which the nurse should be well familiar.

"I'm very tired," Rose said when the older woman's plate was empty of meat. Tossing her napkin onto her own plate that was barely touched, she stood. "I'm going to lie down."

Metal springs squealed in protest; deep inside her, dark emotion continued to swirl.

Pain. Anger.

A loss so profound, it threatened to swallow her whole.

The muted roar of voices vied with the drum of water.

Rose wondered who they were, those people who stood in the pummeling rain.

Her mother? Her father?

Her brothers?

Jack?

But she could not think of Jack. All she could think about was Jonathon and the love he had stolen from her.

A gentle snore rippled the air.

Rose left the bed in which she had slept alone for eleven years.

The nurse was slumped down in the green-velvet-covered armchair.

Curiously removed from the consequences of her actions, Rose reached into the apron pocket in which the nurse kept her keys.

Dark motion fluttered outside of her peripheral vision.

Rose's lashes snapped upward.

Eyes dilated black with opium stared into her eyes.

Their faces were so close, Rose inhaled the other woman's breath: It smelled of roast beef and the spicy-sweet tang of laudanum.

"You drugged me," the nurse said thickly.

"Yes," Rose said.

She had drugged the nurse while weaving around her the illusion she had wanted, to sample the riches which she envied Rose.

Every woman had her weakness.

"Did you kill me?" the nurse asked.

Fear swirled underneath the opium-induced lethargy.

Had Rose overmedicated the nurse?

"I don't know," Rose said.

The woman closed her eyes. Rose unlocked the door.

A thick rose-patterned runner muffled her steps.

Childish giggles and shushes chased up and down the flickering hallway.

It was an aberration . . . the distortion of protesting voices and pelting rain . . . but for one moment Rose imagined the children she would have borne if Jonathon had not contracted the mumps.

He would have been a loving father. She would have been a faithful wife.

An oak balustrade gleamed in the grayish-green gloom.

Rose grasped cool wood.

The third and tenth steps creaked.

There was no one to hear her descent.

Laughter drifted up from the kitchen, the servants enjoying their evening meal.

Later she would be hurt that not one of the men and women she had hired had bothered to help her.

Not now.

Not when she was about to confront the man she should have confronted twelve years earlier.

Silently she pushed open the door to Jonathon's den.

An overhead brass reflector light softly hissed; water rhythmically pelted glass and brick.

Rose closed the door and leaned against hard oak.

It was quiet and peaceful here at the back of the house.

The small, walled-in garden that adjoined the masculine room was obliterated by sheets of rain. The ghost of a woman peered through a French door at Rose.

Or perhaps the pale ghost peered at the wing-backed leather chair in which her husband sat—also reflected in the glass door—trying to see the man she had married.

Jonathon leaned over a glass-topped cherry desk, sensitive face somber. Light and shadow alternately silvered and darkened his baby-fine hair.

It took her a long second to recognize the crimson and gold shards of porcelain that lay scattered in front of him like a puzzle: It was the Oriental vase she had dropped when the men he'd hired had seized her.

"The pieces won't fit," Jonathon said without looking up, as if he had all along been expecting her.

Black beads and heavy silver winked: Her reticule leaned against the ashtray that had been a wedding gift. An opened newspaper adjoined crimson and gold shards; a dull, metal gun barrel dissected her name. A gold ring circled a pale face that bore her likeness. The band matched the white skin that marked her ringfinger.

Calmly, Rose asked, "Are you going to kill me, Jonathon?"

Jonathon raised his head.

The pain inside his sky blue eyes stabbed through her womb.

This was the man who had made her laugh with happiness, but now he laughed no more.

"The pain must end, mustn't it?" he asked, just as calmly.

"Yes," Rose said.

Chapter 43

The clang of the Division bell echoed throughout the eleven hundred and some odd rooms that comprised the Houses of Parliament.

Jack had eight minutes to enter the House of Lords before the content doors locked.

Three MPs dawdled outside the chamber.

"Where's the Lord Chancellor?" Jack asked shortly, folded umbrella raining water.

"What the devil, Lodoun," the first man said, graying head jerking around in surprise. "Made a wrong turn, old fellow: The Commons is due north."

Jack knew exactly where he was.

"Is he in the Content Lobby?"

The equivalent of the Ayes Lobby in the House of Commons.

"Yes, but—"

Wool coat flapping, Jack strode in between red-leather-upholstered benches. The House of Lords was as pompous as the

House of Commons was austere. Overhead, the blackening skylights and stained glass windows were stark against hissing, popping chandeliers. The oak door to the left of a gold, canopied throne pushed inward at the slap of his hand.

The voices of milling, guffawing men slammed into him.

"Sir, you cannot enter here," charged a key-brandishing clerk.

MPs were falling into a long row between Division desks.

Jack fought against a sudden surge of claustrophobia.

"My Lord Chancellor," he called out.

A sixty-four-year-old man—a former criminal barrister and now Chief Justice for the Court of Appeals, the most powerful court in England—turned.

Recognition flared inside his eyes. "How dare you, sir, enter the Content Lobby."

Jack shrugged aside restraining hands, purposefully striding forward. "Answer me one question, my lord."

One by one the guffaws and the gossip died.

The Lord Chancellor snapped: "This is neither the place nor the time—"

Jack ignored the gazes of lords—those born to the title and those honored by the title—that needled his skin.

"The Queen's Bench just ruled that a husband has the right to capture his wife and forcibly detain her in his home. I ask you, my Lord Chancellor," Jack stridently challenged; this was Rose's last legal hope, "does an English subject have such a right . . . of his own motion, whether it be his wife or anyone else . . . to imprison another English subject?"

Chapter 44

"I loved you, Rose, the first moment I saw you."

Rose saw in Jonathon's eyes the love he had felt on a warm summer day.

"Your hair shone like newly minted gold." Gold glinted in the hair of the pale ghost who peered into the window of their lives. "You were such a loving woman. Even angry as you were with your brothers, you were so gentle. I knew then I wanted you to bear my children."

In the summer of their courtship she had been blinded by the sun.

But now the rain obliterated the sun.

"You wanted me to bear your sons," Rose flatly corrected him.

A half-dozen boisterous boys, just like her brothers.

"I have four sisters," he unexpectedly divulged.

But Rose already knew that: Monthly she had invited his family to dinner.

"I had five brothers."

Rose had not known he had brothers.

More secrets.

"They were stillborn," Jonathon explained, eyes bleak with their loss. "My mother came from a family of women. She was not fashioned to carry male children."

Rose fought the crippling pain, facing the truth.

It had hurt not knowing, but it hurt far more knowing.

"And so you married me," she managed, "because I come from a fertile family of men."

Jonathon closed his eyes against the pain he caused; dark shadow hollowed his cheeks. "You've never heard them, have you?"

Rain like tears dribbled down the face of the pale ghost.

"Heard what?" Rose asked.

"Their laughter."

The laughter of the children he could not sire.

"You never heard, either, Jonathon," Rose said.

Jonathon opened the dark lashes she had once tried to count: Puzzlement clouded his sky blue eyes. "What?"

"My tears."

He searched her gaze. "Did you cry for our unborn children, Rose?"

Rose could no longer deny the truth. "I cried because you didn't love me, Jonathon."

"I've ached for you every night these last eleven years," he said.

Rose crossed her arms over her stomach to contain her pain. "Then why did you let me lie alone in the darkness, crying out for you?"

"Because you love me," he said simply.

Rose struggled to hold down the realization that was blossoming inside her: Truth would not be suppressed; it clawed at her insides like a living beast. "And so you deliberately withheld your love."

"Yes."

"You forced me to sleep alone," Rose reiterated, wanting him to deny what was suddenly so clear, "so I would take a lover."

Her pain was reflected inside his eyes. "Yes."

Silently he waited for her to put together the pieces he could not fit.

"You wanted me to get pregnant with another man's child," Rose concluded.

The child Jonathon could no longer give her, but which he still wanted from her body.

Jonathon did not deny it, because he couldn't.

"Yes," he said.

For one moment Rose couldn't breathe for the raw pain that ripped through her. "And you *think* that is love, Jonathon?"

Her pain flashed inside his eyes. "Do you *think* I enjoy the thought of you lying in Jack Lodoun's arms?"

"*Fucking* Jack Lodoun, you mean," Rose said unsteadily.

Hurting. Raging.

Both the hurt and the anger seeking an outlet.

"Yes." Her rage flashed inside his eyes, sharing the emotions he had caused—her love, her pain. "*Fucking* Jack Lodoun."

Fucking rang out over the hiss of gas and the drum of rain.

The gentle ghost stared on, a silent witness.

How do you know, Mrs. Clarring, that passion isn't just a splendid fuck? Jack had asked.

Rose now knew the answer.

But there were many things of which she was still ignorant.

"How did you learn that I was wearing a Dutch cap?"

"You overpaid the doctor." The gun on the table darkly gleamed like the hour hand on Big Ben, waiting to shoot forward. "He sent the refund—and a copy of the bill—to my office."

The memory of throaty laughter danced on raindrops.

The gynecologist's scrawl had been a three—his wife's first impression—instead of a four.

Rose had paid in cash, so she had not provided her address.

The newspaper article inside *The Globe*, she remembered, had mentioned Jonathon was employed by the London Stock Exchange.

"And you received it when?" Rose asked.

How long did it take to plan and execute the abduction of a wife?

"Monday," he said, unaware that each word hit her with the force of a hammered nail.

Fleetingly she wondered what she been doing while he planned to destroy her life.

"In the morning post?" she quizzed.

While she breakfasted.

"Yes."

She had been abducted at four in the evening.

"So it took you . . . how many hours . . . to find the type of men who would do what you wanted them to do?"

"We use a security firm at the office."

How convenient it was to be a man, working among other men.

"Did you love me, Jonathon," Rose asked, throat tight, "when you hired two men to abduct me?"

"A husband cannot abduct his wife."

As attested by the constable who had walked out of Jonathon's house, while Rose remained a prisoner inside.

The pain of the dual betrayal—the law and her husband—whipped through her.

"You watched them seize me," she forced out the words.

"They didn't hurt you."

"I have bruises, Jonathon."

"I instructed them to be gentle."

The pain shock had dulled surged through Rose.

The bruising fingers. The strain of being lifted up by her arms.

The jarring reality of being betrayed by the man she loved.

"You don't think I didn't hurt *here*, Jonathon?" Rose pressed fisted fingers against her breast that Jack had suckled, but which Jonathon had viewed only as an organ to nurse his sons. "I thought you were going to commit me to an insane asylum."

"I wouldn't do that to you," Jonathon denied.

Jonathon forgave Rose; Rose would never forgive Jonathon.

"What you did was far worse."

He had taken something from her that could never be replaced.

"You knew I wanted a child," he said.

The cry of a twenty-one-year-old boy who had dreamed of a family.

"You knew I wanted to be loved," she returned.

The cry of a twenty-one-year-old girl who had laughed with happiness.

"And I will love you every night of your life," Jonathon said earnestly, "if only you give me a child."

With purple-blue eyes.

"What if it had been I, Jonathon, who was sterile?" Rose remembered Jonathon's pregnant secretary. "Would you still love me?"

The uncertainty that flowered inside his eyes hurt him almost as much as it did her.

"Did you ever, for one moment," Rose asked, "love me instead of the children you thought I would give you?"

"Did you ever, for one moment," Jonathon riposted, "love me enough to give me the children I wanted?"

For one fleeting second Rose heard the faint wail of an unborn baby.

"No," she said.

The pain inside his eyes matched the pain she felt.

"Let me go, Jonathon."

Please.

But she would never again say *please* to this man who had betrayed her on every level a man could betray a woman.

"I can't, Rose."

"Why not?" she asked, suddenly not certain she wanted to know the answer.

"Contraceptives aren't foolproof." For one brief moment self-loathing equaled the determination inside Jonathon's eyes. "Someday, Rose, you will get pregnant. As long as I am your husband, I will have legal custody of your child."

It should not be possible to feel even more estranged from her husband: It was.

"We could have adopted, Jonathon."

There were so many orphaned children who needed love.

"I want *your* child," he repeated. "I want to feel its heart beat inside your stomach."

"Because you love me," she said bitterly.

"Yes."

But this wasn't love.

Rose needed to understand the man her husband had become.

"It must have hurt, Jonathon, to have seen my name in the newspaper."

Flickering shadow darkened his face. "I knew you would someday take a lover."

Knowing the pain it would cause her. *Knowing* the pain it would cause him.

"Will not your associates at work ridicule you, Jonathon?" she asked, tears scalding her eyes.

Had she ever touched this man?

"I am a valuable asset at the London Stock Exchange."

"Will they not laugh behind your back," she asked, "knowing that the only way you can keep your wife is by imprisoning her?"

"They already laugh behind my back," he said, his voice devoid of emotion, "married for twelve years with no children."

"Is that why you want a child so badly that you raped me," Rose asked, "so men won't laugh at you?"

"I've never touched you against your will," he instantly denied.

Still he did not understand what he had done.

"You would force me to bear a child, Jonathon," Rose said, invisible fingers squeezing her heart and her lungs. "That is the worst violation a woman can endure."

"You love me!" he suddenly cried, unable to shed the twenty-one-year-old boy.

"I will always love the happiness we shared, but I do not love the man who abducted and raped me."

"You could be pregnant."

"No."

"You don't know that."

Rose stepped forward toward the shattered segments of the past. "There is a pill inside my reticule, Jonathon, that will bring on my monthly courses."

His head snapped back. "You would do that?"

Rose took another step forward.

The pain had to end.

"Yes," she said.

"You would deprive me of my right to be a father?"

Jonathon's rights. But not Rose's rights.

"Sometimes, Jonathon"—Rose took a third step forward—"when I lay alone at night, listening to the sound of passing carriages, I hated the mumps."

Smiling blue eyes flashed through her mind's eyes; they did not match the eyes of the man who stared up at her.

The twenty-one-year-old girl reflected inside the window cried at the loss.

"Other nights, Jonathon"—hard wood bit into her lower abdomen; the shattered vase laid scattered between them—"I hated you."

The emotion Jack's flesh had held at bay—telling him she had blamed herself for Jonathon's pain—reared upward in all of its ugliness.

Rose had read that hatred was the other side of love: The books lied.

Hatred was the other side of guilt.

"You didn't love me." The vicious cycle of emotion burned a trail down her esophagus. "Every night I blamed myself for wanting to be loved. So I hated you. And then I hated myself."

Her heart pounded inside her chest. It was so loud it echoed in her ears.

Thud. Thud. Thud.

"I will not go through that again." The pounding of her heart vibrated the wood that pressed into her abdomen. "The pain will end tonight, Jonathon."

"Then end it, Rose." His pale, sensitive face was somber. Blurred skin and metal flashed between them. "For both our sakes. Pick up the pistol and end it now."

A carousel of voices flashed round her mind.

Wilt thou have this man to thy wedded husband . . . so long as ye both shall live?

You were always the bravest of my children.

I suggest you murder him . . . because no barrister can win you a divorce.

The betrayal she had felt at being seized assaulted her anew. It was chased by the rage of being raped with a doctor's speculum.

The gentle tears of the twenty-one-year-old girl who peered through the patio door were in stark contrast to the violent emotions that thrummed through thirty-three-year-old Rose: The twenty-one-year-old girl would always love the man who had made her laugh with happiness.

But Rose was no longer twenty-one.

She thought of Jack, and the simple intimacy of watching him brush his teeth. She thought of Jonathon, and the eleven years he had forced her to eat and sleep alone.

Simply so he could have the child he wanted.

Rose picked up the pistol, fingers curving around an ivory grip, middle finger instinctively sliding through a metal loop.

The gun was lighter than she had expected: It fit her hand as if it had been made specially for her.

Thud . . . thud . . . thud pounded her heart.

"I will never let you go, Rose."

Rose read the truth of his statement inside his eyes.

"I will follow you wherever you go. I will seize you when you least expect it.

"I *will* have your child," Jonathon promised. "Because I will always love you."

Thud. Thud. Thud.

"And you will always love me."

Thud. Thud. Thud.

"The only way we will ever be free of our love, Rose, is if you pull the trigger."

Rose saw again the marble statue of the woman bearing Bacchus's head.

She understood now why the woman had decapitated the god.

The wine and the ecstasy had to end.

In the end, that is what matters: That you do the right thing. Regardless of the consequences.

Rose pulled the trigger.

Chapter 45

The first shot stopped the rain. The second shot stopped Jack's heart. The third shot flung the black-haired butler who barred the doorway backward.

The fourth shot catapulted Jack forward.

The fifth shot slammed open a closed door.

The sixth shot stopped him short.

Gray smoke coiled around glinting gold.

Rose's hair. Rose's shots.

Jagged glass framed her head and black wool-clad shoulders. Over a straggling topknot, he saw Jonathon Clarring.

Jonathon Clarring, Jack realized, did not see him.

"The girl you loved, Jonathon, is dead," Rose said calmly, as if she did not hold a smoking pistol.

Jack saw his face reflected in glass; there was no glass where Rose and Jonathon Clarring should be reflected.

Rose had not shot her husband, he realized; instead she had destroyed the image of the girl she had once been.

Ignorant of men.

Silvery rain slanted through empty square panes.

"I will always mourn the love we had," Rose continued, voice devoid of the emotion that lashed jagged glass and pelted oak wood, "but I am not responsible for your pain."

Clattering footsteps slid to a halt behind Jack.

Jonathon Clarring did not move.

"I do not forgive you." Protesting voices drifted down the hallway. Rose and Jonathon Clarring were impervious to all but each other. "From this day forward, you are not my husband."

Metal impacted wood.

"You are dead to me, Jonathon."

Cold, wet wind buffeted his cheeks; simultaneously a newspaper whipped past him.

"You cannot hurt me anymore," Rose said.

Jack knew differently.

Rose would always hurt for Jonathon Clarring, just as he would always hurt for Cynthia Whitcox. But he would love Rose until their pain went away.

Just for a moment.

Rose turned in a swirl of crumpled black wool.

"Take me home, Jack." Her eyes were so bright a blue they hurt him. She walked into his arms. "Please."

Other women must have said *please* to him: He could not remember them.

Jack cradled the vulnerable nape of her neck and buried his lips in soft, clinging hair.

He had almost lost her.

Squeezing shut his eyes, he inhaled her scent, of roses and the unique spicy-sweet fragrance that was hers alone. His heart skipped a beat, feeling her hands slip inside his coat and the heat of her arms hug his waist.

It could have been a sound—or it could have been the utter lack of sound—that abruptly lifted his head.

Sky blue eyes snagged his gaze.

On Jonathon Clarring's face was the realization of what he had lost.

Rose loved him, but she did not choose him.

"The Court of Appeals rescinded the Queen's Bench ruling," Jack coldly asserted. "No man will ever again be able to imprison his wife."

Jonathon Clarring showed no reaction.

Jack held Rose close for one painfully short second before letting go. "Let's go home."

They stepped out of the den; a constable stepped inside.

A lone masculine voice drifted down the hallway.

Rose halted, forcing Jack to face her: Puzzlement darkened the brightness of pain. "You said he had the legal right to force me to live in his home."

Jack tucked a trailing curl into a hairpin.

Anxious gazes prickled his skin.

The men and women who stood outside the front door could wait. Jack would no longer deny his need for Rose.

"The law is a living body," he explained; his hand trembled. "It can be changed, and now it has."

"Because of you," she said.

"Because of *you*," Jack corrected her.

And Jonathon Clarring, her husband. And James Whitcox, the husband of his former lover.

She closed her eyes, lashes a dark fringe on pale cheeks, and leaned into his touch. "I wanted to kill him."

Jack did not know how he would react if he were held a prisoner, simply because of legal entitlement. "Did he hurt you?"

Pain knotted the bridge of her nose.

Jack smoothed away the tiny furrow.

A small hand reached inside his wet coat and tunneled inside his waistcoat. "He said one day the contraceptives would fail and I would get pregnant."

It was a possibility.

But Jack did not say what she already knew.

He cupped the back of her neck and forced up her head.

Rose opened her eyes and met his gaze. "He said he would not divorce me, because as long as we're married he would have the custody of any child I might have."

Jack's fingers tightened until the pain of his touch replaced the pain Jonathon Clarring had caused. "A separation will give you all rights to your person, as well as to any child you should choose to have."

Sharp fingernails dug into his bare skin. "But Parliament still will not grant me a divorce."

"Someday, Rose"—Jack took the pain as well as the pleasure she gave—"I will win you a divorce."

"When the laws change."

Jack did not apologize for Parliament.

"Yes."

"Because another woman is abducted by her husband," Rose assayed.

Or beaten. Or mutilated. Or murdered.

"Yes," Jack confirmed.

Sudden tears drenched her eyes. "There is no difference, Jack."

Jack sucked in chill, moist air. "Between what?"

She held his gaze. "You cannot have a splendid fuck unless there is passion."

His eyes suddenly burned with her tears.

Rose lowered her lashes and firmly tucked his shirt back into the waistband of his trousers. "I think I killed the nurse."

"How?" he asked alertly.

"With laudanum."

Jack would not regret the death of the woman who had aided Jonathon Clarring, but he did not want Rose to suffer any more pain.

"Is she in your"—but it was not *her* bedroom; their bedroom was in a small, cozy row house filled with furniture they had chosen together, he still boneless with orgasm, she entranced with the pleasure she had given him—"where he kept you?"

"Yes."

"Stay here."

Reluctantly Jack pulled free of Rose and took the stairs two at a time, footsteps muffled by a rose-patterned wool runner.

The faint odor of roast beef drew him forward.

Her bedroom was papered in roses; there was no sign of Rose in the overly feminine decor.

The nurse—a woman in her late fifties, starched white hat designating her profession pushed low on her forehead—was slumped in a green velvet armchair. The round oak table beside her held an empty plate. Opposite the setting, a napkin covering the plate did not hide congealing food.

A low snore accompanied the drum of rain.

Distastefully, he felt the pulse in the nurse's neck: It was strong and steady.

She would live.

Quickly he exited the bedroom that had brought Rose nothing but pain.

Rose was surrounded by her family: five brothers, five sisters-in-law, her mother and her father.

Six women and six men—coats dripping water—flanked the front door.

Jack met hazel eyes that were black with shadow.

A woman in a red silk gown briefly stood between Jack and the man who was her husband; slowly she faded in the flickering gaslight and encroaching night.

James Whitcox stood beside the woman he loved. Jack took his place beside the woman he loved.

Acknowledgments

In *The Lover* I wrote: "We ain't come that far, baby!" Materially, we really haven't: Our Victorian ancestors had indoor plumbing, electricity, telephones, department stores, amusement parks, commuter trains, *toilet* paper, effective contraceptives. . . . Women for the most part had the same conveniences then that we have now. *But*—and that's a very big but—they couldn't vote.

I didn't fully understand the ramifications of legal disenfranchisement until I wrote *Scandalous Lovers*. Women, I then discovered, could not serve as jurors. In a court of law, women were judged not by their peers but by men, male jurors who routinely exonerated husbands from domestic crimes simply because a beaten or murdered wife disobeyed or "sassed" back.

The government—a body of men charged to protect the liberty of women—allowed this sexual discrimination.

Well, I eat my earlier words. Legally, we *have* come a long way, baby. While Rose Clarring is a fictional character, her story was inspired by a very real woman—and a man, a member of Parliament—who challenged the law and changed the course of history for all married women. Thank you, Emily Jackson and Hardinge Giffard, First Lord Halsbury and Lord Chancellor. And thank you, Mary Lyndon Shanley, for your very illuminating book *Feminism, Marriage and the Law in Victorian England, 1850–1895*. You are the inspiration for

Cry for Passion. If I had not read your book, I would not have known about this landmark in the history of women.

I also would like to thank Valerie Weingart at the Northwestern University Law Library in Chicago who very kindly took me underneath her wing, and made it possible for me to get a copy of the original *In re Jackson* ruling as printed March 28, 1891 in *Justice of the Peace, And County, Borough, Poor Law Union, and Parish Law Recorder.*

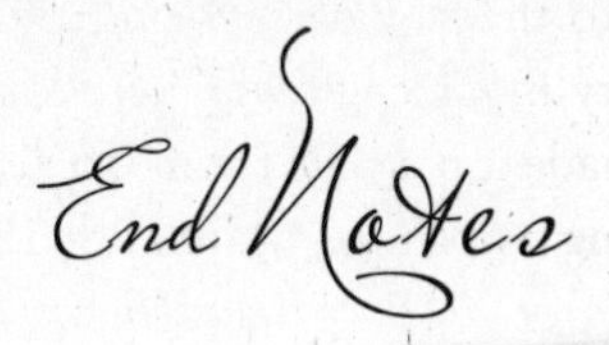

1. Sometimes fact is more incredible than fiction. Well, actually, it often is, which is why I write historical fiction. I wrote in my "Acknowledgments" that *Cry for Passion* was inspired by the real-life case of Emily Jackson *In re Jackson*. The annotated statements in Chapter Forty-one were taken directly from this case, as reported in *Justice of the Peace, And County, Borough, Poor Law Union, and Parish Law Recorder*, Volume 55, March 28, 1891.

2. Emily Jackson's family actually did "picket" outside the house of Emily's husband: I thought it would also be something that the Men and Women's Club would do for one of their own members. The following poem is fiction, written by me through Jane Fredericks. It is Jane's tribute to Rose, and it is what Rose hears in disjointed sentences while she is imprisoned in her husband's house.

   Free the rose
   that blossoms and grows,
   free of the blight
   that is every woman's plight.

   Free the rose
   to flourish in a meadow,
   free in the beauty
   that is a woman's liberty.

Books in The Men and Women's Club Series

SCANDALOUS LOVERS

"THE MEN AND WOMEN'S CLUB" IN *PRIVATE PLACES*

CRY FOR PASSION